BLINDSIDE

JOHN R. CARROLL is the author of a number of thrillers, including *Cheaters*, *The Clan* and *No Way Back*. He lives with his wife in Melbourne.

BLINDSIDE

J.R. Carroll

ALLEN&UNWIN

First published in 2004

Copyright © J.R. Carroll 2004

Allen & Unwin
83 Alexander Street
Crows Nest NSW 2065
Australia
Phone: (61 2) 8425 0100
Fax: (61 2) 9906 2218
Email: info@allenandunwin.com
Web: www.allenandunwin.com

National Library of Australia
Cataloguing-in-Publication entry:

Carroll, John, 1945–.
  Blindside.

  ISBN 1 74114 206 7.

  I. Title.

A823.3

Set in 11.6/12.6 pt Bembo by Bookhouse, Sydney
Printed in Australia by McPherson's Printing Group

10 9 8 7 6 5 4 3 2 1

1

October 1992

Mitch Alvarez pushed the electric blue aviator sunshades to the top of his significantly domed forehead, raised the Canon 12 × 50 binoculars, adjusted the focus and quickly pinpointed the imposing Petrakos residence. There she sat—one spectacularly grandiose pile couple of kilometres off, built into an excavated slope alongside a pretty little valley of velvet green pasture and a network of white fences surrounding a neo-colonial homestead and a complex of outbuildings and paddocks. On the homestead's front fence he could read its name: Corringal Downs. There were various working vehicles and floats visible, and a sleeping brown dog on the front step, but no potential witnesses anywhere. Since it was one o'clock, Mitch figured they were probably in having lunch. In the paddocks he could see a horse grazing, its chestnut coat flashing in the sun, and a new foal on wobbly legs nuzzling its mother. This was prime stud country, home to the legendary former American stallion Express Train—sire to many a serious stake-winner over the years.

Mitch Alvarez knew a thing or two about horses. There was a time when he'd been passionate about them. It had cost him dearly.

Not any more, however. Shifting his gaze back to the Petrakos place he studied the three-metre high wall that enclosed the residence and its acreage. The main entrance was a formidable pair of high iron gates, on either side of which gold-painted bulls' heads sat atop Corinthian stone columns. The gates were more suggestive of a sanatorium or mental asylum than someone's home. Inside was a long, semicircular driveway of raked white gravel lined with cypress trees and roses of every colour in full bloom. Following its sweep with the binoculars led Mitch's eyes to the house itself, and that was something else again.

Built with large sandstone blocks from South Australia and designed in the style of a medieval castle, it featured a high central ivy-covered clock tower complete with ramparts and crenellations. Above it the Greek and Australian flags hung limply in the windless air. There were four levels, three wings and over forty rooms in the main building, most of which contained George's vast collection of furniture, antiques, art works and all manner of artifacts from every corner of the world. In the grounds there was a moat and a complex system of interconnected waterfalls and cascading rock pools set amid a spectacular jungle habitat, complete with an array of exotic birds, including a pair of pink flamingoes. There was also a large pond fringed with bulrushes that was stocked with fingerling trout and perch. At horrendous cost, fifty mature palm trees had been flown down from Queensland and planted all over the property, just so George could pretend he was living in a tropical oasis instead of the rustic backblocks of Lancefield, in central Victoria.

Mitch knew all this detail because the house—and its owner—had been featured in a popular glossy magazine a few months earlier. More recently he had also cropped up in a TV gardening program, which Mitch happened to see. George had taken the viewers on a guided tour of the mansion and its grounds, which had been most helpful of him.

'All nice and quiet,' Mitch said, and handed the glasses to Andy Corcoran, kneeling behind him, his arms folded over the front seats. Andy scanned the scene.

'Idyllic,' Andy said. '*Perfectomento.*'

A third man sitting next to Mitch, name of Shaun Randall McCreadie, was moving his tongue around inside his mouth, making wet sucking sounds. When Mitch turned and looked at him his lean and still-youthful face creased into a slow smile, revealing white, level teeth that were slightly gapped. Shaun ignited a Lucky Strike, using his gold Zippo lighter with the Harley-Davidson insignia on it, and drew in deeply.

'Okay,' Mitch said. 'Everyone clear on procedure? Go through it one more time?'

'No need,' Andy said. 'We-all's ready to rock on down the road, baby.'

Drumming the wheel with his fingertips Mitch said, 'No problems, Shaun? No . . . second thoughts? Can't go back after this, mate. This is where we cross the line forever.'

'Already crossed it,' Shaun said, blowing out smoke. He pointed to the side of his head. 'Up here.' Always a somewhat taciturn person, Shaun gave a convincing impression of cool confidence. He didn't show it except in small ways, but Mitch sensed he was nervous and tightly coiled under that composed exterior. But why wouldn't he be? It took a great deal to stir him up, to bring him to this point. Who'd have thought it would ever happen? Not Mitch. Even now he had trouble grasping the realities that had caused everything to converge here. It felt like someone else's life now, not his. He was behind the wheel, but not driving.

At the opposite end of the spectrum to Shaun was Andy Corcoran. He was bullish, twitchy, pumped-up; right now there was a fine sweat film on his forehead, on which a swollen Y-shaped network of veins stood out, and he was constantly fidgeting with the binoculars or wiping his hand across his mouth. Understandably too, Andy was on a continuous slow burn nowadays, given to intermittent outbursts of white rage. The state of his veins sent a clear signal that a violent storm was on its way. He was a worry: he could tip over big time if things went pear-shaped, which could so easily happen today. It was Mitch's responsibility to control him in that case.

'All right, team,' Mitch said. 'Let's hit it. The wife should have fucked off by now.' He fired up the van, slipped it in gear and moved on, travelling north along the two-lane back road. They hadn't gone far when a dirty white Ford Galaxie overtook them, screaming past flat chat, throwing up gravel and dirt on a section that was under repair—though no work was being done today. Graders and earthmovers sat idle, unmanned, on the shoulder.

'Book the bastard, Mitch,' Andy said, and laughed at his own joke. Mitch stretched his lips in a grim smile, and Shaun didn't respond at all.

As he cruised along, Mitch thought about the Golden Greek, George Petrakos. He was going to get one hell of a rude shock very soon. George was a high profile, big-mouthed, controversial success story, a displaced victim and an orphan of World War II who stepped off the boat with nothing but the shirt on his back, a cardboard suitcase tied up with rope and an empty stomach. It was 1945; he was around fifteen years of age, alone except for an uncle, and didn't know anyone in this distant, empty land. Because the village where he was born was largely destroyed in the war, George's exact age was uncertain. It was a tragic chapter in the family history: both parents and his younger sister were tortured and killed by the Nazis, and George had only survived because he'd hidden down a well all night long, listening to their hideous screams. The way George told it, he could hear the soldiers' voices and see the flashlight beams as they searched for him, laughing and calling his name. The horrors from which he emerged were unimaginable. The Petrakos family was from Crete, and George was always at pains to point out that he was *Cretan*, not Greek. 'I am the Bull of Crete,' he had repeatedly proclaimed on the gardening show, trying to sound like Mohammed Ali. For the benefit of the camera he'd then driven home the message with an upward-thrusting stiff-armed gesture.

George Petrakos had gone into the used car business as a very young man, flogging cheap, worn-out bombs with blown differentials and transmissions that were stuffed with sawdust or banana skins, and always on the never-never. George famously called it 'selling old problems to new owners'. He made his first million from the hire-purchase boom in the sixties before progressing to a second-hand prestige car dealership. That was when he really started raking it in, selling mostly European or British brands that were gleaming and magnificent on the outside, but grossly overpriced when the interest rate and future repair bills were factored in.

As a matter of routine, George—like most used-car dealers at the time—doctored the odometres, reducing them to a fraction of the actual mileage. The cars came with a twelve-month warranty that excluded almost every major component, once the fine print was examined. But of course the customers didn't worry about that—until afterwards, when it was too late. The way George looked at it, the quality of the car's finish, its gloss, was everything. It was the one thing that had to be perfect. He would repair a dented panel with filler or respray a whole car rather than spend a cent on any of its moving parts. He maintained that cars were like women—image is all; no-one worries about what they're like under the bonnet. 'It's the same as sex—if you're getting into bed with a beautiful doll, you don't care if she has brains or not,' he had said in the magazine piece.

It was a principle he applied to his personal life—George was currently married to Stephanie Small, the shapely, photogenic, social-climbing daughter of a retail baron. Stephanie was a former model/actress who, in her pre-George days, was forever displaying her impressive cleavage on magazine covers. She had once posed naked bar an unzipped leather jacket and some chains—sitting astride a motorcycle, a sliver of her dark beaver tantalisingly exposed—in a *Penthouse* magazine centrefold. One summer she was voted 'Miss Wet T-Shirt' at Coolangatta, and she'd also appeared in several soft-core porn movies in which her splendid talents were comprehensively showcased. At the height of her career she even scored a part in the fifth sequel of a Hollywood teen horror franchise, in which she was mostly required to remain in a state of near-undress—and scream the rafters off their joists.

Stephanie's love life filled the soap magazines: it was a case of one wild-spirited, substance-addicted rock star after another. Then, after she met and fell in love ('for the first time') with George, the supposed makeover was sudden and dramatic, as if she'd made a conscious decision to put the raunchy lifestyle behind her and devote herself completely to her husband. Sainthood in Stephanie's case didn't cut it with the tabloids, however, and there were veiled suggestions that she was also mindful of George's fortune—estimated to be upwards of $100 million. In a post-wedding TV interview she made the announcement that, despite his 'mature' years, George had no need of Viagra, that he still 'came up trumps'. According to the *real* lowdown, however, not nearly often enough: she had toy boys by the dozen on the side and paid them handsomely to keep their mouths shut.

The wedding had taken place five years back amid a multimillion-dollar carnival of extravagance and razzle-dazzle in which inevitable comparisons were made with the union of Onassis and Jackie Kennedy. It was 'The Fairytale Wedding of the Golden Greek and his Siren Goddess', according to the magazine with exclusive rights to the big event. It was drawing a long bow, but George was impressed. These days the domesticated Stephanie gave the impression she was a different social animal altogether as she ingratiated herself into all the establishment families of the inner rural blueblood district: the Gisborne-Macedon-Riddells Creek-Clarkefield polo and dinner party circuit.

George had two sons from a previous marriage: the first-born, George junior, had suicided by plunging his throat onto a power saw at the age of twelve; the second, Stan, was a convicted cocaine dealer and standover merchant—an *enforcer*, as he preferred to describe himself. His idea of a fulfilling life was to hang out all night with mid-level criminals and nightclub proprietors, deal and use hard drugs, plan violent crimes, flash inch-thick wads of cash, carry guns in his car and, in general, behave like a man without a future. In underworld circles it was commonly believed that Stan Petrakos was on a hit list drawn up by certain detectives—although, to balance that, he was also allegedly friendly with one or two well-placed plainclothes officers, to whom he paid kickbacks in exchange for favours—including protection.

On top of all that, George's first wife, Iris, had her life tragically shortened in a helicopter crash back in 1973. Questions were raised as to whether it was an accident—the marriage was under stress at the time—but the burnt-out wreckage and incinerated remains scattered in the North Warrandyte hills provided no answers one way or the other. So, for all the untold wealth, Gulfstream jet, fleet of Ferrari cars and his cutting-edge Swedish whitegoods, George's life hadn't exactly been a fairytale journey. And now it was about to take another left turn.

Mitch steered off the main road into a narrow lane that ran behind the Great Wall of the Petrakos place, where they could not be seen from the stud farm. Here at the rear of the property there was a modest tradesman's entrance alongside a pair of iron gates and sculpted bulls' heads that were identical to the ones at the front. A HAZCHEM sign was fixed to the wall, as well as another sign that said NO HAWKERS OR CANVASSERS. Scattered about inside were gardening and tool sheds, hothouses for the propagation of seedlings, a conservatory, a row of stables and, some distance away, several garages. The rear gates were mainly there for the convenience of Stephanie whenever she went off to point-to-point meetings in nearby Clarkefield. Stephanie was big on Country Club, dressage, the hunt and point-to-point; she had some wonderful ponies and certainly looked the goods in her tight vermilion jacket, tan corduroys and shiny black boots. During the season, meetings were held on the first Wednesday of every month, and today being Wednesday, October 3rd, she would definitely be gone—leaving George alone in the house. Stan lived in a Carlton penthouse, and at this time of day he would be snoring in an alcoholic or drug-induced stupor. There were plenty of part-time gardeners, grooms, mechanics and whatnot, but no live-in servants. And the team of house cleaners came on Mondays and Fridays.

The thing about George Petrakos was, he was a caveman when it came to managing money. From an early age he had largely avoided banks and financial institutions, firstly because he mistrusted them; then, as he became richer, to conceal income and so avoid paying tax. Apart from cars he made money from all kinds of suspect activities, and used a variety of legitimate fronts—flower shops, a vineyard, a video store franchise, a cheap mail-order jewellery and cosmetics business—to process the flow of cash. He was known to keep large—very large—amounts on the premises, inside the walk-in strongroom, like a bank vault, next to his billiards room. According to Mitch's information there could be upwards of seven figures sitting in that strongroom at any time—all used, untraceable bills waiting to be knocked off. According to his research, the alarm system was ultra-sophisticated, but at present deactivated during the day because there were always tradespeople or deliveries coming and going in this constantly evolving grand folly of his, this 'San Simeon of Lancefield', as a back-page newspaper columnist had called it. Strangely, no guard dogs either: just some small, yapping poodle-type creatures belonging to his wife. It seemed a brilliant set-up, really, and Mitch sometimes wondered why it hadn't been done before. It seemed too good to be true.

Mitch parked the van, switched off and reached around to the back seat for the canvas Country Road bag sitting next to Andy. By now there was a palpable atmosphere of nervous anticipation inside the van. He unzipped the bag, revealing a silver, long-barrelled .357 revolver, a snub-nosed .38, a Beretta .32 semi-automatic and a sawn-off .410 shotgun with its stock fashioned into a pistol grip. There were also speed-loaders, clips and boxes of ammo, loose shotgun cartridges, three rubber ski masks, three pairs of black kid leather gloves, some knives, a set of amethyst-encrusted brass knuckles, rolls of insulation tape and three other Country Road overnight bags, to hold the cash. He gave the .357 to Shaun and the snub-nose to Andy; then he rammed a clip into the .32, slid one into the chamber, set safety and shoved it into his back pocket. Then he loaded a couple of shells into the .410. He also pocketed a flick-knife and the brass knuckles. Shaun opened a box of Winchester ammo and loaded five into his piece, slipping some extra rounds into his pocket; then he spun the cylinder, drew back the hammer and sighted across his forearm, out the van window. Andy used a speed-loader for the .38 and stuck it down the front of his pants, pulling his shirt out over it. Then they each took a ski mask and pair of gloves.

When they were done they all looked at each other, and Mitch said, 'Remember, lads. If he arcs up, don't overreact. Follow the plan. Don't kill the cunt. What we have to do, we scare the living shit out of him, but stay cool. Right? He's not much good to us dead if he hasn't opened the fuckin' strongroom, is he? And be ready for the unexpected. He's a fuckin' tough nut, and he won't bend over, I can promise you that. He won't cop it nice and sweet.'

'We'll make him cop it,' Andy said. 'I don't give a fuck how tough he is.'

Shaun said nothing.

'Okay,' Mitch said, and they got out of the van, a near-new VW Transporter.

Like the weapons, it had been stolen, then given new plates and signage that said *Graham Shillington—Master Plumber*, followed by a phone number. It was a real plumber's name and number, from the *Yellow Pages*, just in case anyone decided to ring it while they were on the road. There were ladders on the roof and enough tools and plumbing supplies inside to pass more than a casual inspection. Shaun and Andy hefted tool-boxes, a pair of short-handled bolt-cutters and the Country Road bags as Mitch got one of the extension ladders off the roof and set it against the wall, next to the sign that said NO HAWKERS OR CANVASSERS. Over they went, taking the ladder with them and leaving it lying on the ground behind some shrubbery as they sauntered in tradesman-like fashion across an expanse of fresh-mown lawn, to the rear door, which was sheltered in a colonnaded porch. Then it was simply a matter of ringing the bell-press, and with any luck George himself would open up. If no-one answered, they'd smash their way in. There was a locked steel mesh screen door, the heavy-duty type that could only be seen through from the inside. Shaun quickly opened it with two well-placed snips of the bolt-cutters. They put on the ski masks and gloves, drew their weapons, and Mitch thumbed the bell-press. Then they stood aside, out of sight.

In a little while the main door opened and a voice that sounded like George's said, 'Who is it?' No doubt feeling safe because of the screen door, he stood there a second too long. From nowhere three hooded men swarmed all over him—screaming, shoving guns in his face, pushing and dragging him back into the house: through the kitchen, down a hall, into a vast living room with a flat, big-screen TV, knocking over pieces of pottery and furniture as they went. Finally they were in a cavernous billiards room with an elaborate bar that would not have been out of place in the cocktail lounge of a five-star hotel. On one wall were two locked steel doors that led to the strongroom. With his forearm against George's throat Mitch pressed him hard against the full-sized billiard table and jammed the .410 directly under his nose, a barrel on each nostril.

'George, listen to me,' he said. '*George!* Pay attention. I'm going to ask you once, very politely. Would you be good enough to open the vault doors—please.' He eased the pressure of his forearm just enough for George to speak. His face was a deep scarlet and his eyes bulged alarmingly as he looked at Mitch and then at the other two, either side of him. Wherever he looked there was a gun aimed at his head.

'Fuck your mother up her filthy pig's *arse*,' George spat, using the American pronunciation.

'Okay,' Mitch said. He wiped the spittle from his face with his shirtsleeve.

Shaun and Andy held an arm each as Mitch put the shotgun in his left hand and reached into his right-hand pocket. When he brought it out again a moment later, George did not even see the brass knuckles come crashing into his left ear. It happened with such swiftness and savagery that every bone in his head seemed to crack and echo around the walls; the ear itself was transformed into a shredded, bloody mess spread right across the side of his face. He slumped back against the billiard table, knees buckling, blood now streaming from his earhole, but Mitch pulled him up straight, measured him off and then delivered a mighty kick deep into the pit of his stomach. George made an appalling noise and slid down, gagging, whereupon Mitch clipped the back of his head with the brass knuckles and put him face down on the slate floor.

They gave him a few seconds to recover, then hauled him up by the blood-drenched collar. Mitch got right in his ex-ear and said through clenched teeth: 'I fuckin' *warned* you, you

stupid fuckin' wog *cunt*. *Okay?* Got the message now, George?
Are we on the same program?'

George was bleeding freely, slipping in and out of consciousness, wheezing and in extreme pain; there was a vile-looking
yellow substance oozing from his lips and dripping from his chin
as they propped him up against the table and held him there.

'That's for openers, mate,' Mitch said. 'Next time, I promise
it is going to fuckin' *hurt*.'

George tried to focus on Mitch. His eyes were full of
tears—tears of pain that spilled and rolled down his ugly,
puffed-up, bloodied face. Looking at him, Mitch saw for the
first time that his hair had been dyed a sort of russet-red, teased
to a fine coiffure and then held in place with hairspray.
He could smell the spray. The result made him look more like
a sleazy old faggot than the Bull of Crete.

'Open the doors, George,' Mitch said quietly. 'And we'll
be gone, out of here in ten minutes.' Gripping him by the front
of his shirt Mitch drove the .410 into George's neck, right on
the main artery. 'If you fuck us around once more,' he went
on, 'we're gonna damage every part of your body, then wait
till your wife comes home and get started on her too. And I'll
make *fucking* sure you'll have a front row seat.'

'You'll be able to watch her suck my cock,' Andy said.
'I hear she still gives terrific head, George. To all and sundry.'
He stepped into the picture and slapped George a couple of
times, hard, over the back of his skull. Shaun stood off the
action, the long-barrelled .357 loose in his gloved hand.

George mumbled something.

'What's that?' Mitch said.

'Nothing.'

'Say again?'

'Nothing. I give you . . . *nothing*. Kill me . . . I don't care.
Fuck you.'

'Okay, you faggy little fuck,' Andy said. 'That's what you
want. Here.' He jammed the snub-nose in George's ruined ear,

cocked the piece, and from his body language Mitch thought he really meant to pull the trigger.

'Wait on,' Mitch told him, and gently pushed the snub-nose away. 'Cool it—right?' He locked eyes with Andy, giving him a piece of his mind, and Andy glared back before calming down a fraction. But he was really pumped—the gun quivered in his hand.

'Got an idea,' Shaun said. 'C'm here, George.' He grabbed George's left wrist, spreading out the fingers on the blue baize of the billiard table. Then he turned the Magnum around in his hand, so it was butt-first.

'What I'm gonna do,' he told him, 'I'm gonna smash each finger, starting with your thumb, every time you say no. Okay? And remember: if I have to do your right hand too, you won't be *able* to open the fucking doors, so we'll *certainly* kill you—and your lovely wife. After we've gang-banged her, of course. So—going to open the doors now?' It was a long speech for Shaun. He waited two seconds, then brought the gun-butt down onto George's thumb. It crunched like prawn shell, and blood shot out all over the duck-egg blue baize.

Even Mitch flinched at the sudden violence of the blow and the sight of the mangled thumb. George screamed as Shaun held his wrist firmly down.

'Open the doors?' Shaun said again.

George was beside himself. He wept and shuddered and howled, tears and snot mingling with blood, his pudgy face distorted beyond recognition and bright purple, that weird-looking red coiffed rug sticking out crazily. His little eyes had disappeared into his face completely. But he managed to get himself together enough to respond.

'Fuck you . . . you . . . *cunts.*'

Smash.

The index finger, which was wearing a sapphire signet ring, went south in an explosion of bone, metal and blood. The ring itself was in fragments, scattered over the table.

George went right off the air.

Shaun waited for him to settle. 'Open the doors?' he said calmly.

George was swaying; only Shaun and Mitch were keeping him upright. But he was hanging tough, Mitch thought, the little bastard. Having survived the fucking Nazis and made himself filthy rich he's not gonna fold for a bunch of home invaders.

Smash.

George's middle finger was no more. The table was a terrible mess.

Shaun was down to the pinkie when, to everyone's relief, George finally saw reason. Mitch was actually surprised—he was starting to think they'd have to go all the way and top him, just take what they could find in the house and clear out. It just showed that everyone, even the Bull of Crete, had a breaking point. They helped him upstairs for the keys—a big bunch on a ring, like a jailer's—and inside three minutes he'd fitted a brass Yale key into the recessed lock, turned it two full revolutions and pulled the door out. Mitch pulled the other one. It was fucking heavy—six-inch solid stainless steel.

What they saw, lined up on the right-hand side, were racks of machine guns, automatic rifles, shotguns, a range of revolvers and semi-automatic pistols and quantities of ammunition. How much of that could possibly be legal? Hanging on overhead hooks were ceremonial Japanese swords, bejewelled daggers, sabers, handcuffs, chains, other surgical-looking metallic instruments, a leather codpiece, some whips and scourges, carnival masks, wigs and studded, lace-up leatherwear.

'Nice one, George,' Mitch said. 'Dirty old bugger. Think Steph uses this stuff on him?'

'You'd think your own private centrefold in the bridal chamber'd do the job, wouldn't you?' Andy said.

'Just no telling, is there,' Mitch said, gazing around at the collection. 'Who'd have thought it?'

In the middle of the room sat a large Chubb vault, about three-quarters the height of a man. 'Open it,' Mitch said. George appeared to hesitate.

'Go on.'

George's hand wavered uncertainly before he started working the tumblers.

'Now we have to wait . . . for five minutes,' he said.

'Okay, we wait five minutes,' Mitch said. He dragged him back to the billiards room, giving him to Andy to look after. Shaun smoked a Lucky, flicking ash on the floor. When the time was up a little ping! sounded inside the vault. Mitch turned the big wheel a half-revolution and slowly opened the door.

In the meantime Andy pushed George roughly into a wooden chair, under the cue rack. George slumped, his smashed hand folded under his armpit. Andy stood over him, the .38 pointing at his stupid-looking ginger thatch. Andy really felt he had to kill George, put two or three in his brain, even if Mitch was against it. George might just be able to identify them—Mitch, at least. He knew Mitch; they had a history, he could probably place the voice and eyes even if he couldn't see the features. George was a smart bastard. Yes, George had to die. Andy was thinking fast, getting the idea set firmly—satisfyingly—in his mind, when from inside the strongroom he heard Mitch say, 'Holy shit.'

In the vault were tightly packed bundles of cash, all high denominations. Mitch, who had seen large amounts before, did some mental calculations: around fifty bundles, say roughly fifty thou per . . . Came to two and a half mill. Minimum.

But that wasn't the end of the story.

Also crammed into the vault were many rows of plastic packages. Inside the packages, each the size of a house brick, was a whitish powdery substance. Around thirty units in all. Mitch walked between Shaun and Andy. He had a pretty good idea what it was. They all did.

'What's one of these worth?' Andy said, hefting one of the packages. 'Weighs about . . . kilo, kilo and a half.'

'Wholesale, it's a hundred, hundred and fifty large per key,' Shaun said. 'Depending.'

Now Andy was doing calculations. 'I make that . . . four, five mill. Depending.'

'Doesn't matter,' Mitch said.

'Why doesn't it matter?' Andy said, still holding the brick.

'Because we're not taking it,' Mitch told him.

'The fuck we're not,' Andy said, and laughed. 'That's a joke, right? Humour.'

'No joke. We take the cash. That's all.'

'Don't be fuckin' *insane*,' Andy said dismissively. 'Come on, let's load up.' He started putting packages into one of the bags as Mitch stepped closer and grabbed his arm, hard.

'Listen carefully, mate. Listen to each word. We are not taking the heroin.'

'He's fuckin' *serious*,' Andy said, pulling his arm free. 'I don't fuckin' believe I'm hearing this. Five mill at least, maybe even *ten*, and he wants to *leave* it. Care to explain?'

'Use your brains,' Mitch said. 'So far no-one knows who we are. And no-one *will* know, *ever*. But as soon as we take this shit, everything's changed. We've fucked ourselves.'

'Bullshit,' Andy said. 'Listen. I can offload this, all of it, *tomorrow*. Then it's off our hands, in the system, *gone*. So . . . what's the problem exactly?'

'The problem is, when you sell drugs, this amount of drugs, you have to bring in other people. Major players. Syndicates. So . . . they will know we did this. They will know where it came from. Soon, every bastard knows. *Cops* will know. Shaun's old pal, Terry Pritchett, will know. I assume you don't want him coming around with his fuckin' meat cleaver.'

'Pritchett? What in the fuck's he got to do with it?'

'Pritchett's a rip-off specialist. It's what he *does*. He gets one sniff of this, he'll be down on the first flight—and that cunt does *not* take no for an answer. Remember what he did to Brian Hamilton a few years ago? Hacked his fuckin' head off while he was *still alive*, even after he'd spilled. Just ask Shaun about it.'

But Andy didn't need to—he remembered the Brian Hamilton case. Big armoured truck robbery gone wrong, a guard and a gang member shot, then in the aftermath Pritchett in his long Burberry raincoat appearing from nowhere, like a ghost, while Hamilton and his partner slept it off in a quiet suburban motel after a big night on the piss. It was a bad, bad scene: even the toughest homicide detective brought up his bacon and egg sandwich that morning. Pritchett's name was all over it, but as per usual no proof and no surviving witnesses meant he remained at large back on his own turf, in Sydney's inner west. The incident loomed large in Shaun's early career because he was one of the first cops on the scene, while he was still a uniform.

'I don't give a shit about Terry Pritchett,' Andy said—but his unusually subdued tone had the clear ring of famous last words, a quality of impending doom, even to his own ears.

Encouraged, Mitch pushed on. 'This is a large consignment, Andy. Think about it. Use your nut. All right, you could sell it to Madame Sing tomorrow. So you involve the Asians too. Dunno about you, mate, but I don't feel comfortable about mixing it with Triads.'

Andy was sticking to his guns. 'You're fuckin' worried about the slopes? Come on, Mitch. We're gonna be far away from those cunts. We're gonna be sippin' margaritas in Acapulco.'

'In a year—*if* we ever make it, if Pritchett, or the slopes, or *someone* doesn't find us first. How many 'ifs' do you need? Even in Acapulco you're gonna be lookin' over your shoulder the whole fuckin' time. Chances are you'll wake up one night with a fuckin' bullet in your mouth or a cleaver in your throat instead of a margarita. But if we just take the folding stuff, stash it till things cool down *the way we agreed*, we're home free.

Our signature is nowhere. It's simple, it's clean—it's cold *cash*. All we have to do is *spend* it. That was the plan, remember?'

'Yeah, but we didn't know there'd be a container load of heroin in the fuckin' vault, did we? That sort of rearranges the plan in my book.'

'No it doesn't,' Mitch said. 'It changes nothing. We take the cash and leave the shit. The shit is bad news. Tell him, Shaun.'

Shaun, standing outside the safe watching George, waited several beats and said, 'I'm with Mitch. I don't want to mix it with that Pritchett maniac ever again, even from a distance. Leave the shit. It's bad trouble.'

'Trouble?' Andy said, snorting. 'Christ, don't make me giggle. You think what we've done so far is *not* trouble?'

Heartened by Shaun's support, Mitch said, 'A quantity like this, there's every chance the drug squad is already onto it. Christ, it's probably been tagged and put under surveillance from the drop. It'll be tainted for sure. Soon as we rip it off, our prints are all over it, we're in the frame. Mate, it's not worth the risk. Leave it, Andy. Let's load the cash and move out.' He glanced at his wristwatch. 'We've been here too long already.'

Andy looked at Mitch, then Shaun. 'Fuck the pair of you,' he said. '*And* Pritchett.' He turned away and resumed stuffing packages into a bag. Then he felt the touch of steel on the back of his neck.

'Stop it, Andy. Stop it *right now*, or I swear I'll fuckin' shoot you, mate.'

Andy straightened up slowly and turned around, so that he was staring down the barrel of Mitch's .32. Mitch's hand was rock-steady; the cold murderous glint in his blue eyes told Andy the man was deadly serious.

'Two can play this fuckin' game, boss,' he said, and brought up the .38. Now they were aiming guns point-blank at each other. Thumbing back the hammer Andy said, 'I believe this is called a Mexican stand-off, amigo.'

For a second there was a void of pure silence in the strongroom, then:'*Hey!*'

It was Shaun, standing in the doorway, holding George by the scruff of his neck with one hand, and waving his .357 at both Mitch and Andy with the other.'Can we please get *on* with things—*please*? I have a fucking *plane* to catch sometime *tonight*.'

Not wishing to take his eyes off Andy, thus handing him an advantage, Mitch did not turn to face Shaun. 'Well, well,' Andy said, grinning insanely. 'Now we *do* have a situation on our hands—a friendly game of three-cornered stud. Whose move, lads?'

On cue came a clatter, like something being dropped on the slate floor.

Heads swivelled.

Standing there, resplendent in her cherry-red point-to-point jacket, ruffled white shirt at her throat and skintight tan corduroy pants, was Stephanie Petrakos. The clatter was her riding crop hitting the deck. She had a hand over her mouth, and there was an expression of uncontainable terror on her face as she looked at her battered and bleeding husband, the bloody mess on the billiard table, the opened strongroom, the three hooded and armed intruders who had violated her home.

Stephanie screamed—hard. And Stephanie was a top-of-the-range screamer. It had been a big part of her acting repertoire.

Simultaneously, three guns turned in her direction.

2

September 2003

Contrary to widespread belief, the Victorian gold-mining township of Buzzards Hut is not named after the bird, which is not found anywhere in Australia. The real story is that in 1857 a Scottish prospector named Samuel Buzzard, together with his younger brother William, made the hazardous 130-mile cross-country journey from Melbourne with three mules and a horse, camping en route in wild bush country and eventually settling in this remote, mountainous location. According to Samuel's journal, along the way William was bitten by a snake, there were encounters with spear-carrying savages, and Samuel himself suffered exposure and hypothermia from the ceaseless rain and freezing conditions they had to endure—and for which they were less than prepared. It didn't help that they'd made the journey in mid-winter, but when the cry 'Gold!' goes out, no-one seems to care what time of year it is. Neither Buzzard had any knowledge or experience of the wilderness—they had soft hands; they'd worked at the family manchester business in the city. Samuel and William were more at home handling bolts of imported cloth, on the tennis court or at the seaside in Sorrento than hacking through bush, dragging recalcitrant animals and heavy equipment up muddy slopes, pitching tents in dense, inhospitable forests and shivering all night under too-thin blankets. When, towards the end of their journey, they hit a serious snowstorm, the brothers said their prayers and prepared to perish.

Miraculously they survived, then prospered when they finally arrived at a level, grassy tract of high country nestling among snow-capped hills. A fast-flowing river—the Goulburn—ran through it; there were dozens of tent-dwelling prospectors scattered around, and some had found good-sized nuggets panning or working the quartz-rich terrain with picks and shovels. In time the Buzzards built a stringybark and mudbrick shanty, then when the alluvial gold ran out they returned to Melbourne, purchased more equipment and animals and returned to the place that was now known as Buzzards Hut. That was when they began deep-sinking, gouging shafts hundreds of feet down with pneumatic drills and establishing the Number One Sarah mine, which was named after Samuel's wife.

The Buzzards made a fortune and in its heyday the town had a population of 12 500, twenty-two pubs, eleven churches and at least as many whorehouses. The Number One Sarah mine became the economic mainstay of Buzzards Hut. It operated continuously—and profitably—for over a century until it was shut down and flooded in the early 1970s. In more recent times a large consortium had tried to restart it. Following some promising core samples millions of dollars were poured into infrastructure before the cash flow dried up, the bean counters apparently deciding that the price of gold was too low and the cost of production too high to justify any further expense. So Buzzards Hut fell back into oblivion.

This potted version of events was contained in a framed newspaper article on the wall of the town's remaining pub, the Stag. It was being read by a man with a pot of beer in one hand and a freshly lit cigarette parked between his lips. He was wearing brown boots, faded blue jeans, a grey windbreaker and, for outerwear, a dark blue, down-filled Paddy Pallin jacket. He might have been anywhere from his late thirties to mid-forties: it was hard to tell because his hair was dark and smooth, swept back and slicked from being outside; his facial features seemed untouched by age. And yet a closer inspection of his still green eyes would indicate that, like the Buzzard brothers, he had been to places and seen some wild things in his time.

The man took a deep drag on his cigarette, sipped his beer and looked over the bar. Standard features: curling, stained photographs of regulars fooling around late at night, the booze well and truly aboard, a mounted stag's head with an impressive set of antlers, some antiquated rifles, a couple of moth-eaten brown trout and, stuck on the ceiling, hundreds of coins from all over the world. All familiar to him.

He rubbed the window with his sleeve and looked outside. It was still raining heavily. This was a consistently solid, vertical downpour that looked like it had no intention of stopping. When he had driven into town an hour or so earlier there was water sluicing across the road and cascading merrily down gutters and around parked vehicles. It often rained this way in Buzzards Hut—at least for nine months of the year according to the publican. The man knew this anyway, but let the old guy talk. He was a bald, slow-moving man in his sixties with a dead, putty-like face that might have been preserved in alcohol or formaldehyde.

Buzzards Hut. The man in the Paddy Pallin jacket said the words to himself, then again, audibly: *BuzzardsfuckingHut*. It had been a long, long time. Pissing down then too, just like this. He sure got wet that day. Nowadays the town seemed even more of a relic, with a population of ninety-three, no school, one pub and one shop—a combined general store and single-pump petrol station with fifty-year-old signs advertising Swallow's ice-cream and C.O.R. and Plume motor spirit.

There was a town cop, but the nearest doctor was an hour and a half away in Jamieson.

The room was not large, more in the style of a cosy snug, with a horseshoe-shaped bar and a crackling wood fire that provided a certain rustic ambience as well as warmth. At the other end of the horseshoe was a crew consisting of three men and two women who—judging from their smart outdoor attire and cultivated voices—were blow-ins from the city. Owing to its remoteness and unspoiled character Buzzards Hut had become a magnet for tourists, and many of the houses in the town were weekenders owned by outsiders. They came in their four-wheel drives to escape the stress of city life, fish for trout or go bushwalking—there were tracks that penetrated many miles into the wilderness.

The one who had caught his attention had short black hair framing an attractive face that had a fine, sculpted quality about it. She was . . . hmm, late thirties, around his age, probably a little younger. It was hard to tell with women—they could do so much to falsify the truth of the matter. Average height, a fit, compact build, nifty little sunshades perched on her head. Full of self-confidence and . . . what was it? *Poise.* She dripped poise, and style. Outfit: designer checked shirt and stretch jeans that looked as if they'd been purchased for the occasion. One word flashed into his brain: *money.* And although they were a team he had the impression from the 'conversation' that they did not know each other well. Certainly the black-haired woman's body language told him she was on the fringe, even bored with the company. She had a glass of J&B and ice from which she occasionally sipped while she listened in. She didn't seem connected to the others at all, and each time he threw a glance at her he caught her peeping back sneakily. Interesting . . .

The dominant male in this outfit was ruddy and fiftyish, oversized but not much bigger than a Kenworth prime mover; he was sounding off at great length about something riveting that had happened back at the office. Evidently he

enjoyed the sound of his own voice, since he used it continuously, with power and conviction. Probably a corporate chief
and his underlings on one of those bonding weekends.
If someone tried to butt in he simply pumped up the volume
a few octaves and carried on as if he'd just swatted a fly—
clearly a man who was used to having everything his own
way. Then the man in the Paddy Pallin jacket caught the
woman looking at him again, and this time he held her eyes
for longer than usual, staring her out, giving her a smile and
receiving one in return, until she turned away and sipped her
J&B, no hurry at all.

The rain still showed no signs of easing—in fact it was
intensifying. He gazed outside through the misted window
while someone put more wood on the fire. Well, if he had to
stay indoors all day it may as well be here. He tipped down
the remains of his beer and ordered another one, preparing to
settle in, and when he checked out the other end of the bar
the main guy was still in control, but there was no sign of the
dark-haired beauty. *Pity about that.* Quite unexpectedly a pang
of real disappointment stabbed him. He lit another cigarette,
inhaling deeply while he thought about her.

It was warm now, too warm for a down-filled jacket, and
he was working out where to put it if he took it off—there
were no obvious places. In the end he tossed it in the corner,
under one of the stuffed trout. Then he smoked and drank
and looked out the window, thinking various things, noticing
after a while that the rain was slowing to an Irish mist that
swirled and eddied through the air like snowflakes. Two young
girls strolled up the street, drenched, heads slicked, wearing no
protective clothing, not hurrying and apparently not caring.
Fourteen or fifteen years old, he guessed. Watching them pass,
the man smiled. Something about their attitude impressed him.
So it was wet out—so what? Sublime youth.

He noticed his glass was empty, and returned to the bar.

'Excuse me,' the female voice said. 'I'm supposed to have

given these up, but right now I could use one. Do you mind
terribly?'

He spun around—she'd come from his left, near the hotel's
front entrance, presumably where the women's conveniences
were located. Now she was right next to him, having sidled
up from behind.

'Of course not. Here you go.'

She accepted one from the pack, then tilted her face
towards him while he lit it with his plastic Bic lighter. It wasn't
perfume, but a soft fragrant soap that wafted over him.

Exhaling away from him she said, 'You're not a local.'

'No,' he said, watching the smoke leave her lips. 'And
neither are you.'

'God, this is so *strong*,' she said. 'I used to smoke Dunhill
lights.'

'Sorry,' he said. 'Been on these all my life. Guess I don't
notice any more.'

'I'm getting a decent kick, anyway. Wow.' She removed the
shades from atop her head and put them on the bar towel.
A deliberate move, he thought—meaning she wasn't leaving
straightaway.

Seeing she'd left her empty glass on the other side, he said:
'Are you ready for another J&B?'

'How'd you know I was on J&B?' she said—smiling.

'I noticed.'

'You always notice what people are drinking?' It didn't
quite have the inflection of a question, but she seemed to
expect a reply.

'In certain cases, yes,' he said, and signalled the putty-
faced barman: 'J&B for the lady. So, what are you up to in
Buzzards Hut?'

She laughed and said, 'Good question. I'll give you three
guesses. Then you can tell me why you're here.'

'Sounds fair. How about . . . corporate weekend away?'

'Nope. My God—what a grotesque thought.'

He'd already decided to play out this little game. 'Bush-bashing in a Toorak tractor?'

'Uh-uh.' Shake of the head. 'Although we did come here in one. Like everyone else.'

'Maybe . . . some gold prospecting?'

She cocked an eye. 'Interesting idea. But, sorry, no cigar.' The J&B was placed in front of her.

'That's three strikes,' he said.

She took a last drag of the cigarette before crushing it out. 'I think I'm cured of those now. Forever.' She swirled ice, sipped. 'No, I'm here for the bushwalking, would you believe.'

'I would, but not in this.'

'*This* wasn't happening when we left. Didn't start till well after Warburton.' That was where the real climbing began.

'It always rains in Buzzards Hut.'

'Really. So . . . you're an old Buzzards Hut hand?'

Again, it was not *quite* a question.

'You could say that. But I haven't been here in a good while.'

'Sounds like there's a story attached to that.'

He looked her directly in the eye. She was very attractive, but something more than that—her eyes were green, the same as his. That was unusual enough, but they were exactly his *shade* of green; they had the same shape and dimensions, even down to the slightly overhanging lids that gave her a deceptively lazy appearance. And the more he looked, the more he saw uncanny similarities in her other features as well—crow-black hair, longish face, aristocratic, slightly beaky nose, the lopsided mouth when she smiled. She might have been his sister—if he'd had one.

'It is a long story,' he said, still locked onto her unblinking eyes. 'For another time, maybe.'

'Time is what I have on my hands,' she said, not smiling, sipping her drink. He felt his stomach turn inside out.

'Same here,' he said, a crack in his voice.

'Can I have another cigarette?' she said.

'Thought you were cured. *Forever*, was the word.'

'Been a recidivist all my life.'

When he'd lit it for her he said, 'Bushwalking, huh?'

'Indeed.' Smoke curled and drifted around her face, blending with the soap scent—a heady mix.

'I have to say you don't look the type.'

'I'm not. I've never done it before.' She sipped and said, 'What type do I look like, anyway?'

He grinned, sensing a trap, but didn't falter: 'The type who'd be more at home doing lunch somewhere in Chapel Street instead of holing up in the wilds of Buzzards Hut.'

That made her laugh. 'Since you mention it, I am not averse to doing the occasional lunch on Chapel Street. You're right—this is *not* my natural habitat.'

He finished his beer and ordered another.

'What about you?' she said.

'What about me.'

'Ever been bushwalking?'

'Once or twice.'

'Around here?'

'Affirmative.'

'Do you recommend it?'

'Sure. Depending on who you're with at the time.'

She looked across the bar at the others. 'I don't actually know these people. Well . . . I sort of know the woman. They belong to the bush-lovers' society or something, and I've just . . . come along for the experience. But I should rejoin them. They'll think I'm very antisocial.'

'Does it matter?'

She smoked and shrugged at the same time. 'Why?'

He said, 'You've just told me they're not your closest pals. So who cares what they think?'

She thought about it, looked over at them—the main man still fully in control—then shrugged again. 'Doesn't matter a goddamn, I guess. It's just my conventional, respectable, upper middle-class background speaking.'

'Another J&B?'

Searching his face, she gave the impression that this was an important decision for her, a turning point. It was his feeling too. One more drink meant she had switched allegiances. 'Oh, why not,' she said. 'But it's my treat.'

Putty-face delivered the drinks.

'Okay, your turn,' she said. 'Why are *you* here, in the . . . what was it? *Wilds* of Buzzards Hut?'

Grinning lopsidedly, he said, 'You don't think I look as if I belong here?'

She ran her eyes over him—the face, youthful but somehow seasoned, the short-sleeved grey windbreaker, the strong, sinewy arms and capable, big-veined hands with long fingers.

'I wouldn't dismiss the possibility,' she said.

'My family had a weekend house here for years,' he said. 'I came here a lot. But the place was sold and, as I said, I haven't been back for some time.'

Watching him interestedly she said, 'But that doesn't explain why you're here now.'

He swallowed some beer. 'Well . . . I guess you could call it a sentimental visit.'

'Uh-huh. But . . . you don't look the sentimental type to me.'

He knew he'd asked for that. 'What type do you think I am?'

She sipped and said, 'I think . . . you are a man of purpose. You do everything for a reason—a practical reason.'

The half-smile dissolved from his face. Christ she was warm there. She had pegged him as well as any sister could. For an icy moment he felt spooked, as if she was reading him better than she was entitled to, as if their meeting here was not accidental. Or was he that transparent? Maybe. He was not too much given to thinking about himself, or seeking opinions or approval from others—he was what he was, and that was that.

She, however, came from a solid middle-class upbringing, she sounded educated—unlike him—and was probably an astute judge of people. So there was no reason to be paranoid—yet.

'Are you staying here?' she said. 'At the hotel?'

'No,' he said. 'You?'

'Oh, yes. We have the best rooms in the place. Sheer, wanton luxury.'

He laughed. 'My accommodation is much more basic. I'm staying at a log cabin down the road. Place called Scotchman's Reef.'

'Log cabin? How . . . invigorating. Clearly you are a true son of the pioneers.'

'Like old man Buzzard himself.'

'Old man Buzzard? You mean there really was such a person?'

'Sure. He was one of the original settlers, emigrated from Scotland in . . . 1857, I believe. Started the Number One Sarah mine.'

She leaned slightly closer. 'I give in—what's the Number One Sarah mine?'

'It's the whole reason this town exists.'

She was watching him intently, rattling ice cubes. 'I thought there had to be a good one. You know plenty, don't you?'

'Yeah, I'm a smart guy. Plus, I read it on the wall over there.'

She tilted her head back and laughed, and he could see the string of J&Bs having their effect. 'There's probably a lot you can teach me about this town.'

He drank the remains of his beer. 'I could punish you severely from here to Christmas. Given the opportunity.'

Two hours after that they were in bed in his cabin—he examining the spartan layout of the room while she half-dozed in the crook of his arm. They'd made love twice, very fast, very satisfyingly, and then, intoxicated and spent, she'd crashed out. Half an hour had passed since then, and she was vaguely coming to. Now he turned, looked at her still face and thought: is this really happening or what? He touched her mussed-up hair, kissed her lightly on the cheek. She moved towards him, murmuring, and he cradled her warm face in his hand and kissed her lips. Her mouth was paper-dry from all that J&B. He raised himself over her and ran the point of his tongue over her breasts and nipples, which were sticky and pungent with semen. Then, as delicately as possible—not wishing to intrude too much on her rest—he moved one of her legs aside and slid his erection partway in . . .

In less than a minute he was all set, but then, somewhere from the deep—the voice rising as if from a dream—came a plaintive murmur: 'Wait.'

He slowed his rhythm, then stopped; she was moving her hands over his sinewy back muscles, then reaching into the clammy space between them and taking his fully charged cock firmly in hand and bringing it out. Now she was fully awake.

'Lie on your back,' she said.

He didn't need to be told twice. Wordlessly she sat astride him, opened wide, worked his cock back inside her and then leaned right over him, pinning his wrists down while she fucked him in her own sweet, slow fashion, twisting and squirming this way and that while brushing his face with her breasts. When it arrived her orgasm was a torrid, violent spasm, thrilling him too with its power as she pressed her supple body against his, finally releasing his wrists and kissing him violently on the mouth, even giving him a nip and drawing blood.

Holding her tight he said, 'Baby . . . I have to let go, *now.*'

After a muted cry of protest she stopped squirming and slowly hauled herself up. Her cheeks and throat were blotched crimson from sexual excitement and rubbing against his five o'clock shadow, and there was a smear of blood on her lower lip. She seemed in no hurry at all. With a cruelly tantalising languor she lifted and then lowered herself several more times before drawing out and gripping his cock. Straightaway streams of bright, pearly sperm spilled over his black pelt of stomach hair. But some had gone inside her too.

She was an unusual woman in this day and age. Halfway through the night she suddenly went down on him, tossing the blankets back and going about it in a blind, almost savage frenzy. This is one crazy chick, he thought, his blood racing, and then she surprised him totally by going all the way and bringing him right off into her mouth. Jesus, when was the last time that had happened? He couldn't remember. One thing for sure— he wouldn't forget this one-night stand in a hurry.

He got up, switched on the bedside lamp. She was so dry-mouthed, she'd said, so he fetched a glass of water from the tiny bathroom. She watched him come towards her in the half-light. He walked around naked as if it were the most normal thing in the world—not showing off, not embarrassed, just . . . nonchalant. The impression he gave was that he had spent most of his life in an all-male environment with shared bathrooms, such as the army maybe. And his physique was, to her mind, perfect—no fat, no excess muscle, lean and rangy like a feral animal. He was sure feral in the clinches.

He sat on the edge of the bed and handed her the glass. She took a deep, thirsty drink, then gasped: it was icy-cold. He put the glass on the bedside table. She ran a hand along his arm, feeling its smooth, clean-cut contours.

'Better?' he whispered.

'Oh, much.'

He reached under the sheet and cupped one of her breasts. It fitted perfectly into his hand. She'd noticed he had a discreet little tattoo high on his right arm, and now she saw what it was: crossed pistols. She was about to remark on it when he said, 'You don't seem too worried about safe sex.'

She smiled. Her hand travelled down his chest and stomach, on which the hair was stiff with dry semen. 'I've been the dutiful little woman forever. Now I'm breaking out. Living dangerously.' Soon she was playing with his cock, which—unusually—was soft.

'I'm afraid you're not in much danger from me,' he said. 'For what it's worth, I've never done hard drugs, and I haven't had any sex in . . . years.'

She gave him the full benefit of her bright green eyes. 'Years? Truly? What happened—did you take a vow of chastity and live in a cell?'

By way of reply he gave a noncommittal little smile.

She was still playing with his cock: apparently trying to get it up, but so far without a lot of success.

'So, why are you cutting loose?' he said. 'I mean . . . why now? Why here?' *Why me?*

She collected her thoughts. 'My husband—soon to be my *ex*-husband—is a lawyer. No, I do him an injustice. He is a very famous and *wealthy* barrister, a top QC. We have the Toorak mansion, a very nice townhouse in East Melbourne, various blue-chip properties all over the country, the ski lodge, the cars, exclusive clubs . . . He is going to be a Supreme Court judge one day soon. He is also a philanderer, with the morals of a stray cat. No, that's unfair to cats. All our married life he has fucked other women. Specifically, blonde nymphets are his weakness. I have known about this and, to my shame, accepted it because of the comfy lifestyle to which I have become accustomed. But . . . recently he went to Sydney, staying with his Sydney pal. It was supposedly a working visit. They hired some whores and spent three days fucking, snorting cocaine and swilling champagne. I found all this out because someone sent me an anonymous letter detailing his activities. Some colleague he'd put offside, no doubt. My husband has a loose and often vitriolic mouth when he's among the fellows, you see. According to the note there was even some . . . *homosexual* activity in front of the girls. That part knocked me for a loop, even though I have noticed in the past how his sexual orientation becomes increasingly blurred when he's loaded.

I always dismissed these tendencies as a natural product of his precious education. How naïve I have been. So, anyway . . . I confronted him with this knowledge, and do you know what he said? "Bit late in the day to start bitching now, isn't it? Do yourself a favour—stay out of my personal affairs." Stay out of my personal affairs! Can you believe it? Oh, the *outrage*! Stay out of my personal affairs? This is supposed to be my fucking *husband* speaking. So I moved out that day. All I took were two suitcases of my clothes and some personal effects. And I'm not going back, ever. Fuck him. Fuck him and his filthy, disgusting little *personal affairs.*'

She was trembling violently with rage. He lifted her and held her tight while she sobbed. They held on to each other, perfect strangers in a cold, primitive room in this remote zone as a gust of wind rattled some branches outside.

In a while they made love once more, and then at around six she said, 'Christ. I have to go, lover.'

'Sure?'

She touched his face with her fingertips and said, 'No, I'm not sure. But I'll go anyway.'

'I'll take you,' he said.

'Oh, yes,' she said. 'Thanks.' She appeared to have forgotten he'd driven her here from the hotel, about three kilometres away, along a rutted dirt track. She seemed to have no idea where she was.

Outside it was cold, the coldest time of day—immediately pre-dawn. The sky was clear, the stars still bright. It didn't necessarily mean a fine day was in the offing. Weather could change suddenly and dramatically in Buzzards Hut. He remembered once as a boy setting out for a walk in brilliant sunshine, no clouds anywhere, then finding himself caught in no-man's land, drenched to the bone with icy rain and shivering under a tree. You always had to be prepared for anything here.

Climbing into his Land Cruiser he fired up the engine and switched on the heater/demister. In seconds it was warm and

snug in the cabin. When she was aboard he looked across. Like
him she was battered, ravaged; her hair was in disarray and her
clothes thrown on anyhow. The hooded green eyes looked
ready to shut down. She stared ahead, focusing, then glanced
at him. She looked ready to pass the day alone in her 'deluxe'
bed at the hotel, not tramping through the woods watching for
native birds and admiring the view. Catching a whiff of sex from
her skin he squeezed her hand, then reversed the vehicle and
exited the property. Scattered about were large, unidentifiable
pieces of rusted mining equipment, displayed like an art
installation. Everything but everything in Buzzards Hut was
connected to gold mining. And although the town relied totally
on tourism, its mindset was still that of the Deep South—
suspicious of strangers, even violently disposed towards them.
You had to watch your step, and your words, in Buzzards Hut.
A visitor was once shot dead in the bar at the pub, simply
because he was an outsider. A local came in with a deer rifle
and put a .308 round into his stomach. It was a strange mixture
of a place—charming in its way, but dangerous. Vulnerable,
even fragile, but a law unto itself: a true frontier town that had
doggedly refused to move forward with the years.

Outside the pub they sat still, motor idling, as if waiting
for a signal. Now that she was here she didn't seem at all
inclined to shift. He put his arm around her shoulder, drew
her closer and pressed their faces together.

'I won't be able to show myself in public for a week,' she
said. 'Look at the rash you've given me.' She had turned the
rear-vision mirror around to inspect her throat, which was
indeed chafed red raw. He felt a nice buzz watching her do
that, giving him her profile.

'Sorry about that,' he said. 'I, uh, lost the plot for a while
back there.'

'So did I,' she said, and kissed him softly. 'I have to say you
were perfectly brilliant in bed, despite your . . . *alleged* celibacy.'

'Alleged? Believe me, I had no option,' he said evenly.

'Oh, I don't doubt it,' she said. The desperate intensity of his lovemaking was enough to convince her he'd been deprived for a long age.

'Hope you enjoyed it as much as I did,' he said. 'Haven't had as good a time since . . . I don't know when. Ever, I'd say.'

'Ever? That's a big call.'

'Ever,' he repeated. 'No *alleged* necessary.'

They fell together again, silently embracing against the sounds of the motor and the heater fan. She whispered, 'Now that I'm here I don't really want to . . . I don't . . . *feel like* . . . *going*. Anywhere.'

'Then don't. Stay with me.'

She snaked her hands inside his down-filled jacket, right around his body, and squeezed hard. 'That'd be something, wouldn't it?'

'Yeah. One for the books.'

They hugged a little longer before disentangling.

'I don't see it somehow,' she said rather forlornly. A brief pocket of silence followed in which he, too, was trying to 'see it'. In a while she sighed, opened the door and gradually slid away from him until she was standing on the road, stretching and looking at him.

'Well,' she said.

'Well.'

There didn't seem to be anything left to say or do, so she shut the door. It didn't close properly, so she opened it again and slammed it shut. He gave it a few moments, waiting for her to turn and go, to disappear from his life. But she was just standing there, watching him with conflicting emotions written on her lovely, tired features, so he bit the bullet, turned the vehicle around in a U-turn and headed back the way they'd come.

3

He returned to the cabin, had a long, hot shower, shaved, drank a cup of instant coffee, packed his gear into an overnight bag, conducted a final inspection, then vacated the premises. He had paid cash in advance for the cabin. As he drove through the entrance a pale light was rising on the eastern horizon, so that the densely wooded hills loomed up dramatically in stark relief. It was all state forest, safe from the logging trucks but not from deer hunters, many of them weekend cowboys from the city who had a habit of shooting first and identifying the target later.

Turning right, away from town, he drove slowly along the rutted track towards the hills. Apart from the ruts and potholes there were sharp curves that had to be negotiated with care. It would not be hard, even with a four-wheel drive, to slew off the greasy surface and over the side. As he drove he kept his eyes peeled. Isolated, inaccessible-looking houses with smoking chimneys occasionally came into view. Every so often the track came into contact with the river, and it was at one of these points he was searching for a landmark—a big old willow that hung over the river, a rope with tyre attached suspended from a branch. It was a popular swimming hole for children; he had swung and jumped from that rope many a time in his green years. Round the next curve—and there it was. Part of the rope was still there, knotted around the branch like a broken noose, but the tyre was no more. This was the very edge of the town limits—ahead was nothing but wilderness and some serious climbing.

He pulled up on the river side, where there was sufficient room to park off-road. There wasn't much chance of traffic here, particularly at this early hour, but the odd intrepid explorer or cross-country motorbike rider could not be ruled out. Standing alongside the Toyota he listened to the singing river and watched the sun inching its way over the hills and into the empty sky. Only the morning star remained—a tremulous point of flame that would soon fade and disappear too. Woodsmoke from isolated houses floated in the cold air like incense as he scanned and listened—nothing other than cascading water and intermittent birdsong. He took a shovel from the back of the vehicle, crossed the track to the high side, climbed a slight embankment, stepped over a sagging barbed wire fence and, shouldering the shovel, started walking into the trees.

It was further than he remembered—and harder to find. At the time he'd tried to fix the route in his mind by taking note of particular trees, but now every tree looked the same. However, he knew to walk in a straight line for fifteen minutes, at which point a holly bush growing out of a gum tree would tell him to turn left. It was all uphill, not steep but steep enough. Soon he was sweating and breathing hard, and even though he was reasonably fit the oxygen deficit was starting to take effect. The fifteen minutes passed, and looking up, wiping perspiration from his eyes, he saw the holly sprouting wildly from the trunk of its host. He paused for a breather, leaning on the shovel, then struck left.

Another ten minutes, this time following the contour of the hillside. Sweat ran freely from his armpits and the shirt was clinging uncomfortably to his skin. Having a down jacket on didn't help. Should've left it in the car. It was a lot easier on the legs, but the trees were so dense it was impenetrable in places, forcing him to change direction temporarily. It was also extremely dark and gloomy, making him feel slightly unnerved—as if some unseen malevolent presence was closing in on him. Then came a moment of near panic when he felt he had lost his way—he had no idea which direction he was heading in, and no sun showed through the heavy canopy to use as a guide. He turned a full circle, and it all looked exactly the same: trees, trees and more trees. Now he *was* spooked. *Shit.* Something flashed past his face, and from the corner of his eye he glimpsed a beating wing—an owl, maybe.

What he needed to find was a massive stringybark with a red spike driven into its trunk at chest height. Problem was, every tree he looked at was a massive stringybark. But it was somewhere here, exactly ten minutes from the holly bush. Landscapes might change with time, but not distances. So where in the blue fuck . . . He found himself rushing like a madman from tree to tree, looking for a red spike that didn't exist. Couldn't have been removed—it had been slammed in good and deep with a sledgehammer. Then a devastating thought came to him: what if the tree had grown over the spike, completely concealing it? Was that possible in the time? Surely not . . . and yet—*where was the fucking thing*? Now he had to grasp his throat to stop himself from screaming.

He decided to get his act together by sitting on the forest floor and smoking a cigarette. In this situation one had to remain calm and *rational*. Big stringybarks with red spikes embedded in them do not simply disappear. He released streams of smoke into the earth-smelling air while a range of thoughts drifted through his mind—mainly, the lawyer's wife with whom he had spent the night. She had slipped his mind for the last half-hour or so. He hadn't been kidding when he'd told her it was the time of his life. His lingering image of her was the final one: standing outside the pub looking at him with an uncertain expression on her face. She was full of rage, that one—and for good reason. He knew he had been a medium for her to get that violence out of her system. She had picked him up for that very purpose—to hit back at the scumbag husband. No problem with that. He would do it all again, anytime.

He reached the end of the cigarette and crushed it into the earth. Looking up he noticed a horizontal ray of brilliant sunlight filtering through a gap in the trees. He followed the sunbeam, which highlighted the trunk of a giant stringybark in a blaze of coppery gold. It was a spectacular sight. Then he narrowed his eyes. The sunbeam was picking up something on the trunk, too—something red.

The goddamn tree was there all the time—how did he miss it? He gripped the spike and smiled, shaking his head. Bastard was trying to make it tough for him, as if he hadn't had it tough already. Every step of the way presented yet another fucking hurdle. Holding the shovel he walked around to the opposite side of the stringybark, pressed his back against it and measured out five regular paces. Then he stood still, looking at the damp, leafy ground beneath his feet. It had been a long and hazardous journey; now it was finally over. He removed the jacket, draped it carefully over a branch, spat into his hands—and started digging.

The permanently wet earth was soft and yielding, but it still took twenty minutes for the tip of the shovel to strike metal. Then it was at least that again before he'd dug right around the chest enough to be able to move it a little. Still, there was a lot more work to do before he would be able to lift it out. It was necessary to excavate a large area around the chest—it had been buried deep, to reduce the risk of accidental discovery by hikers or hunters, or even animals. Muscles burned and his back was aching, but he felt no pain as more and more of the chest became visible. The clash of metal on metal rang through the woods as the small hill of earth alongside him became a sizeable one. The rusted chest was now halfway clear of the ground. He tried to work the shovel under it, but there was a way to go yet. He stopped for a spell, sitting on his haunches, staring at the reward he was about to reap. *And about fucking time, too.*

In a little while he leaned the shovel against the wall of the hole he'd dug, gripped the handle at the end of the chest— and lifted. Christ it was heavy. But it moved. He pulled hard— straining, grunting, swearing and finally lifting the whole base clear of the sucking grave that seemed intent on not giving up its prize without a decent fight. When he had hold of both handles at either end he half-hauled, half-pushed with his thighs and knees until the beast was balanced on the hole's edge. Then he gathered all his remaining strength, took a deep breath and heaved until it was free and clear and on firm ground.

'Well done,' a guttural voice said. 'Good morning, my friend.'

He looked up at the figure that seemed to tower over him. But there was sweat in his eyes and he had to wipe them with his forearm before he could focus properly. Something in the voice, however, had already triggered alarm bells.

'Bernie,' he said.

'Correct,' the figure said, squatting. 'You've worked hard this morning—but not as hard as you're going to work.' He hooked his fingers into one of the trunk's handles and jerked it well away from the hole. 'I almost lost you for a while back there. That was most considerate of you, displaying your blue jacket so clearly. It served as a very efficient beacon.'

'I . . . I heard you'd retired.' The tone was placatory, almost congenial, as if they were old friends catching up.

The man called Bernie said in his distinctive gravel voice: 'News travels fast inside prison walls. Yes, that's right. I have taken the package, as the saying goes. And now I'm taking yours too.'

Bernie Walsh—real name Bernhard Hermann Wolicz, former crack detective and ex-professional prize-fighter who had served at the sharp end in a long and controversial career. Homicide, rape, drugs, armed robbery, Special Operations. In each case he had etched an indelible impression before departing in dubious circumstances, usually for cutting corners and doing things his way. In the rape squad particularly he had been notorious for bashing suspects, on one occasion shoving a rubber hose right up someone's back passage to see how they liked it. More commonly he would take them to the lavatory and beat them half to death with his fists before making them drink piss from the urinal. Not that he was any champion of justice—he also humiliated the victims with his intense, aggressive style of interrogation, which often resulted in tears, nervous breakdowns and official complaints. Like an army officer he carried a brass-tipped swagger stick under his arm, and one of his little tricks was to slam it on the table when the suspect started nodding off after hours of questioning. The fact was, Bernie Walsh enjoyed hurting people.

Now he stood over the man in the hole, vigorously chewing gum. He was fully erect and looked supremely fit for a sixty-year-old. He had on sturdy cotton trousers, hiking boots, a thermal shirt and sleeveless wool vest. On his back was a daypack, and in his hand a revolver that looked very much like a .38 calibre Smith & Wesson Chief's Special.

'Keep digging,' he instructed. 'Dig the hole longer—and deeper. Six feet deep will suffice. Dig until I tell you to stop.'

He dug steadily, not fast but not too slowly either. Bernie Walsh was no fool—he had an unerring nose for tricks, he was a cop who could read hearts and souls, and it would not do to make him angry or impatient. The dirt pile mounted. Now and then he paused for a much-needed rest, wiping sweat and flecks of black earth from his face with his filthy arm. His ears pounded. All the while he was thinking, trying to figure out how to get out of this mess. The future did not look encouraging, however: Walsh held all the cards. All he held was the shovel.

'Come on,' Walsh said during a spell. 'No slacking off. We don't want some fucking animal scratching up your putrid remains, do we? That won't do. Dig deep, my friend. Put your shoulders into it.'

Bernie Walsh called everyone 'my friend', even the prisoners he used to bash. 'Come with me, my friend,' he would say, leading them by the scruff of the neck to the toilet block. 'It's back to school for you.' In truth, however, he had no real friends, only colleagues. Of his personal life little was known, except that he had a slave-wife who apparently maintained the Walsh residence in the spartan manner of an army barracks, ready for his inspection when he arrived home at night. Not that any visitors ever saw inside it. And he had two sons—both clear-eyed, straight-backed young men, one a tax investigator and the other a customs officer: chips off the old block. Walsh had a reputation for drinking vast amounts of Schnapps and eating huge platefuls of pickled pork, boiled potatoes and cabbage—every night for dinner it was the same. Or so the story went.

After three-quarters of an hour he sagged against the shovel and said, 'Bernie, I'm so fucking dry. Have you got some water?'

Keeping the revolver trained on him Bernie swung the daypack from his shoulder, produced a small bottle of mineral water and tossed it over. 'Thirsty work, is it? Never mind, my friend, you're nearly done. Then you can rest . . . forever.'

The deeper he went, however, the harder the ground became. And there were tree roots to be hacked through, which was not easy given his state of near-exhaustion. Progress was slow. But another half-hour went by; the grave was waist-deep, almost long enough for him to lie in with his legs folded. Any second now he expected Walsh to pull him up.

'That's enough, my friend,' he commanded a few minutes later. 'You have done very well indeed. Now comes your reward.'

Blinking hard to get the stinging sweat from his eyes he looked up at Walsh, who seemed about ten feet tall with his legs astride, jaw working, the gun hand extended. The sun was now spearing through the trees and catching Walsh side-on, so that he resembled an Aryan man-god from a Second World War propaganda poster. His taut, muscular cheekbones flashed as he chewed and his military number-one cut glittered like shaved corn.

The soon-to-be dead man stood still in the grave, legs trembling with fatigue and fear, the shaft of the shovel in his left hand, staring at Bernie and waiting for the *crack* that would send him on his way. He was as good as resigned to it.

'Pass me the shovel,' Bernie Walsh said, moving closer, squatting on his haunches and reaching out with his left hand while holding the gun level and steady in the right. He was not smiling, just watching his victim's eyes as the shaft of the shovel was tipped towards his waiting hand. 'Come on, come on,' he said. But then the shaft, almost within his grasp, fell sideways, and in a reflexive movement Bernie made a lunge for it. It was only a split-second, and he barely took his eyes off the victim at all—but it was enough.

The ground was slippery, and he teetered forward involuntarily, becoming slightly unbalanced. In that split-second a grimy, sweaty hand from nowhere clamped around his right wrist. Bernie Walsh's jaw dropped open and his eyes widened. In the next instant he flew face first through the air, into the grave with the intended victim, crashing in an ungainly heap and ending up in a tangle of arms and legs with a mouthful of soil. On impact the revolver spilled from his hand. He twisted around, scrabbling for a hold somewhere, searching for the weapon, then found himself staring up at the man holding the shovel. The expression that froze his face was a marriage of disbelief and terror. How could their positions have been reversed so suddenly?

He was about to speak, to issue an order perhaps, when the back of the blade slammed down onto his face. He saw the blow coming a fraction before the light show exploded inside his skull. A loud metallic *clang* reverberated through the clear morning air. Walsh made a horrible squealing noise, a panic-driven cry, before the shovel came down again and again, a dozen times, fifteen, every blow smashing into him with equal force, until blackness enveloped him and Bernie Walsh's head was a flattened, compacted mixture of blood, mud and brain. At the end, the back of the shovel's blade was thickly encrusted with dark reddish matter, along with teeth and bone shards.

He wiped the blade on Bernie's olive pants before leaning it against the grave wall. A hot, jagged breath seared his throat raw and his heart pumped so hard it echoed in his ears like the shovel smacking onto Bernie's head. Leaning against the wall he rested for a full five minutes while his system gradually recovered from the massive trauma of a near-death encounter. Then he turned his attention to Bernie Walsh. He went through his pockets, removing wallet, handkerchief, keys, a Swiss army knife, some coins, matches, odds and ends. In the daypack was a map of the area, another pistol—semi-automatic—some loose ammunition, a small mobile phone, binoculars, a notepad, felt-tip pens, tin of Dutch cigars, chewing gum packets, a hand towel, toilet bag, soiled socks and underpants. He zipped up the pack and tossed it clear of the grave, pocketed the dead man's watch and gold wedding band and started to climb out. As he was doing so he noticed Bernie's legs moving in a strange, circular, slow motion manner, and a weird, bubbling sound issuing from the place where his mouth had once been. Christ—the man was still *alive*. The brain was smashed to pulp, but the heart and the rest of his body refused to accept the verdict. He grabbed the shovel and finished the job with a welter of blows that put the matter beyond doubt.

Filling in the plot was a lot easier than digging it—in fifteen minutes the job was completed. He then covered the grave with leafmeal, sticks and pieces of foliage until he was satisfied no-one would look twice at it. Just to make sure he hauled a heavy fallen branch over it, arranging it to look like a natural occurrence. Now there was absolutely no indication of anything untoward. Satisfied, he turned his attention to the chest. Using the shovel he broke the rusted padlock, then slowly lifted the lid. He liked what he saw, but did not allow himself to smile. There was a time for smiling, and it sure wasn't now.

With Bernie Walsh's daypack on his back and the shovel over his shoulder he dragged the chest back to the sagging wire fence, checked both ways, then loaded everything including his down jacket into the back of the Land Cruiser. Not far down the road, towards town, was a white Ford Falcon—presumably Walsh's. They would know where to start searching once he was reported missing. Too bad, but since there was nothing he could do about it there was no point worrying. The body was well concealed, and there was no obvious trail to the grave site.

He knelt at the bank and washed his face and arms in the cold river before cupping his hands and drinking his fill. It was very bracing indeed. After he'd dried off in the vehicle, using Walsh's hand towel, he fired up the engine and drove deeper into state forest, where the track became steep and winding. Ominous rainclouds were rapidly filling the sky. On a level stretch he stopped, got out and looked over the side. There was a sheer precipice that went down a long way. Keeping the automatic pistol and spare ammunition, the phone and notepad, he stowed all Walsh's possessions in the daypack, including the watch and wedding ring, zippered it securely and flung it over the edge. It bounced and tumbled down into obscurity and was soon swallowed up by rugged, impenetrable scrub and rocks. The shovel followed, and it too disappeared. Specks of rain began to fall.

It was necessary to drive on along the narrow, dangerous track for some time before he could find enough room to turn around. All the while he had plenty to think about. What was Bernie Walsh doing coming after him in what was obviously a well-planned operation? How did he know to come to Buzzards Hut? He had information, he was thoroughly equipped, and he was armed up and prepared to kill. One thing was for sure: where there was one, there were bound to be two—or more. Bernie Walsh was a soldier, an effective and fearsome one, but he'd never been leadership material. He had to be working for someone. Who the fuck would that be, after all this time? And while he pondered, Bernie Walsh's phone trilled on the passenger seat.

Immediately he hit the brakes, snatched the phone and hit the caller ID button. Committing this to memory he then answered in Bernie Walsh's gravelly monotone: 'Yes.'

The squeaky voice at the other end said: 'Anything to report?'

'No developments at this stage, my friend.'

Silence, then: 'What's the subject up to?'

'Very little—to any purpose.'

'He *must* have a purpose, or what the fuck is he *doing* there?'

'If he has, it is not apparent. Perhaps he enjoys the clean mountain air.'

'Well . . . stay on it. And keep me informed. Make sure you only use this number.'

'If anything happens, my friend, you'll be the first to know.' *Click.*

And who are you, my friend?

Light misty rain blurred the windshield as he drove slowly through town. Approaching the hotel he saw a figure sitting on a bench, a rucksack beside her. She watched him come, and only stood when he had stopped in front of her. The passenger side window whirred down.

'Good morning,' she said, leaning in.

'Good morning. I thought you'd be sleeping.'

'I was. You?'

'No chance. I had something on my mind. It kept me awake.'

'Me too.' Silence, then: 'I figured you'd have to come by eventually, if I sat here long enough.'

'There's only one way back to the real world.'

'I was wondering if I could . . . hitch a lift. I've decided this bushwalking caper is definitely *not* for me.'

'A lift? Sure. Is that all your gear?'

'It's enough.'

He got out and hoisted the brand-new, expensive rucksack into the back. It was heavy. 'That's good equipment,' he said.

'When it comes to luggage in future, I'll stick with Louis Vuitton.'

Inside the cabin they looked at each other.

'Here we go then,' he said.

'Here we go,' she said. Then she leaned over and planted a delicate kiss on his lips. While she did this he snaked an arm around her and lightly squeezed the back of her neck. The scent of her freshly shampooed hair engulfed him.

In a few minutes they were heading down the mountain, swerving between potholes. Sizeable patches of snow were scattered through the impenetrable scrub on either side of the road.

'This is a nice car,' she said, stretching out. 'Comfortable. Plenty of . . . room, to move around, stretch one's legs.'

'Not mine,' he said. 'It's rented.'

Her hand was resting on his thigh. 'So how long have you been out of prison?' she said. She was a cool one.

He checked his wristwatch. 'About . . . twenty-eight hours.'

She looked at him and said, 'It doesn't matter a damn to me. I was just curious.'

'That's okay.'

'How long were you in for?'

'Eleven years, give or take.'

Silence, then: 'Wow.'

'Yeah. Wow.'

She turned half side-on, facing him, and said, 'Incidentally, in case you're interested, my name's Joanna. Joanna Steer. But people call me Jo.'

Joanna Steer . . . Steer . . . Husband a famous QC . . .

'Are you married to Raydon Steer?' he said after a space.

'I am. Do you know him?'

'No, not personally. I know *of* him. I'm aware of his . . . fame, or notoriety.'

'Notoriety is *exactly* the word,' she said bitterly.

Silence descended while they both thought about the top-priced lawyer who was always in the papers, always on a big case, defending some corrupt tycoon with bottomless pockets: the type of upscale client who can afford the very best representation. Then she said, 'And do you have a name? Or will I call you mystery man and best fuck this side of Paradise?'

He laughed unexpectedly. 'You can call me that if you want. But my real name's Shaun. Shaun McCreadie.'

'Shaun McCreadie,' she said, tapping fingers on her lips.

He lit a Lucky Strike while she processed the information. 'Any bells ringing?'

'Nope,' she said.

'Good.'

They broke the journey once for sex, pulling over on a flat, treeless tract of rocky high country that was as wild and wind-blasted as any Scottish upland heath. In the middle distance was a single rundown farmhouse that looked like the façade of a movie set—there were no animals or crops here, no signs of life, just prehistoric terrain that stretched away for miles, against a backdrop of snowy mountaintops. Golden sun showers and intermittent hail swept over the vehicle under an eerie black sky. Sitting astride him on the passenger seat she directed all traffic, her flushed face resting against his sandpapery jaw while he stroked the damp undersides of her buttocks. Soon he slipped his fingers up under her shirt, unclipped her bra and released her breasts, allowing them to sit in his hands while she lifted and lowered herself with delicious, maddening slowness. Outside, rain and hail swished on the vehicle like handfuls of lead shot being thrown, while in the fogged-up confines of the cabin there was short breathing, the rustle of half-removed clothing and the luscious wet sound of lovemaking.

They were approaching Marysville, winter tread tyres whining on bitumen, when she said, 'What's the plan, then?'

'Plan?'

'As in, what are you going to do now? Where are we heading?'

'Thought I'd check into a motel,' he said. Pause, then: 'After I take you wherever you want to go.'

They were passing a battered, psychedelic campervan jammed with holiday gear and a stressed-out, hippie-looking family, with half a dozen bicycles attached, when she said, 'Tell you what. Forget the motel. Why not stay at my place?'

He didn't answer for a while, so she said, 'I mean the townhouse in East Melbourne. There's plenty of space. And I'm the only one there.'

He gave it some thought. 'What about children?'

'We have two teenaged sons, and they're both at boarding school. Wealth does bestow certain privileges.'

'So I've been led to believe.'

'It's a fair transaction, don't you think—a free ride for a free bed? And . . . whatever, on the side.'

'"Whatever"?'

'Yeah.'

He concentrated on negotiating a series of tight curves in the road, but all the while his mind was elsewhere.

'Nice offer', he said. 'But I wouldn't want to crowd you.'
His mind flashed and ricocheted in all directions.

'You wouldn't be crowding me.' She slid a hand along his
thigh. 'Not unless you wanted to, anyway.'

Christ, he thought. She only has to touch me anywhere
and I bar up like a randy dog.

'Deal?' she said. Now her hand was right on his groin, the
hard muscle striving upwards beneath her fingers.

'Deal,' he said.

'And stay as long as you like.'

'Okay. Thanks.'

'You're not a very . . . *effusive* person, are you?'

Smiling at her he said: 'I can be effusive. And I will be soon
if you keep doing that.'

Driving on, cruising through leafy Marysville, she unclipped
her seatbelt and without a word snuggled down comfortably
across his legs while he played with her hair. In less than a minute
she was sleeping soundly. Astonishing. Glancing down at her
serene face he experienced a moment of pure happiness—what
the prison chaplain, Father O'Gorman, would have called 'an
epiphany, when you thank God you're alive'. *Not a bad day's work
for an ex-con: got what I came for, survived Bernie Walsh, hooked up
with a hot woman, and now . . . a safe house. How easy is this?*

Not exactly what the priest had in mind.

4

The 'townhouse' was in fact a classic, two-storey Victorian terrace in high-priced Powlett Street. After he'd driven past it she directed him around the corner to a rear lane, where there was access via a steel garage door which she raised using a remote. Immediately they were inside, a sensor spotlight flooded the entire back yard. The garage was big enough to house three vehicles. Parked in it were a recent model maroon Honda Prelude and a Land Rover Discovery, in British racing green.

'Don't worry, the Honda's mine,' Jo said, noticing his interest. 'Tractor's Raydon's. Mind you, it's never been driven in anger—and I'd say all it's ever *discovered* is the Australia Club.'

It was a lavish residence. Somehow 'townhouse' did not cut it. Large, expensively furnished and carpeted rooms, chandeliers, magnificent curved staircase. Upstairs were four or maybe five bedrooms. Jo flung her rucksack into the main one, which had an en suite jacuzzi, and opened a window onto the wrought-iron balcony.

'Put your bag anywhere,' she instructed.

He dropped it on the floor and joined her on the balcony. From here you could see the MCG, the gleaming white superstructure of the tennis centre complex and suburbs sprawling far and wide.

Jo said: 'Governor Landy used to live a few houses from here before he moved to a slightly more prestigious address. We were on vaguely nodding terms. I said hello to him when he passed by once.'

'My experience of the governor is a bit different from yours,' Shaun said with a raised brow. 'Come in here.'

'Why?' she said, mouth opened slightly, face upturned, as his arm curled around her waist. 'What's on *your* mind, you vicious rampant animal?'

He drew her inside and roughly stripped her off where she stood, arms held out slightly. Even while he was unclipping her bra and pulling down her fancy knickers with a pink rose on the front, she just watched him, head tilted to one side with an insouciant fuck-you expression on her face that made his blood race. But when he nuzzled into her beaver and gave her the point of his tongue she sighed and pushed his face roughly against her with both hands.

They made mad love twice on the luxurious king-sized bed. On the second occasion she sucked his cock for half an hour, but was unable to produce the goods.

'I hope you realise that's the longest I've ever gone down,' she said, rising for air—and a nice long open-mouthed kiss.

'Let me help,' he said. He turned her over onto her back, put it deep in her mouth, cupped the back of her head and delivered in next to no time.

When they were lazing around on the satin sheets afterwards, she studied his face and said, 'Have you noticed how we look alike?'

'I have noticed that, yes.'

She ran a finger down his nose and over his lips to his chin. 'Same green eyes. Not contacts, are they?'

'No. You?'

'Nope. Same nose. Same shaped mouth . . . same profile.' She touched each feature as she mentioned it. 'Slight gap between front teeth, chin cleft, even a crease in the same place—here.' She traced a fingertip down one cheek, which was creased from his habit of smiling on one side of his face. 'Bizarre, isn't it?'

'Yeah. What does it mean?'

She shrugged. 'We must be related. There's a common gene pool somewhere in the dim distant past. What's it called? Six degrees of separation.'

'You can explain it to me one day,' he said.

'Don't they show movies in prison?'

That made him grin on the creased side of his face. 'Certainly not in mine. It's no fucking summer camp, baby.'

Pause, then she said: 'How old are you?'

'Forty-two. You?'

She said, 'Thirty-nine. And I'm not bullshitting—I really *am* thirty-nine.'

'You are also *evil*,' he said, holding her.

'Better watch out then. I might fast-track you to hell.'

'If you did I probably wouldn't care. Anyhow I've seen hell. It doesn't do anything for me.'

In a little bit she said, 'When I saw you in the hotel yesterday, I was instantly attracted. Bang, I thought. That's for me. I want a big piece of what he's got.'

'I was watching you, and then . . . I thought you'd gone. But you came up behind me, on my blind side . . .' *Someone does that inside, it usually means they've got a knife . . .*

'I didn't want you to slip away.'

She touched the whiskers on his face and said, 'I love this two-day growth. Promise me you'll always have it.'

'You're on.'

'How *do* you maintain a two-day growth? I mean . . . how do you stop it becoming a three-day growth?'

'I'll have to work on that one. But I'm sure there's a little man in South Yarra who'll arrange it for me.'

'Oh, without a doubt. And I know *just* the little man.'

Another string of kisses, then she said, breathing the words into his mouth: 'Do you think we're just going to screw each other stupid all the time?'

'Believe it,' he said, hovering over her. She gripped his erection, spread her thighs wide and slid it in. Then he felt her legs cross behind his back as she rocked evenly up and down, up and down. Even though she was slick his cock felt chafed and sore, but he didn't care. In fact the pain made it all the more real and exciting somehow. The more it hurt, the more he loved it. My God, he thought, if this is the road to hell, here I come . . .

While she was having a shower in the en suite, Shaun stretched out on the spacious bed with his fingers interlocked behind his head. Shit, it was a long way from his narrow little steel number in the Barwon Correctional Facility. Turning his head sideways he appraised himself in the mirrored wardrobe. He didn't look bad, considering. Weathered, creases etched deeper into the skin, but nothing too radical. Earlier they had watched themselves fucking in the mirror, which seemed to have been put there for that purpose. She sure had some serious anger directed at Raydon Steer, distinguished QC, to work out of her system. Anger and passion seemed to live together in her, side by side. Well, if she wanted to deal with it with the help of Shaun's cock he had no objection.

There were, however, more pressing matters that needed sorting out—mainly the chest, which was still in the securely locked Land Cruiser downstairs. It couldn't stay there, and in any case the car had to be returned soon. Tomorrow, maybe. He heard the taps go off in the bathroom, and his thoughts returned to their starting point. What about Joanna Steer?

Well, what about her indeed?

Funny how she didn't mind at all that he was an ex-con—in fact that seemed to turn her on. Maybe he was simply in the right place at the right time following her marriage bust-up. Or—a real possibility—maybe she was one of those apparently respectable women who got off screwing men who came from the edge. There was a particular breed of female that went in for that—he had seen them on visiting days, weeping and carrying on for the lowlife loser on the other side of the mesh screen as if he were a holy martyr. But Jo hit on him before knowing what he was—unless she was psychic. Maybe she was.

In any case Shaun didn't consider himself a bona fide *violent criminal*, not by comparison with the real hardcore inmates, the ones who regarded that status as a badge of honour. In the slams he never really connected with the mainstream of prison life. He didn't adopt its culture or code of conduct, which was basically the 'us-and-them' mentality. He didn't make alliances—or enemies—with anyone. His simple philosophy was: the fewer people you deal with, the fewer problems you have. He didn't try to curry favour with screws either. In effect he shut himself down for the duration, as a way of boilerplating himself against the brain-numbing boredom, moronic attitudes, power plays and the ever-present potential for serious aggravation. All around him men responded to their situation in different ways: they built up their bodies in the gym, studied obsessively, became jailhouse philosophers or lawyers, slowly lost their minds down the drainpipes and sewers of the prison system—or discovered God, in one of his many guises. Shaun's attitude was, I'm in here for a long time, and there's nothing I can do about that. I survive by not letting it touch me, not buying into any prison bullshit, and above all by staying clean. Nothing about it made him feel as if he belonged among the deadheads and self-mutilators, the poor innocent victims of a corrupt criminal justice system, the ones who 'didn't do it', and the drug-crazed, delusional lifers with their big talk and big plans. He wasn't scared or intimidated; he felt . . . nothing. He was dead, or dormant, inside. In a way, he wasn't even there. Someone spoke to him, he rarely answered or even acknowledged them. In eleven years he was never involved in a fight or any serious misdemeanour. You had to be 'stand-up', to be sure, even hostile at times, but that didn't mean you had to swing a fist at anyone who came near you. Surprisingly, few prisoners ever gave him grief, even though he'd been a cop. In a way he was almost invisible. And he was *never* going to be anyone's bitch. The only time he was approached for sex he looked the guy over, then told him he had herpes, and that was the end of it. Word spread inside.

Shaun didn't believe he *looked* like an ex-con either. He didn't have that combative, haunted convict's face. He lacked the empty yard stare, the ugly web of tattoos, the don't-fuck-with-me legs-apart stance or the pumped-up upper body and biceps from marathon sessions lifting weights in the prison gym. He did not feel mentally stunted, as he had a right to be after such a long period of incarceration and the sensory deprivation that went with it. Nor did he possess the edginess and paranoia that could tip over into explosive violence. At a pinch he could pass for a rock star of the jaded, brooding variety—except that he lacked the ego and drug habit.

Another thing about Joanna—she hadn't asked what he'd done to score an eleven-year stretch. People always wanted to know what you did—it was the first thing anyone asked you inside. You told them, or you told them to mind their own fucking business. Maybe she was being tactful, but she didn't strike him as a tactful person. Quite the opposite, in fact. It didn't have to mean anything, but it was slightly . . . odd. She would know it had to be a bit more than shoplifting or passing a dud cheque.

Then there was Bernie Walsh, the treacherous, murderous bastard. Shaun might not have considered himself a violent criminal, but there was no escaping the fact that he'd smashed in a man's skull with a shovel that very morning—less than a day after getting out. What choice did he have? Desperate measures were called for. Bernie was going to fill him with bullets and bury him, leave him there for the worms to eat, and Shaun had simply outplayed him. He felt little or no remorse for killing Bernie, although occasionally images of that shattered skull flashed in his brain while he was fucking Jo. And what about that voice at the other end of Bernie's phone? Shaun couldn't place it, but he had a niggling idea it was someone he'd known a long time ago. He had the number—all he had to do was trace it somehow. For the time being he decided to leave the phone switched off.

She came into the room naked, rubbing a white towel in her hair. Some drops of water glistened on her neatly trimmed black beaver.

'What are you thinking, Shaun?' she said.

'I'm thinking this is a dandy little townhouse, Jo. But is Raydon likely to turn up? I don't imagine he'd appreciate catching his wife fucking out of school under his own roof. He might whack me over the head with one of his heavy law books.'

She sat on the edge of the bed, still riffling the towel through her hair. 'Absolutely not. Raydon would never come here.'

'You seem pretty sure of yourself.'

'Well,' she said, 'let me explain. You see, this is an investment property. A first-rate one, yes, but an investment property nonetheless. We actually leased it to this character, some high-flying Indonesian bank executive, who turns out to be on a wanted list back in Jakarta. He was a bosom buddy of former President Suharto's son Tommy, who has apparently scammed around half the GNP of Indonesia. This guy asked no questions and couldn't move in fast enough. He peeled off a year's lease in cash as if he was tipping a bellhop. Anyhow, he vanished a month ago, hours before the police arrived. Left everything— all the furniture and fittings are his, even the premium wine collection downstairs. Have you any cigarettes?'

'Over there. In the pants pocket.'

She dropped the towel on the floor and went over, showing him an appealing rear view—lovely curved back and buttocks which were damp and slightly reddened from sexual activity. When she found the cigarettes she lit one, took a deep draw and turned around, cupping her elbow in her hand as she smoked. She was so damn cool it made his chest bump.

'Raydon would never come here because . . . it would be beneath him,' she said. 'He is a Toorak man, through and through. He would absolutely have to be dynamited out of Irving Road. Raydon comes from old Toorak stock: he is Toorak right down to his Savile Row chalkstripe suits and his Churchill cigars. Oh, and the royal tennis. Don't forget the fucking royal tennis.'

'But his Land Rover's here.'

That drew a half-hearted shrug. 'He must've come to check out the place after the guy—the banker—took off. Why it's still here I don't know. He probably took a taxi into town for a six-hour lunch with his cronies and forgot all about the Land Rover. Raydon owns lots of cars. He's not exactly in the John Laws class, but he's not too far behind. He buys cars the way other men buy shirts. I'd be willing to bet he's completely forgotten where the Rover is. He wouldn't give it a thought.' She flicked ash into an empty vase. 'So you don't need to worry about him showing up. The only communications I'll have with Raydon from now on will be through his lawyers.'

'You're definitely going to divorce him?'

'Shit, yes. Soon as the twelve months are up.' Again she flicked ash into the vase. She could even make a casual, careless gesture like that sexually provocative. 'You said something before—last night—about not having had sex for a long time. Eleven years, I presume. I can't match that, but I'd say I haven't had sex with Raydon for a year or more. Even that would only have been an alcohol-induced three-minute invasion of my sleep. Sex eventually . . . slipped off the agenda. He was either too pissed, too far away or too preoccupied rooting one of his little nymphets.'

'He's crazy.'

She shrugged one shoulder. 'He's a man. Thinks, eats and works with his dick. The definitive, squalid, sex-obsessed, self-serving, ultra-privileged, venal, God-awful Toorak man, complete with carefully cultivated lisp. Rich filth.'

'Rich filth. I like that,' he said.

'That's exactly what he is. Christ, I can't wait to throw him out of my life. The only snag will be the property settlement. He'll pull every devious, nasty trick in the business to make sure I get screwed financially. But we'll go all the way through the courts if necessary. I don't care. If it costs me, it's going to cost him twice as much. And I'll see to it he cops plenty of adverse publicity, the low *cunt*.'

The last part was spat out with a violence that surprised him. Christ, did she have it in for this man.

'Why don't you put that out and come here,' he said.

She dropped the cigarette into the vase, walked over and sat on the edge of the bed again, twisting her upper body towards him and putting a hand on her hip. Just the way she did that gave him a cracking horn.

'What now?'

He reached out and cupped a breast. It was lightly dimpled. He brushed his thumb across the nipple and watched her eyes flicker. 'Something needs your attention here.'

She could see his cock had risen sharply under the sheet. First she felt and rubbed it through the slinky material, getting him good and fired up, then slowly drew back the sheet. Maintaining eye contact with him all the way, she lowered her head, licked her lips and opened her mouth . . .

Late next day, and Shaun ventured out for some air. The previous night had been a fractured mix of fitful sleep and sudden, wild bouts of sex. It was insane and sublime. He could never seem to get enough of her. After a breakfast of fresh-ground coffee and croissants from the gourmet bakery on the corner, he'd soaked for half an hour in the claw-footed bath while the melancholy strains of J. S. Bach floated on angel wings through the airy house. It was a far remove from the noxious rap noise and pounding techno shit from prison ghetto blasters.

He was enjoying his freedom—the idea of it, the fact that he could wander down the street to the corner shop to buy cigarettes and a newspaper, the PM edition of the *Herald Sun*, and exchange brief pleasantries with the shopkeeper. People were so damn civil. On the way back a man with a small white dog on a leash smiled and wished him good evening. There had been a heavy shower, and steam wafted up from the pavement. It felt good to be alive—and free. No screws slapping nightsticks against their thighs, no pig swill served up as food, no electric fences and razor wire, clanging cell doors, lights out and then the tortured sounds of men jacking off in the privacy only darkness provided. No more being caged up all day and night with psychotics and desperate, drug-addicted lowlifes. He was noticing wholesale change, too: the city skyline, which seemed to have been swallowed up by glass-sheathed towers, including the casino/hotel complex that soared over everything on the revamped Southbank; the cars, which—like the glass towers—all looked the same, sleek and futuristic; clothes, cafes, apartments, every damn thing. Even the trams and trains were different. People were younger, fitter and better dressed than they used to be, and most of them had a mobile phone. Everywhere he looked there was evidence of new prosperity and vast amounts invested in property development. It was as if, in the last eleven years, the floodgates had opened and washed away the old drab face of the capital, transforming it into a more glamorous one.

But not here, not in the precious enclave of East Melbourne. In this neighbourhood, early evening sunlight slanted onto the stately homes and solid apartment blocks like rare gold. Even the air smelled special: it was the scent of spring blooms, fresh-washed bitumen and above all money—lots of old money. That was something he thought he could relate to.

He was sitting in a plush leather lounge chair reading the paper with a Heineken long-neck on the table beside him while Jo watched the Channel 10 five o'clock news on the Grundig wide-screen digital TV. It was no more than back-ground noise—his attention had been claimed by a short item on page 5.

Fears Held For Missing Hiker

By Brian Croft
19 September 2003
Police and Emergency Services volunteers commenced a full-scale search this morning for a man believed to be lost in rugged bush country near Buzzards Hut, in the state's northeast. The missing man, Bernard Walsh, was last seen on Tuesday night at the Scotchman's Reef cabins, where he was staying. It is believed he set out hiking early yesterday, and has not been seen since. Sergeant Ken Swabey, coordinating the search, said today that grave fears were held for Mr Walsh's safety.

'We understand he was quite well equipped for a daytime hike, when conditions are reasonable, but spending the night in sub-zero temperatures in rugged, mountainous country like this is a different story. Apparently he is a former police officer and an experienced bushwalker, so he may have been able to survive last night, but if we don't find him by nightfall today his chances obviously diminish rapidly.'

Mr Walsh's car, a recent-model Ford Falcon, was found parked on a dirt road outside Buzzards Hut, from where he apparently began hiking in heavily wooded country. His exact plans are not known, as he was travelling alone. Speaking from their home in

Melbourne, Mr Walsh's wife Rae said she did not know where her
husband had gone.

'He left on Monday night without telling me his plans. It is
not unusual—he often takes off on his own without explanation.
But I can't imagine Bernard ever being in difficulties. He is such
a capable man. It's unusual that he has vanished like this, but I'm
sure he is all right.'

'Look at this,' Jo was saying.

Shaun looked up from the paper. On the screen was a
chopper flying over dense, mountainous bush country.
A reporter sitting inside it was telling the viewers that searchers
had so far found no sign of Bernard Walsh, the 60-year-old
retired police officer who had disappeared. 'A search of his car
failed to turn up any useful information,' he shouted against
the chopper noise. 'No-one knows where he intended hiking
or when he planned to return. It's freezing cold and raining
at the moment down there, and snow threatens. Police say the
overnight temperature will fall to around 7 below zero, so if
he's not found in the next few hours it doesn't look good.'

'That's strange,' Jo said. 'He went missing when we were
there. And he was staying in those cabins—Scotchman's Reef.'

'Apparently,' Shaun said. He was looking fixedly at the
screen, not her—but her eyes were on him and he knew it—
felt it.

'Do you know this guy?' she said softly, significantly, and
sipped from her cut-glass goblet of white wine.

Now he had to look at her, and as soon as he did so it was
as if he had revealed a full hand of cards. Concealment was
not an option now. But . . . how best to play it?

'I *did* know him,' he said. 'Slightly. A long time ago.'

Again she sipped, still watching him—waiting for more.
Shaun was thinking it through, his brain racing, trying to see
ahead, weighing up alternatives . . .

And then it hit him.

If he was serious about her—and he believed he was—he would have to spill everything: the whole, sorry saga.

There could be no half-measures. He had to trust her—*wanted* to trust her. What was the point of being rich and lonely?

She watched him with patience, her face still, expressionless, waiting for him to arrive at the moment independently. He felt as if it were a test. If he lied to her now, it was all over.

'When you picked me up outside the hotel,' she said, 'you were . . . dirty. How come?'

He drank from the Heineken bottle, set it down and leaned forward in his seat. Leather squeaked.

'I was dirty, wasn't I?' he said.

'And you'd been exerting yourself. You were physically spent. As if you'd been . . . working, climbing, or doing some hard labour.'

'That's right. I was. I had been.'

'Did you know he—this Bernard Walsh—was staying at the same cabins?'

'No.' Shake of the head.

Truth was transparent—anyhow she seemed to accept that answer. But why wasn't he keen to tell her more?

'You were a cop, weren't you?' she said.

Clever girl. 'Guilty. How'd you work that one out?'

'From the tattoo—the crossed pistols. It means something special, doesn't it?'

'Well done. Should've been a goddamn cop yourself.'

She nodded, still thinking. Seemingly she was in no hurry to unwrap the intrigue surrounding him, as if it were a parlour game. Now it was her move again. 'So is there anything you'd like to share with me? I mean . . . only if you want to. I don't mean to pry.'

There it was. The matter was now at hand, and a big decision was called for. Crossroads lay before him. He'd been there before, read the signposts, made life-changing choices—only to find out too late that he'd taken the wrong turning.

And now?

Now it was different. He was older, smarter. Firmly in the driver's seat.

He wasn't about to make the same mistake again. And sooner or later you have to trust someone. Who better than the female form of himself?

Fuck it. *Confession time.*

He drained the Heineken bottle and said, 'Wait here. I'll be right back.'

She could hear him coming back up the stairs several minutes later—laboring, as if he were carrying something heavy. When he walked in with an old, rusted chest, an ancient model with cracked leather straps, she didn't say anything, didn't move.

He set it down heavily on the floor, and knelt. She could see the padlock had been recently snapped apart.

'Show and tell time,' he said.

'Okay,' she said in her cool, noncommittal way. Sitting in a Queen Anne-style chair she held one of his Luckies between her fingers, and now she drew deeply on it. He watched the thick smoke plume from her mouth, and then raised the lid.

Joanna didn't say anything. Her face gave nothing away as she stared at the contents of the old chest. There was simply no reaction—it might have been empty.

He was prepared to wait, as she had been. This moment would decide everything.

Thirty seconds passed before she exhaled more smoke and said softly, 'Holy. Fucking. Christ.'

Shaun knelt with his hands resting on his thighs. He didn't speak—there was nothing to say yet.

'How much is it?' she said, eyes fixed on the tightly packed wads of currency, all fifties and hundreds, that three-quarter filled the chest.

'Two point eight million,' he said. 'And some loose change.'

In time she tore her eyes away from the spectacle of so much cold cash and met his gaze.

Shaun said, 'Do you think there'd be a decent bottle of red wine in that banker's cellar?'

'I'm certain of it,' she said. 'How about French? As I told you, he has a second to none collection of premium vintage.'

'Bring it up,' he said. 'I'll tell you a story.'

'This is going to be some story, right?'

'Uh huh. It's never been told before, either.'

'Could take more than one bottle of wine.'

He smiled at last—it was the first crack in her cool, self-assured façade, the first sign she was entering into the contract. 'Could take a dozen. Maybe even the rest of your life,' he said.

5

A good day in Carlton—after noontime, Lygon Street: dappled spring sunshine filtering through the heavily leafed plane trees onto the pavement, plenty of strollers, office slaves out for lunch, babes, regular denizens of the famous strip. Stan Petrakos felt at ease here. This was his turf, he was known by all the main players—restaurant and cafe owners; hairdressers, Percy Jones down at Percy's Bar and Bistro. One of the most important things in life was to be known, recognised—have heads turn in the street and hear the whispers: 'Look—Stan Petrakos.'

Stan Petrakos—cock of the walk: cruising the strip in his vintage Dino Ferrari, the red one with the STAN 1 tag. The car was nearly as recognisable as he was.

Lunchtime, and Stan was ready to eat. He'd got up late and had no breakfast—just coffee and cigarettes. His stomach was growling like the Ferrari motor on a cold morning. He had on the sapphire-black wraparound Ray-Bans, the blue-and-white loose-fitting tracksuit in crushed parachute silk, brand-new orange-and-white Fila cross-trainers. On his hairy chest and shoulders around a kilo and a half of fine gold chains and a couple of shark's teeth set in gold nuggets the size of his little fingernails. The jewellery matched Stan's own teeth, which were seventy-five percent precious metal. He was feeling a bit seedy from a long night at his favourite nightclub—Joe Micek's rave venue, Trader Joe's—but the first drink would fix that. Always did. There was something else troubling his mind, however, that no amount of beer would fix—a longstanding matter that crackled and spat like wires shorting out in the back of his skull. It was a message from the past, pointing the way to his future. This was all carved in stone—immutable and inescapable, and it was why he'd gone out and got smashed at Joe's. It was why he got smashed routinely, sniffed marching powder and sucked down the green Mitsubishi pills, raved all night, punched heads in lavatories and pushed along the Ferrari, clocking 220 km/h on one occasion, according to the police report.

He swung by the restaurant strip just south of Faraday Street, where the effusive greeters proliferated, urging passersby into their establishments. Stan knew them all by name. Even though he was of Greek origin and they were Italian, he had developed a close rapport with these people, and they more or less spoke the same language. When they saw Stan coming they made way, welcomed him heartily, offered him the best table in the place. It didn't occur to Stan that they did the same for everyone. Cigarette lighters were conjured the instant he slid a Marlboro between his lips. They treated him with respect, as if he were a *capo*—a man of importance who could arrange for problems to go away. This reputation stemmed largely from an episode going back a few years—a restaurateur was stressing about this longstanding local hardman, Lou Galvano, doing the biz in his place, actually moving product and receiving cash for all and sundry to witness. This was bad for business. But after a visit from Stan at his rat-hole, Galvano suddenly saw fit to take an extended holiday overseas, and hadn't been sighted since. That cemented Stan's place in the world—at least in his own mind.

Today it was Gianni Palmieri's Ristorante D'alla Umbria, an old-fashioned, upscale eatery in which the waiters wore long white aprons so stiff with starch you could crack eggs on them. Upstairs was the oak-panelled room with the silver service, cut-glass crystal and candelabra, where Stan sometimes dined. It was modelled on the more famous Grossi Florentino in town, but wasn't quite as chic or expensive. All the waiters were middle-aged or ancient—they looked like superannuated Mafia factotums. They were slow, they spoke little English, they smelled of tobacco and hair oil, they didn't smile—but they produced top food and wines. Gianni Palmieri was a Lygon Street patriarch with a polished, severe countenance; his smile was that of a contract killer pulling on the black gloves. Stan was starving as Gianni showed him to his table on the terrace, sunshine streaming in, people walking past, glancing his way and whispering to each other.

He threw his Ferrari keyring, phone and cigarettes on the table and leaned back, stretching his muscles and cracking a few stiff joints. Soon an aged and Brilliantined waiter brought him a chilled Peroni beer and a tall pilsener glass from the refrigerator. With a slightly trembling hand he poured the amber fluid, dipped his head and withdrew—almost backwards, as if Stan were royalty. Beautiful—*fucking* ace.

He took a long pull of the Peroni then, seeing Gianni cruising by, nonchalantly slid a cigarette into his mouth. Gianni was there in an eyeblink, lighter at the ready. There was a slight breeze, and Stan cupped the flame as he leaned into it.

'Thank you, Gianni,' he said, exhaling smoke at the same time.

Gianni nodded once, and smiled his grave executioner's smile. 'Pleasure, Mr Stan—nice to see you again. How is business? Good?'

It was a standard question, nothing more than a formality: a Lygon Street ritual. Gianni had only the vaguest notion of what Mr Stan's 'business' might entail, and no interest at all, but that didn't matter. It was a code word, a conversation-opener.

'Business is just fine, Gianni,' he said. 'Please, sit down.'

But Gianni was already shaking his head, as Stan knew he would. Gianni never sat with the customers. 'Too busy, unfortunately. I have a new chef starting today.'

'Oh? What happened to . . . what was his name again?' Stan had no idea, had never known the man's name.

'Tim. He's opening his own place at the casino. Good chefs—they all do that eventually. Because they can cook they think they can run a restaurant. Crazy—they must be crazy. If you could only have a restaurant with no chef—that would be perfect.' He waved dismissively and departed.

'Crazy,' Stan said to himself. 'Crazy, man. Cra-*zy*.' He drank more Peroni, set down the glass, pushed up the shades with his stumpy forefinger as he noticed a stunningly gorgeous straw blonde stroll into the restaurant. Early twenties, solarium-tanned skin, nice upturned tits. Neat little shades. Professional-looking: expensive outfit, black Gucci handbag, laptop computer slung over her shoulder. She glanced in Stan's general direction, saw nothing of interest, then the ancient Brilliantined waiter showed her to a table on the other side of the terrace. Stan lowered his shades and picked up the menu as her boyfriend came in. He was a bleach-blond surfer-boy in a fancy charcoal suit and patterned silk vest—fucking stockbroker or something.

Stan Petrakos was no conventional chick magnet, although he did possess an animalistic charm in certain quarters—fetishistic women who fancied a taste of the lash or a split lip prior to orgasm. He was ugly-attractive in a way that defied definition, and his features seemed to change according to his mood. Never for him the gallery or cocktail circuit—not with a scarred, pitted face and neck from severe acne, the squat, boxy body shape courtesy of his father's genes and the chronic dead man's breath he'd suffered all his life due to his complete neglect of oral hygiene. For that reason he always carried a pack or two of Pep-O-Mint Life Savers, on his person and in the Ferrari. At thirty-seven years of age his tightly curled black hair was racing backwards like a fucking grass fire, although the rest of his torso—including his back—was as thick with it as a baboon's. This, he learned early, was a definite no-no babewise—one look at his furry birthday suit and they were fucking *gone*. At one stage he'd thought seriously about having it all removed by electrolysis, but now it didn't bother him. To cover the galloping baldness he wore his hair close-cropped, a number two, which revealed several jagged white scars on his cranium from various physical encounters. He wore a pencil-thin beard all the way around his jawline, connecting with a meticulously razored moustache; rows of rings pierced his ears and brows and a tattoo of a star with a fist punching through it hid behind his left ear.

He was perusing the menu, trying to choose between the roasted split bird—*poussin*—and the veal shanks, when his miniature phone chirruped.

'Ye-ah.'

'Hi. How're you doin', Wolfman.'

Stan's gal-pal—Suzen Christopher. Or, as she spelled it now, *Cristofa*.

'Doin' good. Even better soon with some food inside of me.'

'Whereabouts are you?'

'I'm at the Umbria, on Lygon. You know it?'

'Yeah,' she said. 'We been there, haven't we?'

'Yeah, yeah. What're you doin' now?'

'Matter of fact I'm . . . actually I'm just painting my toenails. Metallic green.'

'Well . . . whyn't you get your butt into gear and come and have a bite of lunch?' Suzen lived in Fitzroy—she could be there in ten minutes.

'Gee, you've got a smooth friggin' way about you, havencha, Wolfman?' she said.

'See you soon then,' he said, and clicked off.

Roasted split *poussin*—definitely. But first, another ice-cold Peroni.

'Hey, Claudio,' he called, spotting the waiter, and held up the empty glass.

She was sitting opposite him in fifteen minutes—waiting for the toenail polish to dry took the extra five. Suzen always looked as if she'd just fallen out of bed, and today was no different. Her spiky henna'ed hair stuck out in every direction, but Stan knew it took her a long time in front of the mirror to achieve that effect. Suzen couldn't help herself: she worked part-time as a hairdresser in a salon for the super-cool cats. Stan had visited her there, and it was like being in a giant, canary yellow, cone-shaped space capsule. Today she had on green eyeliner and eye shadow, a heavy application of mascara and dark green lipstick. Contrasting with all this was a dusting of white powder over the face. When she opened her mouth Stan saw three silver studs in her tongue. She had rings and studs—not to mention tattoos and other markings—all over her body. A glittering silver chain swung from an earring to a lower lip-ring. On her upper arms were tattoos of an Indian chief in full headdress, and intertwined serpents, flames spewing from their mouths, and there was a snarling bulldog on her rump. Coils of barbed wire holding a burning candle—the Amnesty International emblem—encircled her ankles, a sexy guitar-playing *grrrl* adorned one of her breasts and there was a flowering orchid on a shoulder blade. Obscure Mayan and Egyptian symbols were scattered over her like an ancient code, and there was a single Japanese character meaning 'happy life' on the small of her back. She even had a scarified tattoo—cut with a scalpel and inked in—of a holy cross over her heart, and a brand across her abdomen, just above the wispy patch of pubic hair. Burnt into the flesh with white-hot wire, it said

PROPERTY OF WILEY—whoever the fuck Wiley was. Had to be some dopey *boyf* from before she knew Stan, but he didn't want to know.

So Suzen was right into body modification and S&M—it was one of the reasons Stan was attracted to her, and vice-versa. She was no babe—like him she had acne scars on her face; she also had a permanent rash, and was scrawny and under-endowed from an unhealthy lifestyle. But she was a wild and willing party chick who'd do pretty much anything—especially if she'd sniffed some blow or popped a Mitsubishi, or shot some horse into her veins. She would swallow any kind of shit he gave her without even knowing what it was. Best of all, she didn't race for the door when she clapped the peepers on Stan's hairy torso. In fact she liked it—called him Wolfman, or the Wolfhound—Wolfie for short sometimes.

They ordered a bottle of white wine to accompany Stan's seasoned split bird, which filled the plate and came with separate bowls of roast potato and parsnip with garlic and rosemary sprigs, and some steamed greens. Suzen nibbled at a piece of his *poussin* and ate a small potato while Stan made an almighty mess of his plate. Suzen had next to no appetite. 'Lunch' for her consisted of pecking at morsels. She might chew a leaf of lettuce or slice of mushroom, or dab at the crumbs from a bread roll, but there was no real *eating* involved. Stan put this down to her drug and alcohol addiction, along with all her offbeat traits. Together they gulped the Passing Clouds, and when it was gone they had another. Stan was feeling a lot livelier by the time they'd reached the bottom of it, and the lights were definitely on in Suzen's evil, Gothic eyes.

When they'd finished Stan called for the bill, dropped some cash on the table and waved *adios* to Gianni. On the sun-dappled pavement he slapped her sharply on the backside and said, 'So—wanna come back to my place or what?'

Suzen didn't need to think about it too long. 'Why not? Might as well trash the rest of the friggin' day.'

In his recently purchased pad—one of the ultra-modern medium-density apartments in Beacon Cove, Port Melbourne—they did some lines of powder, then made their preparations. After showering they applied liberal doses of lubricant onto each other, particularly over—and into—their erogenous zones. The sex-scented oil acted as a powerful aphrodisiac as much as a lubricant. When that was done Stan attached his nipple rings and the navel ring, then inserted a fourth ring in the pierced head of his penis. When that was done he connected the heavy silver chains to the nipples, ran them down to the navel, then the penis—the Full Albert, it was called, after Prince Albert—he was some kind of groover, the old Prince Al. Then he put on a wide studded belt, studded leather gauntlets with exposed palms and a black leather mask that made him look like Zorro. In the meantime Suzen decked herself out the same way. She already had the nipple and navel rings and two on her labia, so it was just a matter of connecting the chains. Then she clipped on a heavy, seriously spiked dog collar. Stan attached a chain to it, wrapping it around his gauntlet, then ordered her onto all fours.

Slapping her on the bare buttock, right on the bulldog tattoo, he began to berate her: 'You dirty little dog. You filthy creature. You pissed on the floor, *didn't you?*'

'No, I didn't,' she whined.

'Yes, you did. I saw you. Next time you do that I'm gonna rub your nose in it, you filthy bitch. You grubby hound. Go on—get moving.' He gave her hindquarters a stinging blow, and Suzen crawled around the room yelping and panting as he carried on upbraiding her. Then he began thumping her buttocks with his slippery erection, hitting her harder and harder with it, the chains clanking and swishing, before ordering her to roll over onto her back. Panting and woofing—the slavering, studded tongue hanging right out—she cringingly obeyed, folding her arms in like puppy paws and lifting her legs high and wide. Stan got on his knees, unclipped his penis from the chains and slid it into her, under the labia rings. Suzen barked and yelped and bucked, but when he saw how much she wanted it he quickly withdrew.

'No,' he said. 'You've been a bad, bad dog. You don't deserve a bone.' He reconnected the chains to his hefty tool.

'I won't be bad again,' she whined, legs pedalling the air. 'Please . . . I'm sorry. Give me one more chance.'

Stan stood over her, cock in hand. 'Whimper, whimper . . . You're fucking pathetic. You make me sick. I wouldn't waste my jism on you. I'd rather flush it down the can.'

So it went on—for over an hour. The aim of the exercise was to continue for as long as possible without succumbing to the inevitable endgame. This took a lot of discipline—and practice. With S&M it was necessary to deprive oneself of easy pleasures. It was all about denial, refusal to give in, with-holding, punishing. Then at long last—reward. What a huge blast it was—infinitely more satisfying than normal sex. You got rocks off you didn't know you had. Today it was Suzen's turn to wear the collar, but when Stan did she hard-rode him around the room, slapping him over the head and cracking him with a jockey's whip. If she felt the Wolfhound was particularly deserving of punishment, she would shove it deep into his rear end and give him a golden shower.

Dusk came down. The scent of lubricant was still strong on their bodies as they lay in bed, but Stan wasn't even slightly aroused—Suzen didn't turn him on outside the S&M scenario. Come to that, Stan's erections were few and far between nowadays, even though he was still a young-*ish* man of thirty-seven—ten years older than Suzen. Only violence, real or make-believe, consistently made his prick come up and stay up. Now it was at rest. They'd napped, then sniffed some more of that lovely powder. Hmm. How could anyone even *think* of eating when there was this stuff around? Now they were downing Bacardi Breezers and watching the news on TV—another string of convenience store robberies.

'That bastard's out of jail, you know,' Stan said in a low voice—like a growl. The old crackling and spitting at the back of his head had started up again.

Swigging on the Bacardi, Suzen thought about it—she was more than a little spaced. 'What bastard's that?' she said, thinking it had something to do with the still-at-large convenience store bandit.

'Well, what bastard do you think? Shaun McCreadie—*that* bastard.'

'Oh, shit—is he?'

'I just said he was, didn't I? Jesus, Suzen, listen up.'

Suzen bit her lip, swallowed more Breezer. She knew what he was on about now. It wouldn't do to annoy him on the subject of Shaun Randall McCreadie.

'I thought he was in for life,' she said.

'He was,' Stan said. 'But the Appeals Court upheld his appeal. Judges ruled—*unanimously*—that there was some doubt about whether he pulled the trigger or not. New forensic evidence, or some shit. They reduced his sentence to fourteen years, which made him eligible for parole straightaway.'

'Oh, that's *fucked*, Stan,' she said.

'Christ, what difference does it make who pulled the fuckin' trigger? They were all in it together, in concert—all equally guilty.'

'Yeah,' she said. She was remembering: a country mansion, a shocking, violent break-in, appalling torture and bloodshed. Guns, knives, hammers—it all put her in mind of Charlie Manson and his insane 'family'. Suzen was a Goth, but not in that way, not in the evil way of Manson's 'girls'. There was a TV documentary, even a book written about the attack on Stan's family. Large quantities of cash and drugs were involved. There were some vital unanswered questions, and it was all a bit hazy in her mind—but the crime scene details were grisly and harrowing. When she'd first met Stan she didn't know who he was, but then he told her his father was George Petrakos, and she'd been horrified. Playing S&M games was one thing, but real violence gave her the cold shivers—not to mention vivid nightmares from which there seemed no waking. *Awful*, shocking nightmares.

Stan said, 'It wasn't in the papers. My lawyer says it was all hush-hush—to protect him from possible reprisals.'

'Fuck.'

'Yeah—protect *him*. Can you believe it? He's free— *laughin'*—but my parents are still dead, aren't they?'

Suzen remained silent. She could feel Stan's anger building. The fizzing in his brain was palpable. She'd seen him explode into terrible rages before—not pretty. And it was always Shaun McCreadie at the bottom of it. Shaun McCreadie was Stan's Charles Manson.

'Nothing you can do about it now,' she said, and immediately regretted her words. Stan turned towards her, small dark eyes afire in his scarred face. Ugliness made his anger so much more frightening.

'Isn't there, Suzen? I can find him and kill him,' he said through trembling lips—lips that were wet with rage and Bacardi Breezer. 'Make the bastard choke on a bullet, or stick a knife in his black heart. *That* would settle it. Wouldn't it?'

'I guess so,' she said.

'I've got to kill *him*, and anyone associated with him,' Stan said in a level, unemotional voice. Suzen gave him a slightly puzzled look. It struck her as a rather odd phrase to use, and not at all one she would expect to come from Stan's lips. He appeared to have withdrawn right inside himself now, in a way she'd seen him do before. If she'd waved a hand in front of his face, she was sure Stan would not have blinked.

Charles Manson. Nightmares.

For Suzen the two went together as naturally as drugs and alcohol, or a dog collar and a good whipping. As a child, she became aware of Manson's atrocities. He became her night stalker, the monster in her dreams—a darkened, evil presence creeping into her room, standing at the end of her bed, knife-hand raised—night after night it was the same. She'd try to wake up, to *scream*, but couldn't. The scream always stuck in her throat. Couldn't even move—she was frozen stiff with fear. It was as if she were pinned down on a slab, ready to be sacrificed and cut up. She'd read *Helter Skelter* many times, along with every other book on Manson, and years later she saw him on TV during one of his parole hearings—a middle-aged, shaven-haired monster with a swastika tattooed on his forehead. He was lapping up the attention and playing sinister mind games with the interviewer. Manson was so psychotic he could not even see that he had done anything wrong—to him it all seemed very amusing. He was also seen strumming a guitar in his cell. Her stomach turned to water watching the man—the vibe of evil around him was shimmering and potent beyond measure. Suzen always felt that if Manson *were* ever released—God forbid—it would be a crisis. He would surely come after her personally, to seduce and kill her. That paralysing vision of the killer at the foot of her bed would make one final, dreadful appearance.

Charles Manson. Pools of blood. Dismemberment, satanic messages daubed in blood, strewn body parts, the painted corpse of Sharon Tate in a bathtub, wrapped in heavy ropes, a murdered unborn baby—the formative images of her teen years. Suzen (still Susan to her parents, though she'd changed it years ago) actually turned to tattooing, piercing, body scarification and S&M as a sort of protective shield or force field against the real violence out there—and in her night world. Together with hallucinogens, Limp Bizkit, The Clash and PJ Harvey, it was her way of coping. The awful, seductive power of Manson was warded off by the scarified cross over her heart. In her mind 'scarification' meant 'scare away', or 'ward off'—such was Suzen's obsession with Manson. She was

simultaneously repelled and drawn by his diabolical presence
in the world.

As for Stan—well, he was an enigma. Ugly, hairy, full of
threatening macho shit, but there was something else hidden
in there: the small child, vulnerable and frightened, with
whom she could identify. She knew he was usually up to no
good, but he'd never done anything to her, and in a bizarre
sort of way they did complement each other. Like her, Stan
had unresolved problems deep in his subconscious. One night
recently he had woken abruptly from a bad dream and
sobbed like a child at her breast. Suzen cradled him with great
tenderness and pity. She had valued that moment—a moment
when he had opened up to her, babbling on incoherently
about his brother and father. He had let slip his tough guy
façade. Stan, too, had fears and anxieties. And after what had
happened to his family, why wouldn't he?

Aside from that, there was an even more compelling factor
in their relationship. Suzen was a person who needed to feel
protected, and Stan Petrakos, she felt, could watch over her
better than anyone alive. Fear/attraction: Manson/Stan. Her
mind—particularly when she was tripping—was full of
polarisations that blurred, coalesced, became one. There were
times she believed she was seriously crazy, clinically insane.
Times also—late at night when he was high with excitement/
anger—when Stan's pocked face seemed to burn with an
intense, volcanic glow, as if all the scars and craters and
capillaries smouldered and bubbled with a slow-burning lava
heated from deep within.

6

Raydon Steer, QC, had a story to tell, an amusing one involving a newly appointed County Court judge who had apparently made an inauspicious debut. Sitting opposite him was longtime friend and fellow barrister Oliver McEncroe. They were ensconced in overstuffed lounge chairs in Raydon's club, the Australia, enjoying fine, sixteen-year-old single malt Laphraoig Scotch whisky, Lagavulin—Raydon's preferred tipple at cocktail hour. Oliver, who had come directly from chambers, had on his grey chalkstripe three-piece suit with the gold fob watch chain, while Raydon appeared more relaxed in his bow tie and the navy alpaca pullover he was fond of sporting lately. He was puffing on his Churchill, trying to get it started, and relating the anecdote at the same time.

'So his honour'—puff, puff—'his honour calls a recess, you see. It's a major case involving this tycoon fellow—what's his name?' Puff, puff.

'You're telling the story, Steer,' Oliver said. 'Or attempting to. Tell me, do you ever actually inhale that monster?'

'Good Lord, no. One doesn't need to inhale one's hand-rolled Punch cigar to appreciate its superior qualities, McEncroe. Don't be such a boor. Anyway, as I was saying . . .'

'Attempting to say.'

Raydon swirled his Scotch and sipped. 'So his honour calls a recess, and all rise. As I said it's a big fraud case, so the court is overflowing with public, reporters and what have you. He opens the door—what he believes is the door to his office—only to find it's the janitor's closet.'

Oliver laughed uproariously, slapping the table. 'Oh, splendid,' he said.

Thus encouraged, Raydon cleared his throat and hurried on: 'His honour promptly plunges his imported, hand-made Italian shoe into a bucket—one of those metal ones with a . . . a sort of squeezing device in it, and then brooms and mops and other cleaner's paraphernalia fall out all over him.' Puff, puff, puff. Guffaws and an inadvertent snort from Oliver. 'Try as he may he can't extricate his foot from the bucket, McEncroe. It's wedged in tight. His honour is now the subject of much stifled chortling and sniggering from the assembled crowd. He is the picture of excruciating embarrassment as the clerk of the court bends his shoulder to the task, burrowing beneath his honour's gown, and together they manage to de-bucket the learned judge whose face, as you can imagine, is now brick-red.' Puff, puff, puff. 'Then, when he arrives at the correct door, he can't open it, because he's locked it, McEncroe, and can't find the key. Much mirth and merriment ensued in his honour's court for quite a time, I can assure you. Even the accused couldn't wipe the smirk off his face.'

Oliver was beside himself with raucous belly laughter. 'Fucking brilliant, Steer,' he said. 'Absolutely first rate. And extra points if you made it all up.'

'On my honour,' Raydon said, affecting appropriate gravitas. 'I swear 'tis true.'

'Then it couldn't have happened to a nicer parcel of goods,' Oliver said.

'There's something else I wanted to tell you,' Raydon said, a decent time having elapsed. 'On a more serious note.'

'Well, I didn't think you'd invited me to your club merely to relate the misadventures of his honour—diverting as they are,' Oliver said. 'But if we're about to have a serious conversation, I insist on more of this excellent Scotch. What is it? It's so . . . soft.'

'Lagavulin,' Raydon said, raising a hand to the liveried steward. 'From the isle of Islay. The secret is age, McEncroe. It takes out the fire but leaves in the warmth.'

'In life, as in Scotch. You're such an unmitigated snob, Steer. But I must say it's an accurate description.'

The steward promptly delivered a fresh round on a silver tray.

'All right,' Oliver said, after sipping. 'What is it? Suddenly there is the distinct whiff of . . . naughtiness in the air.'

'I was in Sydney,' Raydon began. 'Visiting my friend Rumney. You know him.'

'Rumney, yes.'

'We had entertainment in his apartment—a pair of lusty young harlots he'd arranged.'

'I was right,' Oliver said with undisguised glee. 'Go on, go on.'

'Well, it turns out that one of them was . . . underage.'

'No,' Oliver said with a mock gasp. 'By what margin, if I may inquire?'

'She's fourteen,' Raydon said. 'Or so she alleges.'

'Alleges? Come now, it isn't difficult to establish someone's age. That's why we have birth certificates, Steer.'

'All right, she's fourteen.' An edge of irritation had crept into his tone, which instinctively he corrected.

'Shameful.'

'As you say, McEncroe. Anyway this girl has since dis-covered my identity, and attempted to extort money—*blackmail* me—under threat of going to the police.'

'How has she done this?'

'Telephone call.'

'To your home?'

'God no—to chambers.'

'Good Christ, Steer. Who's helping her?'

'I don't know. Someone, presumably.'

'Not Rumney?'

'Rumney? Don't be insane, McEncroe. Rumney's keeping schtum, I imagine. After all, he too is vulnerable.'

'Quite. God, you're such a pants man, Steer. It was destined to be your undoing one day—if you'll excuse a rather feeble pun. So—what was your response?'

Raydon said, 'I did what any intelligent man would do—denied the whole episode and told her to fuck off.'

'Very good. So what's the problem?'

'The problem, McEncroe, is that last night I received a visit from the police. Apparently this little slut has made a complaint against me. All sorts of lies . . .'

'What does she allege, precisely?'

'She alleges I gave her drugs.'

'Did you?'

'Definitely not. There was cocaine on the premises. I don't know if she had some or not.'

'I see. What else?'

'Apparently I induced her to take drugs, then I forced myself upon her while she was in a semiconscious state.'

'Hmm. Forgive my prurience, Steer, but are there unusual sexual practices involved here?'

'What do you mean?' Raydon said, seemingly outraged at the suggestion.

'Well, you know . . . fellatio, or buggery, for example.'

'Don't be so disgusting, McEncroe.'

'I only inquire because I am aware of your penchant for such tasty peccadilloes. Was there?'

'There might have been. I don't remember. A deal of fizz was being consumed.'

'You don't remember whether or not you fucked this young tart up the arse? Come now.'

'All right, all right—maybe once. And the other thing. But with her consent.'

'It's not looking good, Steer. Drugging and sodomising underage girls is not exactly flavour of the month in the courts, you know. Witness the steady stream of scout masters, priests and schoolteachers shunted off to prison for the very same offence. And cricket umpires.'

'Don't be ridiculous, McEncroe. That's totally different. That's . . . child abuse, serial molestation, betrayal of a position of trust for the purpose of sexual gratification. Those people are fucking *paedophiles*, for Christ's sake. Degenerates. This was just . . . sex.'

'I doubt if a jury will draw that distinction, Steer. In the broader context you too abused your position of trust—as an adult.' He leaned forward. 'You're supposed to protect and guide children, not fuck them.'

'I didn't *know* she was a child. I thought she was older. She said she was nineteen.'

'Did she now? Why did she say that?'

'Because I . . . I asked how old she was.'

'So you were dubious. Clearly you had reservations. Yet you went ahead, knowing she'd lied about her age. I'm sorry, but I don't see a jury accepting that an experienced man of the world such as your good self could mistake fourteen for nineteen, Steer. Come off it.'

'It's all trumped up, McEncroe. You know it is.'

'Hmm—perhaps. What did the police say?'

'They said that Sydney police will be applying for my extradition to New South Wales to face committal.'

Oliver said nothing as he swirled his Scotch, staring into it as if searching for answers.

'Well?' Raydon said. 'What do you think?'

'I think you're in the shit, old friend. If she proceeds, you're facing . . . what, three to five?'

'In prison?'

'That's where they send sex offenders, Steer. It won't be the Sheraton Hotel. The big house, the caboose, the slammer.'

'Don't be mad, McEncroe. I'm not going to prison!'

'I beg to differ,' Oliver said.

'Prison? For *that*? No. Good God, man, the slut was a damned hooker.'

'Yes, a fourteen-year-old hooker. And she has your balls in a vice, Steer. How much did she want?'

'Fifty thousand.'

'Maybe you should give it to her.'

'Pay up? But that's extortion.'

'You can afford it, can't you?'

'Of course, but that's hardly the issue.'

'I would have thought,' Oliver said, 'that the issue was staying out of prison.'

'I'm definitely not going to prison. You can forget about that. If it comes to trial, it's her word against mine—who do you think the jury will believe? A Kings Cross harlot or a QC?'

'You don't want it to go to trial, Steer.'

'No, but damned if I'm going to pay the bitch. What's to stop her coming back for more, anyway, once she's pissed all that away?'

'That is a possibility. In which case you'd have to . . . rid yourself of the problem somehow. Tell me, does your wife know about this?'

'Jo? Well . . . she knows part of it.'

'Which part might that be?'

Raydon swallowed some Scotch. 'She found out about the Sydney dalliance.'

'How?'

'She received an anonymous letter outlining what happened. She confronted me with it, and we had a row.'

'An anonymous letter,' Oliver said. 'How clandestine. This sounds like an Agatha Christie novel, Steer.'

'It's no laughing matter,' Raydon said.

'Do you know who it was?'

'No—it was printed on a computer.'

'A colleague, perhaps, with a grudge?'

'Perhaps,' Raydon said. 'I am a strong candidate for the bench in the next round of appointments, as you know.'

'Sounds as if you're being set up. By a rival, perhaps.'

'Well of *course* I'm being set up.'

Oliver said, 'So your wife doesn't know about the visit from the police—last night, did you say?'

'Last night, yes. No, she doesn't. She's . . . well, she's bolted.'

'Your wife's *bolted*, Steer?'

'That's right.' Raydon's face coloured slightly.

'But how could you allow that to happen? One's wife doesn't *bolt*.'

'She's a strong-willed, even wilful person. I couldn't stop her,' Raydon said.

'So we can assume she won't be giving wifely support as you travel to and from the court.'

'I keep telling you, McEncroe, I'm not *going* to court. Can't you get that through your head?'

'Well, you said you weren't going to *prison*, if memory serves.'

'Don't be such a pedantic arsehole.'

'I'm not being pedantic, but you, my old sausage, are not facing facts. The Law Institute takes a grave view of such sleazy matters. And the police will take great pleasure in prosecuting to the fullest. Rozzers are not enamoured of lawyers, as you

are aware—they'd love to see your odious hide twist in the
wind. Then there's the tabloid press. Imagine what they would
do. You know how, in Sydney particularly, they *love* salacious
sex scandals involving prominent lawyers.'

Raydon knew the case to which Oliver referred—it had
dragged on and on forever. He was starting to feel a little sick.

'Your word against hers?' Oliver said. 'Scales of justice?
Forget it, Steer. The press will go to town. Somehow I don't
see INNOCENT BARRISTER DUPED BY GRASPING WRETCH.
No, no—I see TOP QC IN CHILD SEX ROMP. And of course,
your photograph plastered all over the papers. You will be
defrocked, decommissioned, cashiered, black-balled from your
club, run out of town on a rail. Your life will be *over*, Steer.
Am I getting through to you?'

'I want you to represent me,' Raydon said sullenly.

'Represent you—to do what?'

'I don't care. Whatever you see fit. Make it all . . . go away.'

'I don't come cheaply,' Oliver said, a sliver of mischief in
his beady eye.

'Good Christ, man, I know that. Do you think I'd want
you otherwise?'

'All right. I suggest we make contact, pay her off. If it's not
too late,' Oliver said.

'It's never too late to give people money, McEncroe.'

'Quite. More Scotch, please. I still can't believe you allowed
your wife to bolt, Steer. It's very careless. You really don't want
her outside the tent pissing in. That would be . . . unhelpful.'

'I can't say what she'll do.'

A fresh round of Lagavulin arrived. Oliver consulted his
fob watch.

'Nearly dinnertime, Steer. Does your club do an acceptable meal?'

'Oh—soup, roast beef. Pecan pie. Rather unimaginative,
but satisfying. Wholesome.'

'Wholesome—how fitting. Shall we go in after this?'

Raydon nodded. He had no appetite. He'd intended to carry on with the Lagavulin and get himself shit-faced. But he could have a dozen oysters, and perhaps . . . some grilled boned quail to follow.

7

She came back up the staircase carrying two bottles, two glasses and a Waiter's Friend. 'Chateauneuf-du-Pape, no less,' she said. 'There's a pallet of the stuff down there, packed in straw in wooden crates with "Vin Produit en France" stamped on them.'

'Clearly your Indonesian banker is a man of taste and quality,' Shaun said. He was sitting on the bed examining the list of stored numbers in Bernie Walsh's phone. When she approached he switched it off and tossed it aside.

'I'd say it's got "hijacked" written all over it,' Jo said. She deftly removed both corks, and set one of them back in the bottle. The other she held to her nose, sniffing, then shrugged.

'Seems okay,' she said, splashing carelessly into a glass. 'See what you think. I haven't much of a nose for wine.'

'Can't say I have either,' Shaun said, making a show of peering through the glass, sniffing and swirling. There was a fine sprinkling of cork dust on the surface.

'Sorry. I really should have decanted,' Jo said. 'Raydon would be horrified.'

'Don't worry about it,' he said, and took a decent pull on it.

'Well?' she said. 'Is it . . . off?'

'Off? God no. It's terrific. Best stuff to slide down my throat in a long, long time. Sure beats the hell out of prison hooch.'

'It's a 1992 vintage,' she said, reading from the label.

'Very appropriate. That's the year I went inside. And all that time this bottle has been waiting and maturing.'

'Like me,' Jo said. She filled her own glass and, sitting alongside Shaun on the bed, sipped.

'Hmm. Nice—very nice. I suppose we'll probably want that second one,' she said.

'I'd say so.'

'Well,' she said, sprawling feline-like. 'Over to you, mystery man. Give.'

Shaun had been wondering where to start. There seemed to be no single moment when these events were set in motion—unless he went right back to his decision to join the Victoria police force. But in the end, because the image was so insistent, he settled on a drizzling, wintry night when sleep was snuffed out by a ringing in the hall of his bachelor's flat.

'In July 1987,' he said, 'I received a phone call from a mate of mine, Vincent O'Connell. We were at school and then the academy together, before we went our separate ways—although we caught up every now and again. But then he dropped out of sight, and I didn't hear from him for a while—until that call. It was late, after two in the morning. That wasn't unusual for a cop—young guys, we were always on graveyard shifts, and you got used to weird hours. I was on call at the time anyway. Sometimes you had no idea what time of day or night it was. I'd wake up, look at my watch and see it was seven o'clock, and wonder if it was day or night. A few months earlier I'd made it to the armed robbery squad—the robbers. It was a big deal—I was twenty-five, apparently the youngest detective ever to be appointed to the squad. I was over the moon. Just by the way—how did you know about the crossed pistols? Was it from Raydon?'

'No—I read it in the paper. There was something about the armed robbery squad a while ago.'

Shaun nodded. He'd seen the same article in the prison library, about the life and times of a longstanding member. It brought back a lot of memories for him . . . good and bad.

'Having that tattoo done was a highlight of my life,' he said. 'It meant I was part of the elite, the chosen few. Callow greenhorn, and here I was mixing it with living legends, the toughest and best cops in the whole damn country. They took me down the pub for an initiation, got me totally smashed, told me a few home truths . . . The words "loyalty" and "brotherhood" were mentioned a lot, I seem to recall.'

He gave a soundless, ironic little laugh and drank some wine, allowing the memories to dissolve.

Jo said, 'So, what happened to Vincent O'Connell?'

'Sorry. Yeah—the late night phone call. Turned out Vincent was working undercover at the time, trying to bust a major drug baron. I didn't know he was doing undercover work—last I heard he was driving a divvy van in Ferntree Gully or Waverley Gardens, some such place. So that explained why he dropped out of sight. Anyhow, he was a bit shaken up. Said he believed he was going to be put off.'

'Put off? You mean dismissed from the force?'

'No, no, I mean murdered. Dismissed from the planet.'

'Oh. By the drug baron?'

'Vincent was ambivalent. Either the drug baron, or one of his own.'

'A bad cop?' She arched an eyebrow.

'Yeah, a bad cop—a *very* bad cop. The thing about Vincent was, to look at him you'd think he was a street thug—a big, brawny, shaven-haired character. He could pick up two tree trunks, one under each arm, and carry them from here to Sydney without a pit stop. Good kickboxer, too. So it came as a surprise to see him scared—and he was scared shitless.

'We met in an all-night bar, and he told me that the drug baron, a guy named Morris Salisbury, had been in his ear boasting about how he had a very senior detective on the payroll. Vincent was posing as a middle-level supplier and had apparently got to know this Salisbury character pretty well. He wouldn't name the cop, but Vincent put two and two together. This detective was providing Salisbury with drugs that had been confiscated in police raids, and kept as evidence for upcoming court cases. He was removing this stuff from the storage facility, giving it to Salisbury and copping a share of the profits—nice little scam. It had to be a senior cop for him to have access to this particular building, so it was a short list of suspects.

'Not long after that Vincent met Salisbury at their regular pub to do some business, and while they're talking in walks the detective in question. He sits down at their table and gives Vincent the evil eye—doesn't say a lot, but *looks* at him in a very unnerving way. Vincent doesn't know if the detective knows he's a cop working undercover or not—they've never met before. And why was he there? He barely contributed to the conversation. Then he left. Straightaway Vincent starts getting paranoid.

'For pretty good reason, as it turns out. One day his dog has its throat slashed, and in the underworld a dog is an informer—the lowest form of life. Then someone breaks into his flat and leaves a live bullet sitting on his pillow. The message: we can get you anytime, just like we got your dog. Then he receives all these hang-up calls, all hours of the night. It went on and on. Shots were fired at his parents' car in a drive-by one night. They were telling him: we know where your family lives. By now Vincent's nerves are on edge—he sees people following him, his car is vandalised, pre-paid funeral brochures are sent to his home, and he believes he's been blown, that Salisbury is onto him. He fears both criminals and cops. Then he gets a call—someone with a heavily disguised voice telling him he was about to go off. That's when he phoned me.'

He paused to sip—then again, a bigger sip. Christ it was a top drop.

Jo said, 'Why didn't he contact his supervisor, whatever you call it . . . His controller?'

'He didn't have one. It's not like in the movies. Making official contact is too dangerous. The top crims have very sophisticated surveillance and communications gear nowadays. There might have been a tracking device in his car, a bug somewhere in his flat. He was out there on his lonesome for the duration. This was a long-term operation, he'd been at it for six months and had to see it through, simple as that. It's a solitary, high-risk job.'

'What did he say to you?'

'He didn't believe he could trust any of the people involved in the operation. Thing was, if this top detective was bad, who else was in it with him? There's no way of knowing. But since I was an outsider, an old mate, I wasn't tainted. He felt he could confide in me. He told me about the detective, who was an inspector in CI—Criminal Intelligence—and about his cosy arrangement with Salisbury. Could I go to someone about it? Vincent was scared of this detective—he believed the inspector had made the threatening phone call with the disguised voice. He had a reputation, this particular cop—didn't fuck around. So, I said I'd see what I could do. I asked him if he wanted to stay at my place for a while, but he said no, he'd hang in there. He was relieved just to have someone to talk to, I think.'

Jo said, 'This is all going to end badly for Vincent, isn't it?'

With the wineglass held up at eye level Shaun was studying the rich ruby-coloured liquid. 'I've been over it and over it many times, trying to see how I could have handled things differently. The guy was desperate, he came to me for help, and I did the best I could. I still believe I did the only thing possible.' He brought the glass to his lips, sipped, swallowed, and turned his gaze to Jo. She was lying on her side, propped on an elbow, legs folded behind her: watchful, patient. 'But as

I said, I was naïve. Unwittingly, stupidly, I triggered a chain of events that changed the whole world into a crazy place—a madhouse.'

'Maybe it was a madhouse anyway,' she said in a flat voice.

'In the robbers,' he said, 'we worked in three-man crews. My crew boss was a sergeant named Mitch Alvarez. He was about the smartest guy I ever met. Could've been anything. Mitch was a veteran of the squad, seemed to have been around forever, but he wasn't that old. Great detective, feared and respected in the underworld, a well-read, intelligent man, big on opera. He had a law degree, some other degree . . . He had this unusually domed forehead, so prominent he almost looked deformed. People used to call him the man with two brains, but he just loved being a cop. The thrill of the hunt, you know? A dedicated crimefighter. Mitch was always first in the door after the sledgehammer, he personally ran down bank robbers, made the hard arrests, dodged bullets, dealt with death threats, everything. He wasn't a big bruiser by any stretch— quite the opposite—but he could walk into a low dive and hoodlums would call him Mr Alvarez. He had a way about him that made people trust him and want to cooperate with him. That guy was an inspiration.' His glass was nearly empty; he reached over for the bottle and topped them both up.

'Mitch Alvarez,' she said. 'Name's familiar . . . Raydon's probably cross-examined him a few times.'

Shaun continued as if she hadn't said anything. 'I went to Mitch and explained Vincent's situation, told him who this corrupt inspector was and asked his advice. The third guy in our crew, Andy Corcoran, was there too. It wasn't exactly our territory, but . . .' He gave a half-shrug. 'You have to under- stand that working the way we did, in that job, we formed tight friendships. We were like brothers, only more than that. No-one was more important than your partner when you were about to go into a house full of tooled-up cop-haters who were crazed on booze, smack and speedballs. Can be a wild ride.'

'I'll bet,' she said. She was watching him with appreciative, unblinking eyes, piecing together the lurid fragments of a foreign life that had somehow fashioned this man, her *lover*, and cast him across her path in Buzzards Hut. If she had known all this at the start, would she still have gone for him?

'We had long discussions,' Shaun said. 'Mitch wanted to be sure about this corrupt inspector's identity. When he was finally convinced—and he did some homework of his own—he said, right, this bastard's got to go down. Turned out he always suspected the guy was dirty. He went to an assistant commissioner about it, armed with every scrap of evidence he could muster. Surveillance photos of the inspector in the company of Morris Salisbury, recorded conversations, dates when he had signed in at the storage facility, quantities of drugs that had mysteriously gone missing on the same days— Mitch was thorough.

'Nothing happened straightaway. I don't know what I expected to happen, but there was just this dead calm. I had a bad feeling that certain action was being taken, and we were being kept in the dark. I couldn't contact Vincent—the deal was, he'd ring me. It was safer that way. A long time went by, but no word from him or anyone else. Nothing from the assistant commissioner, a guy named Paul Harcourt. I felt we were being isolated, cut off. I thought I'd caught some of Vincent's paranoia.'

'And Mitch?' Jo said. 'Was he paranoid too?'

'I found it hard to talk to him about it, in case big brother was watching and listening. Cars seemed to cruise by my flat all the time. There were strange static noises on my phone. I started searching for hidden microphones and cameras. One night when I came home, I had the distinct feeling someone had been there, but there was no sign of a break-in. I couldn't really tell Mitch about these things in case he thought I was . . . delusional, or losing it. I was beginning to believe that myself.'

He took time to sip, then got up to light a cigarette from the pack of Luckies on the dresser. In the mirror he saw her twist around so she could see him properly.

'But you weren't,' she said. 'Delusional.'

Still watching her in the mirror he said, 'They came pre-dawn, smashed their way in, dragged me out of bed—there was screaming, guns and flashlights in my face, the whole deal. I was thinking, shit, *I* usually do this—what's going on? Is it a fucking nightmare or what?' He dragged on the cigarette, looked around for an ashtray. 'In my apartment they found commercial quantities of heroin, thousands of dollars in cash, illegal guns stashed in the wardrobe . . . they kept showing me this stuff, and all I could do was shake my head. They read me my rights, handcuffed me and took me in.'

Sitting up in the lotus position now, Jo narrowed her eyes and placed an index finger under her chin. 'I seem to recall something like that, some disgraced detectives or something.'

'Same thing happened to Mitch and Andy, all on the same night. In Mitch's place they found a big bag of amphetamines, a stolen credit card and cash. And just for variety, Andy's garage contained some hot electrical goods and other contraband. And in the boot of his car was a travel bag full of cash, for which he had no explanation. They also dragged up allegations of rape against him. They did a terrific job, managed to come up with a range of offences so it wouldn't look too neat, as if it was a fit-up.'

'I do remember it,' she said. 'Three detectives—it was a big scandal. The chief commissioner himself went on TV.'

'To assure the public that any corruption in the force would be torn out, root and branch. I believe that was the expression he used.'

She poured more wine. The bottle was nearly empty, and he passed her the second. 'For a year or more I spent all my time with lawyers or internal investigations people. Round and round and round we went: interrogations, consultations, bullshit sessions of one sort or another. I even had to do psych tests. We were all suspended without pay, so it was a pretty tough time. Just as well I didn't have a wife and family.'

'Yeah,' she said brightly. 'Just as well.'

Smiling, he said, 'Good point. Anyway, in the end this internal investigations goon, a real piece of work called Burns, offered us a deal. Resign, forfeiting benefits and entitlements, and they'd withdraw all charges. We were called in individually, and first we all said to shove the deal, since it amounted to an admission of guilt, but then, it just wears you down, the whole process. Burns knew that. We came around eventually.'

'Between a rock and a hard place,' she said.

'Yeah. In hindsight we should have boxed on, because I now believe they were never going to proceed against us. How unlikely was it—three detectives with unblemished records all going bad to that extent, and at the same time? I think they were shit-scared the whole scam would blow up in their faces if it got to court. I wish we'd called their bluff now.'

'Easy to make rational decisions with twenty-twenty hindsight vision,' she said. 'Done it a bit myself.'

He was sipping and smoking—chain-smoking. 'No convictions against our names,' he said. 'But we were effectively out of business job-wise. Our careers—Mitch's especially, for Christ's sake—were simply flushed down the john. Gone. I drove a taxi. The others did various menial jobs. Mitch worked in a pub for a while, pulling beer. Andy rode shotgun on a garbage truck *and* drove a cab nights. Mitch's wife cracked the shits and left him. Andy had a wife and two young ones and a mortgage. We were a real bitching society whenever we got together for a session on the booze. I sometimes thought that Mitch blamed me for involving him in the first place. He was so . . . intense.'

'What about this assistant commissioner, the one Mitch went to? Could he have set you up?'

'Paul Harcourt? I didn't know him, except from his public profile. He was too far up the ladder for me. But when someone is that senior, you naturally assume he's straight—rightly or wrongly. I would certainly never make that assumption again. It's possible he was dirty, but if *he* was, God's right hand, where does it all end?'

There was no satisfactory answer to that.

'So what happened to Vincent?' she said.

'Vincent never called,' he said. 'Never heard or saw anything of him again. He just vanished.'

'Murdered,' she said softly.

'Seems so. His premonition was apparently spot-on.' Gazing unfocused at a picture on the wall he said, 'Premonitions, gut feelings . . . they're nearly always right. And that guy, the CI inspector, was later promoted for his sins before retiring on a million-dollar super payout. That just about sums it all up, don't you think?'

'I do,' she said. 'So the world seems to turn. But I still don't see what this has to do with two point eight million in a treasure chest, or the guy missing up at Buzzards Hut.'

'Patience,' he said. 'I'm getting there. Story's not half over.'

8

'One night the three of us were in a hotel in Hawthorn,' he said. 'It was the White Lion, our usual hangout. We used to meet there once every few months or so. And out of the blue, Mitch came up with this scheme. Said he'd been mulling it over for some time and was convinced we could do it. He'd worked out all the angles, or thought he had.' He was looking intently at her, giving her to understand that they were about to enter a horror stretch of non-reclaimable territory. Was she up to it?

'Jo, I want to tell you everything. I want to talk like I've never talked before. Why? I don't even know you.'

'That *is* why,' she said, and he knew it was the answer a nanosecond before she said it.

'You're a very private person, aren't you?' she said. 'Keep your own counsel.'

'Up until now,' he said.

'Fine. So go on, Shaun. Share your worst secrets. I assure you I'm no faintheart, if that's what you're concerned about.'

He drank, looking straight at her. 'Okay then. Did you ever hear of George Petrakos?'

'Hmm—no, not really.'

'Wealthy car dealer. Had a huge property in the country, near Lancefield.'

'No bells ring,' she said, and sipped.

They will soon. 'He was married to Stephanie Small.'

He saw comprehension dawn on her face. Her eyes widened, but did not waver from his. '*That* George Petrakos.'

'Stop me if you don't need to hear this, Jo. I can pull up anytime.'

'On the contrary,' she said. 'Too little information is infinitely worse than none at all.'

'Well, years ago Mitch'd had dealings with George, knew a fair bit about him. His story wasn't a particularly happy one. First wife died in a chopper crash—'

'Shit, I remember that,' she said. 'Back in the seventies?'

'Yeah. Seventy-three, I believe. Anyway, they had two sons. The older, George junior, killed himself at the age of twelve by tearing open his throat with a power saw.'

'Christ.' She shut her eyes, put a hand over her face.

'The younger son found the body in George's workshop. Seems the kid couldn't handle the loss of his mother. But even so it was a pretty emphatic statement—something seriously screwed up in the family, you'd have to say. And the other son, the one who found the body, he is this waste of space called Stan. Stan went off the rails as a teenager, rebelling against the old man, no doubt—he apparently ruled with a fist of iron. George was always bailing him out of strife—car theft, assault, this and that. He was always riding for a big fall. Then he graduated to armed robbery. Mitch was running the case when I arrived at the squad. It was how he came to know George.'

She was looking at him, impatient for the whole story to unfold, but knowing it could not be hurried.

'Stan had held up a restaurant in broad daylight, made off

with the week's takings. But it turned out to be a set-up. He was acting in collusion with the restaurant owner, who planned to claim a highly exaggerated loss from his insurance company. Later on Stan would return the money and they'd split the proceeds from the insurance. It was a sweetheart arrangement, but it didn't pan out right. Stan, the fool, was caught splashing wads of cash around the same afternoon as the robbery, the restaurant guy eventually owned up and everything turned to shit. Next thing George comes in with his lawyers, screaming, waving his arms around, claiming his son is innocent, threatens to sue Mitch for wrongful arrest and police brutality. George always made a big noise. He was a bad-tempered little shit—always mouthing off about his rights. He'd had a tough time in Greece during the war, apparently, and believed this entitled him to be a self-righteous prick forever afterwards.'

'But the son, Stan, was guilty.'

'He was red-hot. Full of denials, but the evidence against him was overwhelming. Any jury would have convicted. Restaurant patrons identified him for openers. Eventually, however, George succeeded in having the charges watered down. In the end it was a no-bill, and Stan walked. An indefinite stay of proceedings, it was called. Gave Mitch the finger as he left the courtroom.

'It left a nasty taste,' he said. 'Mitch had put a lot of unpaid hours into that brief, and they pulled the rug from under him. It was an executive decision, nothing to do with justice. You have to understand that this was at a time when police and the underworld fraternity were *not* seeing eye-to-eye. There was a lot of hostility in the air on both sides. Anyway, Mitch and his partner in the case, a top detective by the name of Brent Wollansky, went on a pub crawl and wiped themselves out till the early hours. They finished up being thrown out of Bobby McGee's after trashing the place. That really rubbed it in.

'So, we jump a few years, the three of us are shafted, Mitch saw something on TV, one of those home and garden shows, and George's place was featured on it. That's what gave him the idea.' He drew deeply on the cigarette and swallowed some wine without tasting it. 'It was believed that George kept large sums of cash in his house, always had. And in the White Lion Mitch outlined his plan. It seemed to Andy and me that we'd been royally fucked over and had nothing left to lose, so we signed on straightaway. We were still pretty burned up, especially Andy. So we agreed to hit the Petrakos property and rip off whatever he had squirrelled away.'

'Which was . . .' she said, her eyes wandering in the direction of the open chest.

Shaun looked at it too. 'Two point eight million—our self-funded retirement scheme.'

'I know about the Petrakos break-in,' she said. 'I remember it now . . .' Her voice trailed away, and he saw that in her mind she was racing ahead of him.

He said, 'Somehow Mitch obtained blueprints, a floor plan. We had a stolen van that was fitted out like a plumber's. There was always work being done at the property, so that was our cover. It was going to be a lightning raid, in and out, George wouldn't know what hit him. Then we'd stash the proceeds somewhere safe, go our separate ways and not see each other until exactly a year later, when things had cooled down. We'd retrieve the money, whack it up and live happily ever after.'

'It went wrong, didn't it?' she said in her flat, knowing voice.

He took a gulp of Chateauneuf. At that moment it could have been a supermarket quaffing red. Her eyes were all over his face, switching from one feature to another, then to his hand, observing how he repeatedly flicked the ash from his cigarette with his thumb.

'As we expected George was a hard case,' he said. 'Would *not* open the strongroom. So, extreme force was applied. I have to say I'm not proud of that, but Christ, we were committed—desperate. We were ready to go all the way. It was a crazy, crazy scene, but finally he gave it up. The strongroom was full of stuff—guns, kinky gear, money, drugs. Lots of heroin—more than I'd ever seen—and George was such a bloody righteous son of a bitch. Anyhow there was a heated argument about whether we'd take the dope. Mitch and I said no, but Andy wanted it. He went off his brain. Mitch was ready to shoot him. For a short time anything could've happened. Here we were, facing off, turning guns on each other in the middle of the goddamn heist. And then, during all this madness, in strolls Stephanie.'

'On cue,' Jo said.

'Yeah. And it was exactly the circuit-breaker we needed. She gave us a reason to quit blueing amongst ourselves.' He inhaled, allowing the smoke to float thickly from his mouth as he spoke. 'She was supposed to be away, riding a horse somewhere. Stephanie was into the equestrian scene. But apparently her horse float broke down on the way, so she came home.' He shook his head, laughing with grim humour: 'Yeah, her timing was impeccable. Even the pose and the scream— Christ, she could scream. It was as if . . . as if she'd rehearsed the scene. Anyway, we taped them to a chair each and bolted with the cash. By then Andy had cooled off on the heroin. We left the way we came, switched vehicles down the road and drove straight to Buzzards Hut.'

'Ah,' she said, but then frown lines creased her forehead, forming twisted curves over one slightly raised eye. Noticing them he thought: that's exactly how I look when I don't believe someone.

'Buzzards Hut was my idea,' he went on. 'Because it was remote, and I knew the country pretty well from my childhood. We buried the cash, then stood around, rain pouring all over us, joined hands and made a solemn pledge to return to the spot a year to the day from then—not before. Funny thing—I remember thinking as I gripped their hands and looked into their eyes that one or two of us could come and dig it up anytime before the agreed date. I imagine Mitch and Andy thought the same thing. There was a lot of trust involved—absolute trust.'

She was still frowning as he lit another cigarette. 'But you never did make that date.'

'No,' he said, holding his Bic lighter in front of his face. 'Everything seemed to unravel at the speed of light.' Looking from the lighter to her he said, 'At the time, I had a gold Zippo lighter with a Harley-Davidson badge on it. It was a sort of trademark of mine. But somehow I lost it after the robbery. It must have slipped out of my pocket in the van, because that's where they found it, wedged between the seat and the backrest. Complete with fingerprints. I remember taking off the gloves in the van and lighting up as soon as we hit the road, putting the lighter in my pants pocket . . .'

'Shit,' she said. 'Something as insignificant as that.'

'That's all it ever takes. One clear print—a *part* of a print. I was picked up the same night I came back from Buzzards Hut. They came crashing in the way we did at George's place, only there were more of them. Questioned all night, thrown in the nick . . . I was stuffed. But I wouldn't tell them who my accomplices were. There was no reason why they'd think of Mitch and Andy. It wasn't as if we were close buddies or a rat pack hanging out together all the time. We just had this one big thing in common. And being an ex-cop, I knew plenty of professional criminals I could've recruited for the job.'

'Right.'

'I should never have held out,' he said. 'Should've given them up. If they'd been arrested too . . .'

'What *happened*?' she said, and put a hand on his thigh, spreading the fingers and gripping tight.

He said, 'Two nights after my arrest, Mitch was gunned down in his driveway, sitting in his car. Executed. Then Andy was found in a stormwater drain with his throat cut.'

Long pause while she tried to piece it all together. 'Shit. But hang on . . . you couldn't have done anything about that.'

'If I'd named them they would have been in custody too. That's the only reason I'm alive today. They—the killers— couldn't get at me. And Mitch and Andy would not have known I'd been busted. The cops would've kept it under wraps for fear of tipping off the accomplices. So they had no advance warning.'

'But I don't understand,' she said. 'Who are *they*? Who killed Mitch and Andy?'

'Big mystery,' he said. 'I've thought about not much else for eleven years. The answer is, I don't know. Damned if I do. And on top of that, at about the same time there was the unexplained murder of a Chinese hood, a guy named Johnny Wu. His body was found in a burnt-out car.'

'Police?'

'Don't see what they had to gain. Wasn't their style, and there was no clear pattern. A driveway hit says Mafia, but there's no Italian connection here. And Andy . . . Andy was a different MO again. A throat-slash suggests Asian. Johnny Wu? He had no involvement in any part of it as far as I know, but the investigating detectives seemed to believe differently. The same crew looked into all three killings, as if they were related. Made no sense. To me, anyway.'

'That's a peculiar thing to say, you have to admit,' she said.

Grinning, he said, 'Sure. None of it makes sense. Except this part—the here and now.'

Jo said, 'Just wind it back a little. Didn't you omit some-thing important?'

'I'm telling the story as I know it,' he said. 'That's the only version I have.'

'Okay, you said you were prepared to kill George if he didn't open the strongroom. But George and Stephanie *were* murdered, weren't they? Horribly?'

He drew deeply on his cigarette, nodded and said, 'Their heads were blown off with a shotgun.'

'And you have no explanation for that?'

'It wasn't us,' he said simply. 'As I said, we roughed George up, but no-one hurt Stephanie except to force her into a chair and wrap tape around her. When we split they were both trussed up and gagged. Definitely not happy, but they were very much alive.'

She poured the remains of the bottle into his glass and helped herself to a Lucky. He liked the way she did that. 'So we're talking about four unsolved murders here,' she said. 'Five, counting Johnny Wu.'

He swirled the wine, made an effort to savour it this time. 'I was charged and convicted of the murders of George and Stephanie, because I was all they had, and I was definitely there. There were no witnesses, no weapons—Mitch had dumped them. I drew two life sentences—as in, whole of life, no change given. I went through appeals . . . it was no good; my own lawyers didn't even believe me. And then, three years ago, Emergency Services workers pulled the body of a man from the Yarra—he'd taken a dive off the West Gate Bridge—and right next to it was a bag full of weapons, including brass knuckles bearing traces of George's blood, plans of the Petrakos place and notes in Mitch's handwriting. I'd always maintained that no shots were fired during the robbery—now they had weapons to test. We had a sawn-off shotgun, and it came out clean. There were even two live cartridges still in it. Every gun was fully loaded, and *none* of them had been fired, ever. They were new, stolen from a gun shop, Mitch said.'

'How can they tell after all that time?'

'They can tell. The prosecution argued that we could've had another gun, which was possible . . . and anyway, if we didn't kill them, who the hell did? They were playing hardball because they hadn't recovered the money and drugs, and because Stephanie's family was rich and influential. Then, out of the blue, an investigative journalist revealed that original tests on my skin and clothing had failed to show up any gunshot residue, which should've been there if I'd done it. It later transpired that this important detail was suppressed by a certain detective who was anxious for me to remain behind bars. So the shit flew, and at the end of the day there was just enough doubt in the air to overturn the murder convictions.'

'Money *and* drugs,' she said.

'What?'

'They hadn't recovered the money and drugs. But you said you didn't take the drugs.'

'That's right,' he said. 'We didn't.'

'But the drugs were taken.'

'Oh yeah, they were taken.'

A couple of minutes passed, and neither spoke. He could hear the wheels turning in her head. Then she said: 'And the guy at Buzzards Hut yesterday?'

'He was a retired cop turned private investigator. His plan was to rip off the money and put me in the hole—only it didn't work out for him.'

Pause. 'They're not going to find him, are they?'

'I sure hope not,' he said.

She processed all of this, then said, 'So, summing up: according to you, someone came between the time when your team left and the police arrived—when? How much later?'

'Little over two hours—two and a quarter. Definite window of opportunity there.'

'Killed George and Stephanie and absconded with the drugs.' She gave him another quizzical look.

'I must confess it sounds . . . implausible. Highly unlikely. If I were a cop I'd be slightly cynical. But why would I lie about the drugs when I've owned up to pinching the money?'

'Uh-huh,' she said. 'You could have your reasons. Call me cynical.'

'Do you believe me?'

'Jails are full of people who didn't do it,' she said—stringing him on, he thought.

'Sure.' He lowered his eyes.

'But let me tell you this: I have an infallible built-in lie detector. It's had years of fine-tuning. And the message I'm receiving is that you are not bullshitting me.'

'That's encouraging.'

'It does sound lame—so lame, so far out, it just could be true.' Then, more solemnly:'Although you are capable of killing, obviously.' In saying this, she was also thinking that he was not at all like a convict. There was an air of calm and composure emanating from him, and no edge of bitterness or latent, pent-up aggression. Judging from appearances, you'd think he'd just come back from a Buddhist retreat, not a hellhole.

Shaun said:'While I was digging my grave up there, I was wondering how I was going to get out of it alive, and whether I had it in me to do what needed to be done. I found my answer—from necessity. But shoot two people in cold blood? No. And I don't see why we'd go to all the trouble of taping them up first. Why not just kill them outright?'

'Could have been a last-minute decision. Maybe you panicked. But it's okay,' she said, touching his arm. 'I do believe you. The system got it right—in the end.'

'It's a funny thing,' he said. 'In my dreams I actually *did* do it, vividly—bang, bang. Every night it's the same, no matter how hard I try to change it.'

'You don't need to be a shrink to interpret that,' she said. 'It just means you have a conscience. But tell me, after eleven years of working on it you must have some theory about what went on.'

He gave a grim sort of smile that had the effect of tightening the skin across his face. She saw suddenly that he was very tired. He said, 'I think there was a whole extra dimension to it that Mitch didn't know anything about. We were like actors doing our bit, but the real action was happening behind the scenes somewhere. I keep coming back to the blueprints. I'd love to know how he got them. That must be the key. Mitch maintained no-one else knew what we were planning, but I think he was wrong. We were being tracked and manipulated all the way.'

'Sounds like it,' she said. 'So what are you going to do now?'

'Now? Now I need to start by finding out who killed George and Stephanie.'

'What about Mitch and Andy? Vincent?'

'I've got a funny feeling that'll come out in the wash.'

'Bit of a hazardous mission, isn't it? Why not just keep the money and forget it? Why buy trouble?'

He was shaking his head before she'd finished. 'Because these people aren't prepared to leave me alone. Walsh was acting for someone. And I didn't do eleven years of stir so I could run and hide for the rest of my life. One lesson I did learn inside was the need to face your fears. In that environment you'll have a shortened life otherwise.'

'I see,' she said vaguely, pushing her hand through her hair and looking a little dazed.

'Not a very nice story,' he said, reaching for her. 'Sorry about that.'

She smiled and said, 'Don't forget I'm married to a lawyer. I know all about the evil that men do.'

'Look, I'm certainly no vestal virgin,' he said. 'I did wrong, and I served my sentence. But I don't see why I should serve someone else's too.'

'Can't fault that logic,' she said.

He crushed out a cigarette and said, 'Mitch was a gambler.'

'What?'

'Before I knew him. I heard the stories about how he punted heavily on the ponies. It was his big flaw.' Squeezing her hand he said, 'Once a gambler always a gambler. He believed he had all the bases covered, but the odds will always find a way to beat you.'

'You said you had nothing to lose,' she said.

'I didn't know you then, did I?'

'If you had, I would have pulled you up,' she said. 'But since I don't have a time machine, let's be practical instead: what are you going to do with the cash?'

'Been thinking about that,' he said. 'Got any ideas?'

She moved closer, draped an arm over his shoulder and said, 'You trust me on this?'

'Obviously,' he said. 'Otherwise . . .'

He saw her eyes, close-up, momentarily reflecting his own, then felt her fingertips on his face and the soft brush of her lips across his mouth, back and forth. 'Can't just . . . leave it sitting there,' she breathed.

He was about to say something, but then the slick point of her tongue slid between his lips, he felt himself falling backwards, free-falling, her hands and lips were all over the place, and for a time words didn't seem all that important any more.

9

Fat Man was far from impressed.

Nothing unusual about that: his mood was generally that of a man whose best suit had just come back from the dry cleaners with a hole burnt in it—glowering, dyspeptic, intense piggy eyes withdrawing deeper and deeper into the soft folds of his overfed face. He had made an art form of wiping off longstanding alliances over a single apparently trifling difference—or what seemed to anyone else to be trifling—and, once a person was wiped by Fat Man, it was permanent. He would then badmouth his sworn enemy on the streets and in bars all over town, until the object of his hatred was replaced by fresh meat. There was a sense of inevitability about this cycle, even of predestination. People came and went in his world like migratory birds—only once they left, they never returned.

There were also those who fell to earth with a splat.

Oftentimes the victims of these splenetic fits did not even know what they'd done to deserve it, but it made no difference:

somehow they had crossed him, or *shit in the nest*, as he usually put it. If anyone had the gall to challenge him, he would interrupt and tell him to 'fuck off' in his cracked, high-pitched voice, wave him away as if he were an insect and turn his broad, bristling back.

Whenever Fat Man had occasion to laugh, it was invariably with bitter satisfaction because someone he disliked had suffered grievously, by accident or design—an underworld figure assassinated, a colleague in financial straits, whatever. Normal, hearty laughter at a joke doing the rounds or an amusing anecdote was unknown to Fat Man. From his perspective everything was intensely personal, the delineations clear-cut. If he was in a conversation at a bar and the talk strayed too far from his own domain, he automatically lost interest and turned away.

The cause of his current anger was Bernie Walsh, who was supposed to follow Shaun McCreadie, without McCreadie becoming aware of the fact. Walsh had not only lost the subject, but somehow he'd managed to lose himself too— the useless, jar-headed *dick*. A covert operation had now turned into a fucking police search, for Chrissakes. Where was Walsh? Wandering around in the scrub—dazed and disoriented?

Bull*shit*.

Walsh was dead. Fat Man had a gut feeling it was all over for the Nazi. He wasn't even answering his phone now, and Walsh would never fail to take a call, the uptight, jack-booted son of the goddamn Fatherland, especially in these circumstances—with so much at stake. The phone was disconnected. Why? It had Fat Man stumped. Walsh might disconnect his phone to recharge it, but not for this long—no way. The only logical explanation was that the phone was no longer in his possession.

It was in Shaun McCreadie's.

Dead men had no use for a phone.

McCreadie would only switch it on if he wanted to *make* calls, not receive them. He was no fool.

Fat Man lifted the seven-ounce glass of Carlton Draught to his lips and poured it down his gullet, leaving an even film of froth all the way down the glass. Then he foraged in his pocket for some change and slapped it on the bar towel—his way of capturing the bartender's attention.

The bartender filled a fresh one, expertly snapped off the tap and set the creaming glass in front of Fat Man, who squinted down his nose at him.

'Don't I know you?' he said.

'Doubt it,' the bartender said, returning to the sports pages of his newspaper.

It bugged Fat Man—he was sure he'd seen this punter somewhere. In court, maybe. He'd seen a lot of losers in court over the years.

But back to Bernie Walsh, and the missing brass.

Missing, missing, missing—everything was fucking *missing*.

All right—apply logic. It had to mean that McCreadie had managed to turn the tables on Walsh, killed him, lifted his phone, spirited away the cash . . . where?

McCreadie had no address. He was fresh out of the slams. His accommodation would be temporary. He was a lone wolf, no close family, and he probably wouldn't shack up with friends . . . if he had any left. Eleven years in the slams, he'd kept to himself—it'd be the same story outside. He'd stay in a hotel or boarding house or something. A backpacker place. He would want to remain anonymous.

Maybe—but not with a large amount of spending power about his person. With that, he could afford to stay anywhere—the top-drawer joints. Crown Towers, Hilton, wherever. Live it up. Champagne, caviar, quality girls on tap doing a private dance on his Johnson all night. Why not? In his fuckin' shoes, Fat Man would.

He squeezed his eyes together and again downed his beer

in a single swallow. A seven-ounce glass seemed so insignificant
in his fat, beefy fist—so fat his knuckles were all recessed. They
were *inverse* knuckles, maybe from punching so many heads
over the years. All his life he had drunk sevens rather than
tens, for reasons he could not remember. It was a habit
common among men of his generation who spent a lot of time
in pubs. And he still used British imperial measurements.
He was six-three and a tick over twenty stone. His cock—
what he referred to as his twin Johnsons—was ten-and-a-half
inches with a collar and tie on.

Not that it made much of a wake these days. It was excess
baggage, a passenger: passive, non-fare paying, utterly useless.
Dead meat.

Like Bernie Walsh.

The bartender gave him a fresh beer. Fat Man downed it.
Then he made a circular gesture with his forefinger, indicating
his desire for a refill. McCreadie—fucking Shaun McCreadie.
He was a devious, silent, determined bastard, you had to hand
it to him. Still full of cop smarts. A killer too. Too fucking much
of one for Bernie Walsh.

Fat Man was recalling the last conversation he'd had with
Walsh. There was something not quite right about it—an
uncharacteristic hesitancy in Walsh's speech, as if he was feeling
his way through the conversation. Walsh was confident,
cocksure, never hesitant. It sounded like him, but he wouldn't
be hard to mimic. Was it Shaun McCreadie? Was Walsh already
dead, even *then*?

Illumination flooded through Fat Man.

McCreadie was trying to identify the voice on the other
end. He was stringing him on. Had he succeeded? In any case,
he would certainly know from that little chat that Walsh had
not acted alone. And if he'd identified Fat Man from the voice,
or the phone number . . .

His weighty scrotum contracted, defying gravity.

Why stop at killing Walsh, if he knew the job was only

half-done? He'd never be able to fully relax and enjoy his riches while Fat Man cruised around him like a white pointer. But who was the hunter, and who the hunted? Suddenly Fat Man wasn't so sure. Attracted by movement he glanced at the window—a woman going past.

The late Bernie Walsh had at least managed to do something useful before his demise. He'd noted the make, model, colour and numberplate of Shaun McCreadie's car— a Land Cruiser. Fat Man had checked with the RTA—it was a rental. Subsequently he had contacted the company, Bush Pig Safari Adventures, who had confirmed the renter as one Shaun McCreadie. Vehicle was due back in the next two or three days—the arrangement had been open-ended. Customer had paid in cash—unusual nowadays. But being an ex-con, McCreadie had no credit cards.

So, Fat Man needed to stake out Bush Pig Safari Adventures, whose place of business was in the middle of Mitcham, on the Maroondah Highway. Right now he was in a Mitcham pub, the Plumed Serpent, and if he looked out the gaudily painted window he could see it down the road, on the opposite side: big picture of a boar's head and lots of fluttering yellow and orange bunting marking the spot.

Fat Man's phone went off—Scott Joplin's theme from *The Sting*.

As always he checked the caller's number before responding. 'Where are you?' he said.

'Five minutes,' the caller said.

'Well, *fuckin'* hurry,' Fat Man said, and clicked off.

In nine minutes Wes Ford came in the door—sauntering, hands in pockets, grinning, but Fat Man could see he'd sweated. Once they had a couple of beers in hand Fat Man led him to the window and pointed out the place.

'They shut at five-thirty,' he said. 'Stay here until then. I'll piss off, because he knows me.'

Wes Ford—part-time police informant, former sporting

hero and short-lived media personality—said, 'What do I do when he fronts?'

'You follow him,' Fat Man said. 'Only don't let him see you, for fuck's sake. I need to know where he is. I need to locate his place of residence without his knowledge. Give me that address, you get paid.'

'Fair enough,' Wes said. 'So, I stay here.'

'Stay here—and go easy on the booze. Be alert. Where are you parked?'

'Not far.'

'Be ready to fly when you spot that Land Cruiser—slate grey, V6 3500 model. And call me the *instant* you have the required information.'

'What if he doesn't show?' Wes said.

'Then you come back tomorrow—early, eight o'clock— and do it again. Until he does show. Pub won't be open then, so you'll have to hang around in the street without looking suspicious, if that's possible. If he slips past you and we lose him I will not be a happy policeman, Wesley.'

Fat Man's words were full of significance, especially his use of 'Wesley' instead of the standard abbreviation. Wes had a couple of outstanding matters on his plate, one for waving his wanger in a shopping mall. For some reason this kind of inappropriate behaviour was becoming problematic recently for Wes. He was finding it increasingly difficult to suppress the ever-present urge to put his goods on public display. But then, even when he was playing AFL football the roots of sexual exhibitionism were evident: he was notorious for displaying himself in the rooms for longer than necessary and 'mooning' from the team bus to and from away games. End-of-season trips, there was no stopping him—wandering around the hotel hallway in the raw, frightening staff and such. Couple of times the club had to bail him out of some heavy charges, including an alleged attempted rape of a woman who was later found half-drowned and drugged in a swimming pool. Even though he was innocent of any wrongdoing on that occasion, it was fortunate for Wes that he'd been such a valuable player. Now, in retirement, his ducking and weaving skills were called into service more than ever.

'Will do,' Wes said. Christ, he thought, how easy is this? Softest quid I ever made.

Fat Man departed. Wes camped next to the window, pulled out his Peter Jacksons and his phone and settled in for the long haul. It was only two o'clock.

By five-thirty there was no sign of a grey Land Cruiser. 'Off duty,' Wes said to himself, and decided to go and have a serious drink. Fuck Fat Man. He punched some numbers into his little red phone and arranged to meet a couple of mates at his regular boozer in Northcote. Then he visited the toilet, and was still zippering up when he came out. A woman noticed him and he grinned at her. He could see she was a lush, so it didn't matter. One of Wes's tricks was to casually touch his genitals whenever he passed an attractive woman in the street. The way he figured it, they couldn't do you for indecent exposure if your ferret was still in your pants.

10

Next morning, Shaun purchased three medium-sized aluminium cases, the type used by film crews, from a specialist luggage store downtown. Sitting in the illegally parked Land Cruiser outside the building, Jo made a half-baked effort to dissuade a parking officer from issuing a ticket, but when it was clear he was proceeding with it anyway she lost interest.

When he'd loaded the cases in the back Shaun drove two blocks to a major bank, where safe deposit boxes could be rented. Joanna knew of this because Raydon had one there—though she had no idea what it contained. Since one could not deposit more than ten thousand into an account without the transaction being reported to the money-laundering watchdogs, this seemed the sensible way to go. Clearly such a large amount could not be kept concealed in the house. Options were limited. But with a safe deposit box you had peace of mind, complete security, anonymity, ease of access—similar in principle to a numbered Swiss account. You simply dipped into it anytime during normal banking hours.

Not that it was a simple process. There was a period of waiting, paperwork, identity verification, more paperwork, twelve months' payment to be made, some more waiting—during which he half-expected a bunch of cops to come for him. Finally he was led down into the bowels of the building where strategically positioned video cameras maintained a watchful eye, past an armed guard who was packing a 9mm semi-automatic, through a barred door and into a fluoro-lit, gleaming room lined on both sides with steel boxes of varying sizes, with the bigger ones nearer the floor. No sign of video cameras here—though they could be hidden in the ceiling.

An hour and a quarter after he'd gone inside he returned to the glare of daylight. There was a second parking ticket on the windscreen—Jo hadn't even bothered to remonstrate this time. In ten minutes they were back at Powlett Street, unloading the aluminium cases. The chest containing the cash had been secured in the padlocked wine cellar, to which only Jo—and possibly the departed Indonesian banker—held a key. It was dragged out, and after a generous amount was put aside for current use its contents were divided equally among the cases. It proved to be a snug fit.

'I think,' he said when they'd finished, 'that I should deposit one case at a time. Don't want to attract unnecessary attention from curious bank officials—or security guards.'

'Probably wise,' she said. 'Although I doubt if they give a shit. Raydon probably stores cocaine in his.'

'He's a user?'

'Chronic. But only recreational drugs, and only for personal use. He wouldn't *dream* of trafficking. That's what criminals do.'

'Too true,' he said. 'And now this criminal would like some lunch. The hunger pangs will not be denied. Where do you want to go?'

'Toorak Road, of course. Where else is there but page 59 of the Melways? Only joking—but actually there is a new French bistro I'd like to try. Then we can fit you out with some decent clothes. If you don't mind my saying so, those jeans are definitely ready for the incinerator. They bear the stain of Buzzards Hut.'

She had a way about her that appealed to him more and more.

A good part of the afternoon was passed in that well-heeled strip where brand-new big-ticket vehicles and snow- or solarium-tanned women who could have been fashion models were the rule, not the exception. The French bistro, Millefeuille, was adequate, according to Joanna. But Shaun was far from impressed: his serving was meagre—thin strips of lamb fillet arranged in a radial manner on a large white plate, with three cherry tomatoes, a few rocket leaves and a gratineed potato.

'Better get a pizza after this,' he said while she nibbled on a fillet of baby barramundi that was half as big as her hand. A small mound of straw-thin fries, constructed in the style of a teepee, accompanied the dish. Evans & Tate sauvignon blanc was a snip at $45. During the meal Joanna said hello to two separate female acquaintances and introduced Shaun without batting an eye. It seemed she didn't care at all about being seen in her social heartland with this faintly sinister-looking stranger. Perhaps they thought he was her brother—or perhaps overt extramarital dalliances were commonplace in these circles.

After an hour in various boutique menswear stores he emerged with armloads of expensive threads, which were then flung into the back of the Land Cruiser. Back to Powlett Street for a burst of sex, a shower and change—then to the bank to deposit the first consignment.

Alone now, Shaun left the vehicle in a high-rise parking garage this time and walked several blocks to the bank carrying the gleaming silver case. It felt heavy, solid and highly conspicuous. In his pocket were the two keys to the box, secured to his belt with a chain. He was acutely conscious of the fact that he was carrying around three-quarters of a million dollars in *cash*. Maybe he should have handcuffed the thing to his wrist—but then he ran the risk of having his hand cut off if the mugger was serious—someone who knew the score. Shaun was also keenly aware of the possibility that he was being surveilled. A couple of times—once outside Jo's house—he'd experienced a sudden tingling sensation at the back of his neck, as if he were being watched through a telephoto lens. At traffic lights he found himself glancing nervously around, sizing up men in suits and gripping the case with extraordinary intensity, making his hands sweat. Then he told himself to relax.

After identifying himself at the bank he was taken through a side door, which had to be buzzed open, then led along a passage and down two flights of stairs. At the barred door a hawk-eyed armed guard—not the one he'd seen earlier—greeted him with an unsmiling nod as the bank official swiped open the door and ushered him into the clinically secure, L-shaped area. An inner swing door with opaque, wired glass afforded privacy, along with a number of cubicles, like carrels, on the left at the far end of the room—the base of the 'L'. When he was done loading the cash into his box he pressed a buzzer to be let out, and in a few minutes he was on the street again. The whole procedure had taken a quarter of an hour, much of that waiting for the official to accompany him. In the morning he would deposit the rest of the cash, return the Land Cruiser, then make some phone calls and see if he couldn't extract a favour or two.

Next day, first thing, he deposited the rest of the cash without a hitch, opened a couple of accounts and applied for a credit card, all in the same bank. After some lunch at an Irish pub, Jo followed him in the Prelude to Bush Pig Safari Adventures in Mitcham. It was a long drive in a heavy stream of traffic. All the way he could see her in his rear-view mirror, never more than a few cars back.

Inside the Plumed Serpent, Wes Ford's attention wandered as he gazed out the window, fingering his glass of beer. Then with a shock he noticed a slate-grey Land Cruiser pulling into the Safari place. Shit. A dark-haired guy got out and went into the office. Wes sank his beer, swept up his phone and hurried out into his car, an old Commodore. It had been a new Commodore when he was a star, an all-Australian mid-fielder, but that was twelve years ago now. His fortunes had since taken a dive, and now all he had was this piece of scrap metal with rust in the doors and chronic overheating problems.

Pretty soon he saw the dark-haired guy come out and climb into the front passenger seat of a maroon Honda Prelude. He couldn't see the driver. Soon as he was aboard, the Honda did a snappy U-turn and sped back towards town. Without indicating Wes pulled into the traffic and followed. At *last*, he thought. A man's patience was wearing thin. While he was driving he wrote the Honda's registration number on the back of his hand with a felt-tipped pen. He drew close, but not too close, trying to get a proper squiz at the driver. He had a feeling it was a woman, just from the way she was moving her head around. The dark-haired guy was looking at her, nodding, then Wes saw his arm curl around her shoulder. He drifted back, allowing another vehicle to get in front of him the way they do it in the movies. As they approached a major intersection he punched the speed-dialler on his phone.

'I have the subject in sight,' he said when the Fat Man answered. 'We're on the road.'

'About fuckin' time,' the Fat Man said, and switched off.

'Fuck you too, you mountain of elephant excreta,' Wes said, and put his foot down to make the amber lights. Wouldn't do to lose the bastard now, whoever he was.

The exchange Wes observed taking place in the Honda consisted of Jo saying, 'Why don't we do something left field? Something completely gratuitous and horribly expensive.'

'Ready when you are,' he said. 'What did you have in mind?'

'Well, we could check into a five-star hotel.'

That was when he put his arm around her shoulder. 'Beautiful. Let's do it,' he said. 'The Hilton?'

'Reckon we can do better than that. I don't suppose we can fly to Vegas and stay at the Bellagio.'

'We could. Except I don't have a passport.'

'Hmm—how about the Grand Hyatt then?'

'Excelsior Suite?'

'Naturally,' she said. 'Strictly top floor.'

'Straight there?'

'Di-rect.'

'No baggage?'

'None whatsoever.'

'So what are we crawling for? Step on it, driver.'

She did, downshifting with swift dexterity and an impressive squeal of rubber, barely making it through a green light.

In the spacious bedroom Shaun opened a half-bottle of Moet from the mini-fridge while Joanna channel-surfed, finally settling for CNN. Clothes were draped all over the chairs. 'Violence,' she said. 'Nothing but violence.' Seemed there was serious shit going on all over—half the planet was a war zone. Then Larry King came on, interviewing a journalist who had recently wined and dined with Fidel Castro.

Getting into the huge bed she said somewhat wistfully, 'Watching CNN always reminds me of being abroad. Makes me feel kind of sad.'

'I've never been *abroad*,' Shaun said, emphasising the last word as he handed her a flute of the pale, fine-beaded refreshment. 'Unless you count New Zealand. And I only went there to arrest somebody.'

'Need to get you a passport then,' she said. 'Cheers.'

'Cheers.'

Flutes clinked. They smiled and sipped. Then he leaned over and kissed her. They put down the flutes and reached for each other under the expanse of the luxuriously cool, crisp sheets. Somewhere in the backdrop Larry King droned on about old Castro . . .

Couple of hours later, replete with sex and sleep, they resumed sipping from a fresh bottle. On TV there was footage of the latest suicide bombing in Israel. Joanna surfed, but in the end settled for CNN once more.

Topping up the champagne flutes Shaun said, 'We're going to have to call room service.'

'There's no reason why we have to leave here,' she said, plumping pillows behind her.

'Forever?'

'That'd be something, wouldn't it?' she said. 'You know, I could stand living in a ritzy hotel indefinitely. Like John and Yoko.'

'John and Yoko?' he said. 'Oh, yeah, that was some love-in.'

'So's this.'

'You said it, lover.'

'Was that New York or Amsterdam?' she asked.

'John and Yoko? No, I believe it was Montreal, in fact. But it *should* have been Amsterdam.'

'Yeah. I've never been there. Anything goes in old Amsterdam.'

'We should give it a run one day,' he said. 'When I get my passport.'

Long pause, then she said, 'All they were saying was, give peace a chance.'

'Yeah. But it fell on deaf ears, didn't it?'

On CNN an African warlord was urging his rag-tag army of children into battle against the opposing warlord. The weapons were bigger and heavier than the 'soldiers'.

'Do you miss being a cop?' she said out of the blue, gazing at the TV but not seeing or hearing it.

'Definitely. I think about it a lot.'

'It's a real cop thing, isn't it? That culture of commitment.'

'Once it's in your bloodstream there's no getting rid of it. I was into the job a hundred and ten percent. Just loved catching bad guys. I'd get up every morning with a buzz, wondering what the day would bring. I didn't want to get married or even have a serious relationship because of it. I saw first-hand what it did to others—sooner or later they had to make a choice: family or the job. Either way it wasn't satisfactory.'

'Same applies to lawyers, I'm here to tell you. So, just going back to George and Stephanie . . .'

'You've been thinking about it.'

'I have. How could I not? And I don't see how you could live with it all these years without knowing the answer.'

'I didn't have any choice,' he said, staring at the TV.

'What about cops? Could they have done it?' she said.

'The place was crawling with police. I don't see them all, you know, having a huddle and deciding to do that.'

'No, I mean the first police to arrive, when the alarm went out.'

'The first police on the scene were two uniformed locals who were let in by workers. The killings were done by then— this was corroborated by the Petrakos workers.'

'How did the alarm go out?' she said.

'A groundsman noticed the rear security door had been snipped open. He went in, followed the trail of destruction, arrived at the billiards room.'

'Could it have been him, the groundsman?'

'No. He was thoroughly investigated and cleared with one hundred percent certainty.'

'Was there someone else in the house? At the time you were there?'

'It's possible, of course—four floors, three wings, lots of rooms. It was huge. But there was no evidence of anyone else being in that particular wing at that time. A search was carried out.'

'Surely that's the only reasonable explanation,' she said. 'There had to be someone else present. Soon as you left, they killed George and Stephanie, took the heroin and disappeared. There would've been time for that before the groundsman noticed the back door had been snipped open.'

'Yes,' he said. 'There was time—plenty of time. But who? *Who* did it? How did they get away so easily? And evade suspicion forever after?'

'What about the son, Stan?'

'Stan lived in Carlton at the time. He was *questioned*, but he had an apparently ironclad alibi—he and a mate and the mate's girlfriend were watching videos all afternoon. I don't quite see Stan having the balls for it, and anyway what's his motive? He had a nice set-up, living off his old man's fortune, using his clout to keep him out of jail. Why would he want to fuck with that arrangement?'

'For the inheritance, maybe. Or for the heroin.'

'Blow away his father and stepmother?' Shaun shook his head. 'In any event, he couldn't be placed at the scene, and that was that. Besides—they had me cold.'

She said, 'I'm no detective, but if someone like Stan Petrakos has an ironclad alibi, I would be extremely suspicious.'

'Sure. Bastards like him always have people lined up to swear blind they were nowhere near the scene. They learn that when they're still in short pants. This was his lifelong buddy, a guy named Rick Stiles. His story stood up. So did Stiles and his chick, under pressure.'

Silence, and a reflective sip. Then Shaun said, 'It's a tough one to crack.'

'But you're gonna crack it, right?'

'Bet on that.' This was said with a confidence that he had not felt earlier: her belief in him was having a rebound effect.

'Catch the bad guys.'

'That's all I ever wanted to do,' he said softly. 'But I never thought I'd become one too.'

More silence as they stared at the screen. A pop-eyed Larry King, leaning all over his desk, was 'interviewing' Hillary

Clinton, searching for a tactful way into the issue of her marriage, and her 'new love'.

'I love you,' Jo said in an expressionless voice, her eyes on Larry King. 'I don't care what you've done or haven't done. It makes no difference to how I feel about you.'

He slid her down into the bed and held her. She was warm, sensuous, alive and liquid with desire. 'Could be a bumpy old ride ahead,' he said.

'I don't care,' she repeated. 'This is no crazy fling for me. I don't do this. I'm a good girl. Never strayed outside the marriage bed.' She added, more thoughtfully: 'What a fool.'

'Stick with me and there's no telling what might happen. It might be nasty, though.'

'I'm not scared of the future,' she said, moving nicely under him. 'As long as you're in it.'

'I will be,' he said, holding her tight, kissing her eyes, feeling her heat and her growing need, then the rapture . . .

In the lobby Wes Ford was on his phone. 'Grand Hyatt,' he said. 'They checked in—with no luggage.'

'No luggage,' Fat Man said. 'Sure?'

'I'm sure,' Wes said. 'Valet took the car away and they just rolled up to reception, all lovey-dovey. Practically humping each other in front of the concierge. She in particular was all over him like an alfalfa patch.'

'Interesting,' Fat Man said. 'Hang in there for a while, will you? Watch for any developments.'

Wes sat in a comfortable chair, picked up a newspaper. The Commodore was parked outside in Collins Street, in a taxi rank. Well, bugger it.

In his office Fat Man rubbed his chins. He had already ascertained that the Honda Prelude was registered to Joanna Steer, of Irving Road, Toorak. Putting two and two together he had also worked out that she was the wife of the well-heeled, aristocratic eagle, Raydon Steer QC, of the same address. Now *why* would the wife of such a successful figure want to carry on a dirty little love affair with a no-account ex-con and ex-*cop* like Shaun Randall McCreadie? How did she hook up with him, anyway? Fat Man understood that women of a certain stripe were capable of going schizoid over a filthy scumbag, even to the extent of becoming a willing partner in their nefarious exploits. There was a case recently of a goddamn *policewoman* who 'turned' in exactly that way, robbing a hotel and going on the lam with a convicted murderer and *rapist*, for Chrissakes. There were other well-documented instances too. So Joanna Steer had the hots for McCreadie. Fat Man continued massaging his chins. He couldn't quite see how yet, but he felt sure this was a fortuitous situation—one he could turn to his advantage. What he needed was to think outside the square, come up with a creative plan.

11

In the end they checked out after only one night, mainly due to the problem of not having clean clothes—not that they wore them, except to arrive and depart. They left behind a trashed room service trolley, empty Moet & Chandon bottles all over the bedroom and an atmosphere that was heavily pungent with sex, to a degree normally associated with rock stars and sportsmen. Jo paid with her Platinum American Express card, for which, she told Shaun with satisfaction, Raydon would have to pick up the tab. 'I'd love to be there when he sees the account,' she said. She was enjoying shoving it down his throat. Her stated intention was to use the joint card—which had no credit limit—at every opportunity and make him pay, pay, pay . . .

Shaun was sitting in the courtyard fernery back at Powlett Street with a plunger of fresh coffee in front of him and an L–Z *White Pages* opened on his knees. When he found what he was looking for he switched on Bernie's phone and stabbed the numbers. After two rings a voice said, 'Homicide squad. Senior Detective Gregory speaking.' It wasn't a name he knew, but he wouldn't know most of them now. That didn't necessarily mean Gregory wouldn't recognise his name, however.

'I'd like to speak with Dave Wrigley, please,' he said.

'And your name, sir?'

'Shaun McCreadie. I'm, uh . . . an old friend.' But was he still? He'd find out in a minute. The two men had patrolled a tough inner-suburban precinct together for a year a long time ago, and remained mates when they were both in plain clothes, but was it enough?

'Wrigley,' said the characteristically blunt voice. Shaun had to smile—'Cut to the chase' had been Dave Wrigley's catch-cry. It was a joke that also became his nickname: Chase Wrigley. Or it had been, back then.

'Hello, Dave,' he said. 'It's Shaun.'

'Shaun—shit. I saw you were out,' Wrigley said, sounding somewhat fazed, hesitant.

'Yeah. Few days ago now. How're things with you, buddy?'

'Oh, you know, soldiering on. Flying the flag.'

Shaun laughed. 'That's the way. I heard you made it to homicide—finally.'

Wrigley gave a stifled sort of laugh, not wishing to sound *too* friendly before he knew what the call was about. 'Yeah, finally. Hang around long enough and your number comes up.' There was definitely a defensive tone in his voice now.

Cut to the chase. 'I was wondering if we could meet for half an hour.'

'Well, I'm not sure if that's a good idea, mate.'

For you or me? Shaun said, 'I can understand your reluctance, not wanting to associate with scum like me. You being a distinguished homicide detective and all.'

That induced a long sigh. 'Ease up. All right—when and where?'

Shaun had deliberately selected a squalid corner pub in Nicholson Street, Brunswick, where he could be reasonably sure Wrigley would not be known. It wouldn't do for him to be seen having a cool ale with a rogue cop/notorious criminal, even if he had won his appeal. To most people that meant he'd got off on a technicality. He was tainted forever and a day. So this was neutral territory: Shaun had never been inside it either. He was standing at the bar alongside a ravaged, fifty-something biker in stomped-on leathers and a mangy grey ponytail, and his wraith of a woman, sipping a Toohey's New and listening to their roughhouse bullshit. She was certainly a heroin addict—there was craving in her every movement. From the man's speech and stance Shaun could tell he had done his share of time inside. Ex-cons were marked out in a way that was instantly visible to other felons.

Dave Wrigley showed up ten minutes late with a phone clamped on his ear. He was wearing a well-cut navy suit and crisp white buttoned-down shirt, homicide squad tie and a short, snappy haircut—corporate right down to the buffed black shoes. The force's image had moved with the times and was totally professional these days. On top of that, Wrigley had muscled up enormously since Shaun had last seen him: pectorals, abs, quadriceps and biceps were bursting out all over his frame. Hundreds of hours in the gym lifting weights had transformed a scrawny young street cop into a formidable physical presence with an iron grip. 'Yeah, good,' he said into the phone as he took Shaun's hand. 'Have to go.' In prison this was the type of handshake a man might use if he wanted to pull you towards him so he could butt you into oblivion. Wrigley had no such intention, however: along with the strong, sustained eye contact, his grip said, I'm taking you as seriously as I mean you to take me. Just don't forget who's calling the shots here.

'You look pretty damn good,' Dave said, shutting the phone and putting it away. 'No grey hairs, no visible scars.'

Shaun ordered him a beer. 'Or stripes. Thanks, mate. No new tatts either. But I would never have known you. That body must've cost a packet in steroids alone, never mind gym fees. You heading for the Olympic wrestling team?'

Wrigley laughed easily—having once been a good mate gave Shaun certain privileges even now. 'It's practically a job requirement these days,' he said, and drank from his pot of Hahn Light. 'I swim thirty laps and bench-press a hundred and fifty kilograms every morning, just to stay on top. And it does have practical advantages in certain situations.'

'I'll bet.' The old biker and his scrag, apparently catching a whiff of cop, had sidled away.

Watching them retreat Dave said, 'But I must say it is addictive—like those coffin nails, I guess. Christ, you are in a time warp. Haven't you heard smoking kills?' Shaun was igniting a Lucky Strike. He inhaled deeply and blew smoke over Wrigley's head, in the direction of a Keno screen on which numbered ping-pong balls endlessly popped out. 'Prison is a time warp, mate. It stands still—even travels backwards if you put a foot wrong.'

'I don't doubt it. Anyway you can't sling off. You're looking fighting fit yourself.'

'I guess I didn't have much else to do,' Shaun said, raising a brow as he brought the beer glass to his lips.

Wrigley gave a slight nod, smiling a bit sheepishly. 'Yeah, sorry. Listen, I was . . . real pleased for you when I heard the news. Seriously.'

Shaun smiled. 'So was I, mate. Seriously. Takes some getting used to again, this freedom caper. It's a whole new shooting war out here now.'

'Yeah, I guess. The job's sure different. A lot's changed since . . .'

'Since I went away.'

'Yeah. Since you went away.'

'Eleven years is a fucking long haul,' Shaun said. 'There wasn't one short year amongst it.'

They drank, looking at each other, and Shaun could feel Wrigley sizing him up: *What does he want from me?*

'So, what are your plans?' Wrigley said.

'Find my way around. Catch up. Then I want to put a few things right—if I can.'

'Put a few things right,' Wrigley said.

'Yeah.'

'You mean, things that happened eleven years ago?'

'That's it.'

Wrigley sipped thoughtfully, but his deep brown, attentive eyes never left Shaun's, or blinked at all. 'You really feel the need to revisit all that territory?'

'I do, yeah. Reckon I owe that much to Mitch and Andy.'

'They're long gone, mate. It's all over. You're free now. You survived. Let it go. Move on.'

'That's the sensible thing to do, Dave, I agree. Move on. I want to. But I can't—not while I've still got this . . . shadow hanging over me. It isn't as if I've come back from the war, mate. There are no medals on my chest. You have to see it from where I sit. We were fucked over good and proper, you know that. And believe it or not, we *didn't* do those murders. I need to clear the slate before I can leave it alone. I've spent a heap of time stewing on it. That can drive you nuts.'

'Understand. I don't see what you can do at this stage, though. The case is still *technically* open, but I doubt if it's active any more. It'd require a death-bed confession to rev up any fresh interest.'

'What about the cold-case unit?' Shaun said. He was referring to a specialist team assigned to investigate old, unsolved homicides—with some success.

Wrigley said, 'There are approximately two hundred and eighty unsolved murders, and the cold-case unit is investigating a handful—the ones they believe they have a chance of cracking. I can tell you now the Petrakos deal is not one of them.'

'Yeah, well. It should be.'

'Maybe,' Wrigley said. 'But I have a feeling most of the cops involved in that case believe they had the right people all along.'

'They didn't.'

Wrigley shrugged. 'The answer will probably never be known—not for sure.'

'What about Vincent O'Connell?'

Wrigley was taken aback. 'O'Connell—the cop?'

'Yeah, the *undercover* cop who vanished. Is the cold-case crew looking into that?'

Wrigley said, 'There isn't even any proof that he's dead.'

'That's pathetic, Dave.'

'No body, no case. What can you do?' He made a helpless gesture.

Shaun gave an empty laugh. 'Yeah. And Christopher Dale Flannery is alive and living it up on the Isle of Capri with . . . Lord Lucan.'

'Okay. But there's no evidence, no prime suspect.'

'Christ. What about that drug dealer, Morris Salisbury?'

'He was looked into. It didn't pan out. He simply denied all knowledge.'

'He would, wouldn't he? That bastard should've been nailed to the wall years ago.'

'You've been away from the job a long time, mate. In the old days you could fit up the suspect, no problem, or shoot him, but ethical standards are much more exacting now. Everything is more community-oriented. Your old unit is now the armed offenders squad, because it sounds less threatening.'

Shaun said, 'It also sounds ridiculous—as if it's a squad *for* armed offenders.'

Wrigley laughed. 'I must admit I've never thought of it that way, but there's a certain ring of irony in it.'

When they'd swallowed some more beer, Shaun said, 'Is he still around—Salisbury?'

'He's still around.'

'Active?'

'Guys like him are always ready to deal if the chance comes up. But I heard a bit of a story that he's dropped the ball.'

'What's that mean?'

'Cracked up. Word is, he's gone mental, mate. In and out of the nuthouse.'

'Couldn't wish it on a nicer bastard. And his good mate, former Superintendent Leon Turner?'

'Old "Brick" Turner? Retired up the New South Wales coast somewhere, last I heard.'

'Turner was rotten through,' Shaun said. 'And my feeling is he knows what happened to Vincent. May even have been personally involved.'

'He was close to Salisbury because that was his job.'

'He took it a little further than that, Dave. It was good cover, but he was Salisbury's man, bought and paid for.'

Wrigley said, 'Shaun, believe me. I know you were a mate of Vincent's, but there's no hard evidence, nothing to be done. You have a mindset, and I see why. It all belongs to a previous chapter—and I agree it wasn't a proud one. Present company excepted, of course.'

That brought a pitiful, hollow laugh.

Moment of truth. 'As a matter of fact there's a small favour you can do for me.'

Wrigley shifted slightly. 'Uh-huh. And what might that be?'

Shaun produced a slip of paper and slid it in front of the other man. 'It's just a phone number, Dave. That's all. I need to find out who is at the other end of it.'

Wrigley studied the paper, but didn't touch it. 'You're pushing the envelope, mate. It's privileged information, as you know.'

'It's a simple thing. You can do it in a few seconds. You don't leave your signature anywhere, and there'll be no repercussions. Give me what I want and you hear no more about it.'

'Sure it's a simple thing. But what you might do with the information concerns me.'

'It won't concern you at all. You're not connected. That's a cast-iron guarantee.'

Wrigley swallowed some beer, giving Shaun a straight-on gaze, searching his still, too-serene face for a sign, some clue to tip him over one way or the other. His phone fluttered almost inaudibly inside his jacket: he withdrew it, checked the caller's number and put it away again. Then in a decisive moment he snatched up the slip and shoved it in his shirt pocket. 'I'll do it, Shaun,' he said. 'Just don't make me regret it, right?'

'You have my word as an ex-policeman.'

Wrigley laughed, finished his beer and stood. Giving Shaun his card he said, 'Call me tonight sometime after nine. I'll either be home or on the mobile.'

'I appreciate it, Dave. And I don't ask this lightly.'

'Just watch your step, mate. Rest assured people will be watching *you*, so don't do anything that's gonna put you back in the hole. Don't leave yourself vulnerable.'

Shaun, still sitting, nodded. 'Don't worry. I learned that one the hard way.' He scribbled Jo's number on a beer coaster and gave it to Wrigley. 'This is where I am at the moment. Just in case.'

Wrigley accepted it, turned to go, then said, 'Stay clean, Shaun. And for what it's worth, I prefer to believe you guys didn't do the killings. It was a fucked case right through—too many questions and not enough answers, no murder weapon and no surviving witnesses at all apart from you. Seems a little too convenient for me. But I have to say I'm in a very small minority. Most people I know would cross the road soon as they saw you coming.' He was gone and on the phone as soon as he hit the footpath.

Shaun thought, someone should've told Bernie Walsh.

Mid-afternoon, and Stan Petrakos was still lounging around in his white terry-towel dressing-gown, feet up on a stool as he watched TV. 'Oprah' had just finished and the theme from 'Neighbours' was starting up. He channel-surfed, then killed it.

Fuck TV. Stan's mood had not yet begun to lift after another heavy all-nighter. In his hand was a bloody Mary—his third—which he repeatedly stirred with his finger before sucking it. He always knew exactly when his mood shifted from black to a lighter shade of grey—it was like passing through a solid steel cell door, emerging from deep gloom into clear daylight. This sudden change was invariably accompanied by a sensation of immense relief—almost a rush, whooshing through his bloodstream like a liberating army, scattering the enemy troops. Mood swings like Stan's were hellish. A doctor had told him years earlier that he might have a 'chemical disorder' stemming from the trauma, and he even used the word 'schizophrenia' when Stan questioned him further. Stan didn't believe a 'chemical disorder' could be caused by trauma—it was something you either had or didn't. The doc told him it could be 'brought on' by alcohol or drug abuse, and Stan's habits were not exactly moderate. He never went back to that doctor. Stan knew that schizophrenia sufferers were medicated out of existence and sometimes even subjected to brain surgery.

Music—that might help. He sorted through a pile of CDs, but couldn't decide. How about . . . Radiohead? Fuck that—he didn't feel like sucking lemons right now. Oasis? No-o-o. Nick Cave? Not, not, *not*. What about something more relaxing—The Corrs? He was partial to them. Where was his fucking Corrs? He had a fistful of CDs, then another, finding the right one at last, but he couldn't open the bastard. Then it *snapped* open, crack, the CD flew out, and all the CDs crumpled in his hands and crashed to the floor.

A strange thing happened—Stan started crying. A huge sob, a muffled explosion deep in his chest, then an overflow of tears that rocked him.

He couldn't stop. He sat on the floor, sobbing and snivelling like a baby, covering his face—CDs all around him like trashed toys. Stan was used to bouts of depression—'anxiety attacks'—but this cry-baby stuff was a recent and alarming development.

Stan Petrakos did not cry—he made *other* people cry. If anyone saw him now—Jesus.

He let out a yowl, clamping his hands to his ears.

Then he realised he was sitting in warm liquid—and saw with horror that he had pissed himself. Urine pooled out between his legs on the polished wood floor. He stared—numbed, open-mouthed, powerless to stop his flow as the fluid spread amongst the CDs.

Stan made a pistol with his thumb and forefinger, put it in his mouth and pulled the trigger. Here was the man who sent Lou Galvano packing, sitting in his own piss, blubbering like a bitch. Terrific.

Soon enough his thoughts went back to that dreadful day—or evening, right on dinnertime—when the seven-year-old Stan went to his father's workshop to fetch his big brother George. George, a strapping twelve-year-old, was his hero. He'd had fistfights at school and won them all. He'd started to shave and could grow a moustache. He'd fucked girls before Stan even knew what the word meant. He let Stan tag along wherever he went with his gang, on the prowl. He stood up to his brute of a father, and once intervened when the old man was beating up on his mother, Iris. That was an act of incredible bravery. Stan watched and felt the blows as his father pounded into George on that occasion, punching his face with a sickening force before turning his attention back to his wife, who was desperately trying to stop him. Stan saw from his wild, blazing eyes that his old man was absolutely off his head—a psychotic, rage-fuelled madman. Not long after that his mother died in a helicopter crash.

In his mind Stan pushed open the door to the workshop. He could hear the buzz-saw screeching and wondered what George was up to. When he stepped inside he saw blood and bits of flesh spattered all over the walls and ceiling. He opened his mouth but could not scream—his throat had choked up tight. George was slumped over the saw, his head hanging by a thread as the blood-soaked blade sang on, issuing a fine spray from George's open throat. The workbench ran with red. It dripped from the edge and made a pool on the concrete floor. The pool was growing bigger, edging towards Stan's feet . . .

He turned and ran, finding his voice with a scream that brought his father running from the house.

Stan knew without having to be told that George had killed himself. He was absolutely devastated—but not surprised. They'd both been gutted by the loss of their mother, but George had a bigger burden than that to carry. In retrospect he saw that his big brother, tough and game as he was, had no real option. Stan clearly remembered George saying to him one night, not long before he took that final step, 'Do you want to know a big secret?' Stan had listened, enthralled and horrified, as the words were whispered in his ear. Afterwards they had both cried for hours and hours.

At that age Stan had no grasp of the notion of suicide. How could you take your own life? It was simply out of his range. But George not only understood it, he was prepared to go all the way. *And* in that horribly gruesome, *agonising* way, ripping his throat apart with the old man's equipment, in his favourite place—as if to *spite* his father. One thing Stan knew for sure—if he ever did decide to pull the pin he'd never be able to match his brother on that score.

Half an hour later Stan had popped 15 milligrams of Valium and was soaking in the bathtub, feeling drowsier by the minute. Next to him was a large Stolichnaya—bloody Mary without the tomato juice this time. People slashed their wrists in the bath, but no way was Stan prepared to sit in a warm soup of his own blood. Staring at the water he saw thick strings of red juice swirling through it. This was scaring the hell out of him—was that *real*? *Fuck.* He really shouldn't be alone when the black mood hit—he knew that much from experience. Stan had always kidded himself these so-called 'black moods' were part of his hangover, nothing more. In company, drugs and booze aboard, mixer music thumping, he was alive, a supreme dynamic force, but afterwards—alone— came the downside, the big drop. When he fell asleep his horrors only escalated, which was why he *fought* sleep the way a child does. Sleep gave no respite: sleep was *worse*. Gulping straight Stoli, he eventually gave up and went with the flow, spinning downwards in his Valium-induced torpor. Stan's unconscious interior was a ravaged, blackened battlefield, ripe with the stench of wrecked and unburied corpses. Carnage, death, more death, bullet holes, bloodied stumps where heads once were—everywhere it was the same. He was the last surviving member of his accursed tribe, every other one of them having died violently—even his grandparents in Crete. All night they'd been tortured in front of each other for hiding Australian troops. The bastards had driven a white-hot wire into his grandfather's penis—or so the old man had once told him after consuming a bottle of brandy one night. No wonder he was so fucked up.

Stan had learned to hate Germans and Germany since the day he was born—it was bred and drip-fed into him from day one. Even now when he saw an ancient war criminal being paraded on TV he felt like killing someone—anyone. 'I FEEL LIKE KILLING SOMEONE,' he occasionally said aloud in a crowd for no apparent reason, when the black mood encroached. He had developed a habit of shouting at people—strangers— in the street, for no reason except that he felt bad. 'GO AND FUCK YOURSELF!' was the staple as he marched angrily along the footpath, picking up cafe chairs that were in his road and hurling them onto the street. That, or simply 'HEY, CUNT!' which, together with a pumped, belligerent stance, was usually enough to scare the shit out of a passing citizen. He sometimes felt like a roulette player, desperate to get rid of the last of his cash on one more spin. Stan would never have children, so the family was done for. Why hold out? The time had to come. It was like the overwhelming urge to jump from a cliff.

Stan's heart and soul were eaten away with corruption, but the final step—suicide—was too hard. The act could be postponed for as long as he could find an excuse to avoid it. It was a simple deal: shotgun in the mouth, shut the eyes, trip both triggers. Boom—oblivion. Freedom. *Ecstasy*. But then came the after-image: bits of his brain and skull plastered all over the room, inter-cutting with that everlasting snapshot of George in the workshop. No, he was but a pale shadow of his brother. Of course it was always possible to swallow a bottle of pills, but that was pathetic: a woman's way out. He was therefore caught in a bind. The sad, tragic fact was that Stan *lacked* his brother's stones for the alternative. However, what he had instead was the ability—and the will—to harm others: 'I FEEL LIKE KILLING SOMEONE'. That substitute victim was going to be Shaun McCreadie. Stan's mind was made up. Kill Shaun McCreadie and he bought peace of mind for himself. And anyhow, the bastard cried out for it. He was long overdue. Eliminate him, the little voice said, and push back the nightmare. Lying there in a soporific state he thought, have to lose the blues fast. Pop a few uppers, do some blow, that's the drill.

Appearances counted for a lot in Stan's world. It was important to look the goods even when you felt like shit. It was like show business. Now and then Stan wore a classy suit for no particular reason—just to be seen looking like a success story. People respected you more if you wore good clothes. With regard to his financial situation, he had a plan. He intended to open an S&M joint—dungeons, they were called—where Suzen would operate as a dominatrix. He'd sounded her out and she seemed interested enough, provided there was no actual sex involved. People paid plenty to be whipped, abused and pissed on. Problem was, Stan's convictions prevented his name appearing anywhere on the paperwork.

That was where old Rick Stiles came in. Stan knew a councilman who had indicated he could help with the permit—for a price. That was the way business was done. First, though, Stan needed some start-up money. Where that was coming from he did not know. He had no desire to use his own diminishing funds unless it was absolutely necessary.

In a while Stan's confused and morbid thoughts faded to a soft, fuzzy black, with little starbursts shooting like comets across a darkened screen. He then slid a little deeper into the bath; the solid crystal glass slipped from his fingers onto the tiles—somehow not shattering—his jaw dropped and he began to snore, gently riffling the tepid water that lapped at his chin.

At around nine-thirty that night, Shaun McCreadie switched off the mobile phone that used to be Bernie Walsh's, staring thoughtfully at the little silver piece. Initially Dave Wrigley had been reluctant to reveal the name, since the individual in question was a serving police officer. But in the end friendship prevailed over ethics—he held no brief for the man anyway—and he breathed the two words Shaun needed to hear before disconnecting.

Bill Simmonds.

Big Bill Simmonds: longstanding, knockabout copper from the old school. In his earlier years he was famous for ripping doors off premises by chaining them to his car, a huge Yank tank, and driving away, dragging the door down the street. Stories abounded of his colourful exploits at his favourite watering holes and at the regular Friday night soirees at the home of a famous criminal barrister, attended by senior detectives, judges, socialites and arch villains alike. They were all in the same soup together. This was the era when ethical standards came from the barrel of a service revolver or a brown paper bag, and when suspects exercised the right to remain silent at their peril. During his stint in the long-defunct consorting squad he had accumulated so many underworld contacts it was sometimes impossible to tell which side he was really on.

Over the years numerous allegations of corruption and improper conduct had washed off him like rainwater. A 1974 inquiry into his assets turned up a new Mercedes-Benz, a luxury time-share apartment at Surfers Paradise, an interest in an angora farm, racks of imported suits and a string of bank accounts under dummy names adding up to tens of thousands of dollars. No charges resulted, however, nor was he ever suspended from duty. In 1978 Richard 'Bully Beef' Popadich, a hatchet-headed standover man-turned-police informant whom Simmonds was the last person to see alive, turned up cut into five parts in a tip at Kangaroo Ground. Only his head was never found. A perfunctory inquiry was unable to connect his murder to Simmonds and could only manage to lay responsibility at the feet of 'a person, or persons, unknown'.

Every attempt to bring Bill Simmonds down had come to zip, giving rise to a belief that he had something heavy on every top cop in a position to hurt him. Word was, Bill Simmonds knew where hundreds of bodies were buried, stretching way, way back. This was his long-term investment portfolio. He knew the whereabouts of cadavers that no-one remembered or cared about anymore. And even now the spectacle of his massive bear shape and his ugly scowl filling a bar doorway made the bowels of normally tough, hardcore criminals run like a tap.

Simmonds was a near-mythic figure, widely thought to be the linchpin in a select group of powerful detectives known as The Three. It was supposedly Simmonds, Leon 'Brick' Turner and someone else. The story ran that nothing went down without The Three having a big say in it. No major robbery occurred without sponsorship from The Three, who would use their positions to protect the perpetrators in exchange for a percentage. Even murder was negotiable for a price, provided no civilians were involved. It was all part of a larger scheme of things in which trade-offs were used to maintain control over the underworld, and The Three apparently ruled with an iron fist. This was before organised armed robbery gangs largely went out of business in the eighties, due in part to stepped-up security in banks and the other usual targets, but also to a growing fear of the dawn raid, in which suspects, armed or not, could easily find themselves on the wrong end of a shotgun blast. The whole climate changed drastically in the aftermath of the car-bombing of Russell Street police headquarters, in which a policewoman died, and the cold-blooded execution of two young constables one night in quiet South Yarra.

Fired up by these attacks, major crime—the notorious 'Majors', since disbanded—special operations and armed robbery squad detectives did pretty much as they pleased in an all-out war on crime, targeting names and picking them off one by one. It was a watershed period in which 'old culture' law enforcement—based on booze, bribery and bashing—came to an end and was replaced by the new breed of dedicated gym rat with a university degree and a Hugo Boss suit, so admirably epitomised by Dave Wrigley. Internal Investigations was replaced by the Ethical Standards Department, a new chief commissioner was appointed and the whole force was restructured, rationalised and made more accountable.

And so, with the passing of the old order, The Three had no domain left in which to operate. They faded away like a photograph exposed to too much bright light. And as for the identity of the third member of this shadowy cabal—well, that was forever uncertain. Various names were thrown around over the years. In fact, in some quarters the whole idea of whether or not The Three really existed was open to question. There were those who believed it was a fantasy, a tall tale passed on to young cops like Shaun McCreadie for inspirational purposes and embellished upon over the years.

Inspector Bill Simmonds: oversized, pathologically

combative, vindictive, vile as cat shit—a manipulative bastard never to be crossed, or trusted. Held in awe in some circles, loathed by many, feared by some, and known far and wide— to his intense displeasure—as Fat Man. Simmonds was exactly the low, scheming type of arsehole to dispatch Bernie Walsh on a mission to Buzzards Hut to take care of some dirty business on his behalf. The voice on the phone came back to him—now he had a face to go with it. For such a big man he had an unusually high-pitched voice, and the angrier he became the more it sounded as if his nuts were being crushed in a vice. Shaun had worked in the same building as Simmonds for a short time, but knew him only distantly, by sight and reputation. He was far too intimidating a figure for a raw young uniform to even say good morning to. Simmonds, on the other hand, had clearly made a point of finding out all about Shaun.

12

In the Sportsman's Bar at the Sebastopol Arms Tavern—a shabby but popular early opener on the city's southwestern fringe, and one of a dozen or so boozers around the traps where he was not required to put down any brass—Detective Inspector Bill Simmonds leaned over the table and gave Wes Ford the full force of his grotesque smile. It was a frightening vision even for Wes, who'd had to contend with sixteen-stone human refrigerators coming at him full tilt in his playing days.

In Simmonds' fist was a bottle of Victoria Bitter, his eleventh in two and a half hours, and not surprisingly he was showing signs of wear and tear. In Bill Simmonds' case, that always meant a filthy disposition. It wasn't only the VB, but the Jack Daniel's Old No 7 chasers that were causing the perspiration to burst from his crater-sized pores and seep through his hair and into his too-tight, slightly frayed shirt collar. Judging from the successive sweat rings under his arms, he'd worn the same once-white shirt three or four days running.

Fat Man's wife of many years, so Wes had learned, had finally come to her senses and vacated the marriage a couple of years ago. In her absence the slide had rapidly set in—according to first-hand reports Fat Man's 'living quarters' were now a no-go zone in which the extended families of rodents and other forms of lowlife flourished under cover of wall-to-wall pizza or Hungry Jack's cartons and discarded Victor Bravo cans. The way one comedian told it, Bill Simmonds' standard of house training was roughly equivalent to that of a retarded ocelot, with maybe the ocelot just getting the nod in a tight call.

Right now—oiled, angry and warming to the intensity of his verbal assaults—he was ripping his necktie loose with scarred and blotched fingers, legacy of third-degree burns long ago. His eyes had developed that fixed, glassy stare: an alcoholic's stare, made even uglier by the fact that a vein had burst in the left one, turning it into a blood-filled egg.

'You're a fuckin' pathetic loser, Wes,' he was saying yet again, maybe for the fifteenth time since Wes had arrived. This had become his catchphrase for the day. 'Lo-*ser*, with a capital "L". I've always said that. You're so far down the fuckin' scale of life forms I can barely see you, you grubby little lowdown cunt. You're a goddamn nobody, a *nothin'*—a *zit*. A zit on the face of a maggot.'

He took a long pull on the Victor Bravo, wiped his mouth with the back of his hambone-sized paw and followed up with what was left of the Jack. Ice rattled against his teeth. 'Beats me how you managed to play football all those years. You got no dash, no go, no *cojones*, nothin'. You're a *thing*, Wes. You may believe otherwise, but you are *wrong*. If I saw you *flattened* out there by a fuckin' truck, know what I'd say? I'd say *roadkill*. There's some fuckin' *roadkill*. But I wouldn't bother gettin' a shovel to scrape it off. I'd leave it for the damn crows to clean up—*if* they'd eat it. And that's a big if.'

He paused for a moment, glowing and visibly impressed

with the level of abuse so far as he gathered some ammunition for the next salvo, then added: 'Reckon you were a hard man in your day, don't you? Real tough son of a gun. Got news: bull*shit*, Wes—that's a myth of your own creation. Your daddy was no pistol. Any *coward* can blindside someone and king hit him. I could find any dope off the fuckin' street—any dope I choose—and I *guarantee* he could kick your shitty butt right over this building. Bet on that, you weasel. *Weasel!*' He slammed his fist on the table: everything in the room jumped, even the bartender.

Fat Man had lost it just for a moment after that. His hair was wild, his face had gone purple and there were bits of foam on his lips. Wes kept his trap shut. He knew Fat Man well in this condition and it definitely wasn't worth arguing with the bastard—not when he was owed some cash and a favour or two. Wes just wanted to collect what was coming to him and split, but Fat Man was making him wait, and suffer. Mind games, nothing more. Wes was used to it. It was a yawn.

When he had some self-control back, Fat Man said, 'So, what've you got to say for yourself, Wesley? *Any fucking thing?* Or are you gonna drop your pants and cop it up the rear end as usual?'

Wes drank from his VB, forcing himself to maintain eye contact with Fat Man, focusing on the less horrible one, then said levelly, 'Whatever, Bill.'

' "Whatever, Bill",' Fat Man mimicked. An ugly leer twisted his shiny dial. 'Listen to the lowdown, cock-flashing little piece of pond slime: "Whatever, Bill". Is that supposed to be your *response* to my question?'

'Well, I forget what your fuckin' question was, to be honest,' Wes said, trying for a slight smile. 'Refresh my memory.'

Fat Man stared at him with an intense loathing pumped into every feature. 'Listen, douche bag—first thing, don't call me Bill, right? *Ever.* It's Mr Simmonds to you—or *sir.* Only people who call me Bill are people I *respect.* Not grubs and perverts. Second, you've never been *honest* in your miserable life—right? *Right?*'

'If you say so.'

'I *do* say so. I do indeed. Now, run along and get me another fuckin' beer, you slippery worm. And don't forget the fuckin' Jack. Make it a double this time.'

'Need it like an extra hole in your arse,' Wes said to himself, heading for the bar. He was reasonably sure Fat Man didn't hear him. The barman pulled two VBs from the packed ice, unscrewed the tops, set them on the soggy bar towel, then poured the jiggers of Jack No 7 over a generous fill of ice.

'Nine dollars even,' he said.

Christ. Fat Man never had to dip into his kick here, but he still made Wes shout every other round. More power games.

When he was seated again Fat Man was on his phone, rambling incoherently to someone he obviously didn't care for—another cop, a dodgy acquaintance, one of his many other snitches, maybe even his ex-wife. When he was smashed he treated everyone with the same hostility and contempt. 'I don't fuckin' *care*,' he shouted into the piece. 'Oh, spare me the gruesome details. Just *do* it. *Do it.* I'm not interested in the fuckin' whys and wherefores. Listen to me. Pay attention one final time: have it in the account by tomorrow, *all* of it, or I'm comin' over for a social visit. We'll have a nice cuppa tea together. Understand me? We in synch here? Or not? We marching to the same *drumbeat*? I sure hope so, for the sake of your good health, my friend.' He snapped the phone shut and dropped it into his shirt pocket. 'Prick,' he said. 'One thing I can't stomach, it's a fuckin' welsher.'

Wes swallowed some beer, allowed a few moments to pass, then said, 'I hate to bring up the subject of money after all that, Mr Simmonds, but any chance of a payday comin' my way about now?'

'Payday? You?' Fat Man said, throwing him a puzzled frown. More mind games.

'I did the job, didn't I?'

Fat Man smiled, almost benignly. 'That you did, Wesley, that you did. And I'm a man who pays his way.' He reached into his pocket, removing a crumpled fistful of notes and some change. Coins spilled freely onto the floor, but he paid them no mind. 'Gotta pay your freight in this life,' he mumbled. 'Now let's see . . .' He selected a fifty, seemed to hesitate, then fished out another one and tossed the two notes on the table among the booze slops. 'There you go. Paid in full.'

Wes looked at the pitiful offering. He had fully expected five hundred, given that he'd put two days into the job. Five hundred was nothing to Fat Man. He would *lose* that much during a night on the town, even before he'd hit the casino. He'd put that much on a horse just for interest.

'You've got to be kidding,' he said.

'What's wrong?' Fat Man said, all innocence, drawing him in, eager for fresh hostilities.

Wes stepped around it. 'You know.'

'Don't know, don't care,' Fat Man shrugged, and took a solid belt of his Jack.

'It's an insult,' Wes said. 'Come on, I have to live.'

'Why?' Fat Man said. 'Who says so?'

But Wes had turned away, slowly, silently, his face a portrait of ever-deepening unhappiness. This was a pointless and humiliating exercise. It was what Simmonds did best.

'Wesley,' Fat Man said. 'No-one says you have to live. No-one. Least of all me.'

Wes refused to meet his glazed, shitfaced, one-eyed stare. Fat Man was challenging him, but Wes wasn't about to take the bait. It just wasn't worth it. At the same time, however, he felt he had to make a stand of some sort. There was the small matter of his own admittedly diminished self-respect to contend with—a near-invisible entity lost in the wilderness.

In a while Fat Man said, 'Tell you what. D'you know who that guy was?'

'What guy?' Wes said, finally forcing himself to return Fat Man's reddened gaze.

'The one you were watching for me, you *reject*. You . . . you *waste of sperm*. Come on, *get with it*.'

'No, I don't.' Did he give a toss?

'Shaun. Randall. McCreadie. Do those three words mean anything? Shift any gears in that lowly, primeval brain of yours?'

'No.'

'I'm sure they do. Flashback: 1992. Sprawling country mansion of departed multimillionaire car salesman, George Petrakos, and his equally departed wife Stephanie. Formerly the well-known porn queen with the big, luscious tits.'

Wes sat up. 'Shaun McCreadie? He was one of those bent cops. They knocked off squillions.'

'Yeah. They knocked off squillions, and they knocked off George and Stephanie into the bargain. Remember that part? Boom, boom: up close and real personal. Slaughterhouse job.'

Wes was nodding, piecing it all together in his mind. It was a sensational case—but was it eleven years ago? Must've been. Now McCreadie's out and Wes had tailed him. *Shit*.

'Shaun McCreadie's a stone cold killer, Wes. Killed a man several days ago, in fact. That's right. Now, if you prefer, I'll arrange for him to find out that some *termite* called Wesley Ford has been spying on him, following him around, trying to nose into his private business, and I'll see to it he has your address, phone number, shirt size and all. How would you like that?'

Wes just looked at him, trying not to blink, trying to ascertain how serious he was in his stupor. The damp, overlong hair had fallen over his perspiring brow, making him look even crazier and cock-eyed than he was. Wes couldn't believe he ever remembered anything in the mornings.

Fat Man droned on: 'Because, you see, because I can *do* that sort of thing, Wes. Done it all my life. I've built my career and reputation—my *name*—on the slippery backs of treacherous little bug species just like you. It means nothing—nothing. I chew 'em up and spit 'em out, dime a dozen. You're not happy with your wages, put it in writing. Go and see the ombudsman for bugs. Complain to the bug species union. See how that plays. Or try begging on the floor, why doncha? If I wanted to, I'd squash you like I'd crack a flea with my fuckin' thumbnail. That's what it is to me, Wes—cracking a flea in half.' He finished his Victor Bravo and stood up, steadying himself by keeping his hands on the table. 'Now I'm going to take one of my Johnsons to the can for a drain,' he said. 'When I come back, I want you *gone* from my pub. You've overstayed your welcome, once again.'

He paused at the door of the men's room, turned and said, 'You want more money? Go and get some off McCreadie, Wes. He's got *squillions* to go around. Do that and you're a better man than Bernie Walsh ever was.' Then he laughed, a booming, thunderous blast of noise that rolled in waves through the bar, and shambled inside, swearing as he bounced off the walls.

Wes drove to another hotel, a major gaming venue not far from where he lived in the northern suburbs, and fed his hundred into the machines. Queen of the Nile chewed up the first fifty, and then Inca Sun snaffled the second. Since he was playing maximum lines and three credits per line, the whole process lasted about ten minutes. Wes didn't enjoy any of it. He went to the bar for a beer and reviewed his situation.

Examined from any angle, it did not look promising. As much as he hated copping all that abuse from Simmonds— *Mr* Simmonds—he had no choice in the matter. He needed to stay onside with the bastard, unfortunately. Fat Man did it to plenty of people, Wes knew that, and took it all with a grain of salt. It was his idea of public relations. What did they call it? Community policing. Wes could sit there all afternoon and let the words wash over him with no ill effect. He refused to be roused. Once it started—as it always did—Wes just sort of shut down internally till the storm passed, let him get it all out of his system. Eventually he ran out of steam.

Bill Simmonds had serious problems. Christ he put away a heap of piss. Wes had known him for six, seven years, and Fat Man had always been a heavy boozer, extremely heavy, but he used to be able to hold it. Now he couldn't. He used to boast about how he could drink all day and night and it would have no effect on him, and it was true, but then suddenly reality kicked in. It hit him right out of nowhere. Wes could remember the occasion when he first noticed. Fat Man was sitting opposite him in a bar just like he was today, in the middle of a tirade about something—or someone—and Wes looked at him and saw how out of it he was. He was completely *gone*. His eyes had popped and his big head was sort of rolling around on his shoulders, he was swaying from the waist up, and he was making no sense, none. It was that sudden and dramatic. One minute he was normal, next minute he was a cot case. He had lost it that day—now it was all downhill fast. Wes would not have been at all surprised if Fat Man's liver was shot. His brain certainly was. He sure must've had a lot of dirt on some important people to hold onto that job. He was old enough to retire on a decent pension, as well as what he'd squirrelled away from graft over the years, but he never would, not until he had to. He enjoyed screwing people's lives and watching them squirm too much.

Wes was impervious to Fat Man's insults because *he* knew the truth in his own heart. As a player—an acknowledged champion—he had learned how to control his violent urge whenever someone tried to wind him up. His policy was not to retaliate—not immediately. In so doing he had received more than his share of punishment over time, but in football as in life, what went around came around. When the chance arrived to square off Wes did so with interest, and was rarely reported. The incident Simmonds referred to—the blindsiding affair—was a notorious chapter of the game in which he had shattered the jaw of a star player from behind at a critical time during a final. The player had had it coming for a long while and his number came up when he gained possession following a scrimmage on the half-forward line. It was the perfect set-up. No umpire saw it, and in those days there weren't TV cameras covering every corner of the field. Despite legal threats from the victim himself and trial by media he was never booked, although there was a police investigation that eventually went nowhere. But the incident dogged him and pretty much hastened his retirement that year even though he had a couple more good seasons in him.

So Bill Simmonds' insults didn't matter. Wes's trophy collection was ample evidence of that. The time was coming, however, when he was going to have to sell all those trophies, as a number of sporting champions had been forced to do of late. Trophies and medals were all very nice on the shelves, and they brought back memories, but they didn't pay the bills or put a new shirt on your back. And Wes was staring down the poverty barrel as a result of what the experts called his 'sexual dysfunction'. In his last trial he was ordered to undergo a course in psychotherapy, to which he'd readily agreed—the alternative was six months in the sin bin. It was all words, pure bullshit, as he knew it would be.

Wes was no sick puppy. He was no more deviant than ninety percent of the human race. People got off doing all kinds of weird shit: playing with blow-up toys, flaying themselves, checking out rock spider porno on the World Wide Web, watching smutty or snuff movies, tarting themselves up in ladies' underwear and bras and putting on wigs, lipstick and make-up. Wes had even heard of a guy who stored high-heeled shoes in his freezer: every now and again he'd whip 'em out and have himself some fun. And if one of those psychiatrists on the panel wasn't a goddamn card-carrying shirt-lifter Wes was a poor judge. In this life it's a case of whatever floats your boat, baby.

Wes became a lab specimen as these high-paid eggheads devoted several months trying to get to the bottom of this sexual dysfunction of his—what they also called his 'compulsive disorder'—to discover the underlying cause that drove him to perpetrate these indecent acts on unsuspecting females. They were right about the compulsive part—Wes only ever acted on the spur of the moment. The chance presented itself and he seized it. He did not hide in shadows preying on victims, and nor was he armed with anything apart from his tool. Wes was smart enough to pick up the pace, learn the correct responses and terminology, tell them exactly what they wanted to hear. Pretty soon he could've run the sessions himself. He could have told them all along that there was no big mystery to solve. Exposing himself out in the open in broad daylight was a buzz—simple as that. Gave him a real boner. But of course the psychiatrists wouldn't buy a simple answer. Fact was, he preferred flashing his wanger to a woman he'd never seen before to actual physical sex. What was the harm, anyway?

Experts claimed it did psychological damage, and could lead to more heavy-duty offences—assault, rape, even murder—as the buzz wore off, but that was not so in Wes's case. He harboured no violent fantasies; he had no intention of hurting or *raping* anyone. Off the field he was a pussycat, plain and simple. Christ. Come to that he had little or no interest in actually *screwing* women, or having a 'normal, healthy relationship' with one. Why, he did not know. He'd never had a proper long-term girlfriend, despite the many opportunities to come his way over the years. One-on-one, women completely defeated him. This had been so for as long as he could remember, and it was an issue Wes had no desire to unpack.

For all that he was now marked as a serial offender, and without the services of Bill Simmonds he might easily score a year or two in the big house for his latest transgression.

Simmonds would help so long as Wes could be of use to him, and Wes hadn't let him down yet. Reliable snoops and general dogsbodies—someone like Wes who knew his way around the seamier precincts—were invaluable but becoming rare these days, no doubt because the heavy drug scene had raised the stakes so much that people weren't game to cross the main players. So if Simmonds chose to be the bastard and short-change him, so be it. There were bigger fish to fry.

While he stood there nursing his beer, Wes's thoughts repeatedly made their way back to Shaun McCreadie. Christ, if he'd known who it was he might have thought twice about tailing him. The guy had done some serious time and obviously didn't mess around. He recalled there was something in the news a while back to the effect that McCreadie's final appeal had been upheld, but Wes didn't know the ins and outs of it. Apparently he claimed he didn't shoot George and Stephanie, but then he would, wouldn't he? Some crafty shyster must have come up with a convincing line of bullshit for that one to fly. Wes's own shyster, a useless, smarmy piece of shit with a ponytail and a cheap suit from Sire's, could never deliver that kind of result. For financial reasons, however, Wes had no option but to stick with him. At least he allowed Wes to run up a decent account.

Something else—who was this Bernie Walsh? That name came from left field at the last minute. What were Simmonds' words? 'You'd be a better man than Bernie Walsh ever was.' Didn't ring any bells.

But wait on—Fat Man said McCreadie had killed someone a few days ago. Was he referring to this Walsh guy? Smashed as he was, Simmonds wouldn't come out with that unless it was right. He'd know. There was a definite ring of truth about it. Very indiscreet of him to let that one drop.

Bernie Walsh, whoever he was, *was* dead. Wes was pretty sure of it now. That was why Simmonds had laughed. The misfortunes of others always made him happy. The implication being—Walsh had unsuccessfully tried to separate Shaun McCreadie from his ill-gotten squillions. Was that why Wes had been hired, to replace Bernie Walsh?

Wes Ford was not stupid. Bill Simmonds was wrong to underestimate him. All kinds of crazy ideas raced through his brain while he stood at the bar nursing his Bravo. Gaming machines jingled continuously, bells rang, coins rattled into trays, players squealed and milled around an excited jackpot winner. Wes was too deeply immersed to notice any of that, however. A plan was shaping up in his mind—a dangerous plan. If it backfired he would wind up in diabolical strife. But Wes knew that success came mainly from confidence, and he had always been a confident player.

Sometime later, in the hotel car park, he was about to climb into his Commodore when he spotted a Chinese or Vietnamese woman approaching, purse and car keys in her hand. His brain instantly flashed: ideal scenario—no witnesses. Acting independently, purely on impulse, his fingers started to unzip his fly as the adrenaline pumped through him. Excitement rose. But then—right at the last possible moment—the strangest thing . . . this *voice* at the back of his head seemed to say: '*Whoa!*' His fingers froze on the zipper, which was already partially lowered, as the woman passed serenely, obliviously, by. Confused, Wes zipped up again. He had never suppressed the urge before, never wanted to. His reaction was mixed—disappointment and a sort of *empowerment*—as he fired up the engine. 'Empower' was a word the psychiatrists used a lot. Thick palls of blue smoke discharged from the rusted tailpipe as the vehicle coughed to life: pop-pop-pop-pop-VROOM. He reversed through the haze and his eyes stung and watered as if it were tear gas.

About the same time, 5.30 pm, Raydon Steer was utterly spent. He was sitting—slumping—in the locker room putting on his shoes, and couldn't help noticing how his fingers trembled violently as he tried to tie the laces. It was sheer, physical exhaustion following an hour and a half of royal tennis with that unscrupulous bastard, Oliver McEncroe. McEncroe was so competitive he would never concede a point even if his life and the lives of his children depended on it. Raydon himself was intensely competitive too, but today he had been no match for McEncroe.

Raydon prided himself on his fighting spirit. It was like being in court—a fight to the death, no honour or glory to the loser. Establishing and maintaining an edge against the opposition was crucial. Lately, however, he didn't seem to have much edge.

McEncroe was standing next to him, doing up his tie. He was so damned cool: tall, slender, handsome—with that unruly mop of black hair constantly falling over his eyes—and gave no outward sign of exertion.

Bastard.

Raydon's own hair was thinning noticeably, and he had developed a slight paunch. And while not exactly short in stature, he had a low centre of gravity, which made him appear a touch simian when naked.

'Too good today, McEncroe,' he said. It was a bitter pill, but etiquette required it. A man of Raydon's bloodlines would have said the same thing as he lay dying on the frosty ground, having been mortally wounded in a duel. Form was important.

McEncroe snapped his suspenders over his shoulders and turned to face his adversary. 'To me it didn't look as if your heart was in it, Steer. If heart is the correct word.'

'Well, I *was* trying. I just couldn't play the difficult angles today, for some reason.'

'Steer,' McEncroe said, in the manner of a pronouncement—how Raydon *hated* that—'this game is *all about* playing the difficult, unpredictable angles. If you can't do it you may as well go home and play . . . *carpet bowls.*'

Raydon could feel his face turning scarlet. Sometimes he could kill McEncroe, the patronising shit. He wore victory with all the grace and sportsmanship of a soccer yob swilling a bucket of lager.

'Quite right, McEncroe,' he said. 'It is indeed all about playing the difficult angles. But I wouldn't gloat too much if I were you. Every dog has his day.'

'"Every dog has his day?"' McEncroe said. 'That's some *bon mot*, Steer.'

'Best I can manage right now. I have the odd problem on my mind, as you know.'

'Oh, is that your excuse?' McEncroe said. 'Something on your *mind*? Sure it isn't below your waistline? Swinging between your legs, say?' And he laughed.

'Oh, do fuck off, McEncroe. You are such a pain.'

McEncroe slipped on his dark jacket, viewing himself in the mirror as he shot his cuffs. 'Now, Steer, that won't do. I've been toiling on your behalf, you know.'

'I should hope so. What have you found out?'

'Well, I wouldn't worry too much about the cops here. They're not particularly anxious to cooperate with their Sydney counterparts—no love lost there, fortunately. They seem happy to let it ride for a while. But the Sydney end is cause for some concern.'

Raydon waited. In his own time McEncroe would elaborate.

'This nemesis of yours, this Tamsin Mascall creature, is, as we know, a prostitute operating out of a Potts Point escort service. She is also a runaway and a heroin user.'

'How do you know that?'

'I have my people in Sydney, Steer, same as you. Although I must say my contact is a lot more helpful than your Rumney.'

'Rumney's all right.'

'Anyway, the Sydney rozzers are anxious to see your head on a pikestaff, Steer. This detective spoke very disparagingly of you. They harbour a deal of animus against members of our profession up there, particularly interlopers from down south. Can't imagine why.'

'What about the money—the fifty thousand?'

'The extortion attempt?' McEncroe said. 'Well, that's

apparently being conducted on the side by Ms Mascall and her pimp. I haven't discovered his identity yet—some underworld goon, no doubt. According to my man, it's the racket of the month: compromising distinguished people such as your good self and then putting the squeeze on them. Often these Bacchanalian cavortings are videotaped *with* the victim's consent, believe it or not. I trust you weren't that stupid, Steer.'

'Of course not.' There was, however, a slight trace of uncertainty in his tone, as if a blurred, half-forgotten image had just sprung unbidden to mind . . .

McEncroe continued: 'Most of the victims are only too happy to pay up. There's even some suggestion that the Sydney cops are in on the scam too. It's a sort of pincer movement. Cops threaten to charge, victim pays a 'settlement' to the hooker, cops take a slice. Matter dropped.'

'What are you planning to do?'

'Locate the pimp, see what he has to say. But I can't string out the cops indefinitely. The Sydney press corps, swine that they are, will really want to get their trotters on this. They'll be clamouring at the gates once word gets out. And once it's published in the Sydney rags . . .' He drew a finger across his throat.

Raydon covered his face. 'Find the pimp, McEncroe. Pay whatever he wants. Get whatever evidence they have.'

Outside in the Richmond main strip it was rush hour. It was always rush hour here. McEncroe threw his sports bag in the back of his Mercedes and said, 'Jo's staying at East Melbourne, right?'

'I believe so.'

'You've had no contact?'

'None.'

McEncroe looked towards the city skyline. It was a five-minute drive. 'I might go and pay her a visit. It's best she finds out about this from us rather than via the media—or the cops. If the press hyenas come around she's a loose cannon. No telling what she might say in the heat of the moment. I'll try to present you as an unsuspecting victim of a cartel of criminals. Squeeze some sympathy.'

'That's what I *am*, man,' Raydon said indignantly.

McEncroe jumped inside the sleek, silver ride, then lowered the passenger window and leaned over to speak, his elegant fingers dimpling the soft leather seat.

'Should see yourself. Chin up, old sausage. It's only another day in court, after all.'

Raydon watched him drive off with a solid, heavy sensation, like a block of stone, sitting in his chest. *It's only another day in court, after all.* This was an expression lawyers airily intoned when a client showed a long face after a gruelling day in the stand. Raydon himself used it routinely. It was hollow encouragement intended to prop up the poor devil when he was clearly about to disappear down the S-bend.

13

Shaun had been out having a haircut in Bridge Road, Richmond—not far from the royal tennis courts. It had become a lot more respectable and upscale since the old days when it was a nerve centre of hardcore crime and a permanent headache for local cops. Some of the worst people used to live here: armed bandits, contract killers, standover merchants, drug czars. The Lebanese gang was one of the worst, along with the Vietnamese and Hong Kong triads. Presumably they still operated somewhere. As a uniformed cop Shaun sometimes had to deal with serious assaults and the vicious tactics the triads in particular employed, and had been smashed over the head with a barstool himself in a pub brawl one time. That pub no longer existed—it had been reincarnated as a smart Vietnamese restaurant. There was now a big outdoor cafe scene—something that *never* existed—and many chic clothing stores. People were shopping, shopping, shopping, and the bars and cafes were full. Times had changed a lot.

After the haircut—in an old-fashioned barber shop where the barber had Greek music on his radio and breathed strong coffee and stale tobacco over him—he walked as far as Coppin Street, and had a beer in the Spread Eagle. When he was in armed robbery Shaun used to meet a guy here called Hong Kong Charlie, who was a very wealthy gambler with connections in the Vietnamese underworld. There had been a spate of robberies targeting Chinese restaurants, and Charlie was an invaluable source of information that eventually led to the gang being rolled up. Shaun could still picture him, standing laughing at the bar in his shiny sharkskin suit, dripping with thick gold bracelets, gold Rolex, heavy gold rings on every finger: all the accoutrements of success were on show. There was nothing modest or understated about Hong Kong Charlie, who was actually from Taiwan. He had small, elegant feet on which he always wore hand-made crocodile skin shoes. Shaun wondered what had become of him. He was no doubt gone, along with most of that old, colourful culture.

On the way back he stopped at Oppy's Vine Hotel, where he'd had many counter lunches. Now it was a pokies joint. There were plenty of desperates playing machines and punting on horses, but none of the old crew—a different generation of desperates. And old Oppy himself was long departed. Looking around as he sipped his beer Shaun picked out a few he could tell had been in the slams, and one that he remembered from Barwon. He looked at the guy, and the guy looked back, but he didn't seem to recognise Shaun. Either that or he didn't want to.

Shaun was also thinking about Bill Simmonds, the old, rabid dog that would not lie down. It was a miracle he was still alive, given his history and lifestyle. Clearly he was unkillable: you could chop at him with an axe all day long and what was left of him would keep coming at you, like the Terminator. Shaun was in his crosshairs. All these years he must have been sweating on his release, knowing he was the only person alive who could lead him to the missing stash. Now that he had a slight edge in the battle of tactics, Shaun needed to work out his next move. It made you wonder what his connection to the Petrakos incident was if it weighed so heavily on his mind that he arranged for Shaun to be followed—and murdered—the very *morning* he was released.

And who else was in on it? A cardinal rule in war: *know your enemy*. But first you had to discover who they were. Bill Simmonds had had an extensive network of spies, thugs, ex-cops and semi-legitimate contacts he could tap into anytime. All he had to do was drop into a pub or pick up the phone. At least that's how it was in the old days.

A worrying thought was that he probably knew where Shaun was living, and was preparing to smoke him out somehow. The failure of Plan A would not stop him. Shaun did not want Jo mixed up in any of this, and yet . . . how realistic was that? Being his lover she was anyway, and didn't seem to object, but she had no real comprehension of the sorts of people involved. She might know all about 'the evil that men do' via her husband's profession, but not this—and definitely not first-hand.

He seemed to have two choices: try to evade Simmonds, or tackle him head-on. Crash through his defences and catch him by surprise. And then do what? Make him eat a bullet? That was hardly an option. He could probably be compromised, exposed as corrupt, but dealing with that was meat and potatoes to Simmonds. But if Shaun could somehow infiltrate or undermine his organisation, run some interference, maybe turn his own people against him . . . What was that line from the squad days? 'Mischief, thou art afoot . . . Let slip the dogs of war.' Someone had written it on a whiteboard, alongside a drawing of a pack of snarling pit bulls on chains, straining to rip into some armed-up bad guys in balaclavas.

A big problem was, Shaun was only one man, and Simmonds had numbers—or he used to. In the squad days they were a team: the dogs of war had sharp teeth, and many of them. It might be a problem, but it could also be an advantage. He didn't have to rely on anyone else, he was independent, he could move how and when he chose. Something else—he had money. And bribery was always an effective leveller.

One thing for sure: he could not simply sit and wait to be picked off.

When he let himself in the front door he immediately became aware of a new presence in the house, even before he heard the voice. He stiffened momentarily, absorbing the vibe and listening as he closed the door softly. There was a man's voice coming from the drawing room, to the left. He smelled cigarette smoke—Lucky Strike—then heard Jo say, 'Nice to see you too. How's Eugenie?'

The man said in an affected, cultured tone, 'Oh, Eugenie's splendid. Sends her love.'

'Does she?' Jo said. 'That's nice.'

Shaun relaxed. This was not a man with a gun. He pushed open the drawing room door and stepped inside.

What he saw was Jo sitting in a tan chintz lounge chair with one leg crossed over the other. She was wearing a shimmering green top and a black skirt with a split along the side, so there was plenty of leg on show. Nothing on her feet. She turned her attention to him and smiled warmly, causing the man sitting on a sofa to notice him also. He immediately sprang to his feet, in the manner of a gentleman, but was clearly put out by this uninvited stranger suddenly—*soundlessly*—violating his presence.

'Hi there,' Jo called. She had the poise *not* to stand, but extended her hand as an invitation for him to join her. He crossed the room, ignoring the other man, and enclosed her hand in his as if it were a perfectly normal, everyday occurrence.

'I approve,' she said.

'You do?'

'The haircut.'

'Oh, that.' He ran his other hand over it—it had completely slipped his mind.

'Oliver,' she said casually, waving her free hand. 'This is Shaun. Shaun McCreadie—Oliver McEncroe.'

Shaun separated from Jo long enough to take a step towards Oliver and clasp his hand. Each gave the other a wary nod. Shaun's impression while they shook was that this man's hand had never done any pick and shovel work: the fingers were white, slender and quite effeminate, as was the delicate shape of his lips and chin. There was, however, a surprising degree of firmness and strength in the grip, as if he didn't wish to appear unmanly.

'I'm sorry if I've interrupted,' Shaun said.

'Oh, not at all,' Oliver said in a polite but completely insincere way that was hard to miss. A mop of dark hair fell across his face, obscuring his pale, baby blue eyes. He was tall— taller than Shaun—and thin as a rail. This was a *very* pretty man, and clearly an aristocrat.

'Oliver's an old friend,' Jo said, making the effort to rise. 'He's just dropped in. How about a drink, everybody? It *is* cocktail hour, I see.'

There was a silver tray of various spirit bottles, decanters and crystal glassware on a cabinet. She flourished a bottle of Glenfiddich, which met with nods of approval, then splashed three generous serves into heavy tumblers.

'Cheers,' she said when they were all armed. 'Here's to . . .' she looked at Shaun, shrugging. 'Here's to friends—and lovers.'

'Good health,' Oliver said, but plainly his heart was not in it. Why was he toasting this *interloper*? Nor was his mind on the very fine Scotch.

'Jo . . .' he said, his voice trailing away.

'Yes?' she said, interlocking arms with Shaun and leaning against him.

'I was . . . in fact I was rather hoping to have a word with you alone.' He did not look at Shaun, but concentrated on Jo, as if privately beseeching her to cooperate.

'Oh, don't mind Shaun,' she said, snuggling even closer

to him. 'We have no secrets—do we, darling? And he is the very soul of secrecy, if that's what you're worried about. Wouldn't know who was up who on the social scene anyhow.'

'No, no, it's just that this is personal—and highly confidential—business.'

'But I thought this was a social call, Oliver.'

'It is, of course . . . partly.'

'Come on, Oliver. Loosen up. You look as if you've just been told you've got the clap.'

Shaun burst into laughter, and even Oliver managed an uncomfortable smile.

'Well, if you're sure,' he said dubiously.

'Trust me,' she said. 'Go. No, wait—top-up first. Sounds as if we'll need it.' She grabbed the bottle and swigged some more into their tumblers.

When he was more composed, Oliver said, 'I'm actually representing Raydon.'

'I would never have guessed,' Jo said. 'Sorry. Continue.' She sipped.

'Well, in part I'm relaying a message from him to say how he regrets what has happened, that you saw fit to leave. He certainly wishes to be reconciled, let me stress that.' He seemed to expect a positive response, but there was none, so he went on: 'And to take whatever steps are necessary to put things right again.'

'But things were never *right*, Oliver. Things have been *screwed up* for a long time.'

'Nineteen years of marriage,' Oliver said, 'must amount to something.'

'Nineteen years of marriage amounts to a lot of *wasted fucking years*,' she said.

Oliver opened his mouth, but she cut him short: 'I must say the mantle of go-between does not sit easily on your shoulders, Oliver. And please, don't raise the issue of the children, if that was the next string to your bow.'

'I wasn't intending to,' Oliver said. Every few seconds he threw a glance at Shaun, as if hoping he would take the hint and leave. But Shaun wasn't budging. He now had Jo's arm draped around his shoulder. 'It's somewhat awkward,' he said. 'A confidential legal matter.'

'Having said that,' Jo said, 'you have no choice but to soldier on.'

'Very well.' Oliver braced himself. Shaun watched his array of postures and pouts. It was difficult to tell when he was being sincere, if at all. Which was the real Oliver? There was little doubt he was a barrister, anyway—he was full of courtroom theatrics. 'There is an unpleasant aftermath to the Sydney affair—I mean, the Sydney matter. One of the women in question has found out Raydon's identity and occupation and is currently engaged in an effort to extort money from him. Unless he cooperates there will be police charges and a tawdry, drawn-out court case in which no reputations will be spared the blowtorch.' And he gave Shaun a good, hard look.

'What's that got to do with me?' Jo said. 'If Raydon's being extorted, that's his problem. Pay up, is my advice. Who cares?' She downed more Scotch and added: 'And by the way, *what* police charges? I mean, great as he is, Raydon is not in Jeffery Archer's class. Last I heard he wasn't running for parliament, or Lord Mayor.'

'She is under the legal age,' Oliver said. 'It's a statutory rape charge. And . . . there are accusations relating to illegal drug use.'

'Are you saying my husband hired the services of a child prostitute, plied her with drugs and had sex with her?'

'Not exactly . . .'

'In Rumney's cesspit, presumably.'

'It was at Rumney's place, yes. But the issues are a matter of contention. Raydon emphatically denies—'

'Oh, spare me! "Your honour, my client strenuously contests the charges." Is that seriously the line you are pushing, Oliver?'

'He didn't *know* she was underage, Jo. That's his main claim, and I believe him.'

'You mean, he couldn't see that her too, too tender flesh was *jailbait*? Was he that ripped?' She separated from Shaun and moved towards Oliver. 'Exactly how old is this slut, if I may inquire?'

'She is . . . fourteen, I understand.'

Jo didn't say anything for a long, long time. She just stared at Oliver, whose boyish face was showing the strain of an unenviable assignment. Finally she broke the silence by saying, 'I don't blame you, Oliver. You are a loyal, steadfast friend, even though such sterling, old school virtues are thoroughly undeserved in this instance. You've been sent on a hopeless mission. I now detest Raydon. He is despicable. He is a shit. I detest *myself* for not having left him sooner. He deserves everything coming his way. I will *not* front the media during his day in court, posing as the loving, faithful wife when all I wish is to see him burn. Go back and tell him that, Oliver— that I wish to see him barbecued on a spit, and *slowly*.'

She sipped, then added: 'Oh—and that I will settle for fifty percent of the family fortune, either the easy or the hard way. Up to him.' A parting shot occurred to her, brightening her face. 'One more thing before you leave—tell him I'm doing very nicely, thank you.' She returned to Shaun, put her arms around him and planted a firm and meaningful kiss on his lips. Then she delicately cradled his face in both hands, as if it were a precious and fragile art object. Gazing at him, she added: 'Tell my ex-husband I've found what I've been missing all these years.'

That night Jo's lovemaking was particularly fierce, as if she had a point to prove for Raydon's benefit. Perhaps intoxicated by the Scotch as well as the scene with Oliver, she seemed half-crazed as she twisted and flung herself all over the sheets, squealing and hitting him and at one point tumbling onto the floor and slightly injuring her arm. In the lamplight there was a vibrant sheen of perspiration mixed with cold-pressed olive oil all over her body. Wherever he held her she slipped and slithered from his grasp, but remained pinned to the floor as he sought to manipulate the levels of her pleasure with a mix of slow, circular movements and a sudden riff of vigorous thrusts that made her breasts slap around like soft hands clapping. Her euphoric sighs gave him such a buzz that now and then he withdrew so he could slip in once more, inch by inch. Slowly. How her thighs trembled when he did that. He felt as if he could go on and on through the night in this way without having to ejaculate. In the heat he accidentally tipped in too much of the green oil, turning it into a slip-sliding affair in which it was impossible to maintain a proper purchase in or on any part of her body.

By morning the linen was splotched with heavy stains, both animal and vegetable. A session in the jacuzzi was required to wash the oil slicks from their bodies. Facing each other across the piles of frothy soap they relived the evening in steamy, contented silence. When they had stirred in the pre-dawn the horny scent of her marinated flesh and the way she squirmed and squelched underneath him made him come off straightaway, *whoosh*, even before she'd had a chance to warm up.

'So Oliver's a lawyer too,' he said, stretching out and raising his face to the high ceiling.

'Oh, yes, indeed,' she said rather dreamily. 'Oliver and Raydon go way back, long before my time. They were boarders at school together—Grammar, needless to say. And in case you didn't know, there's only *one* Grammar, old sport.'

'Uh-huh. And you?'

'School?'

'Yeah.'

She told him—it was a major Catholic school for girls in the blue-ribbon belt.

'What about you?'

'Can't match that, I'm afraid.' He named a red-brick school in the western suburbs, run by the Marist Brothers. 'Or as we called them, the Marx Brothers. Not that there was anything funny about the whole experience.'

Jo found the idea amusing, however.

'So what do rich lawyers' wives do with their time, apart from picking up strange men in remote towns?'

'In my experience, they spend their days shopping, getting their hair done, shopping, playing bridge, shopping . . . But as it happens, I have a real job. I teach Italian at Melbourne Uni.'

For some reason this did not surprise him. 'Why aren't you there now?'

'It's semester break. Anyhow I only work part-time—three days a week.'

'Italian,' he said after a moment.

'Oddly enough, although I speak it like a native, I've never been there. Our overseas trips have been restricted to the Home Country, and the US of A. Raydon prefers to do his skiing at Aspen. But I do have some Italian blood.'

'Is that so?'

'Grandparents on my mother's side come from a village in Lombardy, in the northeast. Near the Austrian border.'

'That's interesting,' he said. 'My paternal grandparents come from a town near Turin—in the north. What about your father's side of the family?'

'They're from County Wicklow, Ireland. So I was always doomed to be a Catholic one way or another. Where do your mother's people come from?'

'Tiny village in County Cork.'

'Wicklow is near Cork, right?' she said.

'Got to be—it's not that big a country.'

There was a long pause while they stared at each other across the steam.

'You know, one way or another, we could be distant cousins,' he said.

A big smile filled her face. 'Wouldn't that be something?'

She'd used a similar expression before, at Buzzards Hut, and he liked the way she said it.

Late morning, a little before eleven, he went out for a newspaper and some pastries from the corner shop. Along the street he again had that unnerving feeling of being watched. A lone man was sitting in a car diagonally across from the house, which didn't necessarily mean jack. People sat in their cars for legitimate reasons all the time. But it concerned him anyway.

When he bought the paper he sat on the sunny terrace outside the shop and read for a while. The only mention of Bernie Walsh was a brief item saying that police had scaled down the search, believing now there was no hope of Mr Walsh surviving for this long in the harsh conditions. Then he looked at the back page, and got a shock. There, in the gossip column by noted muckraker Corin Makepeace—if that was his real name—was a paragraph devoted to the 'recently released inmate and former member of Victoria's finest, Shaun McCreadie, snapped by our ever-vigilant snoops going into plush East Melbourne digs owned by a certain high-flying eagle around town. What's the connection, we wonder?' And there was an unmistakable shot of Shaun leaving the Powlett Street premises. Fortunately Jo was not in it.

'Well, Christ on a bike,' he said aloud. It was safe to say his cover was blown—the house was easily identifiable for anyone interested owing to its bright red front door and the climbing yellow roses over the porch, not to mention a profuse camellia bush next to the gate.

When he reached Powlett Street he noticed the man was still in the car opposite, looking vaguely towards Shaun. He was about to ignore him and go inside to give Jo the bad news when he suddenly decided not to. Damn it—this tingling sensation at the back of his neck would not be denied.

He turned and looked at the man, who now had his head in a paper, as if he did not wish to be noticed. Shaun continued along the footpath and crossed the road, out of the man's line of sight, then approached the car from behind on the driver's side. Giving the impression of appearing from nowhere he rapped on the window, and the man jumped right out of his skin. 'Jesus *Christ*!' he said. Shaun rapped on it again and the man wound down his window. It stopped halfway and he forced it the rest of the way down with his hand.

'Scared the living *tripes* out of me,' he said.

'Sorry,' Shaun said. 'Can I help you?'

The man looked up at him for a few seconds, becoming more relaxed when he saw Shaun was only carrying a shopping bag and a newspaper.

'Matter of fact I thought we could probably do a favour for each other,' Wes Ford told him with a wide, friendly smile.

The previous evening, Oliver had wasted little time reporting back to Raydon. Having recovered sufficiently to start his car and arrange his thoughts he speed-dialled on his hands-free car phone as he entered Victoria Street on his way to turning south into the eternal traffic snarl of Hoddle Street. Raydon answered on the first ring. So he was sweating on him.

'Steer. It is I.'

'I know that, man. What?'

'You're not going to like any of this, old cock. Brace yourself.'

'For God's sake, McEncroe, do you have to take such obvious delight in my predicament? Can't you at least adopt a slightly sympathetic tone instead of sounding so damned *exultant*?'

'Afraid not, Steer. I haven't begun to enjoy myself yet. You are so far down the gurgler they're going to need one of those giant cranes to haul you out.'

'Very amusing.'

'The fact is, your wife hates you, Steer. That's what she said. "Tell him I detest him. Tell him I want to see him barbecued on a spit".' *Like a pig.*

'Bullshit. I don't believe you.'

'It's true. I'm afraid your past misdeeds have caught up with you. This last one has simply tipped her over. I was shocked. She is not the Jo of old, I assure you.'

Raydon digested this. 'You explained everything properly?'

'I tried to give it the right spin. She wasn't having it, Steer. Seriously.'

'Fuck.'

'She wants a divorce, and half the estate.'

'Fuck.'

'She wants your blood on the floor. She is hard-hearted to the point of cruelty and utterly unforgiving. She will definitely not do the sham marriage thing for your day in court. I fear she will do the Afghan thing and piss into the former tent instead.'

'McEncroe, I am not going to court. Not for this Mascall bitch, nor for a divorce. You're seeing to that, remember? I am *paying* you for that.'

'First I heard about the divorce part. There's one more thing, Steer. I've saved the worst till last.'

Raydon sighed heavily. What could be worse than what he'd heard already?

'There was a man—a boyfriend—present.'

'You're lying through your teeth.'

'Not just a boyfriend: a *live-in* boyfriend. Let himself into the house with his *own key* shortly after I arrived.'

'Don't be stupid, man. She's only been gone a week. How could she have done such a thing so quickly?'

'Maybe she had him beforehand. Maybe your Sydney fling was just the excuse she was looking for.'

'I don't believe it. She's never had an affair in her life.'

'Well, she's having one now, Steer. Believe it.'

'Who is this bastard, anyway? I'll have him thrown out and arrested for trespassing. I don't suppose she introduced him.'

'Certainly did. With undisguised pleasure and satisfaction. And she threw herself all over him, rather shamelessly, I must say. Behaved like a lovestruck teenager.'

'Who is he? I'll sue him.'

'For what? Wife stealing? I'm afraid that went out with witch burning, Steer. And for your information the man's name is Shaun McCreadie.'

Oliver waited. He could sense Raydon's brain searching for the name's significance.

'Shaun McCreadie . . . now where . . .'

'I'll tell you where, Steer. The robbery and double-murder at the Petrakos place eleven years ago. He was one of the perpetrators. Now he's had the verdict and sentence overturned on appeal. He was released about a week ago.'

'Christ,' Raydon said. Then came nothing for a long while.

'Still there, Steer?'

More silence. Oliver was starting to think he had passed out.

'Come on, Steer. If you can't speak, tap on the handset twice, like they taught you in the cadets.'

'Shaun *McCreadie*. He was a cop, a *detective* in the armed robbery squad. There were three of them. Bad apples.'

'Mitchell Alvarez, Andrew Corcoran—and your wife's new playmate, Shaun McCreadie. Alvarez and Corcoran dropped off the tree early on.'

'That's right. Shit—*shit*.'

'He was cool. Didn't say much. But I thought there was something feral and a bit scary about the fellow. He had the stamp about him. Gave off a bit of a chill.'

'It makes no sense,' Raydon said.

'I agree.'

'How—where—did she meet such a person? Jo doesn't mix with criminals. Killers.'

Well, she does now. 'Take it from me, Steer. She is in this man's thrall.'

'Ludicrous. I won't accept it.'

'There's something else, you know—odd. When they were next to each other there was an uncanny resemblance between them. One would have sworn they were siblings.'

It was too much for Raydon. 'Just what are you on, McEncroe? Buddha sticks? Angel dust? *Magic fucking mushrooms?* Jo doesn't *have* any siblings, as you may recall.'

'I know that, Steer. Anyhow . . . moving apace, I'll be off to Sydney tomorrow on your behalf. You'll be flying me business class and putting me up at the Ritz-Carlton in Double Bay.'

'That's very decent of me. I certainly hope you produce some better results up there, between your canapés and Dom *Perignon.*' And he disconnected without saying goodbye.

14

It was 2 am and Trader Joe's was jumping. Stan 'The Man' Petrakos was standing at the bar tossing down shooters, end on end. He was firing on all sixteen cylinders. Iridescent mauve-and-purple strobe lights flashed incessantly across the room, highlighting faces for a brief moment and giving them a lurid glow, as if they all wore Halloween masks. Stan's eyes wandered over the crowd, scanning the faces. He liked the way the lights did that, transforming the whole scene into a sort of devil's carnival where no one was real. Across the room he could see Suzen flinging herself around with a bunch of women—heads goosenecking back and forth, shoulders swivelling, flattened hands slicing air as if they were mechanised toys. Tonight it was an eighties theme, and they were doing 'Walk Like an Egyptian'. Suzen was off her face as usual—she was one spaced Egyptian.

Stan remained at the bar because the shooters were gone in a nanosecond, and then he had to order another one. He was feeling nicely juiced as the blood pumped in his ears in time with the music, which had now segued into 'Simply Irresistible'.

The thumping, techno-house mix interspersed with an unseen DJ's voice jived perfectly with his mood. He'd had some snow earlier and it was wearing off, but the shooters were topping him up. Tonight he was very much in Superman mode—he could tear the whole fucking building down if he'd a mind to. He checked out the undulating waves of purple faces, searching for one in particular. Then he felt a hand on his arm.

'*Hey!*' Rick Stiles shouted against the din.

'*Hey!*' Stan shouted back. Since they hadn't seen each other for a few days they shook hands five different ways, the ritual culminating, as always, in a make-believe head-butt, then a bear hug.

'What are you havin'?' Stan shouted.

'Whatever,' Rick told him. In no time a shot of Green Chartreuse and Absolut was in his hand. 'What the fuck's this?'

'Down it,' Stan said. 'It'll zap you fast.'

'I like to notice the view on the way sometimes,' Rick said, and downed it.

'Got any decent shit?' Stan said.

'Couple of Mitsubishis. No blow. It's scarce right now. And *fucking* expensive.'

'Fuck. I was hoping for some blow. I used up my last half-gram.'

'Didn't save any for me, you selfish bastard.'

'Give us half of one of those Mitsubishis.'

Rick produced a small plastic sachet, took out a pill and carefully broke it across the middle. 'Here we go.'

'Cheers,' Stan said, and they washed them down with new shooters.

'Zinggg,' Rick said. 'Christ, I see what you mean. *Bang*.'

'Nice cocktail,' Stan said. 'It's a real seven-forty-seven.'

'A *what*?' Rick said, cupping his ear.

'Seven-forty-seven. Put the brakes on and you still finish up in fuckin' Tokyo.'

Rick laughed his head off and ordered a fresh round. 'Simply Irresistible' had now become 'My Sweet Lord'.

A bit later Stan grabbed Rick's arm and said, 'Let's go out for a while.'

'What for?'

'Come on.'

Down the staircase, past the restrooms and out the back was a car park. A big African with a tag clipped on his shirt stood guard at the door. 'No pass outs,' he told them.

'Fuck that . . . *Seraphim*,' Stan said, reading the tag. 'Do you know who I am?'

'Don't matter, mon. No pass outs. It's house rules.'

'Just a minute,' Stan said, and got on the phone. 'Joe? Stan here. Your coon *Seraphim* on the back door is givin' me wax— no pass outs, he says.' He waited, then gave the phone to the African.

'Uh-huh,' the African said, listening. He tossed the phone to Stan, who caught it. 'You boys make sure you practise safe sex now,' he said.

'Fuck you too, you dumb fuckin' coconut,' Stan told him.

They climbed into Stan's Ferrari. Rick lowered his window and took out his soft pack of cigarettes. 'Stuyvo?' he said, and Stan helped himself.

'That cunt Shaun McCreadie's out,' Stan said after blowing some smoke.

'I saw that,' Rick said.

'We're gonna fix his wagon.'

'Who is?' Rick said.

'You and me.'

Rick smoked and flicked ash out the window. 'Ease up, mate. That was a million years ago.'

'We're gonna fix his fuckin' freight all the same, once and for all.'

'Not me. Sleeping dogs, Stan.'

'Bull-fuckin'-*shit*. He's goin' off, and you're in it with me, brother. It's the old team back together.'

Rick was shaking his head and exhaling smoke with a whistling sound.

'You know what this is?' Stan said. 'Three words: Unfinished. Fucking. *Business*.'

'It's over as far as I'm concerned, mate—dead and buried. Along with the old team. There *will be* no revival. Hell will freeze over.'

'Can't jump ship after all this time, Rick. Unless you're a *rat*.'

'I'm not jumping ship. Christ.'

'You a fuckin' *rat*?' Stan said, in his face now.

Rick was unmoved. 'Fuck off, Stan.'

'Oh, yeah? Fuck off? Everything we've been through, now you stiff me, eh?' Stan said, pushing every lever. 'My *brother*?'

Rick threw his cigarette out. 'That was another era. I don't do that shit any more. *Finito*. I have two little girls to support, remember? I got a real job and all.'

'You do want to be part of the new business venture, right? Still want your share of that action?'

'What's that got to do with it?' Rick said.

'Everything. I need you *onside*, mate,' Stan said. 'You help me, and I help you. That's how it's always been. And don't give me that crap about your little girls. Listen: I'm putting out the call, mate. *Are you receiving?* Can't do it alone, it's a two-man job: the old team is definitely *back in town*. And *you* can't afford to say no—right? *Right, Rick?*'

'Cool it, Stan,' Rick told him. 'Just fucking *calm down*.'

But Stan could not cool it. He sat rigid, fists clenched and face quivering in a sort of controlled simmer. Waves of rage and hostility filled the car. Rick turned away and lit up another Stuyvo. *When he's in this frame of mind you either have to bend to his will or fight him. I swear, if I have to I'll fight him, and kill him, because I am not going back down that road . . . Not interested, not*

*helping. And Stan, you cunt, as much as I love you, you have no
hold over me now; no sir—not one itty-bit. So go fuck yourself.*

The journey home was not a happy one for Rick. Three
times Stan phoned him, trying a different tactic on each
occasion: emotional blackmail, financial incentive, then threats
of violence against himself and his wife and two children. That
was when Rick blew up and tossed his phone over the back
seat. He skidded on tramlines and nearly crashed the car.
By *Christ*, he was dirty—it was one thing to deal man to man,
but what sort of animal brings innocent children into it? Rick
didn't believe Stan meant that, about hurting the girls, but he
was crazy, after all. You couldn't trust him because he was so
fucking *volatile*. And he reacted badly to alcohol and chemicals.
He was a complete nut when he got this way. But then, next
day, he was just as likely to call and grovel and beg forgiveness.
He had two sides, both extremes, and neither one was the real
Stan. The *real* Stan was fucked up years ago, by a train of bad
shit that started long before the Shaun McCreadie affair. That
family . . . well, it was *rooted* from day one. Rick didn't believe
Stan would cut him from the upcoming business venture. He
needed an acceptable front man as licence-holder, and because
of his dodgy past Stan would probably not meet the 'fit and
proper person' requirement of the Brothel Act. That's if it even
got off the ground, which Rick doubted.

When he got home Rick settled down in front of the TV
with a half-bottle of Captain Morgan rum and his cigarettes.
Through the plasterboard walls of the stucco-and-timber house
he could hear his wife Gloria snoring and mumbling in her
sleep. She was a lazy wretch but a decent mother with a heart
in the right place. Rick sometimes became annoyed with her
because she had no idea how tough it was earning a dollar
driving cabs, as Rick did night and day, to clothe the ever-
growing, fashion-conscious girls and put food on the table.
To supplement their income he dealt drugs in a minor way,
but even so had the constant worry of selling to undercover

cops. And his wife had no commonsense: when he gave her housekeeping money she bought goods at the corner store for twice what they cost at the supermarket, and wasted it on dumb things like magazines and expensive salon cosmetics and hair products. She was quite pretty, but obsessed with her appearance.

As per usual there would be no sleep for Rick tonight—with special thanks to Stan. He resumed watching an old black-and-white movie he'd had on earlier: *It's a Wonderful Life*, with Jimmy Stewart. Apparently he is saved from killing himself—by an *angel*—and then finds out how much he has been missed: everyone loved the poor sap. What a crock of shit. Rick watched the movie anyhow, with a cool professional eye. He loved Jimmy Stewart in *The Man Who Shot Liberty Valance* and the Hitchcock thrillers, but this Capra guy was away with the pixies. He lived in a world of his own, like Stan.

Rick Stiles was an old-movie buff. His all-time classics, the ones he watched over and over, were *Key Largo*, with Bogart taking on Edward G. Robinson and his band of thugs, and *Twelve O'Clock High*, starring Gregory Peck as the burnt-out air force commander. The opening flashback sequence in that one never failed to move him. But there were scores of others: *12 Angry Men*, with Henry Fonda up against Lee J. Cobb, *The Magnificent Seven*, the movie that launched Steve McQueen's career, and, right up there too, Brando's electrifying portrayal in *A Streetcar Named Desire*. They all rated in Rick's Top Ten, along with *Hud*, *Stagecoach* and *Spellbound*. But right now he was going through a Jimmy Stewart phase. *Northside 777* was next.

Smoking through his pack of Stuyvos and sipping the Captain Morgan, he immersed himself in the movie and tried to put Psycho Stan out of his mind. *Psycho*—another great movie. That guy—Stan, not Norman Bates—was losing it fast. He was definitely a candidate for suicide in Rick's opinion. He was fond of saying, 'I'm living in a world of hurt', which sounded like a cheap line from a movie. If he ever did try topping himself he sure wouldn't get the Jimmy Stewart treatment. There'd be no angels for Stan the Man. They'd shoot the bastard again to make sure he didn't get up, and right now Rick would be first in line to pull the fucking trigger.

Stan wasn't feeling so hot himself as he drove home to Port Melbourne. The E tablet normally made him feel warm and fuzzy, but that wasn't happening now. Warm, fuzzy Stan had gone and crazy Stan had replaced him. He was dark on Rick—abused him out loud for most of the journey, with the window down, so that when he'd stopped at lights a man in the car next to him looked over to see who he was shouting at. Stan shot him a savage glare and said, 'What are you fuckin' starin' at, *Bozo*?' Turned out it was an unmarked cop car, and they pulled him over. It wasn't Stan's night. The two plainclothes officers searched him and went through his car too, demanding to see receipts for a portable Sony CD player, a Palm Pilot and a set of earphones still in their packaging. Stan didn't have any receipts, although he'd purchased them that day. He didn't even know what to do with a Palm Pilot—he just wanted one. When the suggestion was made that he might have come by the goods dishonestly he spat the dummy and said, 'Don't shit me. You cunts know who the *fuck* you're dealing with here?' To which the main cop said, after checking his licence: 'Yeah—Stan Petrakos. Jesus. Not *the* Stan Petrakos? God*damn*. Not the piece-of-shit, two-bit slimebag and cavemouth Stan Petrakos? *That* one?'

Stan said, 'Go tell it to Lou Galvano—if you can find him.'

'Ah,' the same cop said while his partner foraged around in the Ferrari, 'Lou Galvano—another leading citizen. He speaks well of you, Stan. When we had him in the cells once he said you gave the best blow jobs in town bar none.'

'Fuck off,' Stan said. He was on simmer again.

'You had a drink tonight?' the cop said.

'What's it to you?'

'I can smell it on your mangy, cavemouth, piece-of-shit dog's breath. Here, blow on this—unless you prefer something with meat in it.'

The other cop sniggered. Things were going downhill rapidly for Stan. The preliminary breath test showed that he was significantly over the legal limit of .05. They confiscated his car keys, the CD player, Palm Pilot and earphones, some CDs and tools and a few other items for which he had no receipts, and drove him to the nearest police station. The Ferrari was left at the side of the road. At the station they made him empty his pockets and remove his gold chains and his belt before conducting a proper breathalyser test and interviewing him in relation to the confiscated items. Then, because he was showing signs of violence, they put him in a cell while they did the paperwork. It all took a long, long time—they made sure of that. By 6 am when they had drawn up a string of bullshit charges on top of the DUI Stan was not feeling like Superman any more. The shooters and the half-Mitsubishi had worn off completely, leaving him ragged and parched. Bastards wouldn't even give him a glass of water.

'Gonna report you cunts to the Human Rights Commission,' he shouted from his cell.

'Gotta be human first, dickhead,' one of the night shift uniforms replied, triggering guffaws.

Finally they let him out of his cell and sat him down.

'Do you have any complaints about the way you've been treated here?' the station house sergeant said, straight-faced, completed rap sheets and statement in front of him.

'I want my phone back,' Stan told him. 'I want to make a call. You people have made a big mistake. You're all *dead meat.*'

'Are you making threats to kill police officers?' the sergeant said without emotion.

'By the time I'm finished you bastards'll be lucky to crack a job in fuckin'. . . Warrnambool. You'll be cuttin' down the dead coons every fuckin' mornin'.'

Still unmoved, the sergeant said, 'I repeat: are you making threats to kill police officers? I still have room here for additional charges if that is the case.' He waved the papers.

'I want my *phone*,' Stan said.

'All in due course, Mr Petrakos,' the sergeant said. 'First we need to clear up these very serious threats you've made, then you are required to read and sign this statement so we can file the charges—*then* we might consider bail. *Might*.'

So it went on. It was another hour before Stan was allowed to leave. He collected his possessions—excluding the CD player, Palm Pilot, earphones, CDs and tools, which the sergeant said were 'retained as possible evidence, pending'— and discovered that his wallet had been cleaned out. It had contained around $150. He looked at the sergeant and the sergeant looked back at him with the same expressionless face.

'Everything in order?'

'Yeah,' Stan said, and stepped out into the blinding early-morning sun without another word.

Everything in order. Stan had plenty of time and opportunity to reflect as he made the three-quarter-hour-long journey to his car on foot. He considered phoning Suzen, but the dozy bitch would be comatose until noon after a night at Joe's. He was so dirty on Rick he hadn't bothered going back in to collect her. So he hoofed it. He didn't give a shit about the DUI rap—he'd had two of those before and it made no difference. He drove anyway, every single day. Having a distinctive car meant he ran a bit of a risk of being picked up, but so what?

So fucking *what*?

He turned around in the general direction of the police station and screamed: 'SO FUCKING WHAT?' He shouted it a few times and added: 'ALL COPPERS ARE CUNTS!' A young woman hurrying along was his next target: 'ALL COPPERS ARE CUNTS, DARLING! I'M GONNA KILL ME SOME BEFORE I DIE!' She was gone in a flash after giving him a quick, nervous smile—humouring a lunatic on the loose. He hollered at her disappearing back: 'RUN, RUN, RUN, BABY! GO ON, *RUN*!'

Everything in order. Stan considered how he might avenge himself. He could plant a bomb in the cop shop, one of those satchel bombs. Pipes full of gunpowder and scrap metal, with a timer: go in, put it down, leave. Stan was a top-notch hater. Sooner or later he would find a way of squaring it with those cunts. He had their names and they were on his death list— the detectives were Wilson and Janovic, and the sergeant was Blore. He would deal with them. Wilson, Janovic, Blore . . . He committed the names to memory. Bomb in the cop shop played brightly in his mind. He saw the white flash, the shit flying, bleeding bits of copper blown everywhere, the limbless, headless corpses spreadeagled on the road . . .

Headless corpses.

This image blurred into his father and Steph: same old, same old. Everything came back to that. Stan trudged on, eyes downcast, watching his feet crunch the footpath: left, right, left, right . . .

'FUCKING CUNTS!' he screamed at no one. A man across the street glanced at him and Stan stopped, raised his face and went: 'AAAAARGH!' The guy scurried on.

Liquidity problems. Cash flow problems. Cop problems. He reached an ATM and put in his card before noticing it was shut. He punched the ATM twice, walked on, came back and punched it some more, then gave it a flying kick.

That was better.

Cash flow problems. Stan should be rich, not busted. He should be swimming in it. But the old man, the old man . . . George totally fucked it, the whole nut. It was a sorry story and Stan hated remembering it. Stupid old cunt. Stan roared: 'DIE, DIE, DIE!'

George, his father, *was* dead, leaving behind millions for his only surviving son. *Millions*. Then the Tax Office became interested in his affairs. An investigation found that George owed huge amounts in back taxes. They froze everything and tallied up a bill, adding retrospective interest and penalties. Receivers, liquidators, accountants and lawyers swarmed over his activities, uncovering all his hidden cash and his assets, all his cars, planes, properties; his antique and art collections, all the fittings and furnishings, his *wife's* possessions, her horses, even her engagement ring—the lot. Picked him clean as a plucked duck. Everything was sold off, including the never-completed Lancefield mansion on which he owed a long line of tradesmen and sub-contractors vast amounts—for bargain basement prices. Turned out he *owned* very little. It was all done with mirrors, based on chains of unpaid debts going back decades. Hundreds of people lined up to be paid so many cents in the dollar. He'd been nothing but a shifty, sleazy fucking car salesman *all the time*. Stan had retained a top brief to try and stop the flow of cash, but all that did was suck up more money—*Stan's*. That brief vacuumed it all up and gave zip for it. When it was over there was fuck-all left. The liquidators let Stan keep his Carlton pad and the old Ferrari, both of which were in his name, and that was that. The rest was dust.

In the aftermath, however, he discovered an insurance policy on the old man's life, which the authorities couldn't hook their claws into. That kept him going, but it wouldn't last forever.

Stan arrived at his car, which was just how he'd left it. That was a relief. He drove home, popped a Valium and hit the unmade cot. For the next several hours he slept as if he'd been hit over the head with a tree stump. This was how Stan slept most of the time—from the high board of a wrecked physical or emotional condition. *Rest* did not come into it: Stan *crashed* or *collapsed*, usually in an out-of-mind state.

And why did he scream at people in the street, and threaten nightclub doormen? He did not know. Fact was, Stan lacked the ability or even the will to self-diagnose. He functioned mainly at a level of cunning that was laced with a need to either impose his will by any means or deal with whatever or whoever opposed him by blunt force. A refusal to comply with Stan's wishes was an act of provocation that made his blood boil and his fists clench. In the manner of a tethered animal, intelligence only carried him a short distance in any direction, and after that his need to dominate and the abnormal chemistry in his brain—aided and abetted by illegal or controlled substances, alcohol and deviant sexual episodes—took over.

From a deep, troubled sleep he surfaced to the sound of a ringing phone. In his dreams he was trapped in a crawlspace, trying to escape . . . but there was barely room to move and he was suffocating. He was wedged tight and the earth was pressing down on him. There was a powerful buzzing sound somewhere ahead, and he crawled on towards it . . . then there was a trapdoor above, which he tried to open. It wouldn't budge. He pushed and pushed until finally it opened a crack. The buzzing grew louder. He heaved the trapdoor open with all his reserves, dragged himself out of the crawlspace and saw he was in a workshop full of tools and machinery. In front of him was his brother George, slumped over a bench with the circular saw still spinning through him, ripping him to rags and sending a shower of blood and bone all over the shop, in Stan's face, everywhere . . .

He sat on the bed, still groggy from Valium and the residue of whatever else was in his system. His eyes would *not* come open. The phone rang on in the living room. He stood up, steadying himself. He was clad only in underpants and socks, but as usual had no memory of undressing. Scuzzy after-images from the horrible dream flickered and flashed in his brain as he staggered out and searched for the portable handset, which was . . . *somewhere.*

Finally he dug it out from under some porn magazines on the sofa.

'Yeah,' he said, sitting down, rubbing his face and trying to focus on his wristwatch.

'Wolfman?' Suzen's voice said.

'Yeah.'

'You sound like shit.'

'What time is it?' He still could not focus on his watch.

'Time you came out for a drink, maybe,' she said.

'Gimme half an hour,' he said, and hung up the phone. Then he lay down on the bed again, just for a minute, and slept for two hours without moving.

15

'What are you on about, buddy?' Shaun said. 'And who the hell are you, anyway?'

'Name's Wes Ford,' Wes told him through the car window, and waited to see if it meant anything to Shaun. It did to most people, but whether that applied in the big house was another question.

'Wes Ford . . .' Shaun was lowering himself onto his haunches so he was level with Wes. 'I feel I know the name from somewhere . . .'

'If you're interested in football it'd help,' Wes said, smiling. He was feeling quite relaxed so far—the guy was being reasonable.

'Wait a minute, I've got you. Wes *Ford*. Shit, you were a star, man. Number 11. Frank Zappa moustache, white headband . . . Left-footer. Bit handy close-in. Short-arm jolt specialist, if I remember correctly.'

Wes laughed. 'That part of my game has been greatly exaggerated over the years.' He rubbed his lower face. 'The Zappa moustache went out of fashion. And it wasn't a headband, but a bandanna. I had to tie it up, stop it from coming off during the game.'

'You decked Bobby Sharples during the finals series back in . . . '88, or '89.'

'Second semi-final, 1989. Twenty-seven minutes into the third quarter. And for what it's worth, Bobby Sharples was a sly hit man whose number happened to come up when I was alongside him.'

'Right . . . but my memory is that you were somewhere *behind* him.'

'Whatever. People remember incidents in all kinds of different ways, but the result never changes at all.'

'And only results count.'

'Sure feels like it when you're drinking from the winner's cup. You know, in eleven years and one hundred and seventy-eight games I played in two premiership sides, represented the state six times and won a big swag of awards—including this very car, as a matter of fact. I was also reported twice, and acquitted both times. But all people ever remember is poor Bobby Sharples' busted jaw, as if I'd punched out Bambi.'

Shaun was smiling guardedly and nodding. 'People only care about how you finished, Wes. Especially if you screwed it up.'

'Sadly, that is too true.'

They locked eyes, and in that instant Wes experienced a moment when he believed he and Shaun could actually get along—there was a palpable rapport even at this early point. The man was warming to him. This was no big surprise. After his retirement Wes had done guest commentary spots on radio and TV, conducting interviews with coaches and players and, with his 'special comments' during a telecast, providing acute insights into the way a game was shaping up. So, putting Fat Man to one side, there was nothing wrong with his people skills at that level. He had a man-to-man charm and a resonant, testosterone-driven voice, was quick and funny on his feet and *never* nervous or rattled in front of a camera. He was a natural media talent, and was in fact being primed for a permanent TV slot before blowing his chances. After that he was a leper.

'You still haven't answered my first question,' Shaun said.

'Which was, why am I here?'

'I don't believe you parked outside my place so we could have a chat about your life and times, interesting as they've been.' Now he cocked an eye, indicating that he was up to speed on Wes's off-field escapades too. Which was fine.

'Okay,' Wes said, deadpan. 'Does the name Bill Simmonds mean anything to you?'

The effect was instantaneous. The man's smile vanished, and for a moment Wes thought Shaun was going to reach inside the car and grab him by the throat. He remembered: *this man is a killer.*

'You're Shaun McCreadie, are you not? Did I get that right?'

'You seem to be holding all the cards, Wes. All I have is some croissants, which I plan to eat sometime soon.'

'I've been running errands for Simmonds,' Wes said. 'Following you around town, reporting back. He has a major interest in your activities.'

'Is that so?'

'Enough to have you tagged 24/7. I was there when you turned in the rental car over at the Bush Pig place in Mitcham. Then you checked into the Hyatt . . .'

Shaun was still on his haunches, giving Wes his full attention. 'And?'

'He knows where you live.' Wes elevated his gaze, directing it towards the wrought-iron first-floor balcony across the street. 'Knows about your girl.'

Shaun twisted his neck around, following Wes's line of sight. Jo was standing on the balcony, not exactly watching them but casting her eyes here and there. She had on her white satin dressing gown, which flashed in the sun, and a trail of smoke curled up into the still morning air from the cigarette burning in her hand.

'He's got the dirt on a certain Bernie Walsh too,' Wes continued. 'Killed in action at the front, apparently. Not that I'd know.'

Shaun seemed to receive this information in his stride. If any of it touched a nerve it didn't show. After a lengthy pause he said, 'Why don't you tell me what's on your mind? I don't imagine Simmonds would be thrilled to learn you were ratting him out—if that's what you're doing.'

Wes knew his response to that. 'Fuck Bill Simmonds.'

Shaun studied Wes's features, sizing him up exactly how Dave Wrigley had done with him before reaching a decision he would have to live with.

'You'd better come inside, Wes,' he said, standing up.

Wes found himself sitting at a table in a spacious downstairs kitchen, directly opposite the vision on the balcony. Still wearing the satin dressing gown, she was cupping her chin with one hand and dabbing at croissant flakes on her plate with the other. There was some decent cleavage on offer, from which Wes disciplined himself to avert his gaze. It wasn't easy. Shaun was next to her, arms folded on the table. They were both watching Wes, as if expecting him to jump up and do something interesting any second. A clock ticked on the wall, and the air was rich with the smell of freshly brewed espresso coffee.

Wes picked up his cup and sipped. Shaun had introduced him to Jo ('Meet Wes Ford, the man who punched out Bambi') and explained the situation in two or three sentences. Jo hadn't said or done much, except to nod and touch Shaun. From where he sat Wes saw that there was some serious chemistry happening here. Jo seemed to have no problem with whatever was going down, with this stranger suddenly factored into her living space. She was certainly more relaxed than Wes felt. Now she was draping an arm on Shaun's shoulder, still intent on Wes but ensuring that the love of her life wasn't going anywhere in a hurry. For his part, Shaun McCreadie seemed content to allow someone else to make the next move. It was a strange situation, not unlike being scrutinised in a police station interview room.

'What does this Bill Simmonds person *want*?' Jo said. The question was directed at Wes.

'Hasn't told me in so many words. But he's not doing this for his amusement. No doubt he has a big picture, but I'm not in it.'

'But you must have some idea,' she said. Shaun gave her an approving sideways glance, evidently pleased to see her taking the initiative. Then he turned his gaze back to Wes, an eyebrow raised, awaiting his reply.

Wes interlocked his fingers, forming a peak with his thumbs, which he then began tapping together in time with the ticking of the clock. 'When I saw him yesterday—'

'Where was that?' Shaun said.

'A waterfront dive called the Sebastopol Arms. Know it?'

'Yeah. From long ago.'

'It's one of his regular watering holes. Must be tight with the management, because he's on the free list there. Anyway yesterday he was tired and emotional—totally shit-faced—and when he's in that condition he tends to be loose-lipped. He let slip something about a guy called Bernie Walsh, who I gather was on your case, but no longer.'

Shaun nodded, not in agreement, but to indicate he was receiving. Jo gave his neck an affectionate little squeeze before separating her arm from his shoulder, and getting up to fetch more coffee from the still-steaming pot on the stove top. Whenever she moved, the satin dressing gown slipped and slid all over her contours like molten silver skin, giving Wes a cool shiver.

'Is that all?' Shaun said.

To distract himself Wes chewed on a piece of croissant. 'Pretty much, so far. But I got the distinct impression he believes you have a large stash of money. If so, he wants it.' He swallowed, then added: 'One thing's for sure and certain, this is not official police business. He's moonlighting.'

'Bill Simmonds has always been a moonlighter,' Shaun said. 'He made it an art form.'

'More coffee, Wes?' Jo said next to him, on his right side, poised to pour.

'Please,' Wes said. He didn't turn towards her face because he didn't trust himself—the cleavage was *right* there at eye level. In fact the satin material brushed his upper arm as she leaned slightly to top up his cup. Something else, which he had noticed earlier: there was another smell—cooking oil. It was on Shaun outside, now he smelled it on Jo. Strange.

'So you're offering to switch teams,' Shaun said. 'Is that it?'

'Yes.'

'And what would you expect in return?'

'Well, if I can deliver any important information, I'd want financial recompense. There aren't too many employment opportunities out there for washed-up footballers.'

'Does Simmonds pay you?'

Jo was back at her seat and sliding into it sideways. Wes's eyes flicked from Shaun to her, then back to Shaun.

'Simmonds pays *shit*,' he said, more vehemently than he'd intended.

Shaun didn't say anything, obliging Wes to explain some more. 'The reality is,' he said, trying to arrange the words sensibly before speaking them, 'that . . . I've been snitching for Bill Simmonds for a few years now. He doesn't particularly like me—he doesn't seem to like *anyone*—but I've delivered for him often enough. He trusts me to do the job. Believe me, we are not brothers.'

'Why have you snitched for a man who doesn't like you, and who pays shit?' Shaun said.

'There have been fringe benefits,' Wes said. He was prepared to be upfront about this. 'If I happen to have a run-in with the law, say, he steps in and has a word on my behalf.'

'I see. And you find yourself in need of his services at present?'

Wes nodded. 'Unfortunately.'

Shaun sat back in his chair. 'This is becoming complicated, Wes. You propose doing the dirty—*dogging*—on Bill Simmonds, who everyone knows is an unforgiving, disagreeable person. If he finds out you're double-dealing him he will be displeased. He will *certainly* not intervene on your behalf in your current situation with the law.'

'Are you kidding? He'll do whatever he can to put me away for as long as possible.'

'At the very least,' Shaun said. 'I remember a case years ago, a snitch, in fact, named Richard Popadich, who was known to have connections with Bill Simmonds. He was called 'Bully Beef' because he was so tough. They found him cut up into pieces in a tip somewhere.'

'Excuse *me*,' Jo said, and reached for the pack of Lucky Strikes and lighter in front of Shaun.

'Sorry, baby,' he said. 'But I wanted to point out to Wes that he's playing a dangerous game. This Simmonds guy does not fuck around with people who rat on him.'

'I know that,' Wes said. 'But, shit, he's seen better days. He is *not* in good shape.'

'He might be past doing it himself, but he probably has people who would do it for him for nothing. Or for pleasure.'

'I'll back myself.'

'How often do you see him?' Shaun said after a bit.

Wes shrugged, as Jo shot out a plume of smoke over the top of his head. 'He could call anytime. It all depends.'

'So you'll maintain the relationship, learn what you can . . .'

'And pass it onto you.'

Silence descended over the table as all three considered the pros and cons.

'What can you tell me about Bernie Walsh?' Wes said. 'Just so I know.'

'Walsh was an ex-cop mercenary hired by Simmonds to kill me,' Shaun said without feeling. 'But he lost out.'

A light came on in Wes's head. 'Wait on. Is he the dude that's missing up in the mountains?' He'd seen it on the TV news, but not made the connection until now.

'That's him,' Shaun said.

'Jesus Christ,' Wes said. 'I hope he's got thermal underwear.'

Jo exploded into laughter, and Shaun smiled. 'Wouldn't do him any good,' he said.

Outside on the footpath Shaun said, 'Sure you want to do this?'

'I'm sure if you are,' Wes said.

'It'll be bad for you if he finds out. Seriously.'

'Oh, let's not go there again,' Wes said with a grim little laugh. 'At the very least I'd expect a severe kneecapping—but probably worse. I'd probably finish up on the missing list, like your pal Walsh.'

Better hope not, Wes. 'For Christ's sake don't tell anyone what you're up to. Not even anyone you trust. *Especially* not anyone you trust.'

'I'm not that stupid, man. Give me some credit.'

Shaun said, 'You'd be surprised what people do—even smart people—when they get in over their heads. They stop behaving sensibly for some reason. Not that I can talk.'

'I hear what you're saying,' Wes said. 'But don't worry on my account. You haven't seen Simmonds for a while, right? He's a mess, he's a total piss-head. Still makes a big noise, but he doesn't scare me. At all.'

'Don't undersell him. He still carries weight in more ways than one.'

'I know, I know. He wouldn't do it himself. It'd be someone he owns, like me—or you.'

'Just watch your back.'

'Yeah. She's a nice chick, by the by.'

'Yeah, thought you were impressed.'

Wes grinned. 'I'll be in touch sometime.' They had exchanged phone numbers inside. Wes began crossing the road to his beat-up set of wheels when Shaun called, 'Oh, and Wes. Try not to attract attention. If you know what I mean.'

'Who, me?' Wes said, giving him the thumbs-up.

When he arrived back in the kitchen Jo was facing him with one hand in her pocket and the other resting on the top of a chair. Her lips were slightly apart. Even from the door he saw what was on her mind. Without a word he released the cord of the dressing gown and opened it. She wanted to slip it from her shoulders, but he said, 'Leave it on. It's sexier.' Straightaway he was feeling her high and low and then fingering her. When he put his finger in his mouth it tasted of cold-pressed extra virgin and her own natural free-flowing juice. She watched and waited like an attentive pupil while he cleared a space on the table, then sat her on it. With her feet anchored on the edge she lay back and showed him the whole fun fair. He ripped off his shirt, pushed down his newly purchased Polo Ralph Lauren pants and shunted hard into her with such force it rattled the crockery and made her catch her breath. He curled his arms around her, inside the dressing gown, and with his green eyes alight went about it almost savagely, as if he were repeatedly driving a fist into her. A cup fell from the table and smashed on the floor.

'Steady on, wildman,' she whispered. 'No need to wreck the scenery to enjoy it.'

'Sorry, baby.' He slowed down after that, pleasuring her easily and often. That oil film was still working a treat. After a while she gave a sign that she'd had her fill, and he shot nicely into her.

It was all over way too fast.

As he was zippering up she said, propped on her elbows, 'Got some come on your pants.'

He wiped it off with a napkin.

Sitting her up straight he held her tight so her bare chest pressed against his, and he could feel her heartbeat.

'I really wanted to fuck you while he was here,' she said.

'I had that feeling. There was a certain . . . electricity in the air.'

'That would have given him a shock.'

'It'd take a lot to shock Wes,' he said.

After a while she said, 'Sure is some voice, isn't it? What's his story, anyway?'

'Wes? Used to be a champ. Now he's a flasher.'

'Truly? He doesn't look like a flasher.'

Shaun had to laugh. 'And what does a flasher look like?'

'Oh, dirty little guy in a cheap raincoat, loitering around shopping malls and lavatories.'

'Wes certainly doesn't fit that profile. But there are flashers and flashers.'

'I guess. But he sure has an impressive voice. He should be an actor or something.' It was true. Wes's voice was a deep-seated seismic rumble that made windows vibrate.

Shaun could hear her mind ticking before she said, 'Do you really trust him?'

It was a question Shaun had asked himself. 'I believe him.'

'He might be having you on. Simmonds might have told him to do this, to get under your guard. Might be part of the plan.'

'It's possible,' he said. He couldn't help but feel encouraged— and impressed—that she was capable of entertaining such devious thoughts, thereby, in a sense, confirming her allegiance. However, with all his experience as a cop and criminal and all those years in stir under his belt, no-one could teach him anything about reading into the depths of men's hearts and minds through their lying eyes. As far as he was concerned Wes had passed the test. If Simmonds had set this up Wes would hardly have parked outside the house, hoping Shaun would approach him. He would've made the first move. All the same . . .

'I have fallen into dubious company, haven't I?' she said. 'A flasher and a . . . whatever you are.'

'You know what I am,' he said, holding her.

'Do you still love me?'

'I haven't started loving you yet.'

'God, I hope so. It's a whole new life, isn't it? I can barely remember the old one now.'

Shaun said, 'I don't want to remember the old one.' *But I have to.*

In a while she said, 'What happens now?'

Once again she had tapped into his thoughts. 'Now? I have to go on a little trip up north.'

'How far north?'

'Don't know. Somewhere along the New South Wales coast, I believe.'

'When do you leave?'

'Early in the morning. Gonna be a long day.'

16

Unlike his good friend Raydon—and most other people—Oliver McEncroe was not overfond of Sydney. On the rare occasion when he was obliged to go there he made flying visits, attending to business quickly and returning to the comfy bosom of Melbourne on the same day if possible. The fast tempo did not suit his conservative, stodgy disposition for a start, and most of the Sydney business leaders and legal fraternity seemed to be forever tainted with underworld connections. It was hard to know where one *stood* in Sydney: it was chaotic, standards were slipshod; people were *different*, they came from another planet, and Oliver could never relate to their swashbuckling opinions and cowboy attitudes. There was an air of casual *laissez-faire*, of which he disapproved. Having been raised as High Church of England he craved black-and-white moral distinctions, but in Sydney everything seemed to blur and overlap. Scratch its attractive surface and one discovered a nasty can of worms: a never-ending investigation into systemic police corruption, drugs sold openly on the streets, child slavery and prostitution, racketeering at every level, politicians rubbing shoulders with gangsters . . . it was all too rich for Oliver's blood.

If he'd searched more deeply into his heart, however, he would have seen the real reason he resented Sydney: it always made him feel as if he were out of his depth. The fact was that he'd lived a soft, privileged life, and he lacked the steel, the spine or whatever it was to cut it with the big boys in this roughhouse town where rules were made up to suit the occasion. Sydney showed him up for what he always felt he was in the presence of his father: a lightweight—even, at times, a fraud.

As for the restaurant scene, Oliver did not want to think about that. It was simply impossible. In Sydney, even supposing you could find a proper restaurant, you could never count on a decent, satisfying meal. It was all experimental and constantly evolving—what they called 'cutting edge' dining, consisting of 'taste fusions'. The last time he tried one of these establishments he ordered a dish that allegedly contained eight or ten ingredients and promised to be delicious, but when it arrived there was a tiny knob of something that looked as if it had been extruded from a cat's arse sitting in the middle of a large white plate, with some kind of sauce zigzagged across it for artistic effect. It was so disheartening. You couldn't even count on the same restaurants surviving from visit to visit: there was always a new batch replacing the previous. Even now, as he flipped through the in-flight magazine on his way north, he saw references to the 'hot, new crop of restaurants that were wowing Sydneysiders'. They had names like TT, Red Shoe, Picoline, Zat and Shag—'each exhibiting, in a very different way, a daring, almost giddy creativity'. Many of the chefs seemed to be TV celebrities who were as well known for their sex lives as their culinary achievements.

Oliver did not want giddy creativity for dinner. His preference was for seasoned roast beef with gravy and potatoes and some greens on the side—the sort of fare one could rely on. Accordingly, when he visited Sydney he dined either at the Tattersall's Club, with which his own club had reciprocal rights, or at the Ritz-Carlton, where he always stayed. The Ritz-Carlton restaurant was not 'cutting edge'—or it wasn't last time Oliver was there.

His thoughts drifted back to Raydon, whose ridiculous appetites had once again landed him in deep shit. He was becoming increasingly dissolute and irresponsible, as if he couldn't bear to let go of the last shreds of his youth. He was such a chronic pants man, with a penchant for the 'hot and horny young sluts' one apparently found on the Internet, on porn sites and chat rooms—whatever they were. Oliver had no grasp of that. Raydon, however, was right into it. As for Jo getting mixed up with this McCreadie character, well, that was unfathomable. The poor woman must have cracked up. How could she expose herself and her *family* to such flagrant shame and disrepute? Her parents would be devastated beyond belief. They were such fine people, they had always doted on Jo, and now in response she had picked up a handful of crap and thrown it in their faces. Altogether an appalling situation.

Oliver had been unable to withhold the juicy information from his wife, Eugenie, who positively *reeled* upon hearing it. She even clutched her throat. Immediately Oliver's feeling was that he had committed a grave indiscretion—Raydon was, after all, his client, and therefore entitled to the strictest professional confidence. Not any more. Eugenie played bridge twice a week, Fridays and Tuesdays, with a tight circle of girlfriends who would swallow such gossip like a school of starved piranhas. These idle, cocktail sipping women all had husbands in the professions and high places, including one who was a magistrate. *Christ*. The news of Jo's wild affair with a recently released felon—clearly a *killer*, despite the judgement of the Court of Appeals—would rage through their extended social network like a fire storm, and there was no telling where it would end. The more he thought about it, the more Oliver wished he'd shut up.

Too late. There was no way Eugenie would be able to wait for bridge tomorrow night. The phone lines would be burning up nonstop. And just to fuel the issue even further there was that piece on the back page of the paper yesterday.

As the plane touched down he turned his thoughts to more immediate matters. His Sydney contact had managed to provide him with the name of a police officer involved in the Tamsin Mascall case, and Oliver's first job was to talk to this person. He was a detective sergeant named Patchouli, Garry Patchouli. Oliver's contact described him as 'quite a reasonable man', which no doubt meant a sizeable sum of money had to change hands before he would provide Oliver with the help he needed to fix Raydon's problem.

Oliver had come armed with bundles of cash: used, non-consecutive bills. He had a good idea how such transactions were carried out in Sydney.

The taxi dropped him at the hotel at noon. Oliver checked in (the concierge pretended to remember him from a visit eight months earlier: another Sydney affectation), freshened up, changed into a more casual outfit (blue jeans, Italian loafers, white polo shirt, navy reefer), made several calls (including one to Eugenie, who was engaged), then strolled out into the rarefied air of Double Bay. Eugenie loved it here—loved *shopping* here—and every so often would come up with her best friend to wear out Oliver's Visa card. Oliver didn't mind. It took so little to make a woman happy. Over the years as his career advanced, Oliver had been unable to spend much quality time with his family, so a trade-off became necessary. Fortunately Eugenie saw that the good life to which she had become accustomed came at a price, and accordingly he always made sure that if he couldn't shower her with attention he did it with money: a skiing holiday in Europe with the children (while Oliver slaved over hot briefs), fancy clothes, dozens of red roses delivered on a whim. All *that* took was a phone call from his secretary. A new Chanel or Versace outfit was enough to transform his wife into a purring kitten for days. These were all basic management techniques that Raydon should have learned.

He hoped the same principle applied to Tamsin Mascall.

In a few minutes he was in the main bar of the Golden Sheaf Hotel. Not so long ago it had served as an office for criminals and bent cops in which to 'do business', as the parlance went in Sydney. It looked a lot tamer now: just a normal lunchtime crowd, and no sinister-looking suits with suspicious bulges under their jackets. Oliver checked the time: 12.45. Patchouli had arranged to meet at one, but it didn't hurt to arrive a little early. He went to the bar and ordered a Chivas Regal over ice. It was a warm day; the doors were open and a soft, pleasant breeze floated through the pub. Patchouli had said he was a tall man with brown hair who would be wearing a tan sportscoat with a stickpin bearing the Stars and Stripes, so Oliver would have no problem spotting him. He sipped the Chivas, not really wanting it but needing a prop. For some reason he felt nervous, even though he dealt with cops—and worse—nearly every day in court. In his mind he'd rehearsed some lines, but now he'd forgotten most of them. No doubt Patchouli would make the play anyway.

He came in right on one, scanned the room quickly and made Oliver straightaway.

'Garry Patchouli,' he said, extending his hand.

Half rising, Oliver accepted it with his customary Masonic grip. 'Oliver McEncroe.'

Patchouli sat down, perfectly at his ease it seemed to Oliver.

'What'll you have?' Oliver said. From habit he was about to signal for a waiter before realising it was bar service only.

Patchouli glanced at Oliver's glass. 'Hahn Ice. Have to be on the ball this afternoon.'

Oliver fetched the bottle. He never drank beer—it was all proletarian slops to him.

'So you have a slight problem,' Patchouli said with cool understatement. 'I'm sure we can find a way around it.'

'Well,' Oliver said, swirling the Chivas, 'that's why I'm here. My client is prepared to settle on fair and reasonable terms.'

Patchouli smiled. 'Bet he is.'

Oliver felt himself redden. 'Mr Patchouli, let's be honest, if I can use a dirty word. We all know this is a fucking rort, pure and simple.'

Patchouli shrugged one shoulder. 'What can you do when you're caught in a bear trap but saw your leg off?'

'That about sums it up,' Oliver said. 'So let's do what has to be done. What is the procedure for this . . . surgery?'

Patchouli produced a card from thin air and handed it to Oliver. *Smooth operator.* On it was printed 'Henry T. Agar— Private Investigator'. 'Call this man,' he said. 'Tell him I referred you.'

'Thanks,' Oliver said. 'I appreciate it.'

'You can express your appreciation in the form of a broker's fee,' Patchouli said.

'Of course. And how much is this broker's fee?'

Patchouli showed him three fingers. 'Non-refundable, full and final payment. Cash.'

'Naturally.'

On the scale of things it was not a large sum, but it grated all the same to pay off this corrupt bloody copper. He was so fucking *brazen*, so sure of himself. Oliver produced three bundles of a grand each, wrapped in rubber bands, and gave them to Patchouli. He had another two in reserve. The cop didn't bat an eye as he pocketed the cash—a typical day of law enforcement in Sin City.

'You understand there can be no receipt.'

'I understand perfectly,' Oliver said.

'We never met. You've never heard of me.'

'That too.'

Patchouli finished off his Hahn Ice and stood. 'I'd better move. I'm due in court.'

'What's the case?' Oliver said out of professional interest.

'Fraud,' Patchouli said, with no irony at all. 'Solicitor siphoned his clients' funds. Unscrupulous bastard.'

'Reprehensible,' Oliver said to himself as Patchouli walked out the door. He looked down at the card: Henry T. Agar—Private Investigator. It was a name Oliver knew. He wished he didn't.

Back in the Ritz-Carlton lounge, Oliver considered his position. Henry Agar was a notorious individual whose name had long been associated with the worst criminals and cops in the history of Sydney. A famously flamboyant figure, he drove a gold-plated Rolls-Royce and had sired children to dozens of women over the years. In the late eighties a Cambodian princess committed suicide after Agar refused to marry her. Apparently she was carrying his child at the time. There were numerous, in-depth news items, many of which accused him of breach of promise and pretty much blamed him for the young woman's death. In the fallout there was a slew of lawsuits from an aggrieved Agar, who subsequently demanded a six-figure amount from a top-selling national magazine for his side of the story. Upon receiving the advance, however, Agar reneged on the deal—no story was ever delivered. The magazine's publishers found themselves in a bind: if they took legal action to recover the fee they would expose themselves to accusations of chequebook journalism—and poor taste. In the end they kissed goodbye to their money, which Agar claimed to have donated to an unnamed charity.

Henry Agar. One of his closest friends was a contract killer named Barry Edwards, who was tight with a bad bunch of NSW detectives until one day in 1986 or thereabouts, when business tycoon Adrian White's wife was abducted, raped, tortured, strangled and dumped in the bush. Edwards' semen was found in the victim and he went down for life, no parole.

The police's theory was that he had conspired with Agar to kidnap the woman for ransom, but it was a botched job from start to finish because of Edwards' inability to control his violent impulses. Everything spun out of control and in the end they had to cut their losses and kill her. The husband was ready and willing to pay a large amount, but it never changed hands.

In a sensational separate court case police tried to nail Agar for complicity, but there was no forensic evidence and only one witness, whose testimony was deemed unreliable by the jury because he was a drug addict and a compulsive liar who had cut a side deal with police. Edwards had testified against him, but the defence was able to establish that he was merely trying to save his own hide by deflecting culpability, and was motivated by an intense and venal hatred of Agar stemming from other, unrelated, issues. For the prosecution it was a shambles: the case against Agar fell apart and he walked triumphantly from the courthouse chomping on a big cigar. His licence to practise remained intact. And, as far as Oliver was aware, he had never done time, even though his name had been dragged through the mud at regular intervals. In fact he seemed to revel in the heavy going career-wise, and was something of a star on the Sydney chat show and late-night raunchy club circuit. Oliver knew all this because he had read Agar's autobiography (ghost-written by a hack crime reporter from a Sydney tabloid), pretentiously called *Private Eye, Public Life: The Henry Agar Story*.

This was the man Oliver now had to deal with. To do so, he decided, he would need several stiff drinks under his belt, not to mention a high-powered handgun. Any whiff of fear and Agar would slice him into sushi. Oliver would have to stick to his guns and not accept any shit from this person. In the eyes of a man like Agar, indecision or nervousness would identify him as a soft-cock pen-pusher to be taken apart and ridiculed. Agar would spit him out with contempt. Quite apart from Raydon's problem, there was also Oliver's pride and self-respect at stake.

Oliver called Agar's office number first, but the call was

diverted to his mobile phone, at which point he was invited
to leave a message on the voice mail. It was typical of lowlife
bastards like Agar to put himself out of reach, so he could always
reply on his own terms and gain some leverage. A man like
him would never answer a cold call unless he knew who it
was. No doubt he was enjoying a sumptuous lunch in a flashy
restaurant to go with his flashy personality. Oliver obliged by
leaving a short, succinct message stating his name, Patchouli's
and finally Raydon's—just enough information to capture his
interest. He then checked the time: 2.30. He ordered a Chivas
Regal and moved to an armchair near a window, with a sofa
on his left and another chair opposite. He placed his phone on
the table in front of him. It didn't ring.

While he gazed out into the street Oliver wondered what
it would be like living in Henry Agar's shoes. It was said he was
so tough he flossed with tungsten. He was a large, intimidating
figure, a true heavy in the Hollywood B-movie tradition with
a fearsome reputation as a street fighter in the old days, although
these stories had become much exaggerated over the years.
Once—Oliver knew this to be true—he pulled a gun on a
racetrack official who told him to behave himself in the
members' bar, but no charges were laid after the official received
a sum of money and a live bullet in the mail. Everything he did
was like that, as if his life was a succession of crazy stunts from
which he emerged unscathed through sheer charisma. He gave
every impression of being his own Number One fan—a tough
gig to maintain in a town like Sydney where there was always
someone trying to drag him down. On TV Oliver had seen
part of an interview with him in which he came across as a
supreme egotist. He actually enjoyed *portraying* himself, as if he
were a dramatic character in fiction.

Oliver was tempted to ring Raydon, but he had been
instructed not to provide progress reports. Raydon only wanted
to know when it was over. Fair enough, and the news would
only depress him further, but how would one ever *know* it was

over? There were no contracts to be signed, witnessed and exchanged in this shifty enterprise. The old problem with blackmailers: what was to stop them from going back to the well once you'd paid up? Once they knew you were good for it? *Nothing*, was the answer.

After three Scotches Oliver felt more confident, but after four he wasn't so sure. He knew he was getting pissed, but as long as he didn't go overboard that would serve him well, giving him the courage and even a measure of recklessness to impress his adversary.

He switched to Club soda for his next drink. Still the phone did not ring. Time: 4.15. He rang Eugenie just for something to do, then fiddled with the phone before realising he was as nervous as a cat.

The phone rang. Oliver jumped.

'McEncroe.'

'Oliver McEncroe?'

'Yes.'

'Henry Agar. How can I help you?'

Charming man. 'I represent Raydon Steer. There are issues to be resolved concerning one Tamsin Mascall. Garry Patchouli gave me your name.'

'I see. Where are you?'

'At the Ritz-Carlton, Double Bay.'

'Fine. Give me an hour. Be in the cocktail bar.'

The phone was abruptly disconnected.

Damn. Shit!

Oliver had not planned to meet him here. He was going to suggest the Golden Sheaf or somewhere neutral. This was too much like having him in your own home—too close to the bone. But Agar had been too quick for him. Oliver clasped his hands: they were clammy. He ordered another Scotch.

When Agar arrived—fifteen minutes early—Oliver was dismayed to see he had not come alone. That was something

else he hadn't counted on. Agar he recognised immediately
from the photos in his book, but who was the offsider, his
second banana? He was a rangy-looking customer with pale
eyes and blond hair, somewhere in his mid-forties. Like Agar
he conveyed an air of tangible menace without having to do
anything at all.

Shit. They were going to get him in a pincer movement . . .

As they approached in response to his discreet signal, Oliver
was suddenly a touch fearful for his safety. He heard himself
giggle inanely: was that the Scotch? Christ, man, get a grip—
they don't shoot people in the cocktail lounge of a five-star
hotel, not even in Sydney.

'Mr McEnroe?' Agar said. 'Henry Agar.' Intoning his own
name as if he were introducing a distinguished personage to
the royal court, he crushed Oliver's hand for a second or two
and then sat down heavily on the sofa, on Oliver's left. The
second banana sat on the other armchair, facing Oliver.

Agar's attire was pure Sydney: black summerweight suit
over a blue-and-black tropical shirt hanging outside his pants,
which were voluminous to accommodate his muscular
thighs. Black, square-toed shoes with outsized buckles.
Around his neck was a gold choker with three gold crosses
on it. Oliver remembered: Agar was a devout Catholic.
According to his memoirs he accompanied his mother to
Mass and confession every Sunday, apparently reserving
mayhem for the other six days. The three crosses no doubt
represented the Holy Trinity. He also wore solid gold rings
on all his fingers, and a gold watch with a loose bracelet that
slid up and down his wrist. Sleek and fit as a dolphin, he
sported a shaved, spit-polished head and ultra-dark sunglasses.
In the shirt pocket were three Corona-sized cigars.

He lounged comfortably on the sofa with his legs apart,
arms draped over the backrest as he appraised Oliver. The
second banana—Mr No-name—sat quietly. He too wore a
tropical sort of outfit, with a matching suit and open-necked

shirt in midnight blue. His eyes were bright and wide but still, as if they were as unseeing as a blind man's.

The waiter appeared. 'Gentlemen?'

'Same again for me,' Oliver said.

'One Chivas Regal.' He turned to Mr No-name.

'Do you have Chemay?' No-name said. Apparently protocol in these circles demanded his identity remain undisclosed.

'Yes, sir.'

'I'll have that. Served in a large goblet.'

'Yes, sir.'

Agar's turn. 'Still on that stuff?' he said to Mr No-name, who shrugged. 'Okay. Sambuca for me—Romana if you have it. Throw in a few coffee beans, please.'

'Certainly, sir.'

When the waiter had gone, Agar leaned forward, removed his sunglasses and hooked them on his shirtfront. 'So, Mr McEnroe . . .'

'McEncroe,' Oliver said. 'As it happens I *do* play tennis, but I'm not in that class.'

Agar smiled, showing teeth that were far too good to be real. Mr No-name issued a short, explosive laugh: *'Ha!'* Then he blinked slowly, like a lizard. His lids seemed to operate independently from the rest of him, like a mechanical device. Oliver noticed that his upper lip protruded, from a conspicuous overbite.

'Sorry,' Agar said. 'You must get that a lot.'

'I ignore it most of the time.'

'I can understand. Excuse me, but you're not wired, are you?'

Oliver was taken aback. For a moment he thought Agar was inquiring if he was spaced out on drugs, then he remembered from the book: Agar was paranoid about being secretly taped.

He laughed and said, 'Wired? Of course not. Why, do you want to search me?'

'Would you mind?'

Oliver couldn't believe it. Here he was, standing in the Ritz-Carlton lounge being patted down by this ... *person*. He knew what he was doing too. 'Arms out, please,' Agar said, searching all the possible places a man might wear a microphone or mini-cassette: under his armpits, in the small of his back, jacket pockets and lining, including the sleeves, behind his belt buckle, the insides of his legs right down to the shoes. Some customers took an amused interest, further embarrassing Oliver, but Agar didn't seem to care.

Up close, Oliver was overpowered by Agar's smells: a strong, nutty aftershave mixed with alcohol and premium cigar leaf. It was the rich, intoxicating stink of excess and corruption—and of a serial seducer. His face glowed as if it had been massaged with expensive lotion.

Finally they sat down, just as the waiter arrived. Silence reigned while he set down the glasses, together with a bowl of cashew nuts, and poured the Chemay.

'Please forgive me,' Agar said when he was gone, 'but I've been the victim of dirty tricks in the past.'

Victim? Oliver thought. *Try perpetrator.*

'Just before we proceed, might I see some credentials?' Agar said. He drew a cigar from his shirt pocket, unwrapped it and clipped the end with a natty little cutter—gold, naturally.

'Credentials,' Oliver said, getting out his wallet. 'Well, I have a business card, membership of the Law Institute, driver's licence. Will that do?' He gave the question a slightly sarcastic edge, although Agar took no notice: with the unlit cigar in his mouth he moved the three items around on the table, examining them closely as if searching for the fatal flaw that would reveal Oliver's treachery.

'Seems to be in order,' he said, handing them back with a warm and completely false smile. 'You must think I'm a highly suspicious man, Mr McEncroe.'

Oliver merely shrugged, bringing the Scotch to his lips.

'I have to be careful, you see. Plenty of people want a piece of Henry Agar. You could be anyone, after all—a journalist, or an undercover cop.'

Oliver was aghast. 'Do I look like a *journalist*, or an undercover *cop*?'

'You'd be surprised. They come in all disguises.' He fired up the cigar, a process that occupied his full attention for some time. When he was eventually engulfed in dense swirls of smoke he said, 'And now, Mr McEncroe, perhaps you would care to spell out the nature of your proposal.'

Oliver drew breath to answer just as Agar's phone chirped from somewhere in his clothes. Putting up his hand to Oliver he produced a minuscule flip-phone, noted the caller's number and barked into it: 'Yeah.'

Listening, he stood up. His face darkened alarmingly. 'Is that so,' he said, and began moving away. 'Mate, tell that *cunt* if he wants to be a hero, I'll break his fuckin' *legs*. See how that goes down.' He moved right away, to the other side of the room, but Oliver could still hear the expletives. He glanced at Mr No-name, who evinced no interest, except in the Belgian beer.

Oliver's own phone burred.

'Hello, Sharon.' It was his secretary, who had called to give him a rundown of the day's proceedings in an increasingly difficult sexual harassment case they were defending. It had been given to a junior partner as a baptism, but he didn't seem to be handling it well—in fact he was all at sea. Oliver had to concentrate on questions of law and make some important decisions, which was a challenge under the circumstances. When he looked up at Mr No-name *he* was on the phone too, standing at the window punching an endless sequence of numbers as if he were trying to crack the Enigma code. Over the way Agar was drawing attention to himself by gesticulating angrily with his free hand and occasionally firing off profanities into the piece. Watching him Oliver thought: he's doing it deliberately. It's all about ego.

Ten minutes later the meeting had reassembled.

'Pardon the interruption,' Agar said. 'Can't seem to round up the usual suspects today.' Glasses were emptied; the waiter was summoned for a fresh round.

'Can I suggest,' Oliver said, 'that, without prejudice, we are prepared to do business in a fair and reasonable way, provided certain conditions are met.'

'Go on,' Agar said, crunching coffee beans.

'We'll offer a one-off lump sum payment. In return, you will guarantee an end to this campaign of character assassination directed against my client by making all appropriate representations to Tamsin Mascall and to the relevant police; in addition you will hand over any evidence you may have in relation to this matter—in which my client maintains his complete innocence.'

'But he's prepared to cough up anyway,' Agar said. 'Despite his innocence.'

'So that the matter can be brought to a swift conclusion.'

'Understandably. I would too, in his position. Teenage sex rap like this goes to court, and he's shot to high heaven, isn't he? But that was an impressive list of conditions, Mr McEncroe.' He turned to Mr No-name. 'Did you get all that? Oh, excuse me, did I introduce . . . ?'

'Don't believe so,' Oliver said.

'Christ, I don't know—sometimes my manners . . . Terry, Terry Pritchett.'

It was late in the piece for formalities, so a nod on either side sufficed. The name meant nothing to Oliver, and the man himself wasn't very impressive.

'Sorry,' Agar said. For a prize bastard he sure apologised a lot. 'Terry has a lot more to do with . . . what's her name? Tamsin Mascall. In fact I don't even know the lass. I'm more or less the facilitator here.'

'I see,' Oliver said. That made Pritchett the pimp.

'Mr McEncroe,' Agar said, a slightly puzzled expression furrowing his brow. 'Let's get this straight. You hold no whip hand here. Your client, Mr Raydon Steer, *QC*, was caught with his pants down, having sex with a little girl and feeding her an illicit substance, namely cocaine. The victim in this case is Tamsin Mascall, not Raydon fucking *Steer*. The child is fourteen, man. *Fourteen*. That almost makes your client a fucking *paedophile* in my book, old chap. I don't have much time for paedophiles. Take that bastard—' and he named a lifelong child abuser who had recently been put away for many years. 'If I got my hands on *that* dirtbag, he wouldn't live to see another sunrise. So don't come to me with all your goddamn *conditions*, Mr McEncroe. Pay up and shut up—or cop whatever comes next. I personally want to see your boy swing. But—business is business.'

He finished off his Sambuca and puffed on his cigar before continuing. Agar obviously had strong feelings on the subject: Oliver had already seen that he was a man who could become hot under the collar almost to the point of spontaneous combustion in a second. And yet, strangely, he cooled and became civil again just as fast. 'Mr McEncroe, I've had more than my share of trouble and injustice, but I don't complain. I'm an adult and I can fend for myself. But when I see the callous exploitation of helpless children by adults I become extremely angry. Sadly, there are many unfortunates like Tamsin Mascall in this city—and in yours. Usually they have run away from an intolerable domestic situation. I know what it's like—I've been there. Most of them become hustlers, prostitutes and drug addicts; many live on the street or in halfway houses. They die from disease, malnutrition or heroin overdoses in alarming numbers. Child abuse doesn't just happen in the Philippines or the wilds of South America—it's widespread right here under our noses. It's a spiralling problem and a national *disgrace*. Politicians don't give a shit, because these poor wretches don't even *vote*. But when *I* see an opportunity to make a difference, Mr McEncroe, I seize that opportunity. Someone has to.'

Listening to this passionate diatribe, Oliver was casting his thoughts back to Agar's book: in it he boasted of personally sponsoring *hundreds* of disadvantaged children in various countries. There was also some grand plan about setting up a place, a *ranch*, for homeless or displaced children in rural New South Wales, for which he had unsuccessfully sought government funding. He was a crusader—or at least presented himself as one. But Oliver's gut feeling told him Agar was a pathological liar and a criminal; that all his posturing and sounding off about the tragic children of the world was a sort of cover-up for his own villainous proclivities. He *needed* to occupy the high moral ground to feed his fantasies about himself while he carried on a life of violence and extortion. This was a delusional, dangerous man. But he was right: business was business.

'Point taken, Mr Agar,' he said. 'No reasonable person could dispute one word of that. Nonetheless I have to represent my client to the very best of my ability. And whether you accept it or not there *are* two sides to every story.'

'All right, all right,' Agar said. 'I've got that off my chest. So, where does all this leave us, Mr McEncroe? You said something earlier about a sum of money, all parcelled up in legal mumbo-jumbo as I recall it.'

It was the moment Oliver had actually been looking forward to, in a perverse sort of way. He withdrew a thick buff envelope from inside his jacket and tossed it casually on the table, like a trump card in a game of five-card stud. Agar and Pritchett looked at it but didn't seem all that impressed.

'What's that?' Agar said.

'That's fifty thousand. Full and final payment.'

No-one said anything. The envelope sat on the table like a great, unspoken question, almost quivering in its importance.

The waiter arrived; a fresh round was ordered. Agar and Pritchett exchanged glances as the waiter retreated.

'It won't do,' Agar said at last. He rested the cigar in an ashtray.

Oliver's mouth dropped open. 'What?'

Agar shifted slightly, and clasped his hands. 'Let me explain, Mr McEncroe. I am a private investigator. I investigate all the time. Can't help myself. Accordingly, when your client came to my notice, I ran a little search and guess what? I discovered he is a *seriously* rich man. He can afford to shell out till his nose bleeds. So, operating on the user-pays principle, I figure he's good for a lot more than a lousy fifty. He'd put that much up his nose without touching the sides. It's loose change.'

'You can't do this,' Oliver said lamely.

'Oh, I can. I *am*.'

'No, no.'

'Yes.'

'Mr Agar, I came here in good faith, on the clear understanding—'

'You're not in any courtroom now, my learned friend. No statutes or *precedents* prevail here. *Understandings* can change without notice.'

Oliver swallowed some Scotch. Pritchett's gaze occasionally wandered over the other patrons in the room. He showed so little interest in the matter at hand that Oliver felt scared, as if everything had been decided beforehand and he had no say in the final outcome.

'How much more? Out of curiosity.'

'The figure is now two hundred and fifty. Non-negotiable.'

'You're crazy,' Oliver said straightaway. He suddenly felt dizzy: was there something wrong with his hearing? Did Agar say *$250,000*?

Agar gave him an amused little smile, as if surprised, maybe even impressed, that Oliver would dare to say such a thing. 'Crazy? Perhaps. We're all crazy in our own way, Mr McEncroe.

I've been called many things in my time, but no-one ever accused me of being mentally challenged.'

'It's bullshit. We're not paying, and that's that. We'll go to court.'

'I don't believe so. Not after you've seen this.'

Agar produced a package the size of a videocassette and placed it in front of Oliver. 'Personally, I will never understand why people allow themselves to be filmed doing these things. But they do. I guess it's part of the excitement.'

Oliver's stomach turned to water. He'd had the same sensation in court, when an unexpected twist changed the whole complexion of a case. This unpleasant surprise was invariably caused by the client failing to disclose vital information that falls into the hands of the opposition. It was a feeling of betrayal, and helplessness.

Raydon had not said anything about a fucking *tape. Shit*.

'Take it. View it at your leisure. We have plenty of copies. One for each TV station.'

Pritchett gave his short little laugh again. That seemed to be his only contribution.

'We're not paying a quarter of a million,' Oliver said in a dead voice, eyes fixed on the cassette. He'd hit the wall. Where to next? In a situation like this, in which he was outnumbered and outgunned, it was necessary to box clever. He had to produce something special and totally unexpected from his back pocket. It was crucial not to show signs of distress. Nearly every legal wrangle came down, in the end, to a test of will. His mind was spinning into overdrive: searching, searching, *searching* for some way through, or around . . .

'What you mean is,' Agar said, puffing happily, 'that you'll watch the tape, you'll weigh up your chances, and *then* you'll pay.'

Flash. Oliver straightened. Jesus . . . What if . . .?

'Wait on—I have an idea.'

Agar's eyes lit up. The effect was to trigger a wholesale—

and unflattering—change in his appearance: for all his 'suffer the little children' ravings, this creature was every inch the sadistic torturer, *thrilled* to witness his victims' last, desperate writhings. In that instant Oliver thought: *headcase*.

'This is not some *brains trust*, Mr McEncroe. We're not interested in your *ideas*.'

'Why settle for a quarter of a million?' Oliver said with all the sangfroid he could muster at short notice. 'Why not go for the whole nut?'

Agar inspected Oliver's face, trying to decipher his meaning—and the direction in which his mind was travelling.

'And what *nut* are we referring to?'

Oliver was a chess player, not great, but better than most. With the strategy he'd decided on it was necessary to tempt Agar with an offer he couldn't refuse, at the same time staying two or three moves ahead of him and trying to visualise how it would all turn out. Of course it could all explode in his face, but . . .

Fuck it. Too much Chivas Regal had made him too brave. Aware of this, he nonetheless jutted his jaw and delivered his reply with a level of gravitas normally reserved for those rare courtroom moments, defining moments when fortunes can turn around on a single shiny coin.

'We are referring to the missing Petrakos millions,' he said.

He locked onto Agar's intense gaze, waiting for the information to kick in, determined not to be intimidated by his powerful physical presence and unpredictability. Agar draped his arms over the sofa backrest with the cigar burning idly between his lips. A shade of uncertainty crossed his eyes. Oliver watched and waited, but the next surprise was on him: it was Pritchett who responded.

'I know all about that,' he said. 'But I'd sure be surprised if you did.'

A couple of hours later, dining alone on *filet mignon* (there was no roast beef on the Ritz-Carlton menu) and an excellent bottle of Margaret River cabernet sauvignon, Oliver wondered if he had done the right thing. No good lawyer gave in to reckless impulses: victory in law was all about playing the percentages, chipping away at the enemy until the edifice collapsed. Blinding, inspirational flashes were not supposed to come into it except on TV. But Oliver was not in court and nor was he dealing with normal people who played according to a civilised code.

They were dogs. They would tear each *other* apart if someone were to throw a juicy enough bone between them. And *maybe* Oliver had done just that.

Oliver was a believer in serendipity. Shaun McCreadie had entered this tight, select circle at his own peril: now let him deal with the fallout. His unwelcome arrival on the scene had to have a positive angle, which remained hidden until the time came for it to show itself—now. Oliver was surprised at how much Pritchett *did* know: it seemed he'd made a point of following developments in this out-of-state matter. He even knew the names of all the players, and *claimed* to know who topped them all. Of course he was a bullshit artist. They were all bullshit artists in Sydney.

The more Pritchett talked about it the more animated he became. Agar was vague on the subject, but allowed himself to be carried along on Pritchett's enthusiasm and his obvious grasp of detail—no doubt gleaned from newspaper reports. Then again, given he was a professional sleazebag, perhaps he had connections with the Victorian crime scene. In a while Oliver thought: *this* is the real player, not Agar. Agar was a mad and very bad clown. And so he concentrated on Pritchett, priming him with tidbits of information but withholding the most important part: McCreadie's current whereabouts. That was the clincher, his prime currency. They could have it—provided they got off Raydon's case. That was the deal Oliver laid out. Shit—everyone knew the amount stolen from Petrakos was large, and McCreadie was the only person alive who knew where it was. Possibly he had recovered it already. If Agar and Pritchett wanted a piece, they couldn't afford to waste time.

In the end they said they'd consider the proposal and call back. Agar had wanted to keep the fifty grand 'on account', but Oliver had snaffled it—along with the videotape. He was *not* looking forward to viewing it.

Swallowing some of the nice wine, he allowed himself to bathe in self-congratulation. Was that a smart bit of footwork or not? Could he mix it in the same sandpit as the heavy-hitters? No doubt, your worship. Down went some more red wine.

The videotape was every bit as awful as he'd expected.

When it was all over, Oliver felt decidedly queasy—either from the tape, or too much booze, or both.

In the morning, more hungover than he'd been in a while, he wasn't so convinced of his cleverness. In the cold light of sobriety it felt as if he'd made a serious error of judgement. He was playing with fire and could well finish up on the rotisserie. Worse, he had exposed Jo to possible danger if these animals did come after McCreadie. She could be caught in the crossfire.

He was worrying seriously about all this, wondering if and how he could change everything back, when his phone went.

'Mr McEncroe?' It was Pritchett.

'Yes.'

'Give us what we need and your mate's off the hook,' he said, not bothering with social niceties. 'One condition: if we come up empty, you're back on again. Same deal.'

17

It had been a long time between flights for Shaun. He'd never particularly relished the experience, which in the past had unfailingly put him in a cold, clammy sweat from take-off to touchdown. Crashing to a fiery death in a plane was the one thing he truly feared. Now, as the pilot gave it full throttle, he found his hands involuntarily clenching on his thighs and his eyes closing. The 767 Airbus reached optimum runway speed and lifted smoothly, and shortly afterwards came the double bump of the undercarriage retracting. Immediately a high-pitched whistling noise coming from the wing jolted his eyes open and made his heart thump. He'd always believed that if a plane were going to crash it would occur shortly after take-off. That was when things went wrong. Whenever he had read about such disasters that phrase was generally used: *shortly after take-off.* There were many reasons an accident might happen— jetliners were complex machines with miles of electrical wiring, thousands of moving parts and a large surface area that only needed a single hairline crack somewhere for the whole shebang to break up midair. And that wasn't even taking into account the possibility of some wild-eyed band of fanatics suddenly announcing they had a change of plans for you.

Shaun didn't think there was much chance of terrorists targeting a Melbourne–Sydney flight. All the same, you could never completely discount the lone madman. *Why, just a few months ago on a flight out of Melbourne . . .*

The flight was incident-free, however, and since he had only carry-on luggage Shaun bypassed the carousel and made directly for the Hertz counter. Five minutes of form filling, followed by cash payment (he'd applied for, but not yet received, a MasterCard and Visa) and he had in his possession the keys to a spanking new Ford Falcon Forte with all the trimmings, together with an NRMA roadmap of New South Wales. It felt—and smelt—good sliding in behind the wheel. After familiarising himself with the instrumentation and setting the electric mirrors he switched on the ignition. The car was so silent he thought it hadn't started, so he tried again and triggered an awful screech from under the hood. It was a warm, sunny Sydney day, so he turned on the air conditioning. Then he put the T-bar in drive and left the airport, following the maze of exit signs. By the time he was on the open road, pointed north, it was after eight o'clock. Even though he had avoided the city, the sprawling suburbs of the greater Sydney area took some getting through, and the freeway system was largely new to him. Eventually he found himself on his way to Newcastle, so he was at least headed in the right direction. All he had to do was stay on Highway 1 until the turn-off to Nambucca Heads.

Earlier he had telephoned Dave Wrigley. During their meeting in the pub Dave had said Leon Turner had retired somewhere on the New South Wales coast. Shaun had inquired if he could be more exact than that. Dave had said, 'Why, what are you going to do?' and Shaun had told him, 'Nothing. Just chat to him, that's all.' Dave had replied, 'Hold on.' While Shaun waited he turned towards Jo, who was sitting in a lounge chair sipping a cup of coffee and giving him the once-over with her evil green eyes. She had on that same satin dressing gown, loosely held together in a carelessly provocative manner. Since he was only wearing briefs she could see over her steaming cup that he was becoming aroused. Dave had come back on and said, 'Nambucca Heads.'

Words froze in Shaun's throat for a second, and then he'd said, more in hope than expectation, 'Got an address?'

No address. Still, Nambucca Heads wasn't that big a town. It hadn't been, anyway.

He made love to her where she sat. She was an amazingly passionate woman. Even when sex wasn't in his immediate thoughts she only had to give a sign and he was out of his mind as soon as he touched her. When it was over and he was still kneeling in front of her with his face turned against her chest she said, 'How long will you be away?' and he answered, 'Two, three days. No more.' She said, 'Not sure if I can go without that long.' He said, 'I'll call. We can have phone sex.' She made him promise he would.

After five and a half hours on the road he took a right turn-off at a signpost, and in a few minutes dropped down into the attractive coastal village of Nambucca Heads. It gave him an exhilarating rush of pleasure to see the ocean suddenly materialise in front of him. It was a liberating sensation—not just like being released from prison, but something so far greater and more mysterious that he couldn't find a name for straightaway. Whatever it was, it made his heart fly up. And it took him back a ways.

Shaun had been here once before, a long time ago during the summer of '79. That made it nearly twenty-four years. It made him sad to realise that so much of his life had disappeared. For what? What did he have to show? A pile of money, which was stolen, and Joanna Steer, another man's wife. *Could be a lot worse.* He remembered Nambucca Heads as a bit of a pleasant backwater with a fine surf beach, a couple of pubs and a caravan park, where he and two good mates had spent a week at the end of their final school year. Life had been pretty straightforward then—not just his, but everyone's, it seemed. In his memory the days he'd passed here blurred together into a dreamy montage of surfing and sunbathing under a broiling sun during the day, eating greasy chicken, pizza or mixed grills at the pub for dinner and consuming copious amounts of beer through the night. They sat up till late in that caravan, playing music and cards—penny poker and blackjack—laughing a lot and generally having a top end-of-school time. Some nights they'd light a fire on the beach and have a midnight swim.

No sex. Not then.

The town had come on a little bit since those days. It had never been in the same league as the more prosperous resort destinations of Coffs Harbour, Byron Bay or Tweed Heads further north, but as he drove though the main street and unsuccessfully tried to find the old caravan park his impression was that, far from being a forgotten backwater, Nambucca Heads was now a going concern: the pubs were still there, basically as he remembered them, but as well there were various motels, new-looking apartment buildings, B&Bs, an RSL club, some luxury beachfront housing and plenty of expensive boats sitting out on a blinding sea. It wasn't the holiday season, or even a weekend, but there were groups of young surfer types doing the shopping mall shuffle. That mall hadn't existed in 1979.

He checked in at the Blue Dolphin, an attractive double-storeyed motel perched on a hillside amid palm trees, with a commanding view of the mouth of the Nambucca River and the Pacific Ocean. Again he paid cash in advance, which created a minor problem for the manager, who wanted a credit card imprint to cover extras such as phone calls or the bar fridge. This was standard practice, he explained, but when Shaun made it clear he didn't own a credit card but would happily put down some additional cash, the manager waived the requirement. After depositing his overnight bag and freshening up he cruised around for a while until he found an angle park in the main

street, outside a newsagent's. That might be a useful place to
begin. Maybe Turner had the paper home delivered, or bought
his lottery tickets here. It was worth a try.

No joy. The newsagent was distinctly unfriendly, in fact.
Shaun seemed to recall that they mostly were, for some reason.
What was it about running a paper shop that made the
proprietor a pain in the butt? Maybe it was the other way
around—paper shops probably attracted that type of guy
anyway. After that he visited the post office and checked the
phone book to see if there were any Turners. Sometimes doing
the obvious could save a lot of unnecessary detective work.

Not on this occasion, however. No Turners were listed.
Shaun was not surprised: many cops, both active and retired,
preferred a silent phone number. A long-serving senior officer
like Leon Turner would have accumulated many enemies
during his career, and even years after the event it was still on
the cards that some ugly head from the past might surface to
satisfy a long-held grudge.

Leon 'Brick' Turner: so nicknamed, according to police
legend, because he once chased down a burglar and half-killed
him with a house brick when the guy 'resisted arrest'. That
was in the days when you could get away with anything.

Next on the list were the golf club and the RSL. He hadn't
noticed a sign indicating one, but these holiday/retirement
towns *always* had a golf course—often proclaimed to be 'the
best course in the country'. It seemed to be a law that even
people who had never played the game became avid golfers
the day after their retirement, and there was no reason why
this law wouldn't apply to Leon Turner. Aside from the sport
itself, membership provided a social life. Same for the RSL,
and since that was close by he went in there first.

While he was signing in he noticed that the attendant was
one of those hearty, cheerful fellows who so often worked
front-of-house in community clubs such as this. He had
something witty to say to nearly everyone who passed by.

According to the plastic ID tag clipped to his shirt his name was Wally Jacobs, and he was the Assistant Manager. Shaun waited for him to finish exchanging pleasantries with an old guy on a walking frame and then casually said, 'Could you tell me if Leon Turner is a member here?'

'Leon Turner?' Wally said. 'He sure is. In fact he's on the committee.'

'Is that so. Well, I'm not surprised. Leon would always want to be running things.'

Wally said, 'Too true,' and laughed as he waved at someone else going in.

'I used to know him years ago,' Shaun said. 'We were in the same job. I'm passing through town, and I was hoping to catch up with him. Trouble is, I doubt if I'd recognise him after all this time. Do you know if he's here now?'

'No, it's a bit early,' Wally said, eager to please. 'But he won't be long.'

Shaun checked the time: two o'clock.

'Guess I can have something to eat while I wait,' he said, more or less to himself.

'You most certainly can,' Wally told him. 'Best meals anywhere in Nambucca Heads, bar none.'

He thanked Wally and went in amid the brightly lit rows of gaming machines, most of which were occupied. In the room next door there were people sitting at tables eating, so he went in and found a free table. There were no gaming machines in the dining room, just a Keno screen and Sky Channel showing horse racing with the volume on mute. He ordered a king-sized porterhouse, medium-rare, then went to the bar and got a schooner of Toohey's New. He hadn't realised how thirsty he was until he'd swallowed half of it in the first mouthful. Standing at the bar he surveyed the scene: everyone was old and some were ancient. There were a lot of shouted conversations, either because of the racket from the gaming machines next door and the frequent announcements on the PA system, or because they were all deaf.

Wally Jacobs was right about the food: Shaun's porterhouse was two inches thick, a perfect shade of pink in the middle and so full of delicious juice he began salivating after the first bite. It lasted a short time on the plate. A middle-aged waitress with a blonde beehive hairdo came to clean up and said, 'That wasn't too awful then.'

Shaun sat back, wiped his mouth with a paper napkin and smiled at her. 'Best steak I've had in years.' He meant it.

He sat there for a time, toying with a schooner and watching the races. He finished his beer and wandered out into the gaming area. On the far side, near the front entrance, was the TAB section. He positioned himself at a table there, close to the glass doors where he could see everyone coming through. Wally was still at the front counter serving up his bonhomie to all and sundry. Shaun wasn't sure if he would spot Turner or not: he had an image of him from years ago, but age could alter a man's appearance radically. He figured Turner would be around sixty-five by now. In his mind he had a picture of a rather tall man, rangy and straight-backed, with deep-set eyes, a heavily creased forehead and greying, wavy hair. He had the bearing of a strict headmaster from a bygone era, one who wasn't frightened to use the cane at the slightest opportunity.

Just after four a man came in. Shaun tried to overhear Wally's welcome, listening for a name, but the raised chatter and TV noise in the vicinity drowned it out. When the man stepped inside he glanced in Shaun's direction, and almost immediately the question was answered when an old coot called out: 'Hey, Leon!' He was sitting with a group of similar-aged punters a couple of tables from Shaun's. He'd noticed they were sharing bets on the races. Leon grinned and raised an arm before going over to the group and passing some time with them. There was laughter, backslapping and general conviviality all round, so much so that this Leon did not seem

at all like the bastard with a dirty past Shaun wanted to bust.
He felt a little shiver of anticipation.

There was no doubt in his mind that this was Leon Turner.
The ageing process had inevitably changed him, but the
features were essentially the same.

After chatting to the group at the table Leon went to the
bar, where he joined two other men. Shaun watched them
without appearing to. They were all on schooners and
shooting the breeze. Shaun stopped pretending to be
interested in the horses and got up, crossing a space in front
of the bar where the three men stood and heading to the
gaming machines. He selected one from which he could
observe Leon, and fed in a ten-dollar note. He didn't really
understand these machines, but it seemed to be simply a
matter of pressing buttons. He was playing one that featured
black panthers whose eyes lit up when you won something.
Shaun didn't care if he won or lost: he was merely using the
machine as a cover while he kept an eye out for Leon.
Obviously he couldn't approach him while he was with his
friends, but it seemed he was too popular or important a
person to ever be alone here—he was every inch the club
committeeman.

In any case this was not the right environment for a
confrontation. Turner had power here, it was his turf, and
accordingly he would have no problem in turning Shaun
away, even calling security if he had to. It was better to brace
him someplace where he wasn't surrounded by allies, where
Shaun could look him in the eye, watch his reactions. The
best option seemed to be to wait for him to leave, and follow
him to his home. But he had to be on the alert in case the
subject slipped away.

Body language. One thing a stint in prison taught was how
to read and use it. Glancing occasionally at Turner, Shaun
couldn't help but notice how he dominated the group with
his commanding stance—legs apart, arms folded across his

chest when he wasn't holding his schooner, rocking slightly on the balls of his feet. The vibe said: *I am the big fish here.* The other two were clearly pissing in his pocket, laughing on cue and in general falling all over him, unable to stand still in the presence of the big city cop come to grace their town and club. And, just as clearly, Turner was lapping it up. All his life this guy was in charge of others, even into his retirement. He was probably the local scoutmaster and chief Rotarian as well. This was a man who had to have the respect of others in any environment.

Suddenly his machine made a fuss. Shaun hadn't been paying much attention, just pressing the same button every few seconds, but now he noticed there were five dice displayed, one in each frame. The machine went into singsong mode, indicating a major payout, and the credit metre was in overdrive. He heard the man next to him say, 'Christ, I've been playing that bastard for an hour. All it did was eat my money.'

'Luck of the draw,' Shaun said.

The other man simply shook his head despairingly and resumed playing his own machine. Heads turned here and there. People stopped behind him, watching the total go up.

When the noise and credit metre stopped, Shaun pressed the 'Collect' button, expecting the tray to fill with coins, but instead the machine spat out a slip of paper showing how much he'd won: $175. Didn't seem like a lot.

He took it to the cashier's window and collected. Turner's crew had just bought another round, so there wasn't much danger of the subject going anywhere soon.

He played another machine after that, never straying far from the trio at the bar. He had a feeling Turner wouldn't be much longer—a round of three schooners was probably about it for this time of day.

Sure enough Turner put his empty glass on its side on the bar towel. There followed another burst of backslapping, after which the former superintendent marched purposefully out through the glass doors, waving to a few hearty well-wishers en route.

Shaun abandoned his machine, leaving twenty dollars in it for some lucky punter, and wandered out behind him.

Out in the hot car park he put on his sunglasses and sat in the Falcon. It was not a large parking area and he could easily see Turner climbing into his car, a recent model Volvo. When the subject eased out into the road Shaun followed, letting another car slip in between them. Turner drove at a snail's pace, making it hard to stay back as far as Shaun wanted to, so he let two more cars pass him. In a few minutes Turner stopped outside a mini-mart and went inside. Shaun parked and waited. When Turner re-emerged he was carrying a plastic shopping bag, which clearly contained a carton of milk and some other items. Taking great care he nosed out into the thin traffic and drove on, the inevitable parking lights on, crawling along so slowly the Volvo could not have made it out of second gear. So he was the town's champion Volvo driver too.

They climbed a rise at the back of the town, entering a small street that was lined with neat bungalow-style homes with profuse front gardens. Turner swung right into the driveway of a cream weatherboard cottage that had a dense purple creeper overflowing the side fence and lush tropical flowers and shrubs filling the front. When he pulled up directly outside the house, Shaun could see many large pot-plants and hanging baskets on the front veranda. Turner had parked halfway along the drive, and had some trouble getting out of the car because of the creeper, which he had to beat out of the way. By the time he had extricated himself Shaun was standing at the front gate. Turner, the shopping bag in his hand, came around the back of his car towards some stone steps leading to the veranda. Then he noticed he had a visitor.

'Mr Turner?' Shaun said, hands in his back pockets.

Turner stopped. 'Yes?' he said warily, eyes already narrowing.

It was a big moment, but to his surprise Shaun felt no nerves at all. 'Mr Turner, my name is Shaun McCreadie. I was wondering—'

'I know who you are,' Turner shot back. 'I saw you at the club. What do you mean by following me here?'

That gave Shaun a start. He suddenly thought: the panther machine. He noticed me scoring the jackpot.

Round one to Leon Turner.

'I wanted to speak to you. In private.'

'Is that so,' Turner said.

'Yes, sir.' Strangely, Shaun still felt it necessary to address Turner formally, even though they were no longer in the system. The man simply had an aura that demanded it: he wore gravitas as easily as his old-fashioned clothes.

'Well, I have no intention of speaking to *you*,' Turner said, but he stayed where he was.

'Only a few minutes,' Shaun said. 'I would greatly appreciate it.' He was going to add 'sir', but held it back at the last second.

Turner drilled him with his grey eyes. 'I heard you got out,' he said. 'To my mind that was a travesty of justice.'

'The Appeals Court judges didn't agree.'

Turner nodded slowly. 'Sometimes the system fails us.'

'Not in this case.'

Turner still hadn't budged or shifted his intimidating gaze from the object of his displeasure—this *felon* who had dared to trespass into his personal realm.

'I have nothing to say to you, McCreadie. Except this: fuck off. Fuck off and crawl back into your shithole down south, where you belong.'

The outburst was unexpected, but then Shaun remembered that Turner, who was normally a model of propriety, also had a reputation for using rough language when stirred up. That was fine. It meant the gloves were off, reducing the obligation on Shaun to continue being polite. In a sense it gave him an advantage.

'I realise I'm not exactly a poster boy for the police department,' he said. 'But I—'

'Poster boy?' Turner spat. 'Don't try and crack witty with me, son. It won't wash. You're nothing but a piece of shit. You're a smear on the whole human race.' He was warming up nicely. 'You are a living, breathing case for the return of capital punishment.'

'Strong words,' Shaun said.

'They're true words,' Turner said, and glanced over his shoulder at the house, as if his wife might appear, causing him to cut out the profanities. He was the classic dinosaur who could swear a blue streak in the company of men, but not tolerate it for a second if a woman were present.

'All the same,' Shaun said, 'I have some questions that have been on my mind for years. I was hoping you could shed a little light. I don't wish to intrude on you, Mr Turner. Ten minutes of your time, then I'm gone.'

'But you *are* intruding on me.'

'Ten minutes.'

Turner was chewing it over, maybe wondering if he could snow this guy for a while and get rid of him, otherwise he might hang around and make a pest of himself—bother his wife, turn up again at the club, or whatever.

'If you've made a special trip up here to see me, you've wasted your time,' Turner said. 'There's nothing I can tell you that you don't already know.'

'I did make a special trip,' Shaun said. 'But it's a nice place for a visit anyhow, I guess. Maybe I'll stick around for a while.' He tried a smile, which brought no visible reaction from Turner's flint-hard features.

'Go on,' he said finally. 'Hurry up. The clock's ticking down.'

'Morris Salisbury, the drug dealer,' Shaun said.

'Salisbury? What about him?'

'You knew him pretty well, didn't you?'

'I knew a lot of people on the wrong side of the fence. I was in CI. I even knew *you*. So what?'

'There were people who believed you were a bit too close for comfort.'

'I heard those stories—all made by people who didn't have the balls to come out in public.'

'Someone was raiding the evidence storage facility and supplying Salisbury with confiscated drugs.'

'Supposedly.'

'Then the records conveniently disappeared from the facility filing system. An investigation came to nothing. No-one was charged, despite all the accusations that were flying around. Didn't that seem a bit . . . *strange* to you?'

'People always make accusations. They have their reasons. Finding evidence to support them is another matter, however. Plenty of records are lost or thrown out in error. It doesn't have to mean there's a conspiracy. And there wasn't in that instance.'

'All the same, you can appreciate how suspicious it appears—all this shit going off from the facility at the same time you were cosying up to the biggest dealer in town.'

'I wasn't *cosying up* to anybody. Watch your mouth, McCreadie. I might be retired, but I can still bring you to account. You of all people should know you can't rub shoulders with the shit of the world every day and expect to come out smelling like a fucking flower shop.'

'So, according to you, there was no cover-up.'

'There was *definitely* no cover-up. Is that it now? Can I go?'

He didn't move. Shaun wondered why he felt the need to be so adamantly opposed to the idea of a cover-up, but let it pass. Turner was showing signs of irritation and it wouldn't be helpful to push him too far. At the same time, although he obviously resented the intrusion, he didn't mind getting into a scrap, no doubt to assert his superiority. Turner was a warhorse who got off on power, and he didn't get too many chances to flex his muscles in Nambucca Heads.

'What about Vincent O'Connell?' Shaun said, advancing a little closer. 'Got any ideas about what happened to him?'

Turner paused a second, as if he were going to shoot an answer back, then thought better of it. 'No,' he said.

'He was trying to bust Salisbury. Someone tipped him off.'

'It's a dangerous job,' Turner said.

'It is. Especially when you're ratted out by your own people. Do you remember attending a meeting in a pub with Salisbury, at which Vincent was present?'

'No,' came the quick answer.

'Vincent was a good mate of mine. He told me all about it—about you. Staring at him, warning him off Salisbury. Why, Mr Turner?'

'It's bullshit. This interview is over. You'd better turn tail and fuck off while you can, son.'

'Did you threaten Vincent? Arrange to have his dog killed, and his parents' car shot at?'

'Don't be so *fucking* stupid. I was trying to bust Salisbury too. Why would I tip him off and do all these other terrible things you accuse me of doing?'

'But you didn't bust him. Salisbury has *never* done time. Why?'

'It wasn't for want of trying. You can't catch them all, McCreadie. Inevitably some big fish slip through the net.'

Shaun came a step closer, so that he was level with the fenceline. 'But he was a protected species, wasn't he? He was allowed to slip through the net.'

'Complete and utter bullshit. You know, your condition is not uncommon among long-term convicts, McCreadie. They see threats and conspiracies everywhere. It's called paranoia.

And don't come any closer, or I'll fucking well have you arrested for trespass and thrown back in the can.'

'But I wasn't a long-term convict then. I was a serving officer, like you.'

'Excuse me, but you were *not* like me. *You* were a fucking *disgrace*. You still are.'

Voices had become raised. Up on the veranda Shaun could make out the blurred shape of a woman hovering behind the fly-wire screen door. Curious as she must have been, however, she remained indoors.

He dropped his voice almost to a whisper. 'Who killed Vincent O'Connell, Mr Turner?'

'I have no idea.' Turner, too, softened his tone, no doubt conscious of his wife's presence at the front door. He might well have added: *And I don't give a shit.*

'A CI inspector, and you have no idea. That would suggest you have no interest in finding out, either.'

'People disappear all the time.'

'He was a cop. He was one of us. You sold him out, didn't you? Instead of protecting him, you arranged for his execution.'

There was a slight swallow visible at Turner's sinewy and corded throat. 'You're pissing in the wind,' he said quietly. 'Go away.'

'Mr Turner, I know you weren't acting alone, and that you don't want to betray the others. Bill Simmonds, for example. You were both members of The Three, weren't you?'

'Go away now,' Turner said flatly.

'Do you know Simmonds is trying to kill me? He's out of control, Turner.'

'I have no idea what you're on about, McCreadie. You are bad news.'

'You know what happened to Vincent, don't you? You fixed it. You and Simmonds.'

'Shut up.'

'You're holding a lot of secrets, Turner—too many for one man. Sooner or later they'll find a way out.'

Turner didn't say a word. He had barely moved throughout the dialogue, but now he turned to go up the steps to the house. His wife was still peering through the fly-wire.

'Mr Turner,' Shaun said in a slightly conciliatory way. 'If you do happen to remember any details, anything at all, I'm staying at the Blue Dolphin.' He turned to his car, then called back: 'I'm sure if something happened to a good friend of yours, you'd want to clear it up on his behalf. It's the least we can do when the system fails us. And I'm not going to stop until I do just that.'

The temperature had risen in more than one way during the afternoon. Shaun bought himself a pair of Speedos on his way back to the motel, grabbed a towel from the bathroom and headed for the beach. It was only a ten-minute stroll, but the sun beat down so hard he could feel it burning the scalp through his hair. By the time he arrived sweat was streaming down his face and body. *Should've got a hat too—and some sunscreen.*

There were plenty of swimmers and surfers, mainly bodysurfers but some on big boards further out. He stretched the towel out on the pristine sand, removed his sunglasses, flung off his sweat-drenched top and ran into the sea. It had been many years since he'd been able to do that, and it was a delicious sensation. He waded through the shallows, then plunged in and struck through the waves that were crashing down over him and roaring in his ears. He was not a particularly strong swimmer, but he had an overpowering need to throw himself into it anyhow and work off some of the tension and aggravation he was feeling. In a few minutes he was past the breakers and slicing through an undulating swell of green water. When he was out of breath he stopped and turned, treading water as he gazed around him. Alongside, two surfers, boys about fifteen, were on their way in, kneeling on their boards and paddling towards the white tops of the waves.

Water dripped from the shining bleach-blond hair that was plastered over them. By the time they reached the breakers they were standing up, perfectly balanced, brown bodies leaning forward to meet the imminent challenge.

Shaun shook his head to clear the water from his eyes. The sun had a real sting in it out here. He ducked down and came up again. Soon his head and shoulders were on fire. He looked at the beach and the compact little town, rising slightly up the hill towards the highway not far behind it. It seemed a long way off, but he could see it all clearly. He could even see the Blue Dolphin up on the hill. With the surfers gone he was out here on his own, bobbing easily in the sea, taking in a little water every now and then and blowing it out. Then came a cold stab of fear: *Christ—what about fucking sharks?* He swivelled his head around, searching the depths for ominous dark shapes. *Wouldn't see it anyway. They always come from nowhere.*

He dried off, put on his top and the shades, draped the towel over his head and shoulders and began the mandatory long walk along the shore, all the way to the next point. Ahead of him extended a long, unbroken crescent of white sand. In 1979 he had regularly made this journey following a morning session of bodysurfing. Back then, however, he hadn't been alone.

One of his companions on that trip—his main man—was Vincent O'Connell.

The other guy was Derek Whyteford, who went to university that year to study engineering. The last Shaun heard about Derek, he was an ace in his field, building roads in China or Russia or somewhere far away.

The three of them walked this stretch of beach every day while they were here. It became a ritual. En route they usually covered a range of topics, such as what they intended to do with their lives, post-school.

At that time Derek was in two minds: he had applied for both science and engineering, and would wait and see. Shaun and Vincent were set on the police force. It was something they'd discussed on and off ever since a recruiting officer had visited the school. Even now he had a crystal-clear recollection of Vincent asking him as they walked along in the face of a scorching wind why, above all, he wanted to be a cop. Shaun had simply answered, 'To catch bad guys.' Vincent had thought about it and said, 'Yeah. What could be better than that?'

What indeed? How the wheel had turned.

His thoughts switched to the encounter with Leon Turner. Not a lot had come out of the exchange, but it wasn't a dead loss. *I heard you got out*, Turner had stated at the outset. It meant someone had told him. Someone who thought it was important enough to pass the information down the line. Shaun's release certainly would not have rated a mention on regional New South Wales TV, or in the local press. He would not have been the subject of chatter among the members of the Nambucca Heads RSL.

So Turner was still in touch with his old cronies. Still, that was hardly a hanging offence. It could mean something, or nothing.

More interestingly, he gave every sign of being in denial when the matter of a missing cop was mentioned. It's a dangerous job. I have no idea. People disappear all the time. None of this rang true. They were weasel words. A seasoned CI detective with a small army of underworld contacts would certainly have a theory, even if he didn't want to share it with a visitor from the past who brought too many uncomfortable memories—and questions—with him. His off-hand manner was completely insincere. And why become so overheated? Wouldn't an honest cop *want* to know what happened to Vincent?

But all Turner did was deny and threaten, even before Shaun had accused him of complicity in Vincent's murder. And his claim not to remember the pub meeting with Salisbury and Vincent was pure bullshit. Men like Leon Turner never forgot a fucking thing in their entire lives. It was what made them so good at their jobs.

More telling, perhaps, was the way he appeared to lose his bottle in the last few minutes. A common interrogative technique used by detectives is to hit a suspect with a barrage of accusations to see what he comes out with under pressure. Sometimes he will incriminate himself inadvertently, after which it's too late to retract. That's when good detectives move in for the kill. So it was with Turner.

His whole demeanour changed when Shaun accused him of arranging Vincent's execution. And the mere mention of Bill Simmonds' name visibly compounded his discomfort. Straightaway he lost all that bluster, and the colour drained from his face. In the end he turned away as if . . . as if he were admitting defeat, but couldn't face it, couldn't bear up under the weight. His strength had deserted him. Or was Shaun reading too much into the man's reactions? He was getting old, after all, and age takes its toll. All the same, Shaun's last vision of Turner was that of a man who was spitting blood and not travelling at all well.

None of this brought the closure he was after, but the mere fact that he'd put himself in Turner's face was a step in the right direction. Shaun had learned the virtues of patience and persistence in prison, and these were now his main assets. He had not expected a signed confession or anything like it, but the seed was planted. He was now inside Turner's head, whether the old bastard liked it or not. Now Shaun would do what cops the world over do when they've zeroed in on a hot suspect: embark on a program of sustained harassment. Turn up unexpectedly everywhere. Repeat the accusations again and again; embarrass him in front of his friends and make him see he was *never, ever* getting any respite. Rattle his cage; watch him blow his cool. Put him under extreme stress. Pour on the pressure. Drive him nuts. Hound him into his grave if it came to that.

He saw that his fist was clenched tight. *Easy. Not yet.*

Shaun hadn't planned that parting speech about doing something on behalf of your friend when the system failed to deliver. The words had just come out. But now that he thought about it, he could not have said anything more compelling if he'd tried. On his way up to the veranda Turner had stopped mid-stride and copped those words in his back as if they were hammer blows. Then, without turning around, he trudged on with an old man's gait. The message had been sent and received. It had also served to stiffen Shaun's own resolve, if that was ever in question.

Leon Turner could stew for the present. Right now, more than anything, Shaun lusted after a cold beer. He picked up a six-pack of Hahn Ice at a drive-through liquor store and steered the Falcon back towards the motel, but couldn't wait that long and cracked the first marine in transit. All that exertion plus the heat on the beach had given him an unquenchable thirst. Sitting in the car outside his room he tipped up the bottle and emptied the contents down his throat. Now he needed a decent shower to wash off all the salt and sand that had crusted on his skin and hair. In the rear-view mirror he saw that his face was sunburned, which gave him a strange, almost unrecognisable appearance. For many years now he was used to seeing the sun-starved pallor that comes with long-term incarceration every morning in the mirror when he shaved. But the guy in *this* mirror was a stranger.

After showering he put on some fresh clothes—a new white tee shirt and cargo shorts—pulled another Hahn from the refrigerator and started on it. It was hot in the room, so he switched on the air conditioner before stretching out on the bed with the bottle sitting on his stomach. He was stinging everywhere now from sunburn. It didn't matter; it made him feel alive, different, and free. Inevitably his mind reverted to Jo. Joanna Steer—she, more than anything, made him feel alive.

He was sure he loved her as deeply as he could possibly love anyone. The connection he felt to her came from his vitals, right in the hot core of his guts. Now as she filled his thoughts it all started churning around and his heartbeat automatically powered up a couple of decent-sized ratchets.

He picked up the phone and dialled her number. When she answered after one ring he closed his eyes and smiled. From the quick pick-up and the soft burr of her voice he judged that she knew who was on the line, and had been waiting for the call.

'I'm missing you,' he said quietly, without introduction.

'Tell me all about it.' There came the sloshing sound of a drink with ice in it.

He did so. In between times there were periods of expectant silence in which there was only the sound of her breathing. Her lips could not have been closer to the handset.

In a while she said, 'What are you doing?'

'Sitting in my room, staring at the walls. You?'

'Well, I'm actually trying to prepare some material for next semester. But I can't seem to concentrate, for some reason. Did you see that guy, Leon Turner?'

'Yeah, I did.'

'And?'

'Well, he wasn't too thrilled. Didn't exactly throw himself on the ground and beg for mercy.'

'You didn't expect him to, did you?'

'No. Anyway, he knows the score. I won't let up on him.'

There was the sound of a sloshing glass. 'Don't let up on me either, will you?'

That gave him a shiver.

'I haven't even started on you yet, evil one.'

'Can't wait till you do.' More breathing and sloshing sounds followed. So it went for a few more minutes, until he reluctantly said goodbye. He waited with the phone to his ear until she disconnected first, then gently replaced the handset with Joanna still very much in his mind.

To distract himself he decided to switch on the TV, but there didn't seem to be a remote anywhere. He searched the room thoroughly without success.

No remote.

He picked up the phone again and told the manager, who said people often stole remotes for some weird reason, and that he would bring one to the room soon.

Shaun opened the refrigerator and extricated another Hahn from the plastic wrapping. There were three left.

That was fine. In a little bit he would wander into town for something to eat, maybe check out the pubs to see if the counter meals were as good as he remembered them. Drive out of town and down a couple of cold ones at The Pub With No Beer.

He sat on the edge of the bed sipping beer. There came a rap at the door. He put down the Hahn before opening up. But the motel manager wasn't standing in front of him.

Leon Turner was.

18

Shaun was so stunned it took him a moment to realise who it was. This was partly because Turner was wearing a white terry-cloth hat that obscured his eyes. Shaun gave him the once-over to see if he was carrying. There was an uncomfortably silent gap of several seconds during which neither man seemed to know what to say. Finally it was Turner who coughed up.

'You said you were staying here,' he said.

'Uh, yeah—do you want to come in?'

'No—I prefer to be outside. Can't stand air conditioning.'

Shaun said, 'Hold on,' grabbed his room key and came out, shutting the door.

'Want to head for the beach?' Turner said after they'd already started striding out in that direction, down the hill.

'Sure.'

They walked along. Various thoughts swirled in Shaun's brain as cicadas hummed in the dry soil. At this time, early evening, the air was soft and warm, with a pleasant sea breeze coming off the Pacific.

'How did you find me here?' Turner said, looking down at his feet as he walked.

'I still have one or two friends in the job,' he said.

'That surprises me. After all this time.'

'Well, when I say friends, I don't expect to be invited to any dinner parties.'

Turner's face cracked into a humourless grin. 'I don't get invited to too many myself, comes to that.'

Soon they made their way past a front lawn with a sprinkler that sent out a shower onto the pavement, then turned down a narrow, dusty trail to the sea. At the end of it there was an old Moreton Bay fig tree with a root system that twisted around itself above the sandy ground like anacondas having sex. To one side, under its shade, was a wooden bench on which Turner sat. Shaun, still standing, looked out at the water and waited for Turner to say whatever was on his mind.

'Pretty cool bastard, aren't you?' Turner said.

'Not particularly.'

'Sure you are, fronting me like that. Soon as I clapped eyes on you at the club I knew who you were—and why you'd come. Man on a fucking mission, I said to myself. You haven't changed at all, except now you've got that *yard stare*, and the hunted fugitive look about you. You guys, you're always on the run. There's no escaping that. Why don't you siddown, McCreadie? No-one's gonna come up behind you and stick a shiv in your kidneys.'

'I sincerely hope not,' Shaun said, not quite managing to smile. He sat on the other end of the bench, leaving plenty of space in the middle.

'I've lived here six years now,' Turner said. 'And I'll die here. That's no comfort, by the way, knowing *where* you're gonna curl up your toes. Or when. But it's a far cry from chasing shitbags down south for a living.'

'It is.'

'We've got a yacht, up at Proserpine on the Barrier Reef,' Turner said, scanning the sea as if he expected her to sail into view any second. 'She's a sloop—real humdinger of a craft. Built in the USA and brought over here by one of those playboy millionaires with bikini-clad blonde bimbos all over him. I've never been a sailor in the past, but this baby won me over. We don't actually *own* her, we have a share that entitles us to two weeks a year. Tell you one thing, that's two weeks I look forward to for the whole other fifty. It's unbelievably beautiful up there. We just sail around, pop a cold can anytime, drop the anchor and jump in for a swim when it gets too hot, spear fish and barbecue the sweetest coral trout you ever tasted on deck, under the stars . . . It's fucking paradise, no two ways about it. If heaven exists, that's where it is.'

'Sounds all right,' Shaun said. He'd decided to say as little as possible and let Turner rabbit on. Sooner or later he might get to the point.

'Man of few words,' Turner said. 'That's right—Shaun the Silent, wasn't it?'

'Been a long time since anyone called me that.'

Turner fixed him with his battleship grey eyes. Although his face and arms were deeply suntanned, it was a dry, leathery brown that was creased and splotched with darker spots that stood out in contradistinction. Skin sagged at his throat, and he was much thinner than Shaun remembered from the old days. He could see the bones in his upper chest, where his shirt was opened. There was definitely something wrong with him.

'Prostate cancer,' Turner said. 'Had it diagnosed . . . five weeks ago now. If they get it early they can cure you, but mine is too far advanced. It's now at the aggressive stage. It's coming after me with a vengeance. It wants me, it's eating me up— and it'll do the job in two, three months, unless I blow my fuckin' brains out first. Last thing a man wants is to go out in a fuckin' coma, drip-fed and dosed up to the eyeballs with painkillers.'

'Well . . . I'm sorry to hear that, Mr Turner.' And, unexpectedly, he was—just a little.

'Are you? That's not the impression I had back at the house. What was it you said? Ah, never mind. You know, the cruel part about it is that it's so fucking *easy* to nip the bastard in the bud. That's what shits me to tears. You only have to get yourself tested once a year or so. But of course, men of my generation don't do that. We're invincible. I've always been fit and as strong as a bull, never had a day off in my life, so why should anything happen to me? Anyhow, it's unbecoming to have someone shove a fist up your rear end, even if it does save your life. Shit. A man must be *fucking* mad.'

Shaun was silent.

Turner studied his feet and said, 'So, that's that. It's all over rover. I'll never see Proserpine again. I decided not to bother with chemotherapy. Don't see why I should put myself through all that shit and misery, and still pop off at the end of it. No point.'

'I guess not,' Shaun said.

'Dunno how the wife's going to manage on her own. She wouldn't have the foggiest about dealing with lawyers or insurance companies, or the goddamn tax department, or any of that bureaucratic go-round. It's all beyond her. Christ. She can't even write a fucking cheque, or use an automatic teller machine. I've always managed everything right from the day we were married. Every ship has only one captain, right?' He gave a wry little laugh. 'Well, maybe I should've delegated a bit more. But I wasn't any good at that either. I had to run the whole fucking show. It's in the nature of the beast.' He shot Shaun a sideways glance and said, 'Sorry to bore you with all this personal shit.'

'Doesn't matter,' Shaun said.

'No, I guess it doesn't any more.'

'Is that why you decided to come and see me?' Shaun said, trying to point him in a new direction.

Turner's face split into a smile. 'Confession time? Maybe there's a bit of that in it. I'm no Christian, don't believe in God or any of that architect of the universe, Masonic mumbo-jumbo, even though I'm a member, but I do believe this: what goes around, comes around. At the end of the day we all get what's coming to us. And it's got nothing to with divine judgement. It's just the way it is.'

'I can't argue with that,' Shaun said, since Turner's words accorded precisely with his own beliefs. A lot of inmates found God while they were serving time, but they were nearly always lost individuals whose past lives had been a spiritual wasteland, devoted to greed, violence and drug abuse. They were empty vessels ready to be filled with something—anything—to give their lives a purpose. This was known as the 'born-again syndrome'. But having been brought up in a religious system, Shaun was immune to its seductive appeal. With each day that passed he believed less and less in a higher power. The crunch came when he watched the Twin Towers come down on TV in the Barwon common room. His reaction was: If there is a God in charge of this fucked-up world he's doing a pretty ordinary job at it. He knew what the Marx Brothers would reply to that, but then they were not about to repudiate the reason for their very existence.

'So, I cop this killer disease, you turn up, and you bring Bill Simmonds into it: past, present and future. Maybe it's all connected somehow. At any rate it gives me the chance to spit out some stuff. What'd you say back there? I was holding too many secrets, and they'd find a way out. Maybe so. Maybe this is my last chance. They say if you bottle things up it can give you cancer, and if that's true I've already been punished for my . . . uh, transgressions. But Bill Simmonds brings back a lot of memories, I have to say.'

'Did he tell you I was out of jail?'

'No, he didn't. And don't ask me who did, because I'm

not saying. I haven't seen or heard from Bill in years. Is he still a cop?'

'Oh yeah.'

'That surprises me. I'm sixty-seven years old, going on sixty-eight, and he's five years younger. I would've thought he'd have hung up his guns by now.'

'He shows no intention of doing that.'

'He should. Come to that, they should pension him off. Christ, he was a wild man in the old days. Big bruisers—and I mean real tough guys, not the fuckin' pansies and showponies running around nowadays—used to shit their pants when Bill got a hold of them, and with good reason too. They'd have to hose out the interview room after he'd finished interrogating some poor bastard.' That was worth a fond laugh, and a nod at the ground as he receded further into the past. 'We teamed up when we were both in the consorters, way back in the late sixties. Although I was older I was relatively new in the game because I'd already served a stint in the army. At that time Simmonds was a law unto himself, and I was naturally drawn to him—he was a charismatic guy. We ruled the streets. Big Bill Simmonds and Brick Turner—we were a pretty formidable duo. Anybody wanting to pull a robbery had to get our okay first. The plans had to be officially approved, as it were, so no-one got hurt. Christ, they were gonna do it anyway, so it made sense to come to a sort of accommodation. That's how we regarded it, and in a twisted sort of way, the system worked. Violent crime didn't spill out onto the streets as much as it could've. If some hood fucked up they'd cop a hiding they'd never forget. Jesus, I saw Bill drag this scumbag down a back lane once . . .' He shook his head—the rest was easily imagined without words. 'I could fill a dozen books. Matter of fact I had an approach from a crime reporter down south to write up my memoirs—one of those ghost-written jobs—but I told him to fuck off, I'd have to give up too many people. I wasn't dying then. Now it's too late. So consider yourself privileged, McCreadie. You're hearing stories I've never told anyone before.'

'Now you don't care who you give up.'

'Strange, isn't it? I feel a need to set the record straight, even if it's just to one person. It must be part of the process of dying, I guess.' He drifted away into some reverie, rubbed his face with the hat. 'So be it. Anyway, as far as Morris Salisbury's concerned, well, everyone knew he was the biggest dealer in town. But he was useful, because he'd supply us with information and give up people, and we'd make shitloads of arrests and clear up plenty of outstanding cases. In return we allowed him to operate. It was a perfectly sensible arrangement. Hardly best practice these days, but you have to understand it in the context of the times. Strange as it may sound now, we never considered ourselves to be corrupt. It was just the way we operated, to get the job done. Law enforcement was pretty rough and ready back then.'

Shaun was listening intently. Interesting, he thought, how Turner puts himself in a good light—making arrests, solving cases—but doesn't say anything about receiving kickbacks from the armed heists he and Simmonds green-lit. So he wasn't prepared to come clean, not completely. Not yet. One man's *cosying up* was another man's sensible arrangement.

'Needless to say, the system didn't last. I had various postings, and then CI, and Bill moved around, but through it all we were still a team. But then, things got a little out of whack. Greed was the big factor. When you know you can get away with things, the temptation's much greater. I forget whose idea it was, mine probably, but that evidence storage facility started to look mighty attractive. I used to go there often, for legitimate reasons, so I knew the set-up inside out. There was no sophisticated security system, no video cameras or swipe cards such as they have now. You wouldn't be able to get within a bull's roar of it these days. All I did was get some impressions of the relevant keys, have them made up, and I was set. I could get in anytime, and the building wasn't even guarded after hours. You didn't have to be Houdini to get in and out of that joint. I'd have a few beers, then drive over, slip in and help myself to some gear from the vast array of evidence bags. I was smart enough to remove only small quantities from a number of bags, spread the loss so as not to arouse too much suspicion. These cases might take a year or more to come up, by which time, who cared if there was a small quantity of shit missing from an evidence bag? Who could prove anything? Maybe they'd weighed it wrong in the first place. Large consignments were good too: no-one was gonna miss a few lousy grams from ten or twenty kilos, were they?'

'Did you do all this on your own?' Shaun said while Turner went quiet for a minute.

'At first,' he said. 'But then Bill started coming with me. Usually, if we'd been to the boozer—and we were *always* on the piss—we might decide to visit the supermarket, as we called it. We'd take a few cold cans and sit in the fuckin' evidence room drinkin' 'em while we checked out what was on offer. What a joke. Bill'd say, "Hey, marijuana's on special this week". We used to laugh our fuckin' heads off like a pair of jackasses.'

'You'd unload it all through Salisbury, right?'

'Of course. No problems. He was a bottomless pit. It was a piece of piss, and a nice, steady earner. I got so cocky I used to pinch stuff during the day, when I was there on official police business. No-one suspected anything. But then, along came your buddy, Vincent O'Connell. I wondered who this new *dealer* on the scene was, and it didn't take long to sniff him out and discover he was a cop. We had most of the senior drug squad guys onside, but this was different—it was a covert operation. I didn't know who was behind it, and I was concerned that they were after *me*, via Salisbury. They'd bust him, and Bill and I would be caught up in the wash. That was the fear. So yeah, I put the frighteners on him and did a few distasteful things . . . usually when I was oiled up.'

'You gave him up to Salisbury, didn't you?' Suddenly Shaun wasn't feeling even faintly sympathetic to Turner. 'You blew his cover.'

'What I did, I told Salisbury he'd better watch himself, because he was dealing with an undercover cop, and if he went down Bill and I would go with him. If that happened, if he got busted, he was a fuckin' dead drug dealer. He'd be dead before he hit the courts.'

'What happened to Vincent?' The four words hung trembling in the air. Turner took a deep breath and let it out slowly, as if it hurt to breathe.

'One day while all this was going on, an assistant commissioner called Paul Harcourt was given a dossier by Mitch Alvarez. It was all the dirt on me. Harcourt wanted to know why Alvarez had taken it upon himself to investigate another officer, and Alvarez told him you claimed I was out to get your mate O'Connell, who was in my face.'

'So Paul Harcourt was the third member of the group?'

'Harcourt? Shit no. Harcourt was a very career-minded cop. All he was concerned about was how he could get to the top. He wouldn't have had the balls to run with this, because he didn't know if he'd be treading on the wrong toes. Harcourt was a gutless toady. Fortunately, however, he had the sense to pass it on to the right man—an Internal Investigations officer by the name of Nifty Neville Burns.'

'Burns . . . I know him.'

'Course you do. He offered you a cut-and-run deal, didn't he? Do you imagine that came from the goodness of his heart? Nifty doesn't have one.'

Shaun was wondering if there was any part of his life that was *not* controlled by Turner and his cohorts.

'Burns had also come through the consorters, and he knew Bill from before my time. They were still tight, you know, in the manner of old soldiers trading on war stories, and I got to know him too. This was before he hit the goon squad. In that capacity he was very useful to us because he'd pass on command directives, memos, inside scuttlebutt, whatever, and he had the power to divert or even suppress investigations that may have been damaging to Bill and me. Nifty Burns was our protector. He was the silent partner, the Invisible Man, as Bill called him. For his trouble I used to deliver him an envelope every so often, when we'd made a nice score. I'd just drive around to his place and slip it under his front door. He never once gave it back.'

'That's The Three—you, Simmonds and Neville Burns.'

'Right. I was shitting bullets when he showed me this dossier, because I thought it was this covert operation coming after me, but when Burns told me it came from Alvarez and you I thought I could fix the problem. Alvarez had done a top job, he had photos of me entering and leaving the premises at night, shots of me boozing and carrying on with Salisbury, dates when I'd signed in to the facility corresponding with dates they suspected drugs had been stolen . . . Burns told me there was already an investigation under way that had nothing to do with Alvarez. Someone had smelled a rat. It was all starting to come down on us.'

Turner wiped his face with the hat again. Even though it was pleasantly warm he seemed to sweat excessively. He stared across the expanse of sand at the surf rolling in. Shaun thought, all this shit must seem such a world away from here that it didn't really happen.

'I knew I had to act,' Turner said. 'In life, you can sit still and let things happen to you, or you can take the bull by the horns. I've never been one to take a backseat, so I paid one last visit to the facility one night armed with a razor blade, and cut out pages from the sign-in book that had my signature on them. Alvarez had written down the dates, but if his list couldn't be matched against the sign-in book they had fuck-all except some photos, which didn't prove anything by themselves.

'While I was at it I also ransacked the records and took

anything that might vaguely connect to me—files on Salisbury
and other criminals with whom I'd had some dodgy dealings
over the years. In those days records were not computerised,
it was all in file cabinets. There was a mountain of shit in there,
going back years, so the stuff I'd taken probably wouldn't be
missed. And before leaving, I helped myself to some drugs, and
other items such as weapons that had been used in the
commission of crimes.'

'To fit us up.'

'It's a time-honoured tactic: when all else fails, discredit the
witness. We knew Alvarez, you and Corcoran were a tight
crew, so we figured you were all in it together, especially with
you being O'Connell's mate. Anyhow, why take chances? So
we planted the stuff and made a couple of anonymous phone
calls to the detectives investigating the facility break-ins. And
just to top it off I managed to dig up an ex-girlfriend of
Corcoran's who was still dirty on him. I slung her a few quid
to cry rape. That was the icing on the cake.'

Shaun was starting to simmer. 'What happened to *Vincent*?'
he said again.

'Salisbury had this contact from the Chinese underworld.
The Chows normally stick to their own turf, but this guy was
a freelancer. His name was Johnny Wu. He was a hitman from
Taiwan, a real professional. If Johnny Wu was after you, you
were gone. I don't know the whole story, not for sure, but
I believe he abducted Vincent at gunpoint, shot him in his car
as he was driving, and then dumped the body in a construction
site.' He paused, weighed his words and added, 'Without being
absolutely certain, I would say that right now Vincent
O'Connell is underneath a high-rise office building somewhere in the Central Business District.'

'You fucking bastards.' Shaun's fist had clenched of its own
accord, and he was suddenly feeling strangely light-headed. Too
much sun, now this.

'Fair enough,' Turner said. 'It was a cunt of an act. But all

I wanted to do was scare him off. I had no intention of hurting the boy. Salisbury took matters into his own hands, without consultation. He got the wind up when I told him what Alvarez was up to. Christ, I had no idea he'd go that far, kill a fucking cop.'

'You're responsible. The whole fucking bunch of you.' *And God help me, so am I.*

'I can see you're steamed up. I don't blame you. Go on, then—take a swing. Get it off your chest.'

'I'll do more than that, Turner.'

That drew a mock laugh. 'Yeah? What are you gonna do— kill me? Be my guest.'

'Maybe I will.'

'I don't think so, McCreadie. You're still young. Why go back inside? Killing me can't change anything.'

But the fist would not unclench: it seemed to have seized up on him. Turner glanced across at the white knuckles and blood-filled, purple veins on the back of Shaun's hand. He didn't seem bothered by the prospect of a bashing. Why should he be?

'No,' he said, 'but it would make me feel better.'

'Then you'll have a nice long stretch in the big house to feel bad all over again.'

The logic couldn't be faulted, but all the same Shaun didn't know how long he'd be able to stop himself from smashing him in the face. What made it worse was the boastful pleasure he was deriving from it all, as if these war stories were nothing more than harmless anecdotes that brought back a treasure trove of memories. The fact that he was dying gave him a smug, secure attitude—he was past retribution. It was tough to swallow.

Eventually the crisis passed, and Shaun was able to uncurl his fingers. Sensing it was safe to go on, Turner said, 'After you guys were put out of business, we pulled our heads in for a while, till it all blew over. Being an inspector in CI I had

reason to revisit the storage place, but no more sticky fingers.
In a while we regrouped with Salisbury, who had also been
quiet after the Johnny Wu fiasco. Then one day I was having
a beer with him in the Spread Eagle and he let slip that
something big was about to go down, and did we want a
piece of it. Bill turned up and we pumped him for details,
but he wouldn't spill till he was good and pissed. The upshot
was, Salisbury had it on good authority that a large shipment
of heroin was on its way from Pakistan, and the man behind
the deal was the well-known used car tycoon, George
Petrakos.'

Shaun felt a little edgy—he wasn't too sure now that he
wanted to hear the next part. But he was on white water
rapids, heading for the big drop, and there was no stopping.

'How did Salisbury know about it?'

'He got the mail from George's son, Stan. Stan was down
on his old man, so when he overheard him on the phone
arranging the deal he seized the chance to rip him off with
Salisbury's help. It was an attractive proposition, but I had
reservations. Stan was a crazy bastard, for starters. Like his father
he was full of his own shit, ever since he'd supposedly run Lou
Galvano out of town a couple of years before. He was still
trading on that, but there was a solid story doing the rounds
that Galvano left the country for personal reasons without
even being aware that Stan was gunning for him. However, he
did have street credibility, and the information sounded reliable.
Stan was convinced it was a sweet deal, and he'd won Salisbury
over. Being a big shipment, though, it was possible the Feds
were already onto it, and if so you didn't want to fall into a
fuckin' trap. The stuff could be tagged. So we put it on the
back burner for a while. If George received the goods with
no complications, then we'd go for it. This was . . . late August,
in 1992.

'Bill and I spent a lot of time discussing it. He was of the
opinion that if you had a good enough plan you could steal

the pyramids, but then you'd have the problem of finding a buyer.' Turner laughed, then coughed. Sweat dripped from his nose and blowflies were buzzing around him. When he'd stopped coughing he swatted at the flies with the hat, but they didn't go far. 'He once said that to commit the perfect crime, you had to pull it off in plain view without anyone noticing. It sounded impressive, but I didn't know what he meant, and I doubt if he did either. It was just pub bullshit. There was a lot of pub bullshit with Bill Simmonds.

'So we sat on that, and then one afternoon Smooth Wollansky turned up in the Spread Eagle.'

That name clicked. 'Wollansky? The ex-cop?'

'Yeah. He was in the robbers with your *mate* Alvarez.' For some reason that wasn't apparent, he said this with a distinct sneer.

Shaun knew of Brent Wollansky. He'd left for the private sector by the time Shaun hit the squad, but they'd run into each other in pubs, and he was mentioned in dispatches often enough to still have a presence. He'd been tight with Mitch . . .

'Wollansky had a security business which he'd just started up. He wasn't exactly a regular, or one of us any more, but he was pretty well liked. You may remember that famous case he worked with Alvarez, when Stan Petrakos robbed the restaurant.'

'I remember it. Stan walked because of his old man's money. It was a scam—he and the owner set it up.'

'Correct. Alvarez and Wollansky were real shitty about that. Mitch was heard to say he'd do anything to get back at the Petrakos clan. They made him look like a fool.'

Shaun was remembering some of the things Mitch had said long after that case, what he'd do if he ever had the chance and there were no witnesses. They weren't the sorts of comments you wanted quoted back at you by a prosecution lawyer in court.

'That day at the Spread Eagle, Wollansky said he'd had a

visit from Mitch Alvarez. Alvarez asked him if there was any way Wollansky could get his hands on the architect's blueprints of the Petrakos mansion at Lancefield. The suggestion was apparently made that it would be worth his while if he could. But it was all water under the bridge as far as Wollansky was concerned—he didn't want to know. Alvarez made it clear what he had in mind: "That place is awash in cash. It's up for grabs." Stuff like that. He was playing on the fact that they both hated George's guts. Wollansky told him not to be stupid.'

'He refused to help.'

'Absolutely. But while he was telling us this, I could see Bill's mind ticking over . . .'

Turner's words revolved in Shaun's head: *steal the pyramids . . . perfect crime . . . plain view . . .*

Steal the pyramids. Pyramids. *Petrakos mansion . . .*

It was coming together. He was a blind man whose sight was gradually returning, but although he could now pick out objects in front of him, the shapes were still blurred.

Turner closed in. 'The timing could not have been better. What's the word for that?'

'Serendipity.' A vision of Jo in the jacuzzi materialised in the fog, then dissolved . . .

'That's it, serendipity. Bill couldn't wait to get in my ear. I knew he'd already formed a plan three different ways by the time we left the pub. As he explained it, the deal was that *he* would approach Alvarez with the idea to knock off the Petrakos millions.'

'That's bullshit,' Shaun said. 'He'd never have gone for that. Not after what you bastards did to him. To *us*.'

'True. That was the big worry. But on the other hand, if Bill could get the blueprints, help bankroll the job, supply the weapons . . . Alvarez knew Bill had a lot of useful contacts. He could arrange to steal the van and have it resprayed by professionals and done up. So he had a package deal to offer him. He was counting on the idea that Alvarez hated Petrakos more than he hated Bill. It was a pretty fair bet. And on that subject everyone knew Alvarez was a big time gambler. He probably wouldn't be able to resist the odds.'

Shaun didn't say anything. He didn't believe Turner, but he sounded so confident and sure of himself, as if he knew precisely what had happened every inch of the way.

'So Bill called on Alvarez and made the offer. I stayed right out of it, since I was even less of a pin-up boy. The offer was, they'd split the take fifty–fifty. Alvarez listened, but said no, fuck off, he already had two partners. Well, you didn't have to be a fuckin' genius to figure out who they were. But Bill worked on him. He pointed out that with Bill onside he had a much better chance of pulling it off and not getting caught. Bill could offer protection too, you see. All Alvarez had to do was cut the partners loose *after* the job, persuade them to hide the dough somewhere and lie low for a while, then go back and get it on the sly and split it with Bill. When the partners found out later that he'd done the dirty on them, Bill would take care of the problem.'

Shaun had his face in his hands now. *I don't want to hear this . . .*

'The fact was that we wanted the drugs. Any money was a bonus. Shit, we weren't even sure if there *was* any. But Alvarez would never know the real purpose of the heist. He would merely provide perfect cover for the perfect crime. It was brilliant. When Bill produced the blueprints, Alvarez's eyes lit up. He just couldn't say no. Turned out he did hate Petrakos, *and the system,* more than he hated Bill. But he insisted you two guys were not to be harmed. That was big of him, wasn't it? Bill would tell him when it was all set—he'd give him the green light. Timing had to be exact. There was one rider. Bill told him if he came across a stack of heroin in the strongroom to leave it alone *at all costs*, because it was tagged by the Feds, and there was a big swoop in the pipeline. Alvarez agreed. So that was that—it was a done deal.'

Shaun was staring at the sand at his feet. Lying in his cell at night he'd gone over everything from start to finish, again and again, but never once had he considered the possibility that Mitch had sold them out. Even now it didn't feel right. Mitch wouldn't have done that. They were a team. They were *brothers*.

'If it's any consolation,' Turner said. 'I'm sure he agonised over it.'

'You're wrong, Turner.'

'Am I? Come on. Didn't you ever wonder where he got the blueprints, the guns, the van? Do you honestly believe he arranged all that on his own? Whose idea was it to stash the money? Who was against ripping off a fortune in drugs?'

'I'm not disputing that you put an offer on the table, or even that Mitch agreed . . . He might have *said* that, but he wouldn't have meant it. He saw a chance to use you bastards and square off at the same time, that's all. He had no intention of delivering his side of the deal.'

'That is a slim possibility, I grant you. But if so, why didn't he tell you guys about it? Why not come clean, bring you into his confidence, if he had nothing to hide?'

Shaun could understand why, but all he said was, 'He had his reasons.'

Unconvinced, Turner said, 'Maybe. Have it your way.'

'I will.'

'Anyway, Stan duly reported that the drugs had arrived safely. He was constantly spying on his father and listening in to his phone conversations on the extension. The gear was to be concealed in sculptures, marble statues, antiques and so on, so all Stan had to do was wait for a shipment to arrive at the house. They cleared customs without missing a beat. Everything was set. Bill gave Alvarez the go-ahead . . . and you know the next chapter.'

Shaun flashed onto George's bloody fingers being shattered one by one on the billiard table. He knew that chapter by heart, and didn't want to dwell there.

'What happened after we left? It was Stan, right?'

'Stan was there all the time, waiting for you three to fuck off. He, uh . . . did the rest, delivered the drugs to Salisbury as arranged, and Salisbury put them in the lock-up he rented for such purposes. There it would stay until the heat died down. The city would be alive with cops, and it wouldn't do to be found in possession of a big batch of heroin. Plan was, he'd on-sell it to the Asian triads later, when the investigation cooled off. Get rid of it all in one hit.' He smiled to himself and said, 'It was a classic inside-out job. One job unwittingly covering for another.' Nostalgic recollection made his face crease sharply into a half-smile: so *proud* of his cleverness.

'An inside-out job,' Shaun repeated to himself. 'Very smart, Turner.'

'Yeah, I thought so. Too bad—'

'Did Mitch know Stan was part of the act?'

'Shit no,' Turner said. 'Mitch cottoned on to that, he wouldn't have gone one yard.'

'Stan shot his father *and* Stephanie? Why? I mean, he hated the old man, fine, I can go with that, but why Stephanie?'

'Stan's a crazy son of a bitch. Shit, no-one was supposed to *die*. You're right, George is one thing, but . . . Stephanie? Christ, it was unnecessary aggravation. She wasn't even meant to be there. She was meant to be out riding a goddamn horse somewhere.'

'But she had a float breakdown.'

'Yeah. Couldn't have turned up at a worse time, unfortunately for her.'

Shaun said, 'But we left both of them with their eyes and mouths taped over. Stephanie wouldn't have known who was lifting the dope. He only had to fill the bag and go. She would've assumed it was one of us come back. So would George, for that matter. He wasn't in real good shape. I doubt if he could've given an accurate report about anything.'

'Yeah. But maybe Stan did something idiotic in the heat

of the moment, like . . . give the old man a piece of his mind. Wouldn't put that past him. *Then* Stephanie would've known from the voice who it was, giving him no choice.'

Shaun thought about that. It still didn't sound quite right. Something else he remembered, a detail that came out in the trial: the piece of duct tape they'd put over George's eyes was found on the floor. It had to be from George because some of his eyebrows adhered to it. But how did he get it off? He was wrapped up tight—they'd used masses of the stuff.

'What about Stan's alibi?' he said.

'He fixed it with his bosom pal, Rick Stiles, and Stiles' girlfriend. What was her name? Linda, Linda something.'

'Linda Powell.'

'Yeah, Linda Powell. They were supposedly boozing and watching videos all afternoon at her house. All they had to do was stick to their story, and they did. It couldn't be cracked. There was no evidence to put Stan anywhere near the scene. He was eliminated as a suspect.'

It fitted. More than two hours elapsed before the police arrived at the scene—more than enough time to drive to Melbourne, unload the drugs and get set up at the girlfriend's place—especially if you were driving a Ferrari.

A *red* Ferrari. That's a highly distinctive getaway car.

'Stan went up there and back in the Ferrari?' he said.

'No. He wasn't that crazy. Stiles drove.'

'Stiles was a part of it?'

'No. I doubt if he had the full story. Stan persuaded him to be the wheelman for some bullshit reason, something wrong with the Ferrari. Stiles got a big shock later. Dunno what Stan told him beforehand, maybe that they were gonna lift some dope. But he remained staunch. I suppose he had to—he was in it up to his eyebrows.'

But Shaun wasn't interested in Rick Stiles. Turner had opened the door for him partway, and now he had to push it all the way.

Staring dead ahead with his hands tightly clasped, he said, 'Who shot Mitch?'

Turner didn't miss a beat. 'A better question: who left his cigarette lighter in the ditched van, with identifiable prints on it? That was very careless. It meant you were busted. And once you were busted, there was every chance you'd give up Alvarez and Corcoran. And if _Alvarez_ was busted, the shit could really fly—especially since it was now a double homicide. Once Alvarez spilled, it was all over, period. Couldn't be allowed to happen. He was too hot. He was overcooked. So, two nights after you went down, Bill waited for Alvarez to come home and shot him in his driveway.'

After a while, seeing it played out various ways in his mind, Shaun said, 'There was no need to do that. Mitch would never have put anyone in.'

'Maybe, maybe not. It was just safer that way. You know how many of those Mafia-style driveway hits are solved? Very fucking few. If hoods want to whack each other, that's fine with the homicide cops. It means fewer scumbags on the streets. Simmonds said he got the idea of the driveway hit from the Colin Winchester case some years ago. You'd be familiar with that.'

'Winchester?' Shaun was looking at Turner in disbelief: he was saying that a serving cop had modelled a hit on the murder of a high-ranking policeman.

'Yeah, Winchester.' The case Turner referred to was a driveway execution of a police commissioner in Canberra, back in the mid-eighties. It was a long-running, controversial and bitterly contested affair in which there was much speculation about Winchester's activities, before the culprit was eventually put away. There was even a TV movie suggesting—wrongly, as it turned out—that Winchester was more involved with the New South Wales Mafia than he had a right to be.

Turner said, 'I remember Bill saying the guy almost got away with it, and would have except that his victim was a top cop.

It's not Sicily, you just can't have people running around shooting police commissioners. But Alvarez was no top cop. He was a rotten apple, and no-one would give a shit if he was put down.'

Shaun said, 'You're dead wrong about Mitch, Turner. He wasn't a rotten apple, and he would *never* have sold us out to go with your outfit. He didn't tell us about it simply because he didn't want to distract us. He probably thought we would have kicked up, maybe even refused to go ahead with it, once we knew you bastards were involved. And he was probably right.'

'Believe that if you wish. I can only tell you what I *know* happened.'

'It's not true. Can't be.' But even as he said it he was recalling those night-time sessions at the White Lion, when the anger became white-hot, and when he couldn't help but feel that Mitch held him responsible for everything . . .

Turner gave him a sad, long face. 'Let me tell you something, McCreadie. Sooner or later, everyone rats. It's only a matter of *when*, of the right circumstances falling into place. In Mitch Alvarez's case, he wanted revenge on Petrakos and the department that fucked him over more than anything. So, he used you two as his foot soldiers. And you were willing troops.'

This was stated with such conviction that Shaun felt foolishly naïve for never even considering the possibility when it was staring him in the face all the time. Nevertheless he said, without real heart, 'I still don't believe you.'

Turner shrugged. 'Please yourself. But you have to ask yourself why I'd bother lying. Just to fuck you up a bit more? I'm afraid I don't care enough, McCreadie. Don't care about much at all now.'

'Tell me what happened to Andy,' he said, hands clasped, staring down at his feet.

'Uh . . . that was the Chinaman, Johnny Wu.'

That made Shaun sit up sharply.

'What in the *fuck* did Johnny Wu have to do with it?'

Turner let out a long sigh. 'Morris Salisbury was shitting bullets because of the homicides. Apparently he thought that if you and Corcoran were allowed to testify, it might come out that other parties were involved, and Salisbury was holding the drugs, which made him vulnerable. He made an independent executive decision. It had nothing to do with Bill or me. We didn't want Corcoran killed—shit, he was the only one left who could lead us to the money. I think Salisbury was also scared of Corcoran running around loose, thought he might figure out what had happened and come after us. He was a wild bastard. So Salisbury got Johnny Wu on the job. I dunno the details because I wasn't involved, but I believe he cut his throat from behind while he was getting into his car.'

Shaun was thinking, *Johnny Wu, Johnny Wu . . . burned up in a car . . .*

Turner said, 'Johnny's days were numbered after that. Bill was savage. He wanted to kill Salisbury, but he cooled on that for practical reasons, and we settled on Johnny instead. It was a way of sending a message to Salisbury that he was not a law unto himself. You can't hire guys to go around killing people. It creates too much fuckin' stress. So one night after we'd been to the pub, we visited Johnny with an armful of cold cans. We were sitting at the dining room table sinking beers, bullshitting and carrying on. I can remember Johnny had this big cannon on the table, a Dirty Harry .44 Magnum Special— little man, big gun syndrome. I guess that was his way of saying he didn't really trust us.

'Suddenly Bill lashed out. It was so fast and unexpected. People think because he's so big he's slow, but he's not, he's *fucking* fast. Shit he moved. I blinked and missed it. Next thing I see he's got his monstrous hand around Johnny's throat and he's lifted him out of his seat . . . it was amazing, he was throttling him in mid-air. Johnny couldn't reach his cannon, so he was out of business. All he could do was thrash around while Bill choked him. Johnny was a martial arts nut, I think he'd seen too many Jackie Chan movies, but he had no hope against Bill. He went a terrible shade of purple, his tongue came out and he made these squawking noises, like a chicken. After what seemed about an hour the thrashing stopped, and he went limp. Bill just lowered him back into his seat again and resumed drinking his beer. That was when we noticed the bad smell. Johnny's sphincter had opened.

'We bundled him into his car and drove out the back of Deer Park somewhere, in a sort of windy wasteland. I drove Johnny's car and Bill followed in his Statesman. We propped Johnny behind the wheel, doused the inside with petrol and threw in a match. *Whoosh-o*. Did she go up in a hurry.' He gave a short, hollow laugh, as if he'd just remembered something funny. 'Dunno if you've ever seen anyone burn up, McCreadie, but this was weird . . . Johnny was enveloped in flames, and then . . . his head and arms started swaying around in slow motion, as if he'd come to and was struggling against the fire. Anyway, that was another underworld job for the homicide boys to ponder. It sure put the wind up Salisbury. He's probably in therapy now from having too many nervous breakdowns. For a big time drug czar he was a real drama queen.'

Shaun sat quietly, watching and listening to the surf. It was late in the day. Light was fading, and a soft breeze had sprung up. Now that most of the holes had been filled, what difference did it make?

'You should've whacked Stan while you were at it,' he said in a dead voice.

'Stan was protected by virtue of his father's connections. That probably would've started a Sydney-style gang war. Christ, enough's enough. We were cops, not criminals. None of this was supposed to go the way it did.'

'You were so damn clever you ran into yourselves coming the other way.'

'That should give you some satisfaction.'

But Shaun was just staring at the surf, not feeling very much of anything.

'On top of which,' Turner said, 'we got nothing out of the whole sorry saga. *Nothing.*'

Shaun looked at him with a question mark written on his face.

'Yeah? Surprised?' He gave that same short, empty laugh. He was good at that. He probably laughed that way when he watched Johnny Wu go up in flames. 'Salisbury tested the gear. Turned out we were the proud owners of twenty kilograms of chalk dust and talcum powder.'

'Bullshit.'

'Nope. Someone got there ahead of us.'

It was news to Shaun. When he hit the nick all he knew from press reports was that a 'large quantity of *cash and drugs*' was stolen during the raid. During and after his murder trial, police investigators unsuccessfully tried to persuade him to show them where he'd hidden the 'cash and drugs', and in the aftermath, during his long incarceration, little more was said about it. The issue simply died away. It was as if the script had been rewritten after the event, wiping out the very existence of any dope. Shaun always assumed that whoever lifted it had got rid of the stuff straightaway, that the cops somehow got wind of this on the criminal grapevine and realised it was pointless pursuing Shaun. In the end they even seemed uncertain whether he'd stolen the cash as well, since only *one* outfit was supposed to be involved. The impression Shaun had was that the cops were every bit as confused as he was. But there was never any mention of the heroin turning out to be chalk dust. It fitted, but then Turner could well be snowing Shaun for reasons of his own.

Turner wiped his brow with his hat and said, 'That little *detail* was never explained, at least to my satisfaction. Never will be now. There are theories: George might've been ripped off by his suppliers at the Pakistan end, but it doesn't seem likely. It's bad for business—trust is a fragile enough commodity in the international drug trade without resorting to rip-offs on that scale. We didn't know if the shipment was being tagged by the Feds or not, we just *said* that to Mitch Alvarez as a deterrent, so he'd leave it alone, but maybe it was after all. I tend to believe that the Feds *were* tagging it, intending to wrap up the whole syndicate later, but then grew nervous about so much shit maybe getting out of their control and finding its way onto the streets, so they played safe and switched it. That was the unofficial version that did the rounds later. Maybe the operation was called off for some other reason, so they cut their losses. And after they found out about the murders, they didn't own up to any involvement in the whole affair—reputations, careers would be shot down. Strange. I never heard of anyone being arrested for possession of chalk dust. Dunno if George knew he'd been dudded, but it could be that he did. There was a small cut in one of the bags, so it's possible he'd tested the stuff himself.'

Shaun waited a moment, then said, 'You can still be arrested for *conspiring* to import or traffic, whether or not you have it in your possession. Doesn't matter if the cops seize the stuff first—it's still hard evidence.'

'True. Maybe they were planning to bust George, but his son got to him first.'

Shaun sat still. He hadn't been truly angry in a long time, if ever, but something—*something*—was on its way, and he wasn't sure if he'd be able to control it.

Turner said, 'All that careful planning and scheming amounted to zero. You can see how certain people might be aggrieved about that. As I told you, I'm past caring, but others are still waiting for the ship to come in.'

Shaun sat silently, trying to assimilate this new information.

'I hope all that made your trip worthwhile, McCreadie.'

Shaun said, 'Know what I think? You're full of *shit*, Turner.'

'Yeah? Tough guy. Listen, McCreadie, you're the one who

came here looking for answers. I gave them to you. Don't blame me if they weren't the ones you wanted. Once you start stirring up a fuckin' snake pit you want to be careful, son, because something might jump up and bite you in the face.'

Blood surged through his veins. Suddenly there was the roar of something other than surf in his ears. 'Go and fuck yourself, you lying bastard. If you weren't already dying—'

'You don't worry me, son, any more than these fuckin' flies do. Your jailhouse crap doesn't cut it. Old and *sick* as I am, I'd take you on and I'd whip you too. Go home and think about it. Face the truth if you have the guts. *You* got Vincent O'Connell killed because of your fuckin' Boy Scout antics, blowing the whistle and tryin' to be the hero when he was in no real danger. *And* you indirectly caused the deaths of Alvarez and Corcoran because you were *dumb enough to get caught.*'

Turner didn't see or even sense the blow when it came crashing into his face, so he was wide open. Shaun's right fist caught him flush on the right eye and the bridge of his nose. There was the *crack* of bone on bone; Turner let out a muffled grunt and disappeared off the end of the bench, sprawling onto a tangle of exposed tree roots. Shaun leapt up and grabbed him by the front of his shirt. He was a dishevelled mess with blood all over his face, and eyes that flickered on and off. Shaun hauled the old man to his knees and shaped to punch him again. Blood streamed from his damaged eye and nose. In disgust he threw Turner onto the sand, face-first, and kicked him in the ribcage. The blow was not hard, since he was only wearing soft loafers, but it was enough to make Turner squeal and start scuttling away sideways like a sand crab. Shaun twisted his head around: it was a mess of blood and caked-on sand. He hit him five or six times with an open hand. Blood shot from Turner's nose. He shook him and flung him down, then grabbed him again and slapped him around some more. Turner was howling and Shaun's right hand was awash with blood from the split eye and bloody nose. He wanted to shake him until he came apart and died right there on the beach. In the end he satisfied his rage by hitting him one more time, a short right fist in the mouth, then dropped him. Turner groaned and rolled around on the sand, wanting to hold his face with his trembling hands but not able to because of the pain. Shaun marched away without saying a word, heart pounding like a hammer in his chest. Turner's cries and groans receded into the background and were soon lost in the boom of surf.

Shaun noticed all the blood on his arm and hand, and waded into the sea to wash it off. There was no-one on this part of the beach. As he came out of the water he looked back and saw that Turner had dragged himself up to his knees. He seemed to be retching or vomiting. Shaun felt much better for the next five minutes as he made his way back to the motel room. His fist was starting to throb. It was still clenched, and he could not unclench it. He went into his room in a daze and sat on the bed. His chest was still hammering hard. He sat there and waited for it to die down.

19

It had always been Oliver McEncroe's practice to counsel a client with the blunt, unpleasant reality of his prospects rather than give false hope in the face of facts that indicated the opposite. It made sense: no-one thanked a lawyer for losing a case that they were supposed to win. 'It doesn't look too good for us, I'm afraid,' he would honestly say. Oliver made a point of using the plural *us*, to give a false sense of solidarity: nothing bad awaited Oliver, regardless of the verdict. Not that he drew satisfaction from watching his client sink into depression as Oliver's words proved to be correct, but what was the use of bullshitting? If events turned out better than he expected, it was a bonus, and then they *did* thank him for overcoming the odds.

So it was with Raydon as the two old friends sat drinking coffee in a small Italian cafe not far from Owen Dixon Chambers. Despite appearances it gave Oliver no joy to tell Raydon that his Sydney excursion had not been successful. Quite the contrary: his position was even more dire and difficult than it had been. It wasn't Oliver's fault, but that was no consolation.

Raydon's colourless face stared down into his coffee cup. From his pasty complexion Oliver judged he hadn't slept properly in a long time, since this thing dropped in his lap.

'A quarter of a million dollars,' he said in a low monotone. 'And wanted the fifty *on account*? What new *shit* is this?'

'It was a try-on,' Oliver said. 'But I was a tad too quick for them. Your money is safe for the moment. However, I'm afraid the mention of your illustrious name has attracted the extra premium. Serves you right for being so famous.'

'A quarter of a million,' Raydon said again. A waitperson approached with the coffee percolator and, at Oliver's bidding, refilled their cups. When he'd withdrawn Raydon added, 'Why not half a million—or a million? Make it a nice, round figure.'

Oliver remained silent. He knew what Raydon was thinking: that if he coughed up the quarter mill, these people would be back like bears to the honey pot for more. It was a cardinal rule never to pay blackmailers for that reason, but the rule had obviously been formulated by people who themselves had never been blackmailed. It was an ugly business. Every way he looked at it Oliver saw no solution. It was all very well for him to advise Raydon not to pay and to tough it out, call their bluff, but it wasn't Oliver's life and career in the balance.

'It's looking a shade grim,' Oliver said. 'The fact that they've got Henry Agar on board is worrying. He's a heavyweight up there and it means they're in deadly earnest. He *kills* people, Steer.'

'Agar is a lifelong criminal,' Raydon said. 'He should be in *jail*.'

'If that were the only criterion, every other man in that city would be doing time,' Oliver said. 'Including the cop, Patchouli, who was the go-between.'

Raydon didn't smile at the attempt to lighten his mood. He was way beyond consoling at present. In his mind he was watching himself twist in the wind.

'Who's this Pritchett bastard?' he said.

'Some thug—Mascall's pimp, no doubt. Clearly he's worked out he's hit the jackpot and called in Agar to manage the deal, and Agar has upped the ante to cover his share. They probably plan on splitting the quarter mill fifty-fifty.'

'Not to mention the cops: whatsisname, Patchouli, and whoever else is on the fucking payroll. God, McEncroe, I may as well slit my own throat at this rate.'

'Rather messy, Steer. I'm sure there are more civilised means at your disposal.'

'I don't care. And it takes too long to drink oneself to death. Well, come on—what are we going to do?'

Oliver pursed his mouth. He had refrained from telling Raydon that he'd sooled Agar and Pritchett onto Shaun McCreadie for fear it might anger him, but at least this tactic had given them some breathing space. He decided to keep Raydon in the dark. If it turned out well for them, then Raydon would thank him; if not, if something bad happened, Oliver could easily deny all knowledge.

'Do nothing for the time being,' he said. 'The ball's with them at present.'

'I would have thought the ball's very much with us right now,' Raydon said.

Oliver chastised himself for the slip. 'Well, I mean, I indicated that we were not prepared to go to a quarter mill. Leave it where it is for a few days, anyhow. Give them time to rethink the situation. Maybe they'll see they're aiming too high.'

'A few days,' Raydon said gloomily. 'Christ, man—I could be locked up by then. I could be a dead man.'

'When is the list of new judges being announced?' Oliver said. 'Any word?'

'I have it on good authority that the names will be published very *soon*,' Raydon said. 'Imagine the full horror, McEncroe, of being promoted to the bench one day, then thrown in the caboose the next.'

'That would indeed be horrendous,' Oliver said with an

inward shudder. *Now that would be something to slit your throat about.* 'Chin up, old fellow. We're not done yet.'

After midnight, and Stan was sitting in his spare bedroom with a big glass of ouzo and ice. On his lap was a photograph album. Sometimes, usually at a late hour when he was half-stung and overcome with nostalgia, he would come in here and time-travel with the albums and scrapbooks. He had a shelf full of them, going back to when he was born and even before that. He was bare-chested, and as he turned the pages and lovingly touched the aged snaps with his fingertips, a tear might form in his right eye and burst onto his cheek. He gazed at an ancient shot of his mother sitting astride a bicycle on a dusty road, with some trees in the background. She was so pretty in a floral summer dress, and *so* young. Stan didn't know for sure, but he guessed she was probably about nineteen or twenty. Big smile on her face—she didn't have a worry in the world.

Standing alongside with his arm around her waist and a battered straw hat on his head was the empty space where his old man used to be. He had been surgically removed with a razor blade.

Stan pushed his fingers through his copious chest-hair as he gazed at the shot of his mother. Her name was Iris, Iris Barrow.

He turned the page. Here was a picture of Iris watering the back lawn at her home, somewhere in the outer suburbs. There was a black cat nuzzling at her legs, its tail upraised. Iris was smiling at the camera with a splash of bright sunlight across her face. She had on an old-fashioned one-piece bathing suit, and you could see that she had lovely, shapely legs. Stan traced his fingers over the picture, very delicately, as if not wishing to disturb her.

Next to it was a dinner-table shot of the Barrow family. There was an older sister, now deceased, and a younger brother. Stan had no idea what had become of him. He was Uncle Ray in Stan's childhood memory. Uncle Ray used to visit them in his utility, which was always full of tools and building materials. He was a fun-loving, irresponsible sort of guy who was never married in the time Stan knew him. Stan and George junior loved Ray because he brought candy and comics, and because he took them for rides in the utility, always driving too fast and swerving around corners like a daredevil. Stan was never scared, though. Uncle Ray was one of those people who made you feel you were in safe hands no matter what he did. He was a good driver, but Iris used to say he was a mad lair. Once, high up on scaffolding, he pretended he was about to fall just to scare the pants off Iris, who had brought his lunch for him. Stan couldn't remember the last time he saw Ray. He stopped coming after Iris's death and dropped out of Stan's life forever.

Stan took a big pull on the ouzo. He had tears spilling down his face now. He turned the page and pored over some more pictures from about the same era. One of his all-time favourites was a candid shot of Iris sitting on some grass in a park or a yard, leaning on one arm with the other one curled around her legs. Her head was turned slightly, so that she was looking over her bare shoulder, an expression of mock surprise on her face. She had on a white cotton dress and a bonnet with a feather in it that made her look like a movie star. The way she always gazed so knowingly at the camera with wide eyes and a little ghostly smile on one side of her lips never failed to stab Stan in the heart. In this particular shot there was an empty space next to her where the old man had been.

There was a shot of Stan and his brother running in a race at a picnic. Stan remembered that occasion. All the adults finished up drunk, and there was a lot of fighting and screaming by the end of the day.

Over the page, there was a big colour photo of the family at Christmas. Everyone was sitting in front of the tree surrounded by gifts. The tree was fabulously decorated and lit up. Again the old man had been cut out.

Next, a studio head-and-shoulder shot of Iris, looking wistfully off to the side. It was in sepia tones, and the handwriting on the back said it was taken in 1958. Since she was born in 1941 that meant she was 17 at the time. She had the beauty and softness of an angel. In 1960 she married the old man, and she was rarely happy after that.

Stan drank some more ouzo. He was sobbing quietly. With the album on his lap he stared at the wall and thought about Iris. Even now he could see her oval-shaped face, the luscious red lips and manicured fingernails. She was never less than perfect in her personal appearance. Stan remembered an occasion as a toddler seeing her sitting in front of a mirror in her petticoat and high heels, dabbing at her throat with a powder puff. There was a cigarette burning in an ashtray on the dresser, with bright red lipstick on the filter. She didn't see Stan at first. He watched silently as she sprayed on some perfume and brushed her shiny brown hair. Occasionally she paused to draw on the cigarette before replacing it in the ashtray. All her actions—even something as simple as that— were done with style and elegance. When she noticed him in the doorway she smiled in the mirror and offered him the silver brush. Later on he and his brother used to squabble about who would brush their mother's hair while they watched TV at night.

Stan wondered then, as he did now, how someone that gorgeous got mixed up with his pig of a father. He wasn't even rich then—just a car salesman who succeeded in selling himself to a young woman who was way above him in every respect.

'Whatcha doing, Wolfman?' came Suzen's dreamy voice from the bedroom doorway. She had been asleep, substance-affected, with the light on. Suzen had this pathetic need to sleep with the light on. Stan usually switched it off after a while, but being absorbed in his photographs he hadn't yet. Now she was awake.

'Nothing,' Stan said. His glass was empty; he went to the kitchen for a refill.

'I was dreaming,' she said. 'Wasn't very nice . . . wild animal trying to eat me. I was crawling away. Ugh.' She shuddered and hugged herself.

Stan looked at her. She was wearing nothing except her array of strange tattoos and the usual bits of silver metal attached to various parts of her anatomy. In fact she seemed to have even more now. Her hair was a total bird's nest. Suzen's body was so wasted, the tits so scrawny—there was nothing womanly or attractive about her. Even now, at her age, there were spots on her face, from lack of proper nourishment no doubt. She would have to lift her game if she wanted to work in the brothel, even as a Madam Lash dominatrix in leather and chains. Men wanted flesh on a woman's bones, not waif-like creatures with acne. However, when she was done up and in full flight there was a certain animalistic drawing power there, no doubt about it. Despite her physical shortcomings she had a primeval quality that stirred his loins when little else could. Whatever the reason, Stan felt an affinity with her. He didn't really have a handle on it, except that she was similar to him in some ways. And she obviously cared for him.

Walking past her he gave her a slap on the belly. 'Wouldn't get much of a feed, would it?'

Suzen sighed and followed him into the spare room.

'Lookin' at your pictures again,' she said as Stan resumed his seat and reopened the album.

'I was, yeah,' he said. He took a decent pull on the ouzo and set it down. Suddenly he seemed to make a decision. He snapped the album shut and stared at the wall as if he'd spotted a bug on it. Then he opened a drawer and withdrew something—a *gun* of some sort.

'What are you doin' now?' Suzen said.

'Questions, questions, *questions*,' Stan said. 'Go back to bed, Suzen.'

He pushed the gun down the front of his jeans. She followed him out to the lounge room, where he picked up his shirt from the couch and threw it on. As he buttoned it up he said, 'Just goin' to see a friend, that's all.'

'Yeah?' she said. 'With that?'

'Go back to *bed*,' he said again. 'Or something.' He swept up his car keys and was out the door before she could get another word out.

Stan knew Rick would be up even before he saw the light on in the front room. That guy never slept. He always said he didn't need to—never felt tired enough. He'd doze for an hour in the lounge chair watching TV, and that was it. Hardly ever hit the bed. Rick drove a taxi for a living, and sometimes after he'd finished a day shift, he'd go home for an early dinner and then turn around and drive all night too. That's when he wasn't selling dope.

Stan rapped on the door. He heard some shuffling as someone got up out of a chair, then Rick's voice: 'Who is it?'

'Just me, mate,' Stan said.

The door opened. 'Bit late for a social visit, isn't it?' Rick said.

'Sorry, I didn't realise . . . Well, you gonna invite me in or what?' Stan said sheepishly.

Rick hesitated, then went back inside, leaving the door ajar. Stan made a show of wiping his shoes and followed him. His shirt was hanging outside his jeans, so the gun was out of sight. Rick sat in his flea-bitten lounge chair. As usual there was a bottle of Captain Morgan rum and a pack of Stuyvos on the coffee table in front of him, along with an overflowing ashtray, ash all over the place.

'Siddown, mate,' Rick said. 'Want some of this?'

Stan sat on the couch. 'Got any ouzo? I've been on the ouzo.'

'Hate that stuff,' Rick said. 'Gives you brain damage. Destroys your . . . watchamacallit? *Synapses.*'

'Shit, if that's true I'm in trouble. I've been drinkin' it forever and a day. My brain's down the drain.'

Rick grinned at him. 'You said it, not me.'

'I'll have the rum then. That can't hurt me, can it?'

'No way,' Rick said. He went to the kitchenette, rooting around for a clean glass.

Stan looked at the TV. The grizzled face of Humphrey Bogart was on the screen—another old movie. Rick rented them by the dozen. They were scattered all over the floor.

'What's this?' he said.

'*The Treasure of the Sierra Madre,*' Rick said. He poured some rum and handed it to Stan.

'Cheers.' Stan sipped.

'Cheers,' Rick said, but didn't touch his drink. Instead he lit up a cigarette and tossed the dead match in the general vicinity of the ashtray.

'I liked that Schwarzenegger movie, *Collateral Damage*. Did you see it?' Stan said.

'No, mate. I'm not a big Schwarzenegger fan.'

'Fantastic show, mate. Big Arnie shoves it up to those fuckin' terrorists nine ways from Sunday. *Hasta la vista*, baby.'

'I'll bet,' Rick said.

Silence.

'Ever see *Predator*?' Stan said.

'Nope.'

'That is an absolute *classic*. Best movie ever. Fuckin' jungle turns into a monster.'

Rick looked at him. Jungle turns into a monster. What was he on about?

Stan remembered Suzen's nightmare: Wild animal trying to eat me.

'You can't see it, though. It's just . . . *there*. Invisible.'

'Right,' Rick said. He drained his glass and tipped some more rum in.

They watched the TV for a while. Humphrey Bogart was having a fierce argument with an old bastard. They were in the wilderness somewhere, very rugged terrain.

'Rick,' Stan said. 'I'm sorry about the other night.'

Rick dragged on his cigarette and blew out a stream of smoke. 'Forget it,' he said, watching TV.

'I lost it a bit. Didn't mean any of that shit.'

'I know,' Rick said.

'I got picked up by the cops. Spent the night in the fuckin' cooler. Gave me somethin' for me corner.'

'No bullshit,' Rick said. Not much sympathy there.

Stan waited a bit, watching the screen, then said, 'You're my replacement brother, you know that.'

'Yeah.' *Here we go.*

'And I love you like a rock.'

Rick didn't respond.

'Like a *rock*, mate.' He was sitting up, trying to get Rick's attention.

'I love you too, Stan,' he said, turning from the TV.

Stan reached over and put his arm around Rick's shoulder. 'I'd never do anything to hurt those little girls—Christ, I'm their *godfather*.'

It was the first Rick had heard that Stan was the girls' godfather, but he let it pass. This guy had more fantasies than the brothers Grimm.

Stan pulled him closer, so that their foreheads were touching. 'We're family, you and me. We're . . . *blood*.' Now he was massaging the back of Rick's neck, a little too roughly for Rick's liking. 'Right?'

'Yeah,' Rick said. Stan's dark eyes were right in his face. There was no way he could avoid staring directly into them. Close-up, they didn't look like Stan's eyes at all: they were black, shining beads of alarming intensity.

'We have a responsibility to watch out for each other,' Stan whispered.

Rick nodded. His eyes dropped: Stan's shirt had come open a bit, revealing the sawn-off stock of the shotgun in his jeans. Straightaway Rick's alarm system flashed on high alert. He wasn't sure if Stan had exposed the gun deliberately or not.

He decided to play it cool, no matter what. His number one priority now was to somehow get Stan out of the house without stirring him up.

'Haven't we?' Stan said.

'Sure,' Rick said. Stan could sense him wanting to pull away from his firm grip.

'I was thinking about what you said,' Stan said. 'About . . . putting it all behind us.'

'That's right,' Rick said, squirming a bit but trying not to resist too openly. Didn't worry Stan: he merely tightened the screws.

'The thing is, I *want* to put it behind me, I really do. But that guy—McCreadie—stands in the road. While he lives, I can't go on. *I can't go on.*'

Rick tried to twist free, but Stan wasn't having any of it.

'My brother, we have to take him down. After what he did . . .'

'What?' Rick said. '*What* did he do?'

'It's him or me. Only one of us can walk away from this.'

Jesus Christ, Rick thought—*it's* High Noon.

Stan turned to the TV screen. Bogart was in a barroom fistfight now.

'You know so much about movies, don't you, buddy?'

Still in Stan's tight grip, Rick was also watching the screen, the whole side of his face hard against Stan's. Stan's heavy beard scraped him like a sheet of coarse sandpaper. Rick could smell the ouzo and, beneath that, some pungent animal odour that came from the very essence of Stan.

'I've seen a few,' he said.

'Remember that day,' Stan said. 'You told the cops we spent the afternoon watching videos. What were they again?'

Rick said, 'It was a Paul Newman day: *Somebody Up There Likes Me*, *The Left-Handed Gun*, and *The Hustler*.'

'That's right. You had to tell me what they were all about in case the cops quizzed me about 'em. Which they did, of course.'

'Yeah.'

'And the order we watched them in.'

'Right.'

'Not that it *proved* anything, but if I *didn't* know jack about those movies I was supposed to have watched, we would've had problems, wouldn't we?'

'Yeah.'

'You were so smart, buddy, and so solid. I was proud of you that day. You came up aces. And that cute Pommie girlfriend you had then—what was her name?'

'Ah—Linda.'

'Yeah, Linda. She was staunch too. What happened to her?'

'She went back to England.'

'That's right, she did.'

Without warning Stan turned Rick's face towards him and kissed him flush on the lips. Rick pulled away violently. 'Christ, Stan—turn it *up*.'

Stan laughed—he seemed to have embarrassed himself. 'It's all right, mate. I haven't turned queer or anything. Sorry.'

'*Shit*.' Rick swallowed some rum. Then he lit up another cigarette. He wished with all his heart and soul that Stan would leave, but knew he wouldn't. Stan Petrakos was one of these people who, whenever they do wrong, just say 'sorry', as if that fixed everything. Stan said 'sorry' all his life, but never changed. He was now lounging back in the couch, the shotgun stock clearly visible through his partly open shirt.

'I'm livin' in a world of hurt, Rick,' he said. 'You can see that.'

Rick stared at the screen, trying to appear unruffled. But his mind was working overtime.

'I want you to drive, that's all. You're so good at that. We stop outside his place, wait for him to show, I blow him off, and that's it—we're away.'

Rick blew out smoke.

'He owes me too. Big time. He robbed me of everything—my *inheritance*.'

Without facing him Rick said, 'He went to jail, Stan. He didn't have *jack*.'

'What, you reckon he didn't stash it somewhere for later?'

'Yeah, sure.'

'Well, if I can't have it, neither can he.' He sat up again. 'That guy killed my people. He spilled my blood. He destroyed my . . . my *birthright*.'

Rick looked at him. '*What?*'

'He tore my world apart.'

Rick watched him: there were tears filling Stan's eyes.

'Hang on, Stan,' he said. 'We both know *you* did it—not *him*.'

Stan wiped his arm across his face and gave Rick a cunning, narrow-eyed stare. 'But how much do we *really* know, mate?'

Rick was at a loss. 'Listen to me: I'm not going to drive. I'm not going to do anything. I want you to go, Stan. Pack it in. Come on.'

Stan slid the shotgun out of his jeans and cradled it across his thighs. 'I didn't do anything, did I? It was done when I got there.'

'Have it your way, brother. Come on, up. Go home, take two Valium and sleep.' He lifted Stan by the arm, and to his surprise Stan didn't fight him. He seemed to be in a bit of a daze. There was a slightly puzzled expression on his face, as if he'd become confused, and suspicious. Rick led him to the door and opened it. The gun was in Stan's hand, hanging loosely by his side. He didn't seem particularly aware of it, or anything.

'Jungle turns into a monster,' he said in a monotone.

Rick took him outside, right to the Ferrari. Stan looked up at the sky. 'Stars are shining,' he said in the same dead-sounding tone.

'Off you go, mate,' Rick said. 'Drive carefully, and watch out for cops. See you when.'

Obediently Stan de-alarmed the car and climbed aboard. He was still holding the gun when Rick shut the door. As he crossed in front of the car he saw that Stan was staring straight ahead through the windshield. Rick gave him a wave and hurried on in.

Stan sat in the car five, ten minutes. There was a buzzing sound in his brain. Through a hazy glow he watched himself opening the workshop door. He had on short pants and a pair of sandals. The buzz saw was screeching as if it was cutting through something. What was George doing? In he went.

There was George: bent over the spinning circular blade, throat torn away, mouth agape, his horribly contorted face frozen in a moment of unspeakable agony, blood and gouts of flesh flying through the air. His eyes had gone so far up into his head that only the whites were visible . . .

It was done before I got there.

Stan fired up the engine and let it idle for a minute. 'Jungle turns into a monster,' he said to himself. The gun was on his lap. He cruised down the street and turned left. Then he took two more lefts, until he was back in front of Rick's house. He waited, barely breathing, before driving on and repeating the cycle. Three times he cruised around the block. On the fourth occasion he put his foot on the brake and touched the accelerator: the engine gave a low growl, like a snarling beast straining against a short leash. He lowered the passenger-side window, leaned across, drew back both hammers, took aim and blasted both barrels into Rick's front window: *BOOM! BOOM!* The car was filled with an ear-splitting double-roar that reverberated around the cabin as the windows exploded amid flying shards of masonry and timber—it was as if two bombs had been thrown into the house.

'*HOW DO YOU FUCKIN' LIKE THAT YA CUNT!*' he yelled.

With his left foot on the brake pedal he slammed his right all the way down on the gas. The rear Michelins spun and burned, belching dense palls of blue smoke until the car could barely be seen through it. When he suddenly released the brake they gripped, and the shrieking Ferrari catapulted down the road with its rear end waltzing from side to side, as if it were sliding on ice. Neighbours later reported they could hear the vehicle screaming long after it was off and gone. Even when they ventured out into the street amid the drifts of blue haze, the high-pitched roar of its engine was crystal-clear in the still night air, along with the intermittent squeal of rubber whenever the driver changed gears or turned a corner—at least another suburb away.

20

The morning after his return from the coast, Shaun received a phone call from Wes Ford. He was not at his sharpest. When he'd arrived back at 8 pm, Jo had a 'little surprise': a five-star candle-lit 'tasting menu' dinner party for two with all the trimmings, served on the upstairs polished mahogany dining table that seated twelve. An opened bottle of Chablis Vaillon sat in an ice-filled silver bucket, and a 1981 Chateau d'Yquem with a worm-eaten label had been poured into a cut-crystal decanter; on the rosewood buffet a pair of red wines of similar aged appearance stood in reserve, both corks drawn and pushed back in. The food was served on large, mirror-bright, silver-domed tureens and platters: sweetbreads Josephine (invented for his true love by Napoleon, or so she said), a specialty from Boston called lobster Savannah, glazed Cornish game hens, roasted rare venison in a truffle sauce, Frenched veal shanks, breaded racks of lamb accompanied by a mix of exotic mushrooms, creamed spinach, pommes dauphine, plump white spears of asparagus . . .

And so it went on. Various cheeses, fruits and desserts followed, but by that time Shaun had run out of steam and was sticking with the wine. There was no problem putting that away. But it would take at least three days of dedicated gluttony for two people to consume such a spread. At least she had the good grace to admit she'd ordered it all in from a high-end restaurant in Crown Casino: a sample from every dish on its menu. It was sumptuous, decadent and way over the top. What followed in the bedroom was even more so.

During dinner he gave her a rundown of what had happened in Nambucca Heads after they had spoken on the phone. Although he remembered everything Turner had told him, he spared Jo the less important details, purely in the interests of simplicity. More calculatingly, however, he also omitted to mention the beating he'd dished out to Turner on the beach. This careful editing of the facts caused him twinges of concern, since he had no wish to be dishonest in his relationship with Jo. Even as he was working up to that point in the story he couldn't decide whether to leave it in or not. Although he could justify the beating in his own mind, and had little doubt she would see it the same way, he found it a doubtful quantity nonetheless. Turner had given him the full story—what need was there for violence? What would she think of him for beating up on an old, dying man, regardless of what he'd done to deserve it another lifetime ago? It was too hard, so with serious reservations he left it out. It might have been a small thing, but it niggled at him.

In between times he had thought about Turner's claim that Mitch Alvarez had switched sides. Shaun's first instinct was that it couldn't be true, but on reflection—distasteful as he found it—the scenario Turner had described was an entirely plausible one. It explained how Mitch got the blueprints, and two or three other things: one, the guns, two, the van, and three, why he was so adamant about leaving the drugs, even to the point where he was prepared to shoot Andy. In any case, why would Turner lie to him?

Everyone, even usually honest citizens, sometimes lied to protect their interests, but Leon Turner was on the way out— he had nothing left to protect. And it had been Turner's initiative to come to the Blue Dolphin after giving him nothing but abuse at his house. Obviously he had thought about it and decided this was his last chance to clear the decks. There was simply nothing in it for him to lie, except maybe to shove it up Shaun. But that didn't appear to be his motive. His time had come to open up.

Shaun still didn't see Mitch selling them out. His own spin on it—that Mitch was using them as a form of revenge, and had no intention of going through with any deal they thought he had made—still seemed the most likely explanation. It had come to him immediately on hearing Turner's story, as if he were still privy to Mitch's plans—his *real* plans. He knew how Mitch ticked—he would've jumped at the chance to take these bastards down. He was definitely no turncoat. There wasn't a treacherous bone in him. Turner was right—they were a tight crew. The reason Mitch didn't inform them of Turner's and Simmonds' involvement was obvious—he had to keep a lid on it till it was all over. Shaun remembered the three of them standing in the rain at Buzzards Hut with their hands joined. At that moment they were one person, not three. Turner wasn't there, he wouldn't know. He didn't look in Mitch's eyes and see what Shaun saw: total trust. At that moment he would've put his life in Mitch's hands, and if he were alive he still would today.

But what Wes Ford had to report swept all such thoughts from his mind.

'Had a meeting with Simmonds yesterday,' Wes said. 'Bottom line: he wants me to *abduct* Joanna Steer.'

'You're shitting me,' Shaun said.

'No sir. I had a feeling from his voice on the phone that something was on. Told me to meet him at the Unicorn in North Melbourne. It's one of Simmonds' low dives. Publican's an ex-cop. When I arrived there was a school of regular geezers in the public bar, but no sign of Simmonds. Then I saw him coming down the stairs with the publican. They were very buddy-buddy—beers were on the house, except when it was my shout. Anyhow, I was there five minutes and he drags me out the grungy back bar, which was empty. "Snatch the woman", he says to me. Just like that. I said, "What?" I'm not kidding, brother—he was sober and dead serious.'

Shaun's mind was racing. 'How are you supposed to do it?'

'Uh—he gave me a gun.'

'Christ.'

'It's only a replica,' Wes said. 'Browning nine-millimetre semi-automatic pistol. Looks like the real thing to me—not that I know shit about guns, except from TV cop shows. It's a big, mean sucker. When he reached into his jacket and produced it I filled my diapers big time. Thought he was gonna top me right there in the pub.'

'Okay, okay, so you've got a pretend pistol. What's his plan?'

At that moment Jo came in the front door—she'd been down at the corner shop for the newspaper. Shaun looked at her, and straightaway he could tell she realised something serious was going down. She stopped dead, watching him, and he extended a hand to draw her closer so she could hear Wes's voice.

'I'm supposed to wait outside the house until you're not there,' Wes was saying. 'Then I knock on the door, pacify her with a clip on the chin and put her in the trunk of the car.'

Jo's eyes were wide as she gripped Shaun's arm.

'Listen, Wes,' Shaun said. 'I think you'd better get yourself over here ASAP.'

'Fine,' Wes said. 'I'm on the way. Be there in fifteen.'

Inside an hour they were at the kitchen table with a heady mix of adrenaline and fresh coffee in the air. The seating arrangement was the same as the first time: Wes on one side of the table, Shaun and Jo facing him, next to each other. One difference: she wasn't all over him this time.

In the middle of the table was the replica Browning. Shaun picked it up, hefted it. It was a lot lighter than the real thing, and the parts that were supposed to move did not, but it would pass at a glance. No-one was going to argue if it was shoved in her face. He put it down and fired up a Lucky. Jo already had one going.

'Fill us in, Wes,' he said. 'Don't leave anything out.'

Wes was leaning back in his chair, hands clasped across his lap. His eyes repeatedly moved from one to the other as he spoke. 'We left the Unicorn in his car,' he said. 'I didn't know where we were going. When I asked, he told me to shut up. That's the nature of our relationship. I was getting scared again, because it was night and he was heading into a dodgy area— off Lorimer Street, in West Melbourne, past the car auction joints. It's all factories and scrapyards. He turned into this property . . . there was an iron gate with a couple of big padlocks on it. He opened it and we went in.'

'Hang on,' Shaun said. 'How'd he open it?'

'He used keys. I watched him in the headlights.'

'Okay. Go on.'

'It was a container depot—hundreds of them stacked on top of each other. The place was overrun with crap and weeds. It was deserted, derelict, just all these decommissioned containers everywhere. Anyway he drove in and pulled up. Then we got out of the car and I followed him. He had a powerful flashlight, one of those police jobs. He showed me this particular container, made me memorise its number: APG 11988. That's the one I'm supposed to put you in, Jo. Bound and blindfolded.'

Jo shrank back a little. 'I am definitely *not* going in that container.'

'Of course you're not,' Shaun said, as if such a suggestion was not even on the table. To Wes: 'What happens then? Once you've put her in it.'

'I call Fat Man and disappear. He then swings by and checks that she's really there. I guess he doesn't trust me. Then he . . . well, he didn't say in so many words, but once he has Jo in a box he's in a strong position to deal with you, right? To get whatever he wants.'

'Right,' Shaun said. 'Go back—he said that he'd swing by and check she was in it?'

'Sure did.'

'Excuse me—he wants to hold me as a *hostage*?' Jo said.

'That seems to be the plan,' Wes said.

They all thought about it, then Jo gave a contemptuous snort and said, 'Well, fuck his filthy pig's hide. What a total *scumbag*. Who the fuck does he think—'

Cutting her off, Shaun said, 'You deliver her to the container alone, right?'

'Right.'

'There's no-one else involved, just you and Simmonds?'

'As far as I'm aware.'

'How do you get into the yard? Did he give you any keys?'

Wes reached into his pants pocket, produced two silver Lockwood keys and held them up for all to see.

'They'll be the spares,' Shaun said. 'Assuming he's cut off the original padlocks and replaced them with his own, which is probably the case—it's standard practice for an old-fashioned factory B and E. Those keys look brand new.'

'They are,' Wes said.

'If it's a derelict container depot, he can probably count on no-one coming around to discover the locks've been replaced for a while. Even if they do, and change 'em again, it's no problem. He only has to repeat the procedure. It wouldn't necessarily arouse any suspicion. When their keys didn't work they'd just think the locks were fucked and get new ones. Did you happen to notice an office, or shed, where an attendant might hang out during the day?'

'No,' Wes said. 'No buildings, and no dogs either. Just rusted out old containers. It's a dump.'

It sounded to Shaun as if Simmonds knew the premises pretty well. Perhaps he'd used it before.

'What else, Wes?'

Wes produced a bundle of notes from his shirt pocket, all pristine hundreds. He spread them out on the table alongside the replica Browning, like a hand of cards. There were ten of them.

'Compared to the pittance he usually slings me, this is serious money,' he said. 'And I'm supposed to cop the same again . . . on delivery.'

They all stared at the currency, and judging from Jo's expression it might have been laced with rat poison.

'That's what I'm worth?' she said. 'Two lousy grand? That cheap son of—'

Shaun cut in and said, 'When does he want it done?'

'Soon. Tonight. Provided you're not around.'

They all dropped into silence for a while. Shaun was drumming on the table with his fingers. Jo lit up another cigarette and angrily blew some smoke at the ceiling fan.

'Christ,' she said. 'Two thousand. I don't believe it.'

Shaun said, 'What else can you tell us, Wes? Come on, anything at all that might help.'

Wes sat up and shrugged. 'Well, not much . . . only, when he came down the stairs with the publican, it looked to me as if he'd just put something in his inside pocket. Maybe it was the gun.'

'Maybe it was.'

'That's about it. He drove me back to the Unicorn, paid me off in his car outside the pub and told me to get going and get on it. His parting words were that if I breathed one word about this to anyone, he'd wring my neck like a rabbit's.'

Shaun thought, he'll do that anyway. Has to. Stakes are too high to leave loose ends . . .

'I'll tell you another thing,' Jo said. She was mightily pissed off. 'There's no *way* I'm going in the trunk of anyone's car.'

'You don't have to, baby,' Shaun said.

Slightly—grudgingly—mollified, she studied his expression: a faintly amused and self-satisfied one she recognised in herself. Clearly he had a plan. She wondered what it was.

At around 11 pm Shaun swung Raydon's Land Rover right off Lorimer Street, down a darkened area that was almost devoid of street lighting. Simmonds was smart, no question. It was an industrial wasteland: no-one would ever notice whatever he was up to here. In front of him Wes Ford's brake lights came on as they approached a property with a high cyclone wire fence. Shaun drove by, pulled into a driveway, reversed and parked the vehicle some distance along the street. Wes was already busy opening the locks with the aid of his headlights, as Simmonds had done. When he had them opened he pushed the gates inward, climbed back into the Commodore and drove in. After pulling on a pair of woollen gloves Shaun locked and alarmed the Rover and slipped into the yard. Even though there was no-one around, he couldn't help but feel Simmonds' eyes on him from somewhere unseen. The big man was a survivor over a long period. In that time very few people ever got the better of him.

Wes locked the gates again. They both got aboard the Commodore and travelled deeper into the property, among the hulks of disused containers. When he stopped, Shaun could just see the number on the side of the box in front of them: APG 11988. Out they got, with the car lights aimed at the rear end of the container.

There were four vertical bolts, two for each door. They released the right-side pair, allowing them to open the right door. There was easily enough room for a man to enter. They stood there for a second and Shaun said, 'Okay, as soon as you hit the road get on the phone and tell him the job's done.'

'Right,' Wes said. 'Sure you'll be okay?' He was looking dubiously into the open mouth of the box. It was not inviting.

'Fucking hope so, man. I've got a phone, but I dunno if

I'll be able to use it in there. Don't forget, if I don't call you in the meantime, come back and spring me by ten in the morning. If Simmonds doesn't show for some reason I don't wanna stay in this fuckin' coffin any longer than I have to.'

'Gotcha,' Wes said. 'Anything else you need?'

Shaun had a large bottle of water in one hand and a flashlight in the other. 'No. I'll be all right. Where're you going now?'

Wes shrugged. 'Home, I guess. Unless Fat Man has other plans for me.'

'Okay. Well . . . stay tuned.'

Shaun entered the black hole of the container. Wes then shut the door and slid the two bolts home to lock him in. He stood there a second, picturing Shaun inside the container. Wes would never have done that: one thing he couldn't stand was being trapped in a confined space. It was the main reason he dreaded going to prison. How this guy did it for eleven years and came out in one piece he would never understand. He gave the container a couple of bangs on the door and left.

Inside, it was pitch black. Shaun selected a spot near the opening and sat down against a wall. The air was musty and quite stifling. There were loose fragments of rust on the floor. He switched on the flashlight and checked the time: 11.20. He turned it off again, conscious of saving the batteries, and stood it upright next to him. Wherever you were, in whatever situation, you made your camp to suit yourself as best you could. He removed the gloves, unscrewed the water bottle and took a decent mouthful. He was slightly dehydrated from the wine the previous night, so it was essential to drink plenty of water. His thoughts turned to the scores of people who died crammed in a container after travelling halfway across the world in a people-smuggling racket. They died from suffocation and dehydration, and from his current perspective it wasn't hard to see how that could happen.

He leaned his head back against the wall. He was in a void

of perfect silence. All he could hear was his own breathing, and then, the ticking of his watch. He withdrew his cigarettes from the side pocket of the bomber jacket he was wearing and put one in his mouth without lighting it. It was airless enough in the box without advancing the process. In a while he began wondering how long the air would last, how long he had before suffocation began. It would be a slow, insidious process, and through it he would become weaker and weaker, until he passed out. By then it would be too late.

'So, here we are,' he said aloud. He gave an ironic little laugh. 'Out of one bin, into the other. *Woo-woo.*'

He checked his watch at 11.50, then again at 12.20. Time was passing with incredible slowness. He got up and stretched his legs. Wouldn't help if he had stiff joints when the time came—if it came. After a while he sat down again in the same spot.

'Come on, you fat fucker,' he said. 'I haven't got all fucking night.'

He had another swig of water, and poured some over his face. Even though it was a mild night, he was feeling excessively warm now. He felt as if he were generating his own heat. As he sat there waiting, a range of thoughts found their way into his mind, some bidden, others not. He thought about Jo, about how cool she was and about how she was the other part of him, the half he recognised as soon as he saw her in that bar in Buzzards Hut. She saw it too, even then. Across the bar they saw each other, and both knew that was it, end of story. *Wham!* How easily everything fell into place when you both knew that from the start. The whole process was a lot simpler.

And now here he was, sitting in a box.

Waiting.

In a while he experienced his first shiver of fear. He was locked into this box, and could not get out. He was completely dependent on someone releasing him. What if Simmonds didn't show up? What if Wes Ford crashed his car and died?

Jo only knew he was in a container somewhere off Lorimer Street—would that be enough information to find him? Christ. Even if she found the right address, there were so many boxes here . . .

But Wes was not going to crash his car.

Bill Simmonds would come eventually. He was playing safe, turning up in the dead heart of night to be sure of not being seen.

One thought led to another. What about Wes Ford? What if he had double-crossed them? What if . . . he and Simmonds had orchestrated this whole situation, putting Wes inside the house to befriend them, gain their trust? What if the plan was to remove Shaun from the picture so they could snatch Jo? So . . . Wes produces this cock and bull story about him abducting Jo and putting her in a container, *knowing* Shaun would want to turn the scam around, putting *himself* in the box so he could surprise Simmonds when he swung by. Or, if Shaun hadn't come up with that idea, maybe Wes would have. It made sense. Then, when they had Jo stashed away somewhere, they came for Shaun and told him to come up with the cash if he wanted to see her alive again . . .

He'd played right into their hands.

What made him think he could trust Wes Ford? Not much, apart from gut instinct. Gut instinct. It was a crucial asset for any good detective. But . . . Christ, if he couldn't trust Mitch Alvarez—as Turner would have him believe—how could he possibly trust a total stranger with an agenda of his own and angles to play that Shaun didn't even know existed? We believe what we want to believe, no matter what the facts tell us . . .

'You stupid fuck,' he said.

Now he was recalling Leon Turner saying everything was down to him, because he was *dumb enough to get caught*. The truth of this statement had preyed on Shaun for years. It wasn't why he snapped. No, it was the superior, shit-eating way

Turner pronounced it, as if Shaun's shortcomings somehow outweighed or vindicated Turner's lifetime of misdeeds.

'You stupid fuck,' he said again. *Your gut instinct isn't worth shit.*

No-one was coming for him tonight.

They'd leave him in here to rot for a while, then he'd be half-dead and helpless to resist when they did come. But they couldn't let him die, not if they wanted the contents of that safe deposit box. He had the keys to it in his pocket, but they were useless to anyone else because only Shaun knew where to *find* the box, which bank it was in. He had to sign for it before he could clear the contents. Of course there was no reason to assume Simmonds had figured out the money was in a safe deposit box, but it was a commonsense thing to do with such a large amount.

He'd probably ransack the house first, then by process of elimination come to the logical conclusion that it had to be sitting in a box, somewhere in a bank vault. They'd probably find the hundred grand, but would that satisfy them? Not likely.

Sooner or later, they'd have to come for him, because he was the only one who could lead them to the cash . . .

All kinds of wild thoughts swirled around in his brain: what if Jo was in it with them? What if it had been no coincidence that they'd met in Buzzards Hut, but part of a long-range plan, a fall-back position if Bernie Walsh wasn't able to come through?

Bullshit. The money had been stored in the house, it was right there in front of her eyes. That was the time to snatch it, not now.

He lowered his head and chastised himself for even entertaining such thoughts. He was beginning to see how a person could go insane in this situation.

Time check: 1.35 am.

He played the beam around. It was becoming uncomfortably close and foetid. How those people could have survived as long as they did, squashed in the way they were, was beyond him. But desperate people will do suicidal things if there is a single glimmer of hope, if the alternative is worse . . .

He stood the flashlight up in front of him so that it lit up the roof, and withdrew the .32 from his inside jacket pocket. Then, for something to do, he took out all the bullets and carefully reloaded them before ramming the clip back in the butt and working the slide to make sure there was one in the pipe. He hoped he didn't have to use it—if and when Simmonds made his appearance. In a confined space such as this a stray bullet would ricochet off every surface until it hit someone, and the bullet wouldn't discriminate. It would lose plenty of velocity and get banged out of shape, but could still do fatal or serious damage. He put the compact semi-automatic back in his pocket. Just having it was some comfort. Edginess slowly seeped into him, and he tried to squeeze it away.

He decided to call Jo. Somewhat to his surprise the signal was reasonable.

'Hello there,' he said.

'Hello,' she said a touch nervously. 'Are you there? In that thing?'

'I am.'

'God, I don't know how you can do it. How are you?'

'So far, so good. Whose dumb idea was this, anyway?'

'It's creepy,' she said. 'I don't like it.'

'Me neither. But hey, one night in the lock-up? I can do that.'

'Wish you were here instead.'

'Same here. And I will be soon. I'd better go, baby. Anything happens, you'll be the first to know.' *I hope.*

Soon he was face-down on the rusty floor doing push-ups, counting them out all the way to fifty. In prison he did four sets of fifty a day—on his fingertips to provide a tougher challenge. As a result of eleven years of this he had exceptional strength in his wrists and hands, and his fingers were like steel rods.

Next, he did fifty sit-ups, lacing his hands behind his head and stretching forward so that his forehead alternately touched his left and right knees. When he hit fifty he sat up straight and gasped loudly. His heart pounded. He poured some water over his face and into his mouth.

Time check: 2.15 am.

'Come *on!*' he said.

Then: 'All right, settle down. Don't panic.'

He switched off the light and sat still in the total darkness. There was no sound except the ticking of his watch. Then he realised he was holding his breath, and let the air out. If no-one came within twenty-four hours, he would never get out of this box alive. If Wes didn't come by ten in the morning he was history. It was his tomb. He could bang the walls and scream all he liked, but who was going to hear him? *No-fucking-one.* A security patrol might drive by, check the locks and leave a card, but that would be it. What reason would anyone have for coming *in* here? None. It was a container graveyard.

His eyelids began to droop.

No—no sleeping.

But in pitch darkness, it was natural to want to go to sleep. He knew that. It went back to the womb, that instinct. In darkness, one slept.

This womb, his tomb. Crash out here and he would never see daylight again.

Still his eyes wanted to close.

Time check: 2.45 am.

Now it was a full-scale battle to fight that demon, sleep. From deep within him there was a tremendous urge to simply curl up and call it quits. His head nodded, and when his chin touched his chest he sprang to, gasping, as if he'd been stabbed. He stood up, stretched, paced back and forth along the length of the box, back and forth, back and forth . . .

Just how he did in stir.

Now he wanted to scream. Why not? No-one would hear it. He gave a howl for the hell of it.

Time check: 3.10 am.

He'd been here nearly four hours. Shit, it seemed a lot longer than that.

He decided to stay on his feet for a while. Sleep was far too enticing.

But wait on—what was that? Not so much a noise as . . . the *silence* that follows when a car engine has been switched off.

He stood against the door and strained to listen. Very little in the way of clear sound penetrated these steel walls. From far away came the hefty *chunk* of a car door shutting, then later the crunching of a heavy man's footsteps approaching on debris-strewn ground. So he was alone. Shaun braced himself: back against the door, the .32 in his right hand by his side. Now he was wide awake, coiled and ready, *anxious*, to cut loose. But then nothing happened for a long time, and he began to wonder if he'd imagined those noises.

Bang!

It was the sound of a bolt handle being struck with an open palm. The bolts, as Shaun and Wes had discovered, were stiff from lack of use. Which door would he open? Shaun listened: a hand was working another bolt, twisting and wrenching at it.

He was opening the right-side door.

Then . . . nothing.

'Yeah?' he heard dimly, distantly. It was Simmonds' voice. Shit—someone with him? 'I'm here now,' he heard, ear pressed hard against the steel.

No—he was on the phone.

'I'll be there by eleven,' Simmonds said. 'Before the punters turn up. We'll have a powwow then. Leave the side door open.'

That was all. Then, after a short struggle, the second bolt was wrenched loose. Now he could hear Fat Man breathing heavily from exertion. The door came open, letting in some grey light. Shaun pressed hard against the left door, bringing the gun up next to his face. A powerful beam appeared, flooding the interior with bright light. He could see the flashlight, then the hand holding it—the left hand, indicating he had a gun in the right—then the shirtsleeve and jacket cuff . . .

He knew he had one shot at this. Had to be done exactly right, or Simmonds would gut him. One-on-one he'd be no match—the surprise factor was everything.

Out of the dark his right hand locked around Simmonds' wrist. A split second later, he yanked him into the container, at the same time swinging his own body around to face his adversary and gain better leverage. Simmonds seemed to stumble on the threshold as he was propelled inside, pitched forward as Shaun used the weight and momentum to swing him around one-handed in a wide arc before slamming him into the wall: BANG. The whole box rocked from side to side on impact; the flashlight fell from his hand, extinguishing itself when it hit the floor at Shaun's feet. From his other hand something heavy and metallic, presumably his gun, clanged and disappeared in the dark. It took about a second and a half for Simmonds to recover and get his wind, but before he could act Shaun punched him hard and fast in the mouth, twice. The intention was to inflict some damage and give him something extra to think about as he tried to grope around for Shaun. He felt teeth crunch both times as Simmonds' head snapped back against the steel. Grunts and curses came in a rush from his bloodied mouth. Shaun stepped back and put the .32 squarely on the big man, who was wiping a hand across his face and realising he'd been hit right hard.

'Fuckin' low *cunt*—busted a tooth and cut my *tongue*,' he said, and spat some blood and chips into his palm. Clearly he didn't like what he saw, and nor did he seem at all bothered by the fact that someone was pointing a loaded weapon at his face.

'It's a real gun, Simmonds—not a replica. Give me any reason to and I'll drop you with it.'

Simmonds lifted his face from his hand. Even in the poor light afforded by the open door Shaun could see the mess on his lips and chin. He stared at Shaun, not even noticing the pistol.

'That fuckin' weasel,' he said. 'I'll turn him inside out—after I've fixed your liver, McCreadie. I'll haul his slippery arse through his—'

'Shut it!'

As a precaution Shaun took an extra step back, but the gun didn't waver from the imagined bull's-eye in the middle of Simmonds' huge, boar-shaped head. *Impossible* to miss from here.

'You've blown it, Simmonds. You're doing nothing to anyone. It's over for you. It all ends here.'

Simmonds straightened right up to his full size, placing his hands flat against the wall at his sides as he locked eyes with Shaun.

'Get on your knees, bastard,' Shaun said. '*Do it!*'

Simmonds did not reply. Instead he launched himself off the wall and straight into Shaun with a speed that was astonishing for such a big man. It was over and done in a blur. With his head down he charged into Shaun's chest, sending him reeling back into the wall and then off it again; in the process the pistol flew from his hand and a massive paw grabbed his throat. A triumphant roar from Fat Man filled the box as he closed his fingers around Shaun's neck and applied full pressure. Shaun knew instantly he was in a death hold and had to break it soon or go the way of Johnny Wu. Simmonds could've used two hands, but apparently didn't feel it necessary as he continued to exert pressure, his arm trembling mightily, while at the same time slowly lifting Shaun off his feet. With his eyes popping and a fuzzy sensation already filling his blood-starved brain he could just make out Fat Man's face: he was out of it, wide-eyed, bloody-mouthed and delirious with rapture as he watched the life slowly, inevitably drain from his opponent. A bullet between the eyes could not have stopped him now. Shaun's feet were not touching ground and his tongue was a huge, dry gag in his mouth. He spluttered; the lights were going out; he had no time left. Johnny Wu thrashed around in the air before his sphincter opened, but Shaun had longer arms than Johnny Wu. With his fingers spread he galvanized what strength he had left and thrust them into Simmonds' face, the wide madman's eyes an open invitation. The steel rods of his fingers buried themselves in their twin targets, precipitating an appalling, ungodly howl of a different kind from Fat Man. Still Shaun gouged and twisted the fingers in corkscrew fashion, then pulled them out as the grip around his throat loosened. When he extracted his fingers they were dripping, but he couldn't quite see if it was just blood or something else too . . .

With his face buried in his hands Simmonds doubled over, giving Shaun time to get some breath back and regain strength. Blinded he might be, but even a blind Simmonds was not to be undersold. Shaun scrabbled around on the floor, located the heavy-duty, police-issue flashlight and brought it down two-handed on Simmonds' head and shoulders with all the power in his body—once, twice, three times. As it smashed into him on the last occasion the flashlight exploded, bits and pieces and loose batteries flying in every direction. All he had in his hand then was the hollow shell. He tossed it away and searched for his or Simmonds' gun, but couldn't see either weapon anywhere. Simmonds was down on all fours, groaning and bleeding all over his clothes from the open head wounds.

'It's *over* for you,' Shaun rasped again. 'Should've been a long time ago.'

Reaching down he wiped his wet fingers on Simmonds' trousers. He remembered his own flashlight then, in his back pocket, but when he tried to switch it on nothing happened. Damn thing must've been damaged when he hit the wall. Then he saw the glass was broken. He put it back in his pocket and conducted a systematic search for the .32. Wouldn't do to leave it here possibly bearing prints that might identify him. More often than not prints left on guns were smudged and useless partials, but it was a chance he wouldn't take. In a little while he discovered both weapons. Simmonds' was a standard-issue .38 revolver. He left it where it lay and put the .32 in his jacket. Simmonds was face down, moving slightly and moaning like a gut-shot grizzly. Shaun searched his pants pockets until he found the gate keys, then conducted a general search of his person to see if anything useful turned up. There was no notepad or scrap of paper that might connect him or Wes Ford to Simmonds. In his wallet there was a hefty wad of cash, but it was too dark to see what else was in there. He replaced it in Simmonds' pocket and stood over him for a few moments, trying to decide how he felt. Sore and traumatised, pumped, still blowing hard and too fast, but not filled with remorse the way he was after doing over Turner. His only regret was that he'd not had the chance to extract any information from Simmonds. Who was he speaking with on the phone, for instance? Where was he going for a powwow at eleven in the morning?

Shaun had a pretty fair idea on the second count at least.

He stomped on Simmonds' tiny silver phone until it was in shards.

Then he stepped over the heaving, slobbering bear shape and exited the black box. He shut the door and rammed home the two vertical bolts. All around him were derelict, rusted out containers. Without prior knowledge the chances of locating the right one were slim. It was a vast block, and there were so many boxes it would be easy to get lost in the maze.

He walked between rows of boxes until he came to the space where Simmonds had parked. He knew the keys were in it because they were not in the cop's pockets. It was a near-new Statesman, not a police car, in black or midnight blue. After pulling on the woollen gloves he started it up, reversed, and burbled towards the front gate with the lights off. Using Simmonds' keys he opened the padlocks, and as he did so he noticed several business-sized cards on the ground. One of them was folded over, as if it had been wedged between the two gates and dislodged when Simmonds, or maybe Wes, opened them. He put one of the cards into his pocket and drove out, then locked the gates again. There was no sign of life in the street—not even a howling dog—and just a handful of parked vehicles in the vicinity along with the Land Rover. He drove the Statesmen for several blocks, then pulled in and parked outside a die-setting factory that had a For Sale sign on its cyclone wire fence. After locking and alarming the Statesman he made his way back towards the Rover, pausing to toss the Statesman and padlock keys high onto a factory roof.

As he drove carefully back to East Melbourne, ever watchful for late-night police patrols, he pondered Bill Simmonds' chances. They were not wonderful. In his condition he would be helpless to do anything much. Even if he pounded the walls and bellowed until his strength finally gave out no-one would hear zip. Eventually he would give up and go to sleep. In time the rotten smell of a decomposed cadaver would attract attention. If he managed to find his gun, however, he might choose to shoot himself. It was hard to call—this was a man who had believed himself indestructible for many decades.

But it was all over for him now.

When he reached home—what he now thought of as home—it was nearly four. He drove in the back, parked and alarmed the Rover, and let himself into the house. He'd decided against calling Jo in case she was asleep. On top of that he was shaken up, and did not want her to hear him in that state. His throat still hurt from Simmonds' iron grip. For around ten minutes he sat at the kitchen table slowly sipping a glass of orange juice and listening to the clock ticking in time with the drumbeat in his chest. He was way too wired to sleep. Above all he couldn't get over how soon he'd gone stir crazy, despite being an experienced convict. He'd truly thought he'd do it on a break, but no. How Simmonds would cope, boxed in and blind—doubly blind—and with a gun at his disposal, made Shaun wonder how long he could've stood it before turning the weapon on himself. Not too much longer, he suspected. It was a tough thing to find out.

Remembering the business card in his pocket, he took it out and studied it in the kitchen light. Printed on it were the words SKYLINE SECURITY, beneath a graphic of an eye watching over a metropolis of skyscrapers. There were phone and fax numbers, along with a dotcom address.

When he felt ready he mounted the staircase and, as quietly as he could, undressed and climbed into bed next to Jo's motionless form. She appeared to be asleep, but the absence of audible breathing told him she was not. In the dark he turned her face towards him, and sure enough her eyes were wide open. He began to speak, but before the first word was out she pressed a finger to his lips.

'You're back,' she whispered. 'That's all I care about right now. Tell me the rest later.'

He held her tight. Her hair fell over his face and chest. She rustled around until her warm body aligned perfectly with his. Within minutes, to his amazement, the soft flutter of her exhalations told him she had gone under.

By seven, when he arose, he was feeling ragged from the night's drama and lack of sleep. Whenever his eyes had closed all he'd done was twitch and jump, as if he'd been hit with a cattle prod. Now his body was a jangle of warring nerves made worse by the insistent flashing into his mind of Bill Simmonds' mad-eyed face when he tried to choke him to death. Jo offered him a tranquilliser, which he declined on the grounds that he needed to stay on his toes for some time to come. Couple or three things to do, and soon.

First off, a call to Wes Ford.

'Did I wake you up?' he said when a bleary-sounding voice answered. It was twenty after seven, and Shaun was on his third coffee.

'Uh—not exactly,' Wes said, but yawned anyway.

'It's all cool,' Shaun said. 'You don't have to do anything.'

'Right.' Wes's senses gradually came to. 'Ah . . . Simmonds is in the box?'

'Yep.'

Silence. 'Man,' Wes said. The enormity of what must have transpired was dawning on him. 'Shit.'

'Yeah. Shit.'

'Rat's in his own trap.'

'He is. And far from happy about it.'

'Wow.' Down the phone line Shaun sensed conflicting sentiments: initially relief, satisfaction, but then, in the subsequent thoughtful silence, a growing realisation that he had no-one to bat for him when his day in court came.

Shaun said, 'Listen, Wes. Might be a good idea if you moved out of home for a while. Got anywhere you can go on short notice?'

'Move out? Why?'

'Just as a precaution, that's all. It ain't over yet, buddy. Not for you, or me.'

'Uh . . . okay,' Wes said. 'Got the fistful of dirty dollars, don't I? Guess I can splash it on a ritzy hotel.'

Shaun had a sudden vision of Wes dropping his towel in front of a chambermaid. 'Do that. Call me later, when you're settled. And Wes?'

'What?'

'Keep a low profile—if you understand my meaning.'

Wes sounded offended. 'Who, me? What?'

'Never mind. Just stay zipped up. Keep everything in check.'

'Uh-huh. Got the message. So, what's on your plate?'

'Gonna see a man in a pub.'

'Tough. Catch you later then.'

Shaun suddenly remembered a detail that had been nagging at him.

'Wes—wait on. Still there?'

'Still here, man.'

'Listen, when you went to the container place with Simmonds, did he go straight to it, you know, as if it was prearranged? Or not?'

Wes thought about it. Shaun could hear him scratching his hair. 'Hold on. We got out of his car . . . I followed him, between these rows of containers . . . uh, he stopped a couple of times, shone the flashlight on a box, tried to open it up. Three times maybe he did that, but couldn't open 'em 'cause the bolts were rusted tight. They hadn't been used in so long, he couldn't budge 'em. So, we went on in this vein until he found this one, the one with the serial number I told you, and he could shift the bolts on it. Then he kind of scanned around with the flashlight, as if checking the location, and then he said, "This is it", or "This is the one", something like that. So, in answer to your question, I would say that the container was definitely *not* pre-selected. That any help?'

'Big help, Wes. Thanks—I mean, for everything.'

After he'd disconnected, Shaun wondered if maybe he ought to have apologised to Wes for doubting him back in the container.

What he really needed now was to hit the cot. His stinging eyes—every part of him—cried out for a decent sleep, but there was none on the horizon. The next best option was a session in the jacuzzi, which at least softened the tightly knotted muscles and sinews and quieted the nerves. It wasn't long before his lids began to twitch and close, lights flashing weirdly behind them—like a flashlight beam spinning around in a dark space—and then his head gradually succumbed to gravity, as it had done in the box. Soon enough he descended into an uneasy slumber and subsided into the froth, surfacing only when the scented water began to lap into his open mouth.

More caffeine and a shot of Benzedrine from Jo's store of pharmaceuticals and he was good for another twenty-four hours. Now there was shopping to be done. With Jo at the wheel of the Rover they headed into the city, a Dick Smith electronics superstore being the object of the visit.

21

The Unicorn Hotel was a sad, soot- and grit-encrusted pub that had long been a favoured venue for railroad workers who, when they came off shift at the North Melbourne or Dynon yards, trudged with their Gladstone bags to the nearest watering hole and drank as much of their pay packets as they could before weaving home to the ball and chain. More than anything it was its convenient location—easy walking distance for an army of willing boozers—that kept the Unicorn's cash registers ringing even in more recent years, when the old blue-collar traditions had begun to fade. An unusual, wedge-shaped building, it was located on a hill, adjacent to a railroad bridge, which accounted for its heavy coat of soot, dust and grit that had accumulated for over a century, going right back to the age of steam.

Nowadays it was a pit, frequented mostly by the current, dwindling generation of thirsty railway men and local pensioners who had come there all their lives. The price of a beer at the Unicorn had remained constant for years, and there were no visible signs that a single cent had been invested in modernisation or refurbishment since before World War II. Even the carpet gave the impression that it was held together with a sticky compound of beer, blood and cigarette ash. The reason it had escaped the ever-watchful eyes of developers was the same one that had been its *raison d'être*: a run-down location alongside unsightly spaghetti lines of railroad tracks and the derelict, boarded-up shopfronts that used to serve the local community before the advent of megastores and strip malls.

When Shaun arrived at ten to eleven it was bright and cool. No breeze. He wore a black-and-white check shirt hanging loose outside his black jeans, and a pair of black Rivers boots. The heavily tinted windows gave no view of the interior. A painted sign said, HAPPY HOUR EVERY DAY 6–8PM $1.20 POTS. Around a dozen silver barrels were lined up on the pavement, waiting to be taken back to the brewery—so business was still reasonable. The main door was locked as he'd expected, so he walked around into the narrow side street. There he found an inconspicuous door with a wire mesh-reinforced window. The door opened when he pushed his fingers against its steel plating. As soon as he was inside he had the feeling he'd come to the right place. The grit floating in the air and the full ashtrays along the base of the bar reminded him of the dives he had often had to attend as a uniformed cop, when a brawl had broken out. It felt so long ago he could hardly believe such places still existed.

Once inside he turned right from a short passageway into the main bar, past a fireplace that smelled of embers burned a long age ago. There was no-one around, but muted noises rose from somewhere deep in the pub's bowels. He placed both hands on the bar, leaned over and saw that a rubber mat had been moved so that the cellar trapdoor could be lifted. He remained silent and waited patiently for whoever was down there to show himself. It was nearly eleven. He lit up a cigarette, and the sound of the lighter snapping on and off abruptly stopped the sounds below. Sure enough, a figure emerged through the trapdoor—first, a tousled head of thick white hair, then a plump, ruddy face that was overhung with winged, black eyebrows. Shaun knew those ridiculous-looking brows. When he was halfway out the man gave Shaun the once-over and said, 'You're a bit previous. We're not open yet, pal.'

'I know that,' Shaun said, blowing out smoke.

The man climbed out and lowered the trapdoor before taking a proper squint at his early bird customer. Between the fingers of one hand he carried three bottles of Johnnie Walker Red, which clinked together as he straightened up. It seemed to take a long time for recognition to dawn, but Shaun was in no hurry. When he realised who it was, the publican narrowed his gaze. This had the effect of making the winged brows darken his face dramatically. Shaun watched closely: first there was surprise, a split-second of shock—then glowering, blue-eyed hostility.

'Hell're you doing here, McCreadie?' He put the spirit bottles on the counter next to the sink.

'Public house, isn't it?' Shaun said.

'Like I said, we're not open.'

'Why don't you bend the rules, Burns? You've always been good at that. Be a gent and pour me a pot.'

Neville Burns, former Internal Investigations goon, hesitated as he sized up his options, then picked up a glass and moved to the tap. This was all done with a measured slowness that suggested he was buying time. He took his eyes off Shaun for just long enough to fill the glass and shut off the tap. The first pour of the day was not one for the scrapbook.

'That's a pretty ordinary beer, Burns. Why don't you put a decent head on it?'

Burns put in a few extra squirts to produce some froth. Shaun took a mouthful and set down the glass. In moments the head had completely dissolved.

'That beer's flat,' he said.

'System's not hooked up properly yet,' Burns said. 'That's left over from what was in the pipe.'

Shaun crushed out his cigarette, picked up the beer, leaned over the bar and tipped it down the sink.

'It's piss, probably from the slops tray. You'd be up for that.'

Burns didn't say anything.

'Give us a can of Victor Bravo,' Shaun said. 'Something you can't contaminate.'

Burns opened a dairy case door and produced the can, which he popped before setting it down.

'Two dollars fifty cents,' he said.

Shaun dropped some coins in front of him, but Burns made no move for them. He hadn't taken his blue eyes off Shaun since pouring the flat beer.

'I repeat my question. What are you doing here?'

Shaun took a slug from the can. Then he produced his cigarettes from his shirt pocket and lit up before dropping the pack and his lighter on the bar towel. Burns' eyes momentarily fell on them before switching back to Shaun.

'How long've you had this dump?' Shaun said.

'Five years.'

'Bit of a comedown, isn't it?'

'It does me.'

'You must miss the old days, Burns, pushing people around, stitching them up. All you can do now is toss out the pisspots.'

Burns had no comment.

Shaun walked around the room, examining the yellowed photographs of old-time footballers in their heyday, going back to the twenties and thirties. In addition there were pictures of various racehorses standing with their proud owners, also long dead and gone.

'Whyn't you spruce the joint up, Burns? Attract a better class of customer.'

'Whyn't you mind your own business?'

'But I am.' He returned to the bar and took another slug from the can. Burns stood still, watching over Shaun as if he thought he might lift something otherwise.

Neville Burns had to be sixty now, slightly younger than Simmonds. Ever since Shaun had known him he'd had a mop of grey hair. He'd probably had it prematurely in his twenties, along with the bushy brows. He was of medium stature and built like a bulldog, with watery eyes that were perpetually red-rimmed. Shaun had always assumed that was caused by excessive boozing, but later he'd been told it was a medical condition that required him to put drops in his eyes every day. It seemed his lids didn't function properly, which caused the chronic redness. Now, with the ruddy complexion and thicker waistline, he looked like a retired pug who had somehow managed to avoid major rearrangement of his dial. He also consumed far too much from the top shelf nowadays, if the purplish, roadmapped nose was any indication.

Shaun threw down his cigarette and said, 'So, you stay in touch with any of the old crew, Burns?'

'Not particularly.' It was an instant response, as if he'd been waiting for the question. Shaun could see Burns was trying to read his face, but Shaun wasn't giving him anything to read.

'That's not strictly accurate, is it?'

Burns shrugged one shoulder. 'Nothing to do with you, who I see or don't see.'

Shaun checked the time: quarter after eleven. 'Matter of fact, I had a call this morning from your old partner in crime, Bill Simmonds.'

'Is that so?'

'Yeah. Said he had something of mine, and if I wanted it back to meet him here at eleven. Sounds a bit mysterious, doesn't it?'

Burns shrugged again. But the mention of Simmonds' name had wrought a definite change in his manner. One of his brows arched, and there was a slight smile at the corner of his lips, as if he knew something Shaun didn't—as if the odds in this little standoff had suddenly shifted to his corner.

'Well,' Shaun said. 'I'm here, and it's after eleven. Where is the cunt?'

From around a corner he heard a door open—the same one he'd come through. It closed, and then came heavy-sounding footsteps.

'Careful what you wish for,' Burns said, unable to resist a broader smile now. 'Might be him now.'

Shaun looked down at his beer can. Both his hands were on the bar. A shiver of dread swept right through him as the footsteps approached from behind. If it's Simmonds, he thought, I'm not leaving this hotel alive. But how could it be . . .

He didn't dare turn around, fixing his gaze instead on Neville Burns, as if he were a mirror. Burns looked over Shaun's shoulder at the new arrival. From his expression Shaun tried to ascertain if it was indeed his nemesis, but before he could decide anything the man was alongside him at the bar.

'Well, well,' the man said. 'Who have we here?'

Shaun looked sideways. It took two seconds, maybe three, but he tried not to show that he was either surprised or ruffled in any way. The whole plan was to let the cards unfold, play them as they were dealt.

'Brent Wollansky,' he said.

'Got it in one,' Wollansky said.

It was no mean achievement, given that he hadn't seen Wollansky for fifteen or sixteen years. Brent Wollansky: former armed robbery squad detective, and Mitch Alvarez's sideman before Shaun's time. Wollansky was an operator in the professional sense, a class act and the designated public face of the squad because of his smooth delivery and sartorial good looks. He was a departmental fashion plate well before it became mandatory among the new generation. In fact, his nickname in those days was 'Smooth' Wollansky. No-one ever called him Brent, although Shaun did on the odd occasion they'd met socially, because he never knew him in the job. Wollansky worked the Stan Petrakos case with Mitch, and when it snapped back in their faces like a slingshot everything changed for both cops. That famous night when they trashed themselves at Bobby McGee's and had to be thrown out was effectively the last rites, whether they knew it then or not. Wollansky left the robbers soon afterwards and rotated through several other squads to get his twenty years up, then quit and started his own security company.

As far as Shaun was aware that company had grown from its humble, one-man origins to a prosperous business. His appearance certainly gave that indication—he wore a quality single-breasted charcoal suit, a crisp, white Oxford shirt with French cuffs and antique gold cufflinks, expensive black shoes that were polished to a high shine. The straight, perfectly combed jet-black hair for which he was so famous was now seasoned with silver, making him every inch the top-level CEO. He had to be mid-fifties, but his face was as classically handsome as ever—bright, brown eyes, aquiline nose, even a cleft in his chin—and the smooth, close-shaved skin was so evenly and deeply tanned it had to be a sunlamp job.

His manner was friendly enough, but significantly he did not offer his hand. Keeping his own on the bar, Shaun noticed a quicksilver exchange of glances between Wollansky and Burns before Wollansky returned his attention to Shaun.

'How's it been for you, Shaun? I saw that you were ... among the living again.'

'Yeah. That's a good way of describing it, Brent. This's a lot better than the other place, I'm here to tell you. The place of the living dead.'

Wollansky was studying him intently. 'You were at Barwon, right?'

'Mostly. Pentridge, Metrop Reception Centre, Barwon ... I honestly can't recommend any of them, Brent. No money, love, hatred or revenge is worth one day of it.'

Wollansky nodded. He was paying close attention. One of his great skills—a major asset to any detective—was that he was a terrific listener. When you engaged him in conversation he made you feel as if you were the only person in the universe who mattered at that moment. It was an effective technique—and a highly seductive one that made suspects *want* to confide in him.

'Were you in protective custody? I mean, being a cop . . .'

'Yeah, I was for a fair bit of the time. It's only a different kind of punishment, Brent. Might've saved my life, but what life was being saved? You have to ask yourself that—is it worth it? I preferred to take my chances out in the open.'

Wollansky nodded again, and Shaun felt the former detective's eyes assessing him without appearing to. What did he see? An ordinary guy in a check shirt and jeans, having a beer before noon in a pub that wasn't even open . . .

Wollansky's mind was almost visibly working. Shaun could feel the buzz of his circuits and synapses hard at it, as if he were plugged into the same power board. There was an intense force field around Smooth Wollansky that was every bit as palpable as flesh and bone. But Shaun's brain too was working hard—assessing, readjusting, arranging words and planning moves, all under cover of some polite chitchat that mainly served to give both men some breathing space.

Shaun said, 'How's business, Brent? I hear you've got the game stitched up.'

'Making a dollar,' Wollansky said. 'Can't complain.'

'Got a card there? You know, in case I'm out of a job, man.'

'Shaun, I can always use good staff,' Wollansky said benevolently. He flipped open a black billfold with gold corners, in which the banknotes were held by a gold clip. After fishing around he found a card and handed it across. It said SKYLINE SECURITY.

Pocketing the card, Shaun said matter-of-factly, 'What brings you here at this early hour, Brent? You don't qualify as a desperate, and our friend the publican informs me that he isn't even open yet.'

'Obviously that didn't deter you,' Wollansky said, glancing at the Victor Bravo can and smiling. The smile tightened the skin across his unblemished face, making it shine. He looked like a million dollars.

'No. Well, would you care to join me?' Shaun said. 'I wouldn't try the leftover slops in the pipe if I were you.'

Burns, who had stood immobile and silent, bridled and seemed on the cusp of chipping in with a comment before Wollansky cut across.

'I'll have what he's having, Mr Burns. Provided you have no objection.'

Burns wordlessly popped a can and set it in front of him. Wollansky didn't bother putting out any cash, and Burns didn't seem to expect it. He leaned back against the dairy case and crossed his arms.

'Here's to it,' Wollansky said, and lifted the can to his lips. When he'd had a hefty swallow he gave a satisfied gasp and put the can down, slowly twirling it around and studying it in a way that indicated he was deep in thought, and not altogether comfortable with the current situation, not too sure which way to jump.

'You didn't answer my question,' Shaun said.

Wollansky turned to him. 'No, I didn't, did I? You know how it is with cops. We *ask* the questions—we don't *answer* 'em.'

Silence filled the room. Shaun finished his can and indicated he'd like another, which was duly served. This time Burns didn't take for it.

'I'll make it easy for you,' Shaun said. '*I'm* here because Bill Simmonds told me he wanted to see me. He didn't say why, though.'

'Really,' Wollansky said, studying his beer can.

'Yeah. Said to be at the Unicorn at eleven. It's now . . . eleven-thirty. He's late.'

Interested as he transparently was, Wollansky didn't take his eyes off the can. 'Not like Bill Simmonds to be late.'

'You obviously know him better than I do,' Shaun said.

'Well, considering your enforced absence, that would be true in relation to nearly anyone.'

'That's true, Brent. Good point. So, *why* is he late? And what's going on? What's he want?'

'That I can't tell you,' Wollansky said.

'I am in the dark,' Shaun said. 'I wish *someone* would enlighten me.'

'No doubt all will be revealed when he arrives.'

'*If* he arrives. I have the feeling I've been stooged for some reason.'

'There'll be an explanation,' Wollansky said dubiously.

'You were expecting him too, weren't you, Brent?' Shaun said, tightening the ratchet a couple of notches. 'I mean, that's why you're here, right?'

Wollansky looked at him. 'I don't know why you would think that. I'm here because I'm here, to visit my old comrade-in-arms, Mr Burns. There's no mystery.'

Shaun decided to throw in a wild card while he had Wollansky slightly off-balance.

'I've just been up north visiting your other old buddy, Leon Turner.'

'Turner? That so?' Wollansky said. Very good, Shaun thought, very good indeed—total surprise feigned with impeccable sincerity. Or, wait, maybe he really didn't know . . .

'Brick Turner, yeah. Lives in Nambucca Heads now. Did you know that?'

Wollansky considered before obviously deciding that was something he could reasonably be expected to know. 'I did, as a matter of fact. He's been up there for a few years now.'

Shaun swallowed some beer. 'He's dying, as you probably realise.'

Wollansky nodded grimly at his VB can. 'Yeah. Prostate's got him,' he said.

'Told me he had maybe three months left.'

Wollansky nodded again. 'Most unfortunate. Can happen to any of us. Well, maybe not you. You're still a bit too young for that one.'

Now Shaun nodded. 'Only on the outside, Brent.' He was thinking, Wollansky knows Turner is dying. But Turner himself only got the diagnosis five weeks ago, so they've been in contact with each other recently. Probable conclusion: Brent Wollansky told Turner that Shaun was out of jail . . .

It felt right, but a direct question would no doubt elicit a denial delivered with all the panache and conviction of a leading man on the set. He decided to try for it anyway.

'Have you spoken to Turner?'

'Didn't I just admit to that?'

'Not exactly, no. You said you knew he was dying. Someone could've told you. How'd you find out?'

'Well, if you really need to know, we spoke on the phone recently. Is there a problem with that?'

Shaun put his hands up. 'Hey. No offence, Brent. I've been out of circulation a long time. Just trying to get a handle on some things, that's all.'

'Like, what things?'

Shaun drew some breath. 'Oh, you know, who's up who, who hasn't paid rent. Who wants a piece of me, and why.' He looked sharply at Wollansky and added, 'Mainly, what the fuck's going down, Brent? You're here because you're here? Don't give me that shit.'

'All right. I won't,' Wollansky said. 'I won't give you *any* shit.' He glanced at his watch.

'Brent, listen to me. Don't spit it. And don't worry about the fucking time. I've been in the dark so long now I can see like a cat. But I'm no wiser.'

'Who among us is?' Wollansky said.

'When you phoned Leon Turner recently, was my name mentioned in dispatches at any point? Give us a straight answer on that.'

Their eyes met and held fast. It was a testing moment, and they both knew it. A door would either open or remain shut forever. Wollansky, Shaun saw, was weighing up his chances of lying convincingly to someone who, like him, was a trained lie detector. But he also had to take into account the fact that Shaun had survived for years among pathological liars and psychopaths, so his skills in that area would be honed to razor sharpness.

Wollansky was astute enough to see that the chances were shit.

'I believe you were mentioned once or twice,' he finally conceded. 'Is that all right?'

'Maybe. What was said? That I was on the loose?'

'Yeah, that's about the size of it. It was a news flash, that's all.' He gave a half-hearted shrug.

'Sure, I understand.' He lit up a cigarette to give himself some time. Wollansky had to be played with great care, or he would be gone. 'You know,' he said, 'I can't get over the fact that the three of us are here together right now—three ex-cops, with a shared slice of history. What a coincidence.'

'It's not that big a one,' Wollansky said.

Shaun drained his can and ordered another round. Wollansky did not object, so they were set for a stretch yet.

'When you were a cop,' Shaun said, 'you didn't believe in coincidences, did you, Brent?'

'That was then,' Wollansky said. 'Your problem, Shaun, if you'll forgive me, is that you've spent too much time inside your own head. You're seeing things.'

'Can't argue with that,' Shaun said. 'I see things all the time. But, come on—the three of us intersected at a pretty special time, wouldn't you say? Throw in Simmonds, who is here in spirit, and that makes four of us, all connected by that same inglorious series of events. See what I mean?'

'Your point,' Wollansky said, 'appears to be valid. When you express it so colourfully.'

Shaun swallowed some beer and said, 'Ever go to the Spread Eagle these days?'

'The Spread Eagle? In Richmond?'

'That's the only one I know of.'

'No, not really. It's not part of my zone any more.'

'Oh? Where is your zone?'

'The head office is in Clayton.'

'That's many a mile from here.'

Wollansky had a slug of his can. 'It certainly is. But I'm meeting some people for lunch over at South Melbourne anyway. Is that all right by you?'

Ignoring the jibe Shaun said, 'Do you remember one time at the Spread Eagle—'

'So we're back at the Spread Eagle now.'

'Yeah. This was 1992, June or July. You'd left the job and started up—'

'Jesus Christ, Shaun, ace it up. 1992? I have trouble remembering what I did last *week*.' He laughed, and even Burns' surly face showed signs of a smile.

'Yeah, well, that's how it is with everyone, Brent, as you know. But most people can remember what happened years ago, even trivial stuff. I'm sure you remember the occasion I'm talking about. Bill Simmonds and Brick Turner were there, and you told them that Mitch Alvarez had approached you to see if you could help him with the Petrakos job. Now that isn't something you'd report every day, is it?'

Wollansky nodded slowly as he revisited that afternoon. 'I do have a hazy recollection of that day,' he said.

'Mitch wanted you to get some blueprints. You told him no.'

'I sure did. Mitch Alvarez . . . I loved Mitch, he was a top guy and a top cop, too. None better. But . . .' He shook his head.

'But what?'

'It was a crazy idea. He was on the road to self-destruction.'

'Yeah, but he didn't destroy himself, did he? Someone did it for him.'

'That's true,' Wollansky said, nodding. 'I didn't mean that literally.'

'Someone shot him in his driveway,' Shaun said. 'Same deal as the Winchester killing, remember?'

'Yeah,' Wollansky said with a sadness that seemed genuine. 'I thought at the time it was similar to Winchester. What a tragic waste.'

'It was more than similar, Brent. Try identical. It was a cold-blooded execution modelled on the Winchester murder. And as you know, the executioner in Mitch's case was never caught.'

Wollansky stared at his can, nodding imperceptibly as if locked into his own memories, before sneaking a glance at his watch. Shaun could sense time was running out—Wollansky had his lunch excuse to leave anytime.

'I don't blame you, Brent,' he said quietly.

'What?' Wollansky was visibly taken aback—why *would* he be blamed?

'Brent, listen. I know all about it. Turner told me. He's dying, he doesn't give a stuff anymore. You didn't realise that day at the Spread Eagle—'

'Oh, we're back *there* again!'

'Yes! Simmonds and Turner already had a job planned on the Petrakos place, didn't they? The scumbag son Stan tipped them into it. There was a big heroin shipment they were gonna lift. Morris Salisbury was gonna move it. Am I right?'

'Why don't you shut your trap?' Burns said.

'Oh, welcome to the conversation, Mr Burns,' Shaun said. 'Feel free to jump in anytime.'

Wollansky wasn't saying anything.

'Here's a reconstruction,' Shaun said, 'Indulge me, please. At the Spread Eagle you told Simmonds and Turner about Mitch's proposal, which you rejected. Then, later on, you had a surprise visit from Simmonds, who had hatched a neat double-play. You know how Turner described it? An inside-out job: one scam unwittingly covering for another. Bill Simmonds invited you in, didn't he? Get those blueprints—being in the security business you'd be in a position to break into an architect's office, maybe even under cover of patrolling the premises—and give them to Simmonds. Maybe you arranged to supply the guns, too. Just nod if any of this hits the spot, Brent. I wouldn't be surprised if you did use your . . . *resources* to steal those weapons from a gun shop.'

'You don't—' Wollansky started.

'Wait on. You get your chance in a minute. So you give all this shit to Simmonds in exchange for a share of the proceeds. Simmonds takes it all to Mitch, sells him the idea that he can help him pull off the Petrakos job, which he knows Mitch is burning inside to do. So, the pact is made. Except: Mitch doesn't tell Andy or me about it. But that's part of the pact, isn't it? We do the heist, leave the drugs for Stan to rip off, and there's the inside part of the job. Without realising, we covered for Stan.'

He drank some beer and lit a cigarette. The one he'd been smoking had burnt itself out in the ashtray.

'You should write novels, Shaun,' Wollansky said. 'You'd be good at it.'

'It all fits, Brent. Why would Turner lie?'

'I can't account for Turner.'

Shaun made a bold move, putting a hand on Wollansky's arm and turning him around so he had to look Shaun directly in the eye. Wollansky didn't like it, but didn't try to shake the unwelcome hand off his fine threads.

'Tell me, Brent. You were prepared to work with Simmonds and his bunch, but not with Mitch. Why? You two had been through a lot together. You were a team. You *knew* you could've trusted him with your goddamn *life*, for Christ's sake. I did. Come on, Brent, talk to me, will you? It was years ago—I don't hold any grudges now. Used to, but not any more. Please. Help me out. *I need to know.*'

It was a turning point, an all-or-nothing roll of the dice. Shaun maintained intense eye contact, not even daring to blink. In his peripheral vision he was aware of Burns fidgeting and shifting—was he going for a weapon? Chances were he had more than a phony gun on the premises of a dive like this.

Slowly, with great care, Wollansky detached Shaun's fingers from his jacket—one by one.

'Take it easy, man. You're creasing the fabric. Cost me a fortune.'

'Sorry.' Still his eyes did not deviate from the other man's.

'Mr Burns,' Wollansky said. 'Can we have another round, please?'

Two cans were popped and placed on the bar towel.

When he'd had a sip Wollansky said, 'Mitch was twisting in the wind. He was . . . out there. You're right. Under normal circumstances I would've trusted him with my life. But these were not normal circumstances. Mitch was driven at that time. He had the fire in his belly but not much else. He was . . . a rogue cop. You don't need to be told that when a cop crosses and tries to work the other side of the street, he puts himself in no-man's land. Neither side respects him. Mitch Alvarez had no protection, no back-up . . . just you two guys, who were also twisting.' He swallowed some more beer. 'A job on that scale, you're gonna go down for it unless you have the official seal of approval, Shaun. Mitch didn't have it. Simmonds did.'

'That's why you went with him?'

'I had no personal involvement, and the potential payoff was huge. It was a no-brainer. I thought about it for maybe a minute.'

'Watch what you're saying,' Burns said.

'No, Shaun's right. It's all history now.'

'You supplied the blueprints, and the guns?'

'Yeah.'

'Watch your *mouth*,' Burns said.

'Cool down, Burnsy,' Wollansky said. 'What's he gonna do—arrest us?'

'Did you supply the van too?' Shaun said.

'No, no—that was Bill, through one of his connections in the hot car biz.'

'Brent, what did Mitch say? About the pact.'

'I don't know. I never saw or spoke to him again after that first approach. Simmonds handled it all, with his redoubtable powers of persuasion. You don't believe Mitch would've sold you two guys out?'

Shaun nodded.

'Yeah, we always want to believe we can trust those closest to us, don't we? But we never know. Not really. Mitch? He was loyal, sure. But his overriding need, as I saw it, was to get back at the Petrakos clan and the police department, and this was his big chance to do both at the same time. According to Simmonds . . . I don't know, Shaun. He agreed to the pact, and that's all there is to it now.'

'According to Simmonds—what?'

'He said, "Alvarez is ours". Those were his exact words.'

'Mitch might have said that without meaning it. Putting it over him.'

'Possibly. Pretty tough to fool Bill Simmonds, though. Graveyard's full of mug punters who've tried.'

Shaun said nothing as he processed what Wollansky had given him. It sounded as if it came from the heart. Wollansky raised his can to his lips, held it there in a contemplative pose, then put it on the bar towel again before turning to Shaun.

'Simmonds is not coming, is he? You know that. That's why you're here.'

'I can't honestly say, Brent. But I hope to Christ not.'

Wollansky thought about it.

Shaun said, 'Wherever he is, I hope he's suffering mightily.' A thought suddenly occurred to him. 'You know he killed Mitch, don't you?'

Wollansky spun around. '*What?*'

Christ. He really didn't know.

'Turner told me, Brent. After I was arrested, Simmonds was concerned that I'd give up the others and that Mitch would subsequently name names. So he had to go.'

'Bullshit.'

'No, it's right.'

Wollansky stared ahead with his hand on his barber-smooth jaw. He appeared to be trying to come to grips with it—with something.

'What about you, Mr say-nothing Burns?' Shaun said. 'Were you aware of that?'

Burns' eyes flicked from Shaun's to Wollansky's, but he didn't respond.

Wollansky said, 'I just assumed it was an underworld hit. A rip-off merchant, or . . . someone Mitch had crossed somewhere along the line.'

'Big, brave Bill Simmonds hid in the bushes and waited for him to come home. He shot him in the head before he got out of the car and then vanished into the night. It was a replica of the Colin Winchester hit, except Simmonds didn't use a .22 rifle. *And* he was never caught. Was he, Mr say-nothing Burns? Because he had influential allies in the system, didn't he? People who'd go down *with* him if they didn't cover his big, ugly butt.'

A heavy silence descended into the room. Burns looked to be on the verge of saying something, but couldn't quite bring himself to do it. Shaun knew he'd come around eventually. Powerful men like Bill Simmonds and Brick Turner—and the third wheel, Burns—were given to boasting about their exploits, because they lived off it, they believed in their own invincibility. And anyway, what was the point of possessing secrets if you didn't reveal them to anyone? The buzz was power, the power to *tell*. It was the unmaking of many a felon.

Shaun decided to try and draw in the ex-goon. He leaned over the bar and said in a confidential tone, 'Come on, Burns.

No-one's going to hurt you. We're just shooting the breeze here. Get with it, can't you? Shit, even if it was given a red-hot chance, I don't think the present administration would want to dig up these old bones. They've got enough problems with the drug squad to worry about.'

Wollansky gave a snort. It had been an inglorious time for the now-disbanded squad. Major prosecutions were on hold pending investigations into the detectives involved. All kinds of rorts had been uncovered, and some ex-members were going down for forgetting which side they were on.

After a long moment's deliberation Burns said, in a surprisingly small voice, 'Mitch Alvarez was a fallen angel. He burned himself.'

'Spoken like a true prophet, Burns,' Shaun said, equally restrained. 'You ought to be full bottle on that. But tell me: did you hesitate for any longer than a minute before accepting that first pay envelope from Simmonds? Way back when?'

'I didn't hesitate at all,' Burns said with surprising candour. 'It was a bonus simply for doing the job I was paid to do anyway. I often prioritised cases, put 'em on hold, or filed 'em in the WPB. A blizzard of paper hit my desk every day, so I was in an ideal position to run interference. I just had to be discriminating about it, once I was on the team.'

'The fixer,' Shaun said. 'The insider.'

'Yeah, the fixer,' Burns said with some puffed-up pride, which came across as rather comical given his present situation. 'Bill Simmonds was the man. He had power. He had respect. He ran the streets and put the thugs in their proper place when no-one else had the balls to. It was the Wild West in those days. Nobody fucked with Bill—or if they did, they paid the price.'

'That's what it was all about,' Wollansky said. 'Being on the right team, I mean. Everyone understood the system, including Mitch. As you may recall he used to be a big-time gambler, so when he switched sides he was simply exercising his better judgement, like a jockey going with the form horse, the one with the black-type pedigree. It was a living certainty. Should've been, anyway. All he had to do was stay in the saddle and steer it. Instead it was a royal fuck-up, from go to whoa.'

Ignoring all that, Shaun said, 'Remember a guy named Johnny Wu?'

'Johnny Wu? Chinese gangster?'

'Yeah.'

'I remember him. He crashed and burned too, didn't he?'

Shaun studied Wollansky. His puzzled brown eyes were not lying. He didn't know.

'Yeah. In a big way.'

It was becoming clear to Shaun now that Brent Wollansky had been a peripheral player all along: a provider of plans, weapons and other services, such as suggesting a useful container depot for which his company had the account—but what else?

He didn't know Simmonds had shot Mitch.

He didn't seem to know that Johnny Wu had wasted Andy, and that in turn Bill Simmonds had put Wu to the torch.

He was apparently removed from the hot centre of action.

Shaun returned his attention to Burns.

'Burns, you knew Simmonds and Turner were robbing the evidence storage facility, didn't you?'

'Of course.'

'You shared in the profits?'

Burns laughed. 'Who are you, the chief prosecutor? Yeah, I took a cut.'

'An equal third share?'

'No, I got less than that. Just some walk-around money, basically.'

'And you knew Simmonds and Turner planted that evidence to crucify Mitch, Andy Corcoran and me?'

Burns shrugged. 'It was a case of you or me, buddy boy. A no-brainer, as the man said.'

'So, the bottom line is, you aided and abetted a conspiracy to pervert the course of justice.'

'Well, if you wanna put it that way, Mr Clean Hands prosecutor.'

'How would you put it?'

Burns drew a deep breath. 'It was survival, McCreadie. That's all. You bastards didn't realise what you were letting yourselves in for. Your fatal mistake was that you got in Bill Simmonds' face. That was the start of all your troubles, sunshine. Once you did that, there was no way back. You were fucked and far away.'

Shaun lit another cigarette. Again, the one he'd been smoking had been forgotten, and burnt itself out.

'What about now, Burns? Has Bill Simmonds still got you under his thumb?'

Burns was visibly miffed. He had an almost effeminate way of showing it, by performing a sort of shoulder-shuffle with his arms folded across his chest. 'It was never that way. It was always a mutual arrangement.'

Somehow Shaun couldn't see anything mutual about it. Once Simmonds had an Internal Investigations detective by the nuts it would be one-way traffic. Simmonds would have no respect, only contempt, for a man like Burns, a glorified pen-pusher and paper-shuffler who was anxious to ingratiate himself into the company of real cops, real men. Even when he was in the consorting squad he probably didn't cut it, not really. He simply didn't have charisma. He was a pathetic hack, constantly seeking approval.

The third wheel in The Three.

'We're all here right now because of Simmonds,' Shaun said. 'But does anyone know why?'

Wollansky shook his head.

'Said he wanted a powwow. That's all I was told.'

'And when he calls and says he wants a powwow, you drop everything? Even now?'

Wollansky drained his can.

'Shaun,' he said, 'what you fail to understand is that once you sign on with a man like Bill Simmonds, that's it. It's like joining the fucking Mafia. You don't tender your resignation. He can get rid of *you*, but it doesn't work the other way. What's the line in that Eagles song, *Hotel California*? Something about checking out, but never leaving. That sums it up. And the only way you can check out is with a label tied to your big toe.'

'And you've got no idea what he wanted today.'

'Nope.'

'What about you, Burns?'

Shaun was thinking: Simmonds called Burns last night at three. He said, 'I'm there now', meaning Burns knew where he was and presumably why he was there. Burns had to know about the planned abduction of Joanna Steer.

Burns' body language told the story. Shifting his feet and jutting out his jaw in a sort of defiant pose, he said, 'Not really.'

Shaun's right fist began to clench.

'Not really,' Shaun said levelly.

Burns looked everywhere in the room, except at Shaun. There it was, right there.

'He isn't coming, Burns,' he said softly. 'Understand?'

With great difficulty Burns was finally able to return Shaun's intense, unforgiving stare.

He nodded.

'So you're free. You're off the hook. His time is over.'

Wollansky looked at Shaun, clearly trying to decide if it could be true or not. But he knew Shaun was a serious guy, doing a serious job.

A man on a mission.

And Wollansky had to believe him.

'Well, what about one for the road, Mr Burns?' he said after a while. 'Then I have to go to lunch. Not that I have much of an appetite now.'

Shaun checked the time. It was past noon. Two green cans were popped and placed on the bar towel.

Wollansky picked up his can and regarded it for a moment.

'I feel we should toast something, but I don't know what,' he said.

'End of an era,' Shaun said.

'Yeah. End of an era. Good riddance.'

They touched cans as Burns watched. Shaun knew that without Bill Simmonds calling the shots, Burns was nothing. He was a eunuch.

There came the sound of someone trying to open the front door. An elderly man was peering through the tinted glass, a hand cupped around his eye.

'Time to open up, Nifty,' Wollansky said. 'You've got a paying customer out there.'

Shaun reached behind him, under the shirt, withdrew a pistol from his waistband and placed it casually on the bar. For a long moment no-one breathed. As soon as he saw it, Burns closed his eyes, as if in prayer. Alarm filled Wollansky's features, but he did not move or make a sound.

'Relax, Brent,' he said. 'It's a toy.'

'Doesn't look like one,' Wollansky said—relief only too evident in his voice.

He picked it up, demonstrating its harmlessness before turning it around butt-first and offering it to Burns.

'Your property, I believe, Burns,' he said. 'I'd lose it if I were you. Someone might think you want to pull a stunt with it.'

He lobbed the piece at Burns, who caught it awkwardly on his chest. He was visibly shocked as his mind grappled with the question of how it had ended up in Shaun McCreadie's hands. Minds raced, but no-one said anything for a full minute as Shaun and Wollansky finished their cans. They went out together and stood on the pavement next to Wollansky's car, which was a brand-new anthracite Jaguar XK8 convertible, with the hood down: risky in this neighbourhood, but it showed Wollansky was rich enough not to care. He had the key in his hand, but hadn't yet de-alarmed the car. Shaun could see how anxious he was to get inside it and drive away, but he wasn't quite ready to let him leave yet.

'How do you think that went down, Brent?' he said.

Wollansky studied his car key for a moment before meeting Shaun's unrelenting green eyes. 'You certainly make your presence felt, don't you?'

'You okay about it all now?'

Wollansky nodded. 'Yeah, I'm perfectly okay about it.'

'Understand the issues involved?'

'Yeah, I have a grasp of that.'

'What about Burns?'

Wollansky snorted. 'I wouldn't worry about Nifty Burns. All he wants is for his customers to go away so he can hit the Johnnie Walker.'

'Yeah, I guess,' Shaun said. 'He's a right mess, isn't he? A sack of crap, one might say.'

'Has been ever since he gave the job away. That created a big hole in his life, which can only be filled with the JW, apparently.'

Shaun lit a cigarette. 'Yeah. Listen, Brent, before you go.'

'What?'

'Have you had any, uh, return calls from Leon Turner? Since I was up there, I mean.'

'Nope.'

'He told me a lot of stuff, you know. I had my doubts for a while, thought he might've been running off at the mouth, big-noting himself, but I don't think that anymore. He gave me the whole fuckin' deal, inside-out and every which way, and he managed to touch off a few raw nerves along the way. At the end I, uh, lost it a bit and gave him a decent old pasting. We were on the beach, talking, and I just . . . lashed out and into him, old and near-dead as he was.'

'I guess you had a lot of pent-up anger.'

'Pent-up anger, yeah. I didn't think I was carrying any of

that, but it turns out I am. I wanted to put him down, right there on the fuckin' beach. I mean, I was fuckin' *savage*. Out of control.'

Wollansky was nodding, wondering what the point was.

Shaun stepped closer, so he was right next to Wollansky's face. They were about the same height, and stared straight into each other's eyes. To Wollansky's credit he didn't waver, although at that range he didn't have much choice.

'I don't want any repercussions from what went on in there today, Brent. None.'

'You won't get any from me, mate,' Wollansky said straightaway.

'Good.'

Wollansky moved towards his car.

'There's just one more thing,' Shaun said. He produced the business card Wollansky had given him and put it in front of his eyes. Wollansky glanced at it before he returned his gaze to Shaun with the shadow of a cumulous cloud crossing his features.

'Does your company have responsibility for an old container depot off Lorimer Street?' he said softly, aware that Wollansky's eyes were watching his lips move. 'Don't lie to me, Brent.'

Wollansky ran his tongue around his lips. There was a dry, clicking sound coming from inside his mouth. Shaun would never have thought Smooth Wollansky was a man who knew much fear, or could ever be stood over, but he was showing signs of distress right now. It seemed material success had made him soft.

'We look after some places down that way, I guess so, yeah,' he said.

Shaun put the card in Wollansky's shirt pocket. Then he dug out the other one, the folded-over one he'd found at the site, and held it in front of Wollansky's concerned face.

'See, Brent, I don't need your card, because I already have one. And you know where I got it, don't you?'

Wollansky swallowed and nodded.

'This is just so you know the whole score, Brent,' Shaun

said. 'You gave certain information to Bill Simmonds very recently that was grievously harmful, possibly even fatal, to my wellbeing. Maybe he put the screws on you, I don't know. But where I've been for the last eleven years that sort of minor detail would not matter. The offender would be cut open and then strung up with his own guts. Are you with me?'

Wollansky continued nodding. The safety of that Jaguar was a million light years away.

'Remember, Brent. I know you did that. I'll give you a pass on it—for now. I'm prepared to give you the benefit of the doubt, because you're not a complete and total cunt, like Simmonds and Burns. At least you have some redeeming qualities, plus I believe you are genuinely remorseful about your part in what happened to Mitch. He got himself caught up in the mangler in a way that perhaps you didn't anticipate. Even though you should have. Lie down with sluts and you *will* get up with the pox. So, don't push it, Brent. I've still got plenty of that pent-up anger to go around if I get one breath of grief from your general direction. *Ever.*'

Shaun was now so close Wollansky winced as if he thought he was going to be head-butted, and was bracing himself for the impact. But then Shaun stepped back, evenly balanced on the balls of his feet, arms loose at his sides, ready for anything. It was the classic prisoner's stance: poised, locked and loaded.

'You've got nothing to worry about from me,' Wollansky said. 'That's a pledge.'

Now Shaun was nodding, measuring the sincerity of Wollansky's words and overall demeanour. Then he reached out, squeezed his arm lightly—significantly—and released him.

'Nice chariot, Brent. Given your current status, I don't think you would welcome an investigation that's gonna put you in the stand and dredge up a whole bunch of real bad shit from the old days. Am I right?'

'Definitely,' Wollansky said automatically.

Shaun edged slightly closer, holding the other man's eyes. 'Just between you and me and that bag of garbage indoors, I wouldn't bother going anywhere near that container yard. Scratch it off the list. Nothing there for you except a hard road to a place you don't wanna be in, believe me.'

'What container yard?' Wollansky said, dry-mouthed.

Shaun continued to claim his eyes close-up for a significant moment before giving him a wide smile.

'That's all I wanted to say, Brent. Go and have your lunch. Enjoy the rest of your life.'

He turned, walked away and was gone around the corner before Wollansky had time to climb into the open Jaguar, where he let out a long, deep breath and sat stunned for three whole minutes before he could bring himself to put the key in the ignition.

'Holy fucking *Christ*,' he said, and whistled soundlessly as he accelerated down the street.

The first thing Shaun did when he got home was to remove his shirt and have Jo cut through the brown packing tape that was wrapped twice around his body, holding the miniature cassette recorder firmly in place on his six-pack stomach. Once she had used the scissors he unpeeled the tape from around his back, then gritted his teeth before separating it from his mat of stomach hair with one painful rip. If he'd been a real professional he'd have shaved his body first, but then, what was a moment of discomfort in the overall scheme of things?

The Panasonic recorder was the smallest and most expensive one he could buy at Dick Smith's. From it a wire— also taped over—ran up his chest, so that the miniature, acutely sensitive microphone was about level with his second-top shirt button. When he had his shirt on and buttoned up there was no sign whatever that he was wired for sound.

As he'd followed Brent Wollansky out of the Unicorn he had surreptitiously slid his hand up inside his shirt and pressed the Stop button, so that the exchange on the pavement was not recorded.

The tape ran for around forty-five minutes, and throughout the sound quality was outstanding for an amateur effort. To his layman's ear it was as good as anything on radio. All three voices were clear, distinctive and could be readily identified, especially as Shaun had made a point of using names frequently so as to avoid any possible confusion. And yet, although there were many incriminating admissions made during the session, he realised that the tape would never be admissable evidence in any court of law. Apart from the issue of proper authorisation and authentication, there were numerous occasions when statements were made as a result of glaringly leading questions, and there were also times when Shaun had virtually put words into the speaker's mouth. And so, even though the confessions from both Wollansky and, later, Burns, were perfectly clear and unequivocal, and damning, any defence attorney worth his fee would be able to convince a judge to throw them out for a variety of legal and technical reasons.

But that wasn't why Shaun had made the tape.

If a time ever came when the Petrakos case was reopened, or if there was ever a more wide-ranging inquiry into police corruption in Victoria, then the tape would serve as a reference point, a useful tool for investigators running down instances of abuse of power, dereliction of duty, graft, bribery, extortion and murder. One revelation would lead to another. History showed that once a juggernaut like that got moving there was simply no stopping it. The choice was to get on board, or go under and get chewed up. Witness protection programs went into overdrive, old loyalties were forgotten as everyone got their stories straight, amazing reports hit the papers daily and, of course, lawyers had a field day. This was what had happened in the long-running Independent Commission Against Corruption in New South Wales. The lid was lifted, and the air became ripe with hot denials and counter-accusations.

Not that Shaun believed such an inquiry would ever be instituted in Victoria. As he had said in the pub, it was in no-one's interests to dig up old bones. There was no political mileage in it for anyone.

However, it was an extra string to his bow. Although he believed neither Brent Wollansky nor Neville Burns posed any threat, it was essential in such circumstances to have extra insurance, a Plan B to fall back on. And so, he would make two copies of the tape, send one to Wollansky and another to Dave Wrigley, to be played and acted on only in the event of anything unfortunate happening to Shaun. The original he would hold on to.

The way Shaun now saw it, Bill Simmonds initially hired Bernie Walsh to recover the lost cash with a hit-and-run mission, and when he failed to deliver he roped together the old, trusted team for one last payday. Burns was on tap and had a pub, which served as a useful rendezvous and centre of operations. *Must've* been Burns on the other end of Simmonds' phone at the container yard, confirming the arrangements. Maybe at that hour the publican was too pissed to remember what they were, and had to double-check. Shaun had little doubt the plan to abduct Jo was hatched in the Unicorn between the two old cops. Trouble was, Burns was now a lush and a has-been who couldn't cut it any longer. He was anything but *nifty*. For his part, Wollansky came over as a reluctant conscript. He had a thriving business, so why would he want to get involved in this shit after all these years? The answer had to be that Simmonds strong-armed him into it. On top of that, Brick Turner had one leg in the grave, and former drug czar Morris Salisbury was nuts.

His private army of followers was no more, but Simmonds couldn't accept it. He was living in dreamland. Now Shaun had to sweat for a while and hope he did not appear again in the real world, anywhere, anytime.

Sydney Private Eye Henry Agar Found Dead

By Louise Dhouma

Homicide and arson squad detectives are sifting through the burnt-out wreckage of a Milson's Point office building in the search for clues regarding the violent death yesterday of prominent Sydney private investigator Henry Agar.

Firefighters were called to the premises at around 10 P.M. last night as the fire threatened to spread to a high-rise apartment building next door. Three units took over five hours to subdue the flames.

According to a police spokesman, the victim's burnt remains were found in a bathroom area at the rear of the office. 'We don't know the full story at this stage, but we believe Mr Agar had been brutally attacked and mutilated with a sharp, heavy weapon such as an axe or a cleaver before the perpetrator set fire to the building, apparently in an attempt to cover up the murder.'

The 58-year-old Agar, a flamboyant personality and a familiar sight in the Double Bay area in his gold-plated Rolls-Royce, heavy clusters of jewellery and trademark black clothes, has long been associated with Sydney's sleazy underbelly. When challenged by a reporter over his extravagant car, he once quipped: 'I like to have a decent set of wheels under me.'

Supposedly under the patronage of bent detectives and leading organised crime figures, Agar's name has been linked to serious offences going back to the 1970s, including the rape and murder of Penelope White in 1985. Although his private investigator's licence was under threat many times, he was invariably able to beat any charges, often due to the unwillingness—or inability—of witnesses to testify against him.

Perhaps the lowest point in his turbulent life was the suicide of Cambodian Princess Soong Ran, who was pregnant to him, in

1988. The couple were to be married, but Agar cancelled out after the substantial dowry he expected was cut off by her parents, who bitterly opposed the marriage.

In more recent times Agar tried to have a movie made of his life, based on the biography by Sydney crime reporter Jack Pace. Producer Martin Braddock recalled that Agar approached him with a screenplay he had written himself.

'It wasn't all that bad,' Braddock said at his office this morning. 'We had some discussions, I suppose you'd call them. He seemed to believe he could get his movie made using tactics you might expect on a construction site. I remember he insisted the only actor who could play him was John Malkovich.'

22

By mid-afternoon, Shaun was showing signs of becoming unglued in new and different ways. His skin and hair hurt to touch, his overwrought brain was in a continuous swirl, he'd developed a tic under his left eye, and a violent twitching had started up in the depths of his stomach. It was as if something trapped in there was trying to kick its way out. Whenever he shut his eyes he felt as if he was spinning backwards into a black void with no lifeline.

There were moments right now when Shaun thought he was heading in the same direction as Morris Salisbury—down that one-way road to the funny farm.

Under continuous pressure he had to crash and burn. Staying cool all those years was now exacting its price. He could visualise himself sitting out on the green lawns in a trance, lobotomised or doped up to the eyebrows: the richest inmate in the asylum.

Bull*shit*.

He got up from the sofa, did fifty push-ups and fifty sit-ups without raising a sweat, then undressed and treated himself to a coldish shower, standing under it with his face upturned for ten whole minutes. When he had dried off he put on clean clothes and went out into the courtyard where Jo was sitting in an oversized white shirt and blue jeans, reading what looked like a textbook and sipping a 'gin-ton', as she called it. He leaned over and kissed her on the lips, and straightaway felt brand new.

'Better?' she said. She touched his five o'clock shadow.

'Much.' He could taste the gin from her lips. Nice.

'Sit down,' she said. 'I'll get you something. What do you want?'

He put his hand between her legs. She responded by opening up a little. A mist seemed to rise from within her and cloud over her green eyes. Shaun withdrew his hand from the warm place and cupped the back of her head, bringing her flushed face against his.

'Oh, my *God*,' she sighed, crumpling into him.

'Love you, baby,' he whispered into her bunched hair. 'Love you . . .'

'I know,' she whispered back.

'Always and always . . .'

She nodded against his face. 'Yeah . . . scares me a bit.' He held her tight and wasn't sure if it was his heart or hers he could hear thudding. Maybe it was both. But he understood what she meant. He, too, was scared: that she might come to her middle-class senses and terminate her flirtation with the wild side as suddenly as she'd bought into it.

When they separated he said, 'One of those will do it.'

'What?'

'Gin-ton.'

'Oh. Yeah.' She smiled and got up, brushing him with her body as she passed. He sat in one of the iron chairs and looked around at the garden. It was a sort of rockery with a variety of spring flowers in bloom, and tiny birds were chirping and darting in and out of the trees and shrubs. The air was still and warm. Life was pretty damned good.

From inside he heard the phone ring. Jo picked up, but he couldn't quite hear what she was saying through the open door. After a moment she appeared, brandishing the portable handset and said, 'It's for you. Dave Wrigley.'

Shaun's heart nearly stopped. Bill Simmonds, he immediately thought. He's got out, or they've found him. It's all gonna turn to shit, right now . . .

In the doorway she gave him the phone and began moving away, but he grasped her wrist. She needed to be part of this, whatever it was. She was one step up from him, so their eyes were about level.

'Dave?'

'Yeah. How's it going, man?'

'Travelling. What's up?' His eyes were fixed on Jo's, jumping anxiously from one to the other. His grip slid from her wrist to her hand, which he squeezed lightly. She edged so close she could hear Dave's clear cop's voice.

'Well, there was an incident last night, a drive-by shooting. Did you hear about that?'

'Nope.'

'Someone put a couple of shotgun blasts through this guy's front window in the middle of the night. No witnesses. The shooter vamoosed in a high-powered vehicle, left burnt rubber marks on the road. Neighbours said he smoked the street before taking off at a million miles an hour.'

'Yeah.' Curious as he was, he had no intention of hurrying Dave. Jo moved even closer, nestling her head on his shoulder as he slipped his arm around her waist, inside the loose shirt. Her back was soft and warm. His fingers moved up and down her lower spine.

'When he was interviewed, the victim claimed he had no idea who it was, who would do such a thing. He was in a state of shock, but obviously lying, apparently. And as we both know, attacks of this type are *always* carried out by a close associate, or former close associate, of the victim—right?'

'Right.'

'The victim in this instance was one Rick Stiles.'

'Yeah? No shit.'

'No shit.'

Shaun had a pretty good idea who the other party was, but he was happy for Dave to spell it all out for him. He was doing a top job so far.

'Anyway, this morning, guess what? Mr Stiles has a change of heart. Calls us to say he is prepared to nominate the shooter. That's one thing. But then, the kicker: he also says he wishes to retract the evidence he gave in relation to the murders of George and Stephanie Petrakos.'

Shaun suddenly felt as if he'd been dropped in a hole. His stomach leapt up, and he tightened his grip on Jo's waist.

'Christ.'

'Yeah. Stiles, as you remember only too well, was his main man back then. But no longer. For some reason they've had a major falling out.'

'Always just a matter of time,' Shaun said.

'Yeah. You might be right, man. This could turn out to be one for the cold-case unit.'

'If he goes through with it. These people have a way of changing their minds back again when they've had a chance to cool off.'

'Right. He sounded adamant, though. Word I got is that he is seriously aggrieved, in fact. Wants the shooter's nuts in a jar two days ago. Stiles has a wife and two little ones who were in the house at the time. Fortunately no-one was hurt apart from Stiles. He copped some small fragments of glass. He was coming out of the bathroom when the shots went off. Been watching TV, right in the line of fire. Would've been turned into sushi if he hadn't gone for a squirt.'

'Lucky man.'

'Anyway, the cold-case unit is flat chat right now. They probably won't get around to him until sometime next week.

Local CIB will handle the drive-by separately. Just thought you might be interested.'

Wrigley's words seemed to be reaching him via an echo chamber, from somewhere far removed both in time and space. Sometimes the echo actually got ahead of Wrigley's words, completing his sentences before he had uttered them. Shaun was well aware, however, that the distortions were occurring inside his own head, like a déjà vu effect induced by his over-eagerness to embrace the reality of what Wrigley was telling him: the whole can of worms might yet be reopened.

'I'm very interested, Dave. Having trouble getting a grip on it. Uh . . . is he in the phone book? Stiles?'

'Yeah. Caversham Drive, Moorabbin. You can't miss it. It's the only house with the front blown away.'

'Thanks a million, Dave.'

'Just hang cool, man.'

'I will. Don't worry.'

'And I never called you.'

'Absolutely not.'

Dave Wrigley disconnected. Shaun drew a deep, deep breath, and slowly let it out.

'Did you get all that?' he said to Jo, arm still tight around her.

'Yep. It means they'll have to reopen the case, doesn't it?'

'If Stiles stands up. If Stan doesn't get to him first. If the DPP decides it's warranted. There's a whole bunch of ifs to get over yet. But, it's a start.'

'What are you going to do?'

'Gonna have a chat to Mr Stiles. While he's still hot to trot.'

'Not now?'

He had both arms around her. 'No, no; not now. Tomorrow. *Now* I want that gin-ton.'

While Shaun was sipping his drink, mulling over Dave's words and their possible implications, Stan Petrakos was cruising the streets of East Melbourne. It wasn't a big suburb—hardly a suburb at all. You could walk around it in half an hour.

On the front passenger seat of the Ferrari was a copy of *The Age*, turned to Corin Makepeace's Back Page column. Stan was alternately glancing at the photograph of the house from which Sean McCreadie was leaving, and the houses either side of the street as he drove slowly along. He was searching for a two-storey Victorian place, painted off-white, with a red front door and yellow roses all over the pillars that supported the porch.

Underneath the newspaper was his sawn-off shotgun.

Soon enough he turned into Powlett Street, and immediately something told him he was in the right ballpark. He slowed even more, examining each house. There were a lot of Victorian terraces. The few people he saw were old and genteel-looking. The whole area seemed to be an enclave for rich greyhairs, seeing out their days strolling around the neighbourhood and messing around in their gardens.

Stan stopped outside a large house with a red door. He held up the newspaper, eyes darting from photo to house, back and forth, matching up the details until he was sure he'd hit paydirt. He dropped the paper back on top of the shotgun just as two teenaged girls in school uniforms crossed the road in front of him. They both looked at the Ferrari, and at Stan, who stared back at them: *go away, little girls*. They wandered off, one of them giving Stan a last glance over her shoulder.

He drove on, passing the girls so slowly they looked a little nervously at him, as if he were going to try to pick them up. But the girls had already gone from Stan's mind as he turned the next corner and did a lap of the block. He was now fully pre-occupied with thoughts of Shaun McCreadie, tapping the wheel with his fingertips as he tooled along the quiet streets. When he re-entered Powlett Street he made a decision to park well short of the house and wait for however long it took for McCreadie to show. Problem was, there were no spaces. This didn't worry Stan: he double-parked alongside a Commodore and settled in for the wait, his motor idling. He turned on the radio and listened to golden oldies on 104.3, his eyes glued to the house in question. Fifteen minutes passed, then half an hour. Stan began to fidget. Patience was not his long suit. He surfed through the radio stations before coming back to the golden oldies: Lovin' Spoonful's 'Hot Time In The City'. *Gonna be hot for you, McCreadie—real soon I hope. Wanna see the look on your face just before I—*

'Excuse me,' a man's voice said beside him. 'Would you mind moving? I have to get out.'

Stan looked at the guy: at least seventy-five, tweed jacket and hat, thick glasses, pocked nose. Looked like a retired professor or something. Then he noticed that the old coot was not looking at Stan anymore, but past him, at the newspaper. Stan took one look and said 'shit' under his breath. Part of the weapon was clearly visible—and this old bastard had clocked it. Stan quickly covered it up and moved forward enough for the Commodore to get out. He watched the guy in his rear-view mirror. He took an eternity getting into the car, and then sat looking at the Ferrari for an equally long time. *Go on, piss off, you prick.* Eventually he drove away at a glacial speed. Stan was more than a little concerned now: while he was sitting in the car all that time, the old guy could've written down Stan's registration number. Nosy old bastards like him were always doing things like that—he was probably the big banana in the local Neighbourhood Watch.

Fuck it. Stan now saw that he'd missed his chance. There were three people who could testify that he was at the scene prior to the killing of Sean McCreadie. As much as he loved the Ferrari he cursed it now. And he cursed Rick Stiles as well, the weak bastard. They could've done the job in Rick's taxi, the perfect getaway car. There were hundreds of them, and they were all the same.

As he motored west along Victoria Street, on his way back home, Stan worked out a plan. At least he knew where to find

McCreadie. But he could move anytime—maybe he had already, because of the newspaper thing—so Stan would have to shift his arse. Tomorrow he'd hot-wire a car, an ordinary old bomb no-one would remember. Then he would come back and put McCreadie right out of business.

As soon as he'd turned into Caversham Drive at around nine-fifteen in the morning, Shaun spotted the address in question. There was a tradesman's vehicle out the front, from which two men were unloading a steel shutter. A third man was standing at the gate with his hands on his hips. Shaun drove slowly past the house and saw that it was a white, turn-of-the-century stucco-and-timber bungalow with an untended lawn, on which children's toys were scattered, and a dilapidated wire fence. There was shattered glass and debris and a gaping hole where the window had been. Shaun knew the scene inside would be a lot worse. A cold shiver ran down his spine. Even though he had never fired one outside of a police gun range he'd seen enough to realise that no weapon short of military hardware was more devastating or frightening than a shotgun. He parked in front of the next house and got out.

The man at the gate was maybe late thirties or a bit older, unshaved with terminally overlong sandy hair, denim jacket and worn-out jeans. Shaun remembered him vividly from the trial, and had no doubt it was Rick Stiles. Didn't look to have aged much in eleven years. But then, this was the type of dude who would never change his image, even when he was on the pension—if he made it that far. As he approached, Shaun thought, this hippie bastard perjured himself and put me away for life.

He waited until the tradesmen had carried the shutter onto the lawn, then said to the man in the denim jacket, 'Rick Stiles, right?'

The man zeroed in on him with eyes that zoomed in and out.

'Yeah,' he said warily, scanning the street as if to see if Shaun was alone. Understandably, he was jumpy and nervous. Shaun saw that he had a band-aid on his neck, and another one on the back of his right hand. Up close he saw deep vertical creases etched into Stiles' face, on which there were also lots of tiny cuts, like shaving nicks.

'I'm Shaun McCreadie.'

Stiles focused on him, crossing and uncrossing his arms and shifting his weight from one foot to the other, as if he expected Shaun to take a swing at him. The guy was hyped to blazes. He was on something for sure.

'Holy shit. So you are.' He put his hands up defensively. 'Hey, don't shoot, man. I got enough bad shit to deal with here.'

'I know,' Shaun said. 'Don't worry, Rick. I'm not gonna give you any more problems. I just want to talk to you is all.'

'How'd you know about it?'

'Little birdie told me.'

Stiles' pupils were dilating wildly. 'What you wanna talk about, man? Jesus, I can't believe it's you.'

'It's me all right, Rick. Eleven years later.'

'Yeah,' Stiles said. 'Eleven years.' Now he was unable to maintain eye contact. Shaun noticed he had dirty fingernails and a couple of tattoos on his arms, mostly concealed by his jacket sleeves. 'Well,' he said, and his attention wandered back and forth, 'I dunno what to say, man. Sorry doesn't cut it.'

'No, it does not. You lied on oath. If things hadn't panned out differently I could still be inside, forever.'

Stiles squeezed his lips together and nodded. He had no words. All he wanted was for this person, this ghost, to leave him alone. Say his say, then go.

'Listen, man,' Shaun said. 'I didn't come here about that. I'm not after revenge. It's over and done with. All I want is to hear your side of the story. I want to know what really happened that day. Understand?'

Stiles continued shifting around, running hands through his greasy hair, rubbing his chin, turning to spit on the pavement. Every gesture was indicative of his nervous, hyped-up state. Still, he was entitled to be nervous after having the front of his place shot to pieces. 'Well, I'm the one that can tell you, that's for sure.'

'Wanna go for a little stroll? These guys are okay on their own, aren't they?'

'Yeah, sure, I guess . . .' He glanced back at the workmen, who appeared to have matters in hand. But Stiles was far from sure about anything.

'Come on then. This'll be about an hour of your life, then I'm gone.'

'Guess that's not too much to ask, is it?' Stiles said, and laughed vacuously. Shaun touched his arm and led him along the pavement. Not far down the street there was a small park containing some benches and a children's playground. Shaun was anxious to get Stiles started while he was high. He had no doubt the guy would run like a tap once he was turned on.

They sat down on a wooden bench, and straightaway Shaun produced his cigarettes and offered one to Stiles: an old cop's tactic to win the subject over. When they were both alight, Shaun said, 'You were pretty damn lucky the other night.'

'Lucky? Christ, it was a fuckin' miracle. I was coming out of the can when I heard the shots. Couldn't fuckin' believe it, man. If I'd been back on the couch, a few seconds later, watching TV . . .' He shook his head and then sucked deeply on the cigarette, as if it were a reefer.

'It was Stan, wasn't it?' Shaun said.

Stiles nodded. He was staring at the ground, reliving the horror of it.

'Didn't think he'd ever do anything like that,' he said. 'Shit. I got two little girls, man. They could've been injured or killed.

And he's supposed to be their *godfather*. Wife's gone half-crazy . . . She's taken 'em off to her mother's.'

'Well, that's probably not a bad idea, while things get sorted out.'

'I know, but shit . . . I just can't *believe* he'd do that. Even now.'

'You two used to be good mates.'

'We were more than that,' Stiles said. 'Much more.'

'No longer, though,' Shaun said.

'He's a very disturbed, dangerous person. Should be put down.'

'You're prepared to testify against him?' Shaun said.

'Bet your balls on it. I want to see him removed from this world. I'm not scared of him, 'cause I know him too well for that, but . . . shit, he's a fuckin' worry, isn't he?'

'He sure is,' Shaun said.

Stiles sucked on the cigarette one last time, then flicked it away. 'We've known each other since school, down the peninsula. We were always together. Where you saw one of us, you saw the other. But he wasn't crazy in those days. A bit on the wild side, but not crazy.' He produced a crumpled pack of Stuyvesants from his shirt pocket and shook out two, one of which he offered to Shaun. With a slightly trembling hand he got them both ignited, then carried on. 'It was one of those . . . doomed families, you know, like that Kennedy crew. When Stan's mother was killed in the chopper crash, he was just completely and utterly fucked, beyond salvation. Stan loved her so damn much it was indecent. I think he was . . . sexually obsessed with her, to be brutally honest, and when she died it left a hole that could never, ever be filled. He never got over it. That was bad enough, but it was worse than that—a lot worse.' He inhaled a lungful of smoke and let it drift out of his nose and mouth as he spoke.

'As you probably know, his brother George took his own life when he was twelve years old.'

'Yeah, I did know that,' Shaun said. 'It was pretty gruesome, wasn't it?'

Stiles nodded. 'Awful. Shocking. Tore his throat apart on his old man's power saw. Beats me how anyone can . . .' He shook his head. 'I mean, what pain must he have been feeling inside, if *that* was the better option?'

Shaun didn't say anything. Stiles was really just thinking aloud, he realised that.

'One day, not long after George died,' Stiles said, 'Stan and I became blood brothers. You know how it is. We cut our wrists, pressed them both together, and swore to be loyal and true to one another forever. Jesus, you wouldn't do it these days, would you? Finish up with Hep B, or HIV.' He laughed, and so did Shaun. He was getting a bit of a feeling that Stiles wasn't a bad person—he was someone who had made a few wrong turns in life and was still paying for them. Becoming Stan Petrakos's blood brother was definitely a major one. But then, he had long been Stan's best buddy, and in a way it was to his credit that he had stuck by him, been loyal and true, through all the tough times.

'Stan had a big secret,' Stiles said. 'He was busting to spill it, but wouldn't, because it had been given to him by his brother just before the suicide. He was sworn to silence, but it was too much. It was eating him up inside. One day we were drinking some of his old man's wine, and he finally let the cat out of the bag. He was in tears while he was saying it, but he *had* to get it out. Sure explained a lot. *Shit.*'

Stiles threw down his cigarette and massaged his face. When he took his hands away his eyes had filled up. He sniffed, staring at the ground, and Shaun watched the teardrops fall. When he had straightened himself out a bit he took some deep breaths, and wiped his face with his sleeve.

'Sorry about that,' he said. 'Still gets me right here.' He hit himself in the chest.

'It's okay, man,' Shaun said. 'No hurry.'

'You have to understand some of the family history,' Stiles said. 'Stan's mother, Iris—well, she was truly a wonderful person, and beautiful too. Too perfect by far for old George. It was not a happy marriage. A clash of cultures, I suppose. She was Australian-born and he was a Greek, and as far as George was concerned that meant he ruled the roost. He was a proper bastard. Stan told me he used to slap his mother around if his meals weren't on the table at six sharp, or his favourite shirt wasn't ironed, whatever. Stuff like that. He used to belt the boys too, just because they were on their mother's side. It was a concentration camp. Stan used to say he couldn't help it, he was fucked up from the war. And then . . . one night, the old man was bashing her up in front of George and Stan because he believed she was having an affair. He was right off his scone. Anyway, young George has a go at him, and his old man gave him a proper hiding, using his fists, with Iris trying to drag him away. You can picture the scene. He beat the shit out of his own son. The Bull of Crete, he called himself. He was the *pig* of Crete.

'A while after that, the old man was gonna buy this country house, you see, a bed and breakfast place up near Mansfield. Had his own helicopter and employed a pilot, who was a nice guy. I remember him. George told the family over dinner that he was leaving in the morning and would be back during the afternoon sometime. Young George . . . he really had it in for the old man. You can't imagine how much he must've hated his guts. Now he saw his chance. So, he got up before daylight, and poured some sand into the fuel tank of the chopper. He was so fixed on killing his dad he didn't even care that the pilot would go down too. As long as the old man died, that was all that mattered. And then he went off to school without saying a word to Stan.

'Trouble was, in the morning, something came up and the old man couldn't go. It was some business problem he had to attend to. So, he sent Iris to look over the place instead. They got some distance before the sand blocked the fuel lines, and down she came in the North Warrandyte hills. The chopper

burst into flames on impact. When they called George from
class that morning he expected to be told his father was dead,
but when they said it was his mother . . . well, you can imagine
the reaction.'

Shaun was feeling a little stunned. 'I can,' he said.

'That was the big secret George told Stan later. He made
him swear he wouldn't tell anyone. When Stan told me, he made
me swear I wouldn't tell anyone. And I haven't—until now.'

Shaun said, 'And that was why—'

'Yeah. That was why George aced himself. Couldn't live
with it. Shit, how could he? How could anyone? Imagine—
you set out to kill the person you hate most in the world, and
end up killing the one you love most instead.'

Shaun had nothing to say. He was suddenly seized with
thoughts of Vincent O'Connell. Leon Turner was dead right:
with the best intentions in the world he had sent his friend
to a stupid, unnecessary death. It was something he would
have to live with now. He decided he would just sit tight and
let Stiles get on with the story in his own fashion. Shaun had
an idea there would be one or two more jolts to his system
before the ride was over.

'Jump-cut a respectful interval, and George marries
Stephanie Small,' Stiles said. 'Pin-up girl and porn movie star.
She couldn't have been more different from Iris. It was so
stupid. George was filthy rich by this time and thought he was
Australia's answer to Onassis. So he goes into overdrive, has
this ridiculous multimillion-dollar wedding, flies in guests from
all over the world. Then he decides to build this . . . monstrosity
out at Lancefield. It was supposed to be a symbol of his love
for her—a palace for his princess. What did the magazines call
her? "The Siren Goddess." Well, the way George was throwing
his money around it was obvious she had him by the shorts.
Whatever Steph wanted, she got. I dunno why she'd be all that
impressed, though. Wasn't as if she crawled out of the gutter,
was it?'

Shaun said, 'Did you know her?'

'Steph? Yeah, I met her—or should I say drooled over her—plenty of times. Seems a bit hard to believe, doesn't it? A bum like me, mixing it with the rich and beautiful. But I was coming in on Stan's coattails. We were close then. Blood brothers to the last, especially so after George junior . . . Stan used to say I was his replacement brother, and that's how it was. I had nothin', but Stan had more than enough cash for both of us. Drugs, booze, women, parties . . . it was wild. We were eighteen or nineteen, and he'd splash it around just like his old man. Crashed a brand-new Porsche once, and just left it there, abandoned it. Couldn't care less. Then he started hanging around with some dangerous people, having run-ins with cops, getting into fights. It was pretty obvious to me that he was not travelling.

'All this time, he was fighting with his old man. Bitterly, sometimes violently. You wouldn't believe the stuff they said to each other. When he got really wound up, George would slip into Greek, which Stan couldn't understand, and that would drive him around the twist. But then after the storm would come the attempts at reconciliation. It was very bumpy. When George and Steph moved to Lancefield, Stan stayed in his Carlton pad, even though there were rooms to burn up at the new place. Stan didn't want any part of it. He was part of the Carlton scene, anyway. But the old man used to get him up there on Sundays for a family lunch, you know, doing his best to hold it all together. Stan hated going, but went under sufferance. Sometimes he'd get me to go with him for moral support. They were very interesting occasions, I can tell you. It was always a matter of when, not if, the blue would start. They would argue about absolutely anything and everything. There were shouting matches across the table. After we'd eaten, when Steph was in the kitchen cleaning up, George would start on the brandy, and that was more or less a declaration of war. I can remember he'd bring out an unopened bottle of Metaxa and three glasses, which he would fill up. You'd only get halfway through it and he'd top up your glass. No-one was allowed to leave the table until the bottle was empty. In the end it was a total shambles. And then Stan and I would have to drive back to town. Shit. How we did that sometimes . . .' He shook his head, pupils zooming in and out.

'It was a test of manhood,' Shaun said.

'A test of something. I dunno what that was supposed to prove. But anyway, the Sunday lunch became an institution, a ritual. Even though he hated going, Stan could never resist because he wanted to attack his father. It was a fight to the death between them. How sick is that? I dropped out. It was too much for me. And then one day Stan drops a bombshell. He was good at that. He revelled in the telling of it, too. Told me he was screwing Steph.'

'Oh,' Shaun said. 'Shit.' What did this mean? Where was it going? He couldn't see, but it had to tie in somewhere . . .

'Having it away with his own stepmother,' Stiles said. 'Now I know that's not incestuous or evil or whatever, and she *was* hot stuff, but even so . . . Christ. How fucked up can one family get?

'The way Stan tells it, he goes to the bathroom during lunch one Sunday. He opens the door and there's Steph, sitting on the can. "Oops, sorry", he says, as you do, and she stands up and steps out of her pants. Without a word she pulls her sweater off over her head, and she's got nothing on under it. Picture that, Pilgrim. Then she tells him to snib the door. So Stan gives it to her, right there in the toilet. When they've finished they go back and resume eating lunch with the old man. And that was how it started.'

Having run out of Stuyvesants, Stiles crumpled the pack and tossed it towards a bin. When he missed, he got up and dropped it in. Shaun offered him one from his own nearly depleted pack. When he had it burning Stiles remained standing, with one foot resting on the bench. Shaun waited patiently for him to go on.

'Steph was hot,' he said. 'All that talk in the magazines about how she had changed, how she'd turned into a nun and was dedicating herself to her home and marriage—it was all complete bullshit. Stan couldn't wait to get up there after they'd broken the ice. The place was so big they had no trouble finding a room to do it in. They even went around the world in the marriage bed while the old man was downstairs pissed. They'd go out in the stables for a roll in the hay. Huh! When she wasn't riding horses, Stan was riding her. Steph said she didn't even care if George found out. She was so desperate for it she used to trawl around the city at night in a rented stretch limo, pick up guys from outside nightclubs and bars, do 'em in the stretch and then sling 'em to shut up.

'The old Bull of Crete . . . well, he couldn't get it up anymore. Not unless Steph used the whips and that on him, and she wasn't into that. She just wanted the sex, without all that, uh, heavy lifting. The bull's pizzle was a fizzer. Had been for a long time, she said, since a year into the marriage. All George wanted was to get smashed on Galliano every night. Used to put down bottle after bottle of it. Often he didn't even come up to bed, he was that legless. Must've had a cast-iron constitution though—he was up and at 'em at the crack of dawn seven days a week, fifty-two weeks a year.'

A chattering little girl and her mother walked by the park. Stiles whipped his head around, as if to check whether they belonged to him: evidently not. He switched feet on the bench, from the left to the right, rocking back and forth while he sucked on the cigarette. He seemed to be trying to organise his thoughts before putting them into words.

'I knew all that,' he eventually said. 'Understand. What I'm going to tell you now I found out later . . . a lot later.'

'Okay,' Shaun said. The vibe: *Get ready for anything.*

Stiles flicked the butt away and plunged his hands into his back pockets.

'Did you ever see *The Postman Always Rings Twice?*' he said. 'There are two versions—you've probably seen the Jack Nicholson one.'

'Yeah, I've seen it,' Shaun said.

'It's not as good as the original,' Stiles said, 'with John Garfield and Lana Turner. The gist of it is, they decide to bump off her husband and live happily ever after.'

'I remember,' Shaun said. 'It all goes to shit.'

'Of course—it's a James M. Cain novel. Anyhow, life imitates art, right?'

'If you say so.'

'I dunno who brought it up first, but Stephanie and Stan decided to get rid of George. Stan said it was her idea, but you know, he would, wouldn't he? Maybe it was the marriage of true minds, united in the face of a common enemy. So let's say she's the *femme fatale*—Lana Turner with brown hair. But Steph was more like Jane Russell in *The Outlaw*, especially when she's rolling around in the hay. I can see her doing it. We can say what we want about her now, can't we, since she's dead? She was trapped in a bad marriage. George was an old tyrant. He'd never let her go. He'd lose too much public face, not to mention the divorce settlement he'd be up for. The only way out was to snuff him. So she got Stan onside. Might've been why she started screwing him. The plan was, he'd do the hit, and then they'd live happily ever after. But as we know, that script never works out, does it?'

'No,' Shaun said, sitting up straight.

'Jump-cut several months,' Stiles said. 'They're in deep, and Stan's done his nuts. Who wouldn't? So one day during one of their little trysts, Steph informs him that she's overheard George on the phone talking to someone long distance about a drug shipment coming from overseas. She had no idea he was involved in this scene, and neither did Stan. Eager to please,

Stan says, don't worry, leave it to me, sweetheart, I'll fix it with my cop contacts. We'll rip him off. We have to kill him too, Steph says, and Stan sees how he can do both at the same time. But he's not stupid, Stan—he can see he's a logical suspect, so he needs a plan—a good one.

'He goes to Simmonds and Turner. Doesn't like either of 'em, but they're bent, they'll go for it. They bring in Morris Salisbury, and now we have a full cast list of arch villains. But it's not quite there yet. Stan doesn't tell them he plans to whack George, doesn't know how that will go down. And he's still iffy about it, he's still the suspect. They all wait for the dope to arrive: D-Day. Old Steph's constantly on the extension, eavesdropping on George.

'In the meantime, a major coincidence pops up. Cops—at least the ones in movies—don't believe in coincidences. They believe everything's, you know, destined to happen, it's written, it's all out there waiting to unfold. So how *ironic* is it when Mitch Alvarez, ex-*cop* and sworn enemy of the Petrakos clan, appears on the scene with a plan to rip off George's stash? Man. Simmonds has Alvarez champing at the bit. But he doesn't know about the *real* job. Doesn't know about the heroin. Doesn't know Steph and Stan want to put George down. Alvarez doesn't know shit. And neither do his two sidemen, right?'

Stiles was visibly captivated by his own narrative skills at this point. His grin was loose; the zooming eyes danced and bobbed. He was one spaced out, wired-up piece of business.

'As I said, I didn't know any of that until after the shit had flown. Until *after* what went down that Wednesday in October 1992.'

'As you say.'

'Hey, man, I'm no killer. If I'd realised—'

'It doesn't matter now.'

'Matters to me. I know I lied at the trial. But I had to. Understand—'

'I *do* understand. You and Stan were tight. And he had you. Get on with it.'

Stiles sat down again. 'Got any more cigarettes? There's a shop down the corner.'

'Got some, not many,' Shaun said. There were three left. 'Here.'

When Stiles had his hit of nicotine he made an effort to settle himself down before continuing.

'On that morning, the Wednesday, Stan calls and says he wants us to go up to Lancefield. Pretty unusual, since it wasn't Sunday, but I figured he was gonna jump on Steph's bones. Still . . . why would he want me along? I press the point. He says his car has engine problems, and will I drive. Sure, why not? I didn't have any plans for the day. I wish I did have. I wish I'd been up in Kakadu fishing for barramundi. I wish . . . but I wasn't, was I? So I chauffeured him up to Lancefield. And all the way there I had this uneasy feeling in my gut that something was not right about this. Stan was so tense, so goddamn *quiet* . . . so I pumped him, and eventually he says he's gonna rip off some dope. I bought it, but all the same I thought—'

Shaun suddenly remembered something.

'What were you driving?'

'At that time . . . I had a Ford Galaxie. Used to be my dad's, and he gave it to me.'

'What colour was it?'

'Safe family car colour—white.'

In his mind Shaun was back in the pretend-plumber's van with Mitch and Andy, heading for Lancefield on a secondary road that was under repair. A car rushes past in a big hurry, showering them with dust and stones, and Andy jokes: *Book the bastard, Mitch.*

The car: a white Ford Galaxie.

'I saw you,' Shaun said. 'Saw you on the road.'

'Yeah? Should've stopped me. Shit. Wish to Christ—'

'Get *on* with it, man.'

'Sorry. When we got there we stopped around the back—'

'At the double gates?'

'No, no—there's a single gate further around, near the stables. It's more inconspicuous, and there's good cover between it and the house. I dropped him there and he tells me to be back in an hour. He's carrying an overnight bag. I watched him slip inside, then went to the drive-through liquor store in Lancefield and bought myself a bottle of Tequila. Stopped on a back road, sluggin' it down. I was shittin' blood, bad. By the time I got back to the house I was half-tanked, but, man, I needed to be. Stan jumps into the car, throws his bag on the back seat and says, "*Drive! Go!*" Shit. So now I'm Steve McQueen in *The Getaway*, except I've got this big, ugly bastard next to me instead of Ali McGraw. When we were moving I looked across at him. I knew he'd done something terrible. He was heaving, there was blood smeared on his right hand, there was this . . . fine red *mist* on his face, hair and clothes—everywhere—as if he'd been spray-painted. He was *staring* through the windshield, absolutely rigid. He wouldn't say shit, but I pushed and shoved and slapped him, and then he . . . he turns and gives me this *maniac* stare. I'll never forget his words: "I did it. I killed my parents. Mate. You've got to help me. I've knocked 'em both!" "Bullshit!" I says, but I know it's got to be true. It's all over him.'

Stiles sat down and covered his face. Shaun had one cigarette left. He didn't want Stiles going to the corner store in case the thread was broken, so he lit it and gave it to him.

'By the time we hit town I was full bottle,' he said. 'Only by then, I didn't wanna be. The way Stan told it, he and Steph cooked it up together—*apart* from Simmonds and Turner. They didn't have a clue it was even on the menu. It was a private arrangement: Stan'd have his revenge for the death of his mother and brother, and Steph . . . Steph scored a quick, clean divorce. And afterwards . . . they'd have each other.'

'That fits.' Shaun was reminded of Turner's words: *No-one*

was supposed to die. What a fucking disaster: the 'classic inside-out job' had more inside dimensions than even the chief architects realised . . .

'Go on.'

'Plan was: Steph would go out riding as usual, except she'd have a float problem. Stan fixed it so the axle would run dry. So, Steph unhooks the car and heads home. See, being the widow, she would naturally be a suspect in her old man's murder, so they *arranged* it so she would arrive back at the house while all this shit was going on, someone robbing and killing her husband. She'd put on an act, and Stan'd give her a proper biffing. Cops would then believe she had blundered innocently into this, uh, violent scenario. That was her cover.' He sucked hard on the cigarette.

'He gave her a bit more than that, didn't he?' Shaun said.

'Like I said before, Stan might be clinically insane, but he's cunning with it. He realised that with George gone, Steph would inherit everything, the whole box and dice. Given the father–son relationship, this was a fair assumption. He wouldn't get a cracker. On top of which he *must've* seen that he was no catch, that Steph, beautiful *nympho* that she was, would drop him for the first pretty boy that came along. Shit, he must've seen she was probably only using him to get what she wanted. But Stan *loved* her. She was his squeeze. It's the old, old story, seen it in a bunch of movies: if he couldn't have her, well, no-one could. So he decided to dump her before she dumped him. He waited upstairs while you guys robbed George and gave him shit and, at the prearranged time, in strolls Steph. She, of course, is expecting to see *Stan*, not three hooded bastards playing merry hell. She panics. Stan waits, maybe hoping you'll fix the problem for him, but when you're gone he rushes downstairs and sees George and Steph both trussed up, eyes and lips sealed with packing tape. First he fills his overnighter with the dope, then removes the tape from his father's eyes so George can *see* who is on the other end of the shotgun that is in his face. Imagine how much he must've hated him. George apparently says one word: "*You*." Then Stan takes off his head at the stem. Steph's wriggling like crazy, she must've sensed it was all wrong. Stan doesn't help her, or even give her a biffing. He does a lot more than that.' He dragged on the dwindling cigarette, holding it inside his hand as if it were a roach. 'At least she didn't see it coming. He spared her that.'

Stiles threw down the last butt. Shaun was remembering Stephanie's entrance. It was a funny thing, but even at the time, with everything that was going on, he instinctively thought there was something odd about the way she performed. She seemed puzzled, or confused, more than genuinely shocked. Now he knew why: there were three intruders, not one. And none of them was Stan—she would've known him even in a ski mask. She must've seen then that somehow she'd been fucked over. It was a scene from a melodramatic movie, and Stephanie played it like the third-rate actress she was. That was, until she found out Stan had a different ending in store for her.

Poor Steph.

Poor, *stupid* Steph, for trusting in Stan. On countless occasions—in real life, not just in movies—women had exploited their magnetic power over men in exactly the way Steph had done, but few of them ever got anything except pain for their trouble. Every case was different, and yet they were all the same. Shaun was reminded of an episode some years earlier, in which the town cop was on with a farmer's wife. She prevailed upon him to bump off the farmer, so they could be together. The chemistry of sex and murder was a potent, irresistible mix: the cop shot the farmer, then attended the scene in his official capacity. An itinerant intruder was blamed, and they got away with it. They were home free. But then she discovered he was having it off with someone else on the side, so she gave him up, fully aware that she'd go down too. Revenge for his sexual betrayal was far more important to her than twenty years in the slammer.

He became aware that Stiles had picked up where he'd left off.

'. . . while we drove back. We delivered the dope to Salisbury's place, then zapped over to Stan's apartment in Carlton. He had a shower and put his clothes in a plastic bag, which we tossed in a factory dumpster on the way to my place. I'd worked out what to do by then. I was pissed enough to go with it. Anyhow I had no choice by that time: I was already an accessory. The alibi was that we were watching videos all afternoon. I got the idea from *12 Angry Men*—ever seen it?'

'Uh—doesn't ring a bell.'

'Top show. Classic, in the true sense. Son is accused of murdering his father. Nice ironic touch. Everyone on the jury except Henry Fonda assumes he did it, open and shut. It's a sweltering day, there's no air conditioning and they just want to find him guilty and get the hell out. The boy's alibi is that he had been to the movies, but when questioned by police he can't remember what he had seen, or who was in it.

'At that time I was in my Paul Newman period. I had three of his early ones at home: *Somebody Up There Likes Me*, *The Left-Handed Gun* and *The Hustler*. We stopped at my place to pick them up, but couldn't stay *there* to use the alibi because people may have seen me leave earlier, my car wasn't in the drive, so I couldn't have been home watching movies, could I? Instead we went to my girlfriend's place.'

'Linda Powell.'

'Yeah, Linda. She was a Pommie, and a schoolteacher, but she was all right, Linda. Loved a root and a cool drink. We bought a case of Victor Bravo and some more Tequila and dropped in unannounced. She lived in East Preston, in a neighbourhood where cops are the natural enemy. So we got stuck into the piss and watched vintage Newman. When she'd had a few I said to Linda that if anyone inquired, we'd been with her all afternoon. That was all. She was cool. I had to coach 'em both on the storylines to avoid the *12 Angry Men* problem, the boy not knowing what he should've known. Turned out to be a good day: I even jumped in the cot with her while Stan got smashed on the Mexican and VB chasers, watching Fast Eddie towelling up Minnesota Fats, potting ball after ball and saying, "How can I possibly lose?" God, I love that movie.'

Shaun looked at Stiles. He wasn't trying to be witty. The guy was nuts. Crazy in his own harmless way, but dead-set crazy all the same.

'Have you made your statement to the cops yet? About the drive-by.'

Stiles came out of his reverie. 'Uh, no, not yet. When I rang they said . . . they'd send someone around. Hasn't happened so far. Typical. Where's a cop when you need one?'

'You want to watch out for Stan. He might come back, especially if he finds out you're gonna blow the whistle on him. Word travels in the wind.'

'Yeah, I know. Still, what can you do? Shit, I might have to go into witness protection. Either that or go on the run. Otherwise I could finish up fish bait.'

After a silent spell, Shaun said, 'Why'd he do it?'

Stiles looked at him. 'What?'

'The drive-by.'

'Oh. Well, as a matter of fact, he plans to bump you off. Wanted me to assist, reprise my old driver's role. Must think I'm Ryan O'Neal. Anyway, I refused. Stan doesn't appreciate being refused. Not the Godfather. The *Godfather*. Christ.'

'Why would he want to do that?'

'Put you off? It's a strange thing . . . He actually blames *you* for the death of his parents. By that I guess he means George and Steph. Somehow, in the bizarre depths of what's left of his conscious mind, the part that hasn't been eaten away, he has managed to exonerate himself completely. He's now the bereaved son, out for revenge. *He actually believes he didn't do it.* Not only that, he's also managed to morph Iris and Steph into one and the same. It's his twisted way of dealing with the guilt, right? His *conscience* has simply collapsed under its own weight. So, put it on someone else. Get rid of it. And you're the obvious candidate, my friend.'

'I see that. But if he can't find me, you'll serve. Because you're *there.*'

'Yeah. And refusing to help him, refusing to play along with his bullshit, that's a slap in the face. It says: come on, you did it, Stan. *Face facts, man.* And he can't. Can't cop it. He's a fuckin' psychiatrist's dream, no doubt. There's a thesis in that guy.' He pushed a hand through his unwashed hair, sighed and said, 'I don't hang with Stan as often as I used to, which means I can appreciate how far he has deteriorated whenever I *do* see him. He's livin' with the pixies. Maybe he hears little voices. Maybe he's schizo. Guess it's in the genes—George was pretty damn warped. Then again, he's cunning . . . could be playing mind games. If so, he's a fuckin' good actor—better than Brando ever was.'

'What are his plans for me?' Shaun said.

'Drive-by. What else?'

Oh, wonderful. *Does he know where I live?*

If not, he can find out. Driven psychopaths like Stan always do. Then he remembered: shit, it was in the fucking paper.

Silence descended on the tiny playground. Shaun felt he was on information overload. He was also starting to feel a little unsettled. Different thoughts flashed through his mind— some connected, others not. With all the pieces apparently in place, it was now clear that everyone involved had a bit of it, but no single person, not even Stan, had the whole picture.

Stiles snapped him out of it. 'You know what?' he said. 'Stan used to babble on about the Menendez brothers, Lyle and Erik. Dudes that shot their *wealthy parents* over in LA, remember?'

'Yeah. Of course.' The names in that sensational case were almost as well known as O.J. Simpson's. There were obvious parallels with Stan. Amazingly, the name Menendez had jumped unbidden into his mind one second before Stiles had said it.

'They were his fuckin' heroes, man. His *inspiration*. Can you grasp that? I remember . . . he used to say they *almost* pulled off the perfect crime, except that they started throwing money around straight after the murders, when they should've been in mourning, and then the younger one went to water. Stan said he wouldn't spend up—he learned his lesson in that restaurant robbery, when he was busted for doing the same thing. You'd probably be familiar with that.'

Shaun nodded. Their major problem, as he saw it then, was that there were *two* of them sharing this terrible secret. The younger, weaker one—Erik—cracked early on and spilled his guts to his shrink. Then they started arguing with each other, after which it was only a matter of time before the whole scam came apart. Stan didn't have the problem of a weak accomplice, but that only meant he had to tear *himself* apart—along with whoever else was in range.

23

Suzen Christopher was inspecting herself. Swaying slightly in front of the full-length mirror that covered the wardrobe in Stan's bedroom, she put her face so close to the glass it misted up. Even through the mist, and in her stoned condition, she was impressed with what she saw. Jet-black, dead straight hair fell over her forehead like a raven's wing. Under the fluorescent light there was a slight metallic sheen to it. Her eyes were a Gothic marvel: black, pencil-thin brows, long, curling black lashes, kohl (imbued with specks of silver glitter) painted on the lids, and a heavy dose of mascara underneath. Suzen wore ice-blue contacts, which gave her that living dead, vampiric quality. Her naturally pallid skin—which saw little daylight, let alone any sunshine—was a ghostly white in contrast. She had applied a compact powder of the palest pink, partly to emphasise the ghostliness but also to conceal her acne scars and the chronic rash on her forehead and chin. Her lipstick was of the purest matt black, applied with great care so that the lips appeared thinner than they were.

The overall effect, combined with her full array of silver facial adornments, was stunning. She thrust out her overlong tongue, displaying the three silver studs.

'You are the living dead,' she whispered at the misted-up glass. She peered at herself with the vacuous, chemical eyes that were completely encircled with black: eyes that stared out of an open grave.

Suzen had given herself a complete makeover.

She spread her hands, admiring the nail job. In place of her real nails, which she was prone to biting, she had long, perfectly shaped silk wraps, polished to a high black gloss. They were too, too brilliant: long, tapering talons that looked as if she'd dipped her fingers in a vat of black blood.

Her toenails were also black.

Black, black, black: the new black.

'Wicked,' she whispered to her reflection.

The new dress she had on was a black velvet, body-hugging sheath with velvet buttons down the front, and long sleeves with lace ruffles at the cuffs.

The entire makeover had cost her a bomb, but she didn't care. The hairstyling and nail job set her back two hundred and twenty, and the dress was a hundred and fifty. The contacts . . . well, the whole deal had nearly cleaned her out, but it was worth it.

She lifted the dress and pushed down the fishnet pantyhose: she'd trimmed her beaver to a small, perfect triangle, immediately below her PROPERTY OF WILEY tattoo. Through the even mat of hair her two labia rings glinted.

'Sexy beast,' she breathed, swaying giddily.

She went out into the lounge room. There was Stan, sleeping on his side on the couch in his tracksuit pants, the black and white satin ones with the press-studs down the seams. His mouth was open. Snores rippled the air. A bottle of Smirnoff was on the floor next to him, along with an empty glass. He'd been watching 'Saturday Night Live' on TV and dozed off. It was 1.30 am.

'Hey, Wolfman,' she said. 'Whyncha go to bed?'

No response.

Earlier in the evening they'd been watching a dirty video. Stan had suddenly come on to her like a man possessed, but couldn't raise it. Suzen threw everything she could at him, but to no avail. It was friggin' hopeless. In the end she gave him a hand job, and even though he never had a halfway decent boner from go to whoa, he wanted it *bad*, so bad he wouldn't let her stop, even for a spell. God, her wrist ached. So, half an hour later . . . but then, even when she *finally* got him off, all he could manage was this sad little dribble.

The spirit was willing, but the flesh wouldn't do squat.

The Wolfman was losing his bite. But right *now* he was snoring.

Stan the Man. One more 'a' and *Stan* became *Satan*. The words coalesced nicely in her stoked brain.

Suzen wandered into the spare room which, as well as serving as a storeroom, accommodated Stan's iMac computer. It was the same outdated model as Suzen's. Her fingertips trailed lightly over it, giving her a nice buzz: that hard plastic was so friggin' *tactile*. As far as she was aware he only used it to surf the Net, especially the porno and underground sites. She'd been with him a couple of times when he'd browsed some bondage sites, looking to push the boundaries. There were also bookshelves containing some books, CDs, 'zines ('The War Against Terrorism', 'Guns and Ammo'—ugh!), newspapers, his precious photo albums and a pile of school exercise books with red binding that were full of old clippings. She bumped against the computer: *Whoops*. Stan/Satan didn't like her going near his stuff, even being in the room, but Suzen was cool and brave about it—as long as she could hear him snoring. She was *so* trippy and ultra-sensitised: earlier, before the dirty movie, they had smoked some dope. It was *excellent* shit, lovely green ganja with no stems or stalks in it at all. It was also laced with heroin, and that was a *real* bonus. Man, it packed a punch. It was the first time Suzen had 'chased the dragon', but it wouldn't be the last. Stan told her he got it from his hairdresser in Carlton. Some hairdresser! *Get me some!*

On top of that she'd consumed more than her share of wine, beer and whatnot.

Being a seasoned substance user, Suzen had no fear of 'addiction': she was instinctively *receptive*, able to trip the light fantastic and push it to the max without tipping over into the abyss—same way a committed alcoholic can somehow function right through a total bender without ever lapsing into unconsciousness. Every so often something weird flashed across her vision—vivid snapshots she only glimpsed for a split second. What *that* was all about, she had no friggin' idea. Just go with it. Embrace it. Love your drug and it will love you back. This particular boost was having an unusual and *very* interesting hallucinatory side effect, as if she'd tripped on acid or mushrooms and was experiencing momentary 'insights' and 'revelations'. And her visual perspective was *way* distorted, as if she were trapped inside a goldfish bowl. There it was again: some tiny creature scurrying from the corner of her eye. *Whoa.*

She sat down on the ergonomic computer chair, tapping her talons on the keyboard. She *loved* that sharp sound: *click click click click.* For something to do, she decided to check her e-mail: the whirr of the computer coming to life was such a turn-on. When she was in, there were only the usual messages: 'FURRY NAKED BARNYARD FRIENDS!!!', 'GET THE DIRT ON ABSOLUTELY ANYONE!!!!!', 'UNDERAGE NASTY SLUTS SWALLOW CUM', 'BRITNEY TAKES IT UP THE ARSE'.

She switched off the machine. For a few moments she was transfixed by the intricate circuitry that was visible through the monitor's transparent plastic shell. That was *so* cool. Stan/Satan was still blowing air. Sitting in the chair, she swivelled from side to side, casting her fish-eye contacts around the room: *what next?*

She picked up one of his exercise books with the red binding, and flipped through it. What was with all these friggin' newspaper cuttings?

A headline jumped out at her:

Following the Trail of the Menendez Brothers

Yeah? She remembered the name *Menendez* from somewhere . . .

She started reading the piece. It was dated 11 March 1990.

'. . . Los Angeles Homicide Detective Les Zoeller was up against it in his investigation of the murder of Jose and Kitty Menendez in their Beverly Hills mansion . . . Jose Menendez had many enemies and almost anyone could have done it.'

'. . . A friend of the family said, "I have no basis for this, but I wonder if the boys did it."'

'. . . Police observed as Lyle and Erik went through a million dollars in the three months after the murders . . .'

Hmmm—now she had it. These were the two little charmers who murdered their friggin' parents over in L.A.

'. . . After watching "Billionaire Boys Club" on television, the boys were convinced their father planned to disinherit them. Inspired by the show, they resolved to kill Jose . . . They did not want to kill Kitty, but had no choice . . .'

'. . . drove to San Diego to buy shotguns . . .'

'. . . disposed of their bloody clothes and shoes, together with shell casings . . .'

'. . . Erik, who had been having suicidal thoughts, told his psychotherapist: "We did it. We killed our parents."'

What was all this reminding her of? Stan said a while ago, *My parents are still dead, aren't they?* But . . . Stephanie was his *stepmother*, not his mother. It was a technicality, but in Suzen's expanded state of consciousness the word *parents* rose from the page and loomed close-up like a revelation in front of her fish-eyes.

Anyhow, what was Stan doing saving a whole bunch of cuttings on the friggin' *Menendez* murders? *Shotguns . . . bloody clothes . . . shell casings . . .*

She flipped through the pages: it went on and on.

Profiles of the Brothers: Their Luxury Lifestyle.
Erik: 'I couldn't shoot my mother . . . when she tried to get away,
Lyle shot her.'
Erik confesses to psychotherapist.
Lyle: 'We've got to kill him and anyone associated with him.'

More of the same followed.

Wait. Waitone friggin' minute. What was . . . She went back until she found what she wanted. There it was: *Lyle: 'We've got to kill him and anyone associated with him.'*

Christ. Didn't Stan say that—*exactly* that—when they were in bed that time?

Those words were originally spoken by *Lyle friggin' Menendez*.

She fanned through several more books in the stack: more Menendez stuff. Police investigations, legal proceedings, expert witnesses, profiles of the victims, transcripts of the 'secret tapes', testimony, cross-examinations.

So it went on.

The remaining exercise books in the shelf seemed to deal with the Petrakos murders, and their aftermath: *Mansion Break-in. Bloody Crime Scene. Rural Peace Shattered on a Sunny Wednesday.*

Suzen flicked through, mainly scanning headlines and studying the accompanying photographs:

'Death in the Afternoon.'

'Curse of Petrakos Clan Has Roots in War.'

Life of Screen Goddess 'Pointlessly Snuffed Out'.
Stephanie Petrakos 'Was Unfaithful'.
Culprit: Arrest and Trial of Shaun Randall McCreadie.
. . . Promising police career 'ends in disgrace and ignominy'.
QC: Shaun McCreadie 'Only Surviving Gang Member'.
Verdict in Petrakos Kill Case.
Judge: 'Despicable, callous crime.'
Parents: 'No punishment can bring back our beautiful daughter.'
McCreadie: Life Without Parole.
Final McCreadie Appeal Turned Down.

A rustling sound came from the lounge room. The snoring had abruptly stopped. Suzen hurriedly shoved the books back, spilling a couple of them onto the floor in her haste. When she went out she saw that Stan had changed his position: he was now flat on his back with one arm flung across his eyes, shielding them from the light, with the other dangling onto the floor near the Smirnoff bottle. She watched and waited: he was still asleep.

She switched off the light. It was after two, and Suzen was suddenly *very* tired. Her depleted physical reserves could only fight sleep for so long when she was tripping. On the way to the bedroom she killed all the lights in the apartment, leaving on only a pair of wall lights on either side of the bed. They glowed with a yellow, foggy glimmer. With her brain still flashing she wriggled out of her velvet sheath and fishnet pantyhose, letting them both drop to the floor. She disconnected the silver chain from her earring and lip-ring and put it on the bedside table. When she crawled inside the sheets, under a featherweight doona, her eyes were already closing over the persistent images from the paper clippings. She curled into a foetal position and slid her hands under the pillow.

They came into contact with something: a hard, metal object.

Suzen slid it out.

Christ. It was a friggin' *gun* . . . a *shotgun*, with the barrels sawn off, and the wooden stock shortened, so it could be held like a pistol.

The gun she'd seen him with the other night when he went out 'to see a friend'.

Suzen gazed at the weapon with weary, doped-out eyes. It was heavy. *What's 'is friggin' gun doin' here?*

She flashed onto a studio photo of Lyle and Erik Menendez: clean-cut, handsome college boys. *Jose would be proud . . .* Chemicals played over her synapses. Then she snored once: a sudden violent explosion in the back of her throat. Her eyes snapped open with a start. She realised she had dropped off to sleep with the gun still in her hand, resting across her chest on top of the doona.

'Ugh.' She hefted it onto the bedside table with her face chain.

When she shut her eyes again she dropped immediately into an underworld of horrid dreamscapes. She saw the naked body of a woman closely resembling Sharon Tate in a blood-spattered bathtub, wrapped in heavy ropes. Her eyes were empty sockets staring out of a blood-smeared face. There was a vertical slash in her stomach, under the ropes, from which heavily slicked birds slithered out into the bathtub. They tried to flutter their wings to get away but could not climb the slippery sides of the bathtub and repeatedly fell back into it. More and more birds appeared, desperately but unsuccessfully trying to escape from the bathtub. Then the body itself began to move . . .

Suzen gasped.

In a subconscious attempt to dislodge the image, she rolled over so that she faced the other way, her head buried under the pillow. When she'd descended again, however, grotesque pictures of repugnant animals ripping apart a man's corpse rushed to fill her headspace. They were fighting each other over pieces of the cadaver the way jackals or hyenas do with the remnants of a beast left unattended by lions. As they growled and slavered over the flesh these ugly brutes sometimes swivelled around as if watchful for predators, throwing out sprays of blood and gout from their disgusting snouts as they did so . . .

Several nightmare sequences followed, including the one in which she—as a teenager—is thrown into the trunk of a car by a man without a face. In the dark, enclosed space she screams silently as the car speeds to its destination. When the trunk door opens the faceless man helps her out, and she sees she is on a desolate, windswept beach. Instinctively she recognises the place, just as she senses that the man without a face is her father. He has taken her to the end of the earth, but . . . why? Suzen's father had never done anything to harm her. She walks towards the water, knowing she has to wade in and drown. At the shallows she turns to see that the faceless man and the car have disappeared, and she is alone. Waves crash over her. She is underwater, battling the undertow as it drags her far from land. Down she tumbles into the green water, seaweed entangling itself around her throat as she fights to hold her breath . . .

Suzen wakes up with a loud sob. She *had* been holding her breath. Her heart pounds so hard it hurts, and her body is slippery with perspiration. But there is no seaweed around her throat.

'*Oh*,' she sighs, and falls back onto the pillow—relieved beyond words, and utterly exhausted. '*Oh*.'

Suzen hated the beach. It was a bad place where people went to drown. Although she was too young to possibly remember it, she was rescued from the surf at Point Hicks, East Gippsland, one summer. She was only three years old at the time, but nevertheless the experience was embedded in her brain forever.

At least three times a week now she dreamed that dream. Strangely, it had only begun when she was in her late teens, after a gestation period of about sixteen years—from around the time when she became a serious drug user. Although she found it puzzling, Suzen was astute enough to know that every dream contained a full set of meanings, whether you grasped them or not. It was all encoded in there somewhere. Dreams stemmed from one's fears and anxieties, and in her case that was a deep, irrational fear of death—at Manson's hands.

Soon she was asleep again. One good thing about addiction: no matter how often she surfaced during the night, it was always only a minute or so before she was back under.

A man was coming towards her from far away. At first he was just a dot in the distance, then a tiny, shimmering human form. He was carrying something over his shoulder. Suzen couldn't see who it was, but stood still, waiting for the figure to come properly into view. She started to recognise certain significant details, but the traveller's identity remained hidden from her. She understood she had to wait for him—to turn and walk away was out of the question. Despite a feeling of growing apprehension she remained rooted to the spot as he drew ever closer. Now she could see it was a guitar slung over his shoulder, one with a beaded, hippie strap attached to it. Instinctively she knew who it was, and began to cry. When he was a short distance from her, the man stopped. His forearm was held across his face, as if to shield her from the awful truth, but then she realised he was only playing with her. He wore loose ragged robes, like sackcloth, a leather, studded bracelet on his wrist and Roman sandals on his dirty, battered feet. It seemed to Suzen he had travelled a long way through both time and space to reach her, and now the journey was over at last. She waited for him to lower the forearm from his face.

At the foot of the bed Suzen's night visitor remained motionless for a long moment. Then, as the arm came down, the first thing she saw was the shaved, shiny skull; after that the swastika tattoo in the centre of his forehead glowed in the dull glimmer of the wall lights.

With his arms now outstretched towards her Manson's face was overspread with his mischievous, seductive grin, revealing teeth that were as uneven and rotted as old tombstones. The evil, playful eyes glittered insanely, entrancing her and pinning her to the bed as he moved in closer, alongside the bed with his arms extended in an embracing gesture. Suzen clutched her throat and tried to scream, but as always the sound died before it was even born. The swastika glowed with a magical iridescence as the maniac's bright, luminous face closed in; then, from somewhere inside his robes Charles Manson brandished a long-bladed, silver saber. The weapon glinted momentarily as she watched, horrified and unable to wrench herself from the grip of his spell. Suzen's hand was on her chest, feeling the maddened thump of her fearful heart. *Now I am in his thrall; now it comes . . .*

Holding the saber in both hands Manson raised it high above his head. In a moment of clarity Suzen thought: *Am I dreaming? No, no, it's real. It's happening. I'm going to be butchered, right now . . . have to friggin' do something . . .*

Savoring the occasion of his triumph, Manson held his position. Suzen pulled her eyes from the maniac's glittering stare. She tore her right hand from her chest and flung it sideways, where it struck the bedside table and caused something on it to rattle heavily. Under the wall light she glimpsed the gun. In a reflex action she grabbed it, swung it around and grasped it in two hands. Aiming at Manson's midsection, she clenched her eyes shut and pulled both triggers, hard. And screamed.

BOOM BOOM.

There was a brilliant flash; the gun bucked upwards as the kick from the simultaneous detonations of double-aught, 180-grain buckshot bounced her head hard against the plasterboard wall. An ear-splitting double-roar engulfed the whole world. Suzen's scream rolled on and on, marrying with the unending reverberations around the room and inside her own head. When her eyes jolted open she glimpsed Charles Manson, his upper body a mess of bloody, shredded rags, being lifted clear off his feet and hurtled backwards into the mirrored wardrobe in an almighty explosion of shattered glass. After he had slid down to the floor, bloodied, sword-shaped glass slivers dropped onto him while he lay sprawled and motionless among the debris. Suzen's scream ran its course, died, and then all was silence.

Suzen sat up straight. The gun was still in her trembling hands, her fingers curled around the two triggers. Smoke drifted from the barrel. There was a . . . sort of *haze* in the room. Putting down the weapon, Suzen crawled to the foot of the bed. With her hand over her mouth she gazed upon the wreckage. The huddled mess on the floor was not Charles Manson at all. He was not wearing sackcloth robes, and nor was there a guitar or silver saber. Instead she recognised Stan's black and white track pants, which were partly blown off his legs. A vivid rash of pellet wounds peppered his exposed, hairy thighs. The main mass of his body was eviscerated: only reddish, splintered rib bones and strands of intestinal and other tissue showed through in the stomach cavity. Suzen was repelled and riveted by the horror of it. The shattered wardrobe and the ceiling wore a patterned spray of the victim's shredded inner organs. What she could see of his bloodied head was stabbed and slashed with glass spears. It wasn't possible to identify the face, but Suzen knew this was no bad trip, and nor was it a nightmare. She was quite serene about it as she came to terms with what she had done. Shock moved silently, inexorably through her nervous system, but just for the moment she could deal with this. She had killed Stan. *Fine*. She had blown him to bits with his own shotgun. *Yeah*.

In a minute or two the shock started to register. Soon she was shaking so violently she was sure she was having a heart attack. Her body racked and convulsed as the smell of burnt gunpowder and the appalling reek of the quivering, disembowelled corpse mingled in the air. Suzen got off the bed and ran. She ran into the lounge room, grabbed her head and hyperventilated. Her breath roared in her ears. Then she ran down the hallway, into the bathroom, and proceeded to vomit in the bathtub. Since there was little of substance inside her she only managed to bring up a string of brown material, but continued to retch uncontrollably until there was no strength left in her frail body. Pain burned with a scalding heat in her chest. In the end she sagged over the bathtub, sobbing hysterically as her bladder opened and a pool of urine spread around her knees.

24

Shaun parked the Land Rover in the street outside the Powlett Street house. Normally he drove around the back via the laneway and secured it in the garage, but he had formed the idea in the last half-hour that he and Jo would go somewhere for lunch on this perfect spring day. The sky was a clear-blue expanse, and the breeze—such as there was—blew in occasional soft riffles from the northeast. It could've been the first day of summer. He'd been to a post office, where he'd dispatched copies of the taped conversation at the Unicorn Hotel to Brent Wollansky and Dave Wrigley, with a covering note to Dave explaining what it was all about.

The previous evening Wes Ford had phoned to inform him that he would be domiciled in the downtown Sofitel for as long as his funds held out, which he estimated to be five or six days. Would that be long enough? Shaun told him not to worry about it, that *he* would take care of the bill, since this was his idea. Wes was silent for maybe a second or two—from surprise rather than indecision, probably—before graciously accepting his offer. He was also gratified to learn that Bill Simmonds remained on the missing list. It was a case of 'so far, so good'.

It was now 11.30 am Friday when Shaun turned the key in the front door. When he'd left an hour earlier, Jo had been on the receiving end of a heavy-sounding phone call from her distinguished father-in-law, Hugh Steer, who was urging her to 'cool off', 'come to her senses', and 'consider everyone's best interests'. From her responses he understood that he was offering to act as intermediary, and do *whatever she required* to 'sort out this spat' and 'get the marriage back in shape.' She had rolled her eyes at Shaun as he went out, gaily waving him off as the High Court judge subjected her to the benefit of his wisdom on the subject of reconciliation. Despite her cavalier attitude, she would have to be strong to resist his weighty influence and whatever else the Steer family came up with to try and get her back onside. This was what they did every day, and they were very good at it.

The second he stepped inside and closed the door he instinctively felt that something was out of place. The house was still and silent. To the right of the vestibule was a passage leading to the downstairs bathroom and kitchen, while to the left an L-shaped passage led to the lounge room via a small sewing room. Dead ahead was the staircase.

The normally placid air had an *edge* to it, one he could feel *and* smell.

It was a man's cologne or aftershave.

Why was everything so still? There was a sense that if he made a single wrong move, the consequences would be catastrophic.

'Jo?' he called, without moving from the vestibule.

No answer. But she was here—her presence was as palpable as his.

'Jo?' he called again—louder this time.

Nothing at first, then: 'Here.'

It came from the lounge room. But why was her voice so strained, so . . . tentative?

She was not alone. Jo was never tentative. Whoever she had for company was *controlling* her. Justice Steer, perhaps, come to tighten the screws on his wayward daughter-in-law, to protect the family's 'interests' and avert a messy divorce. There was, after all, a great deal—aside from reputations and careers—on the line. Errant wives met untimely deaths for a lot less.

He dropped the keys on an antique wall stand next to the door. There was definitely an unwelcome presence here. Maybe even a threatening one.

In prison, every long-term convict developed certain survival skills. Chief among these was a sixth sense, an ability to detect an impending threat or an *aura of menace*, well before it had shown its human face. If you could not sense that subtle shift in the molecular structure of the atmosphere, you were in serious trouble.

He passed the open door to the sewing room and continued on, through the double-doors of the spacious, expensively furnished and upholstered lounge.

And there was Jo.

She stood facing him, her hands straight down at her sides. Behind her was a man: tall, blond, smartly dressed in black pants and a dark-blue patterned shirt that was buttoned to the neck.

In his left hand he held a stainless-steel carving knife. It was pressed against Jo's throat.

In his right was a heavy-calibre, chrome-plated, semi-automatic pistol, possibly a Beretta or Sig-Sauer nine-millimetre: a seriously destructive handgun. The arm was extended over Jo's shoulder, the weapon held sideways in the manner favoured by Chinese mobsters in movies, and aimed right between Shaun's eyes.

Jo's eyes were wide; her face was the colour of flour.

Shaun froze in the doorway. He had no intention of even slightly upsetting the balance in this delicate and deadly tableau.

That blade was hard against Jo's skin: any more pressure and it would cut into her. The man would tell him what to do, when to do it. Shaun only had to await his orders, and stay calm.

'Keep coming, convict,' the man said, poised and set to slice if Shaun was dumb enough to rush him. 'Put your hands in plain view. Come on.' He gestured impatiently with the gun as Shaun did his bidding: both hands spread in front of him, showing he was no threat.

'Whatever you want, you can have it,' he said. 'It's yours. Just don't hurt her, please. We'll cooperate.'

'Oh, I know *that*, convict,' the man said. 'Stop right there.'

Shaun stopped, hands still outstretched, fingers spread: awaiting orders.

'Right,' the man said. 'Lift up your shirt and do a three-sixty.'

Shaun raised his polo shirt to chest level and did the turn. Nothing in the waistband of his jeans, or anywhere else: a clean bill of health.

'Turn out your pockets,' the man said. 'Empty 'em on the floor.'

Shaun produced his wallet from his back pocket, showed it to the man and dropped it. From the front pockets came change, some notes, cigarettes and lighter, all of which hit the carpet.

He stood still, waiting. Jo's eyes never left his for a second. She was a picture of terror, but he saw and sensed that even though she was under threat her mind was ticking over. So was Shaun's. Now he recognised the knife as part of a German carving set from the kitchen. As he awaited his next order he studied the intruder: straight, dirty-blond hair, boyish face, dancing grey eyes, razor-thin lips, pointed chin. He was one cool son of a bitch: calm, composed, in control. At first Shaun had put his age at mid-twenties, but now he detected signs of ageing on his face and throat. He was mid-forties, older than Shaun, but glance at him in the street and he would pass for much younger.

'Get on your knees. Clasp your hands around your head.'

Shaun did so. From this angle he saw that the blade was pressing so firmly into Jo's throat that the carotid artery bulged alarmingly.

'What do you want?' he said. 'Just say it, you got it. No need for—'

'Shut up, convict,' the man said coolly. Shaun was staring into the black hole of the nine-millimetre. This guy obviously knew who Shaun was, but who the fuck was *he*? Shaun was trying desperately to slot him in somewhere in the database at the back of his brain. He did not believe he had ever forgotten a single face: they were all in there somewhere. This one was vaguely, *distantly* familiar, but it wasn't coming to him yet. He wasn't some hypo off the street—too cool and well organised, and that cannon was rock-steady in his hand. Maybe he wasn't even local. Everything about him cried out *professional*. Shaun was casting his thoughts back to a time when the guy *would* have been mid-twenties, and just as lethal. A man like him did not take up heavy crime later in life with all the expertise of an old hand. He *was* an old hand: maybe from the eighties . . .

'Now pay close attention, convict. You, uh, want to *live*, I presume?'

'Sure.'

'You want the *bitch* to live?'

'Yes.'

'Then listen. You do the wrong thing once—*once*—and I'll open her up. You can watch her bleed out all over the nice floor. Then I'll do something *much* worse to you.'

'If you kill us, we can't give you what you want,' Shaun said. He felt it was important to engage the guy in conversation: the first rule of negotiation. *If he's talking, he's not killing* . . .

The man smiled his boyish, razor-lipped smile. 'You don't understand. If it comes to that, if I have to open her, that means

I don't *care* any more, convict. It means I'll deal with *you* for my *amusement*. Got it?'

'Yes.' He switched his gaze from the weapon to Jo, trying to communicate some degree of reassurance: Hang in there. I won't let him hurt you . . .

'Good. Now, I understand you are in possession of a large quantity of cash, which used to belong to the late George Petrakos. Correct?'

The man was very well informed. This was a major, professional sting.

'Correct.'

'Fine. Now we play a little game. I'm going to ask the bitch how *much* is involved. She'll whisper her answer to me. Then I'll ask you, and if the numbers don't match . . . well, you don't want me to spell it out, do you? *Do you?*'

'No.'

'So, you understand the rules of the game?'

'Yes.'

'Okay. Say a number, bitch,' he said, and turned her lips to his ear using the flat side of the blade. Shaun saw her whisper, but couldn't read it.

'Your turn, convict. Go.'

Shaun didn't hesitate. 'Two point eight million, plus change.'

The man gave him a wide smile. 'That's what she said . . . although she failed to mention the change.' Seeing some alarm on Shaun's face he added: 'But I'll overlook that.'

Now it hit him. Jesus Christ. It's Pritchett. Terry fucking Pritchett. The fucking toe-cutter from Sydney. Oh, Christ. We are in some deep shit here . . .

'Hate you to finish up like Henry Agar,' the man said.

Shaun had noticed an item in the paper about the grisly death of Henry Agar up north. Cops had no suspect. Shaun knew of Agar's exploits over the years, but he had no reason to connect him with Terry Pritchett. Now he did.

'I knew a cop-convict once,' the man said. 'What a busted arse he was. Fell between two worlds, the good and the bad, and neither one loved him. Sad son of a bitch ate his own gun in the end.'

'What happened to Agar?' Shaun said.

'Agar was a bit too hungry. Wanted a fifty-fifty split. We exchanged views, and he, uh, lost the debate.'

Shaun was now absolutely certain it was Terry Pritchett. He was a gangly, grinning reaper who had stepped right out of a bad dream. Shaun only recognised him from undercover surveillance photos shot at around the time of the Hamilton murders, when he was a young, arrogant hood with that *same nasty grin*. He'd hardly changed at all with the years.

It was an image that did not fade in a hurry. Shaun, however, would not have come to Pritchett's attention until the sensational events of 1992 . . .

'So where is it, this . . . two point eight million, *plus change*?' Pritchett said.

'Not here,' Shaun said. 'It's at a bank. In a safe deposit box.'

'Of course—*exactly* the right place for it. Where is the key to this box?'

'In the kitchen.'

'I see. All right, listen. Get up, convict. Leave your shit there. Turn around and lead us *slowly* to the kitchen. Keep those hands clasped behind your head. Any sudden moves and you know what. Go on.'

When they were in the kitchen, Shaun stopped and waited.

'Turn around,' Pritchett said.

Shaun faced Jo and Pritchett. They were much more intimately grouped in here. Jo was watching him, eyes jumping from one of his to the other, trying to read his thoughts or connect in some way.

'Where?' Pritchett said.

'In a canister, on the mantelpiece.'

'Get it.'

Shaun opened the tin canister and removed the small bronze keys, which he held up for Pritchett to see. Pritchett's eyes lit up.

'Fine. Now we reach a critical point in proceedings. You, convict, have the power of life and death in your grubby hands. But that's nothing new, is it? This time, however, your bitch's life is in the balance. Still with me?'

'Yes.'

'Listen. You have precisely three-quarters of an hour to go to the bank, take out *all* the cash, and bring it here. If you are one *minute* longer, she dies. If you try to involve cops, or anyone, she dies. If I even *suspect* you are trying to fuck me up *in any way*, she dies. Are we in concert?'

'Yes.'

He glanced at the bench next to the sink: Walsh's phone was on a charger, still plugged in. Useless. He couldn't see Jo's phone anywhere. His pistol was in the bedroom, nowhere in contention. He had nothing.

'Shaun, take the Honda,' Jo said suddenly. 'It's quicker.'

He held her eyes, nodding as he picked up her keys from the table. Using her eyes she was *imploring* him in some urgent, secret way.

'Clock's ticking,' Pritchett said. 'What are you waiting for, convict? A fanfare?'

'Uh . . . I need the cases to put the money in.'

'Where might they be?'

'In a cupboard, under the staircase.'

More watchful supervision while he armed up with the aluminium luggage.

Through the kitchen window Pritchett could see him load the three cases into the trunk, climb into the maroon Prelude and fire it up. The steel door went up, and he reversed into the narrow laneway. As he drove down the lane the door came down again.

Where the laneway met the street he stopped and thought

it over. Jo had told him: 'Shaun, take the Honda.' They were the first words she'd uttered, and she was using them to *tell* him something. He did not believe she had ever once called him by his name before: it sounded . . . odd, unnatural, when it came out. It was a wrong note. Come to that, he never addressed *her* by name either, except just then. Theirs was a name-free relationship.

It was significant. And the reason she gave for using the Honda—'It's quicker'—was bullshit. It was cover.

There was a message in her words. *What?*

Then he saw it, staring him in the face.

The Prelude was equipped with a carphone. At least, there was the mounting and connection for one. Where was the handset?

There: in the glove compartment.

He pushed the T-bar into 'P'. The car idled soundlessly. The beginnings of a plan rose from the swirling mist of his confusion and panic. Seconds disappeared. Sweat popped under his arms and slid down his sides. Then in a decisive moment he drove around the corner, past the house, and stopped. Quickly he removed the front door key from the key ring, opened the car door and silently, out of sight of anyone in the house, placed the key under the welcome mat. Then, just as silently, he got back in the car, connected the phone and took off for the city.

One thing he knew and remembered about Terry Pritchett: he was an ice-cold killer. A butcher. He chopped up Brian Hamilton and his partner at that motel back in '85, when Shaun was a young constable attending a crime scene. It was the most horrific thing he had ever witnessed, and it was carried out *after* Pritchett got what he came for.

He would certainly do the same to Jo and him when he got the cash. No doubt of it. He was fresh from the butchering and burning of Henry Agar. The man was on a roll. Two more victims would be meat and potatoes to him. A true psychopath, he killed not because he had to, but because he *wanted* to.

The moment he had the cash he would cut Jo's throat and shoot Shaun—with that boyish smile all over his cool, psychopath's dial.

Shaun drove. His mouth was set tight. In his mind he carefully composed some words, then stabbed numbers on the phone as he sped west along Wellington Parade, into the heart of a tight clutch of skyscrapers.

A terrible fear had weighed on him from the moment he'd left the house: Jo was completely at Pritchett's mercy. Forty-five minutes was a long time to wait with a blade at her throat and a gun behind her head.

What if he became restless? What if he decided to turn his attention to her? An attractive woman like Jo . . . he could do whatever he wanted and she'd be powerless to resist. He'd kill her in an eye-blink if she tried, and Jo was the type who *would* fight the bastard, regardless. Christ, what if he went feral on her?

Worse: he wasn't there to protect her. But what choice did he have?

Now he was palpitating.

Sweat streamed down his face as he struggled with the awful possibilities that might greet him when he returned.

Inside the house, Pritchett's mind was starting to fragment. Fifteen minutes had gone by, then twenty. He had already stuffed a tea towel into Jo's mouth and made her sit down at the head of the table, under threat of having her hands trussed if she moved. Unnervingly he stood behind her: a sinister, mostly silent presence made even more unbearable by the fact that he was out of sight. She couldn't see what he was up to. The sharp blade never deviated from her throat. Her instinct was to grab the arm holding the knife, but that would be a fatal mistake. She could hear him breathing and a rustling of his clothes occasionally. She could also smell his strong aftershave.

His occasional attempts at one-way small talk came to zero.

Then he started touching her hair, ever so delicately. A cold shiver rippled straight through her. *It was starting . . .*

His face came down alongside hers.

'No reason we can't be nice to each other,' he said in a vacant, dead voice. 'While we wait.'

She shut her eyes while he curled a lock of her hair around his fingers.

'Convict's gonna be a while,' he murmured. 'We could make whoopee. How about it?'

She arched slightly as his right hand left her hair and started groping her breasts. Where was the gun? *Must have put it down his pants . . .*

'You've got a lovely set,' he said. 'Wasted on the convict.'

Without warning he ripped open her shirt. Buttons flew over the table. She braced herself to scream, but all she could manage was a deep muffled sound.

'Yummy,' he whispered, then deftly used the blade to cut open her bra, between the cups.

Jo twisted and squirmed under his hold while he fondled and squeezed and pinched nipples. Now his tongue was dipping in and out of her ear.

The hand inevitably moved south. When she stiffened he gave her a taste of the blade's edge.

He forced his hand down inside her jeans, popping open the stud, and grabbed her. She clenched her legs together and tried so hard to scream she was starting to see spots.

'Know what I like to do, baby?' he said, and whispered into her ear.

The bile was rising: she was about to throw up. If so, she would surely choke to death.

After a long minute he removed the hand from in her jeans and slid his fingers slowly over her breasts, leaving a smear. Then he trailed them lingeringly over her shoulder.

Her eyes darted nervously. The flat of the blade was pressed so hard against her throat it was cutting off her windpipe.

She heard him unzip.

And that was when she lashed out with everything she could muster.

Down in the bowels of the bank Shaun was shoving wads of banknotes into the cases. His worst fears were rapidly mounting. How would Pritchett be able to resist taking advantage of the situation?

Bastard wouldn't hesitate for a *nanosecond*.

The race was against Pritchett, not the deadline.

In his haste he was spilling wads onto the floor. *Stay calm*, he told himself, but could not.

So much *fucking money* . . .

Twenty-six minutes remained when he snapped the last case shut. He left the building at a fast trot, as fast as he could go without breaking into a run and attracting the attention of security guards: through the revolving doors, banging them loudly with the cases, out into the busy street. The Prelude was double-parked right outside, its hazard lights flashing. No sign of a cop. He threw the cases into the trunk, jumped in, put it in Drive and performed an illegal, squealing U-turn with barely a glimpse at the mirrors.

Twenty-two minutes left.

He drove around the back, scraping the rear quarter panel on a fencepost as he entered the lane, and activated the garage door. As soon as he was inside he killed the motor, popped the trunk and leapt out. Grabbing up the cases he hurried to the door, past the wrought iron outdoor setting. Setting down one of the cases, he opened up and crashed inside with twelve minutes to spare.

The kitchen was a war zone.

Pritchett had her face-first against the window. In one

hand was a bunch of her hair; in the other the pistol: locked, loaded and jammed so hard into the back of her head her nose was squashed into the glass. In the first split-second he saw that her shirt had been torn open, that there was blood on her face. Pritchett's legs were braced apart as he leaned his weight into her. His fly was open, his shirt was in disarray, his hair was wild and he had deep vermilion scratches across his face, right under his eyes. On the webbing between the thumb and forefinger of his right hand the flesh was ripped—Christ, she'd *bitten* him. They were both heaving and gulping, and the air was still charged with the fierce heat from recent, intense violence.

Chairs were upended; the table had been shunted against the wall. The tiled floor was littered with smashed crockery and glassware and other things from the buffet and countertop. *Where was the knife?*

There: on the floor, amongst the rubble.

Pritchett didn't care about the knife any more. He was in gun mode, and spoiling to use it.

'*Pritchett!*' he screamed. '*Pritchett! Don't do it! I've got the cash!*'

But Pritchett didn't even seem to be aware that Shaun was in the room. He saw he was too late, that Pritchett was so enraged and out of it he was definitely going to blow her brains out *right now*. That bruised and bleeding gun-hand was flexed tight; the map of veins and sinews stood out as if chiselled from the spare, bony flesh.

But then, inexplicably, Pritchett seemed to cool off a degree or two. The bright, grey eyes flicked towards Shaun, sweeping over everything they needed to see, then his concentration reverted to the woman under his control. Sweat gleamed on his brow.

'Feisty bitch, convict,' he rasped. 'Don't mind that in a woman. Gets the old mojo revvin', know what I mean?'

'Let her go, Pritchett. It's *here*. *Look!*'

He dumped one of the cases on the table with a loud bang

and snapped it open. The compressed piles of tightly wadded currency sprang up.

That got more of Pritchett's attention.

He gazed upon the riches, in so doing relaxing his grip on Jo's hair. The gun wavered slightly from her head, drifting in Shaun's general direction.

Seizing the moment, she tore away and threw herself at Shaun, burying herself in his arms. Now he saw what else he had done to her, but he believed that patch of blood around her lips was Pritchett's, not hers. She was heaving and sobbing and holding on for dear life, as if being with him was enough to shut Pritchett out of her life.

But even with his arms tightly around her, pressing her hot face into his chest, Shaun knew it was nowhere near enough.

The next five minutes would tell the story.

Pritchett extended his right arm, aiming straight at Shaun's face.

'Man knows my name,' he said, smiling with his empty eyes. 'Clever convict, but for that you *must* go down, obviously.'

'Better check the other two cases first,' Shaun said, coolly as he could manage.

Pritchett lowered the gun, seemingly undecided for a brief moment. He glanced at the two cases on the floor, then back at Shaun and the quivering, pathetic wreck in his arms.

'Get 'em up on the table,' he said, gesturing with the gun.

Shaun separated from Jo, easing her to one side, to his right and slightly behind him. Then he hefted both cases onto the table as instructed, before stepping back with a wisp of a smile. This clearly puzzled Pritchett, who seemed to smell a rat of some sort. Had the convict booby-trapped one of the cases, maybe?

What did he have to *grin* about? Maybe he was too stupid to know any different . . .

'Open 'em,' he ordered.

Shaun counted to three, then stepped up and snapped one of them open. Currency sprang up as before. Pritchett's empty grey eyes were wide; his tongue did a slow lap of his slightly parted, chapped lips. The blood on his hand dripped on the floor, but he didn't notice, or care.

Again he looked at Shaun, as if trying to figure out what his game was. Bastard was *still* grinning.

'And again,' he ordered, and pointed at the third case with the pistol.

Shaun held his eyes, even as his hands moved towards the case. Pritchett was frowning and smiling at the same time. Shaun's fingertips tentatively sought out the clips to spring the case. Pritchett's eyes switched from Shaun's to the silver case. Then he aimed his pistol at it, as if preparing to shoot whatever came at him once the lid was opened.

Shaun caught a blur of movement behind Pritchett.

From nowhere came the sickening crunch of fist on bone; such was the force of the blow that Pritchett's entire head went out of shape, and reddish bits of his teeth spat through the air. Jo found her voice with a glass-splitting scream as Pritchett crashed against the countertop and swayed a second on loose, rubber legs; two gunshots hit the ceiling and a third blasted through the window as his arms swung loosely around, firing at random and, it seemed, without even intending to. Wes Ford came at him, grabbing his throat in both hands and swinging him back towards the table in the style of an Olympic hammer thrower. Pritchett slid over the tabletop, scattering silver cases and wads of cash before hitting the wall hard, flush on his battered face.

The gun spilled from his hand.

Down he went, between the table and the wall, all gangly arms and legs.

Straightaway Shaun pulled the table clear, dragging it over the mix of rubble and currency, to get a clear go at Pritchett. He put the boot in two, three times as Pritchett instinctively curled up to minimise damage. Then he swivelled his head around by the hair.

It was an ugly spectacle. He was a total mess: jawbone and teeth smashed, the jaw swinging loose; tongue and lips reduced to chopped liver; the whole face, even his eyes, were awash with the blood that still spilled from his nose, mouth, even his ear. The whole left side of his face was way up.

Pritchett gave a wet moan. Shaun released the head and let it drop. He glanced around at Wes, who was wringing his unclenched right fist, holding it by the wrist and muttering: 'Christ. *Christ* Almighty.'

Jo stood still and silent now, arms wrapped around her front, staring down at Pritchett.

Shaun came towards her as Wes sucked air, doubling over and wringing the badly damaged right hand.

In that instant Pritchett was on his feet.

He grabbed a chair and hurled it at Wes, hitting him on the arm; then he leapt at Shaun, screaming horribly, the blood flying from his mouth. Before Shaun had time to react or even believe what he was seeing Pritchett grabbed his face, trying to tear the flesh from it; Shaun tried to punch on, but they were too close, Pritchett was all over him, and all he could do was try to wrestle him off. But Pritchett was *strong*: he wrenched and twisted Shaun's face, forcing him sideways, then shoved him away towards the shattered window as he groped among the rubble and cash on the floor for his gun . . .

He brought it up, swinging it this way and that, trying to pinpoint his target through the screen of red. A couple of rounds went in Wes's direction, but Wes had been alert enough to disappear from harm's way, and the bullets thudded into the staircase. Then a third sailed through the window, ricocheting off the garage roof and into space.

He wiped a hand across his eyes, trying to clear his vision. But Shaun had already charged at him, at the *gun*.

They grappled. Wes reappeared with a crystal vase in his

good hand, waiting for a chance to smash it over Pritchett's head. But considering his rangy build and the extent of his injuries, Pritchett's strength and stamina were astonishing. With an insane will he forced Shaun around towards Wes's poised arm, thereby blocking any attempt to crown him, then wrenched the gun free of Shaun's grasp. Momentum then caused him to stagger back against the table's edge, where he again brought up the weapon with a terrible howl.

'*Pritchett!*'

The scream came from his right. Immediately he turned towards the sound of his name, just in time to see the better part of nine inches of high-priced, tempered German steel plunge into his chest. His bloodied eyes fixed on the blade, which had sliced through the soft connective tissue between his ribs and into the left side of his heart, then on the woman's hands gripping it like grim death.

She released the blade and backed away, watching him.

Pritchett looked curiously at Jo, then at the knife with some surprise. Dropping the pistol he made an effort to pull out the blade, but all that did was slash his hands. He slid onto the floor and sat down on a pile of cash. Again he looked at Jo, apparently in an effort to say something, but his eyes had started to flutter and any semblance of life was rapidly leaving his features. He gave a sigh, spasmed briefly as if someone had walked over his grave, then his head fell back. His eyeballs travelled up, his body went slack and then he crossed over into uncharted territory.

They all stood around and watched him go, not quite accepting it until a long minute had passed with no sign of a second miraculous revival.

Wes Ford was first to break the silence.

'Shit,' he said. He was still holding the crystal vase.

Shaun had one arm around Jo's neck, pressing her face into his shoulder. He was staring at the corpse, its eyes and mouth agape, hands flat on the floor at its sides with the cut and bloodied palms turned up. He could feel Jo trembling right through her body, but she wasn't crying.

'Cops'll be here soon,' he said. 'Better do something with the money. Otherwise . . . it's, uh, gonna complicate the whole deal.'

Scads of it littered the floor.

'We should call triple-oh anyway,' he said. 'Got a phone there, Wes?'

'You bet,' Wes said, and tossed it over with his good hand. Jo turned from Shaun's shoulder and drew some strands of hair from her eyes. The carnage was something to behold. She moved a foot and crunched porcelain.

'Pack it all up, put it back under the staircase,' she said. 'Before you call triple-oh.'

They set about it quickly and carefully, picking up currency from every corner of the kitchen, even moving Pritchett's corpse to remove the bloodstained wads he was sitting on. When the cases were safely stowed, Shaun hit 000, requesting police and an ambulance. When the dispatcher had told him the cavalry was on its way he closed the little piece and handed it back to Wes, who was still gripping his wrist.

'You did good, Wes,' he said. Simple words, but Wes understood the weight they carried.

'The way I see it,' Shaun said, 'we were here, all three of us, uh . . . planning to go out for lunch . . . then the doorbell goes, this bastard forces his way in and turns our world upside-down. He holds us at gunpoint, assaults Jo. Uh . . . we have a go at him, Wes and I, he shoots up the place, and in the confusion one of us stabs him.' Glancing at Jo he said, 'I don't mind wearing that, since I'm tainted anyway.'

Somehow he knew what her view on that would be.

'No,' she said calmly. 'I did it, and I'd do it again.'

'Fair enough,' he said. 'So, any problems with the story, Wes?'

'Nope,' Wes said. 'But . . . people in the street might have seen our comings and goings.'

'Fuck the people in the street,' Jo said. 'We stick to our version, back each other up.'

'Sure,' Wes said. 'Fuck the people in the street. We should know what happened.'

'Has to be straight and simple,' Shaun said. 'Try to be too clever, and we're in shit.'

'Got it,' Wes said.

Shaun said, 'Anyhow, I'd say that once they discover who he was they'll be so busy high-fiving each other they won't give a rat's arse about the details.'

'Uh, who was he?' Wes said.

'You don't need to know. Better if none of us does. He's just this . . . *bastard*, come in off the street.'

'No arguments there,' Wes said.

'I'll tell you all about him later,' Shaun said. 'Right now I'm going upstairs, turn the place upside-down like he's ransacked it.'

In a few minutes sirens pulled up outside, followed by a commotion. The bell rang, then came a loud, insistent pounding on the door. There was the crackling of urgent-sounding voices on two-way radios.

'Sounds like the SWAT team's here,' Shaun said. 'Everyone set?'

Jo and Wes nodded grimly. Then Shaun negotiated his way through the chaos towards the front.

25

Five days later . . .

'You know, I can't believe your form has turned around so radically, Steer,' Oliver said as he adjusted his paisley Dolce e Gabbana bow-tie. 'I mean . . . you really cleaned me up today.'

'Situation normal,' Raydon said, slipping into his patent-black English wingtips. '*C'est juste.*'

'No need to be arrogant,' Oliver said. 'Not so long ago you were a sorry spectacle.'

'You're right, McEncroe. I must learn to be more modest and gracious. But as the song goes, it's hard to be humble, especially when one vanquishes the resident champion in straight sets.'

'You had the angles covered this time.'

'I did.'

They went outside into the early evening. The air was soft, uplifting.

'Cocktail hour,' Raydon said. 'How about it?'

'Count me in,' Oliver said.

When they were sitting in a cosy bar with double-shots of aged Scotch on ice in front of them, Oliver said, 'Well, here's to it.'

'Indeed.' Raydon swirled and sipped. 'So, you're sure it's all over with, McEncroe?'

Oliver nodded. 'According to my source, when Henry Agar was murdered, this Tamsin Mascall person developed a severe case of cold feet and disappeared. Hasn't surfaced since. Then when the pimp Terry Pritchett finds himself on the receiving end of your . . . ex-wife's wrath, all the bent cops in Sydney run for cover. My contact Patchouli says the tents have definitely been folded on the whole scam.'

Raydon nodded. But he seemed somewhat distracted.

'How's Jo?' Oliver said.

'Oh, she's fine, by all accounts. Tough as all get out, that one. I just don't understand what this . . . Pritchett piece of *shit* was *doing* there in the first place.'

Oliver shifted slightly. 'Well, he was in league with Agar, remember? They were a team. Agar was a professional snoop: what he couldn't dig up via his devious contacts is nobody's business. But then they fell out, as thieves do, and Pritchett decided to go it alone.'

'I see *that*,' Raydon said. 'But who was his target? McCreadie, or Jo? Since McCreadie is supposedly the one with the stash . . .'

'I'm not sure, Steer. Perhaps he discovered through the criminal grapevine that McCreadie was staying there with your wife. That isn't totally implausible. In fact, it was in the paper.'

'Yes,' Raydon said. 'Still, it's odd . . .'

'The main thing is, he's *dead*, and we are free of the whole affair.'

'True,' Raydon said, and sipped.

'What news of the appointments?' Oliver said after a short, subject-changing silence.

'Monday, according to father. Just has to be rubber-stamped by the Governor.'

'And?'

'And *yes*, McEncroe. It seems I am to be appointed to the Supreme Court bench after all. But it's not official yet. Don't shout it from the rooftops.'

'Congratulations.'

'Thank you.'

They touched glasses.

'You are a lucky bastard, Steer,' Oliver said.

'I suppose in some ways I am,' Raydon said diffidently.

'Things could have turned out a *lot* worse for you.'

'I can't deny that.'

'And once you're on the bench, you can*not* carry on with your wicked ways.'

'I am suitably chastised, McEncroe—and grateful, old friend. Gave me a decent old scare, the whole episode.'

'No doubt.'

'You can expect prompt payment of your exorbitant fee.'

'Oh, don't be ridiculous, Steer. My fee is waived.'

'Seriously? Good Lord. What sort of precedent is that for the legal profession?'

'I'll count it as a credit instead. Who knows? The day might come when I have to approach the Great One on bended knee, cap in hand.'

'As you wish, McEncroe. All I require is that you do so with all due obsequiousness.'

'But of course, your Worship.' He steepled his elegant hands and lowered his eyes.

After a pause, Oliver said, 'Any chance with Jo?'

'Afraid not. It appears she's thrown in her lot with this . . . ruffian. So be it. I bear no ill will. In any case, I wouldn't want her back now that she's become a gangster's slut. Soiled goods and all that.'

'Harsh words coming from you, Steer. She *is* the mother of your children.'

'I suppose one can rise to the occasion. Settle in a civilised manner, make proper arrangements for the boys . . .' He shrugged. 'McEncroe, call me dense if you will, but there's quite a bit I don't . . . *grasp* about this vale of grief and sorrow we live in. But then, I suppose, I'm just a Supreme Court judge after all.'

'Absolutely, Steer. And let's hope you don't put your foot in a mop bucket on your first day in court.'

Raydon exploded into laughter, and after a moment Oliver joined in, uproariously, slapping the table as if it were an Old Boys' night out.

Shaun and Jo were sitting opposite Dave Wrigley in his partitioned workspace at the homicide squad offices in the St Kilda Road Police Complex. Dave was wearing a pale blue lightweight cotton shirt through which Shaun could see the short sleeves of his white tee shirt. He leaned back in his chair with his hands behind his head, making his impressive biceps and pectorals even more apparent. A recent buzz-cut completed the warrior image.

'He was in there for three-quarters of an hour before the stabbing occurred,' he said to either of them, or both.

'That's about right,' Shaun said. 'As I said, we weren't watching the clock, Dave.'

Dave nodded thoughtfully.

'Three-quarters of an hour is a long time,' he said.

'I assure you it seemed a lot longer than that,' Jo said.

'I'll bet,' Dave said, and sat forward again, clasping his hands. His eyes switched from Jo to Shaun. Along with Wes, they had already been subjected to an intense grilling by Dave Wrigley and others, and this was the third go-around in as many days. Dave had called Shaun, saying he wanted to have a separate 'chat', but Jo had insisted on being present too, and Dave hadn't objected.

Shaun was more than happy to have her along.

'What demands did he make?' Dave said.

Shaun said, 'As I said last time—'

'Just indulge me, buddy.' Dave might've been smiling, or not. It was hard to tell.

'We spent a lot of the time trying to calm him,' Shaun said. 'He was pretty fired up, waving his gun around and threatening to shoot everybody. Searched the house high and low for money. Wanted me to go to an ATM and withdraw five hundred dollars. I told him I didn't have a card. But he didn't believe me, and so . . . all this *arguing* went on. We were walking on eggs, Dave. I was trying to negotiate with the bastard. He carried on about how there had to be cash in the house somewhere but, you know, all we had was what we carried in our wallets. Then he turned on Jo, and that was when Wes and I jumped him. After that it was sheer mayhem.'

'That's *exactly* what happened,' Jo said.

Dave nodded again. It didn't mean he was in agreement.

'You were all very fortunate,' he said. 'Terry Pritchett was the nastiest bill of goods to come out of Sydney in a good while. He was a hot suspect in the Henry Agar murder, which I'm sure you've heard about.'

It was the first time the Agar connection had been made to them. They both nodded.

'What was that all about?' Shaun said.

'Dunno,' Dave said. 'Don't care, particularly. Nice pair of slimeballs they were. Good riddance.'

'Yeah,' Shaun said.

To Jo, Dave said, 'Jo, there'll be a full investigation, and a coronial inquest in due course. At this stage I wouldn't worry too much if I were you. It's a violent death, and we have to follow set procedures.' He straightened his conservative homicide tie. 'I have no reason to doubt that you acted in self-defence, and that is was a righteous homicide.' He added, with the tact of a true professional, 'Going on what he have so far, I would not expect any criminal charges to flow from this incident.'

Jo nodded. That seemed to be it.

Dave stood up. Shaun and Jo did the same.

'Might have to go over the odd detail again down the track,' Dave said. 'So don't leave the country yet. Come on, I'll ride down with you.'

When they were outside the building, Shaun lit a cigarette.

'What's the deal on Stan Petrakos?' he said. The grisly death had been all over the papers and on TV.

'Yeah,' Dave said. 'That's a weird one. The girlfriend definitely did it, but she claims she didn't mean to. Apparently she thought he was Charlie Manson come to get her.'

Both Shaun and Jo regarded him with undisguised disbelief.

'Come on, Dave,' Shaun said.

'True,' Dave said, putting up two fingers like a good scout. 'She's a Goth, would you believe, a bit of a wild child. Been obsessed with Manson since forever. A real dope fiend, too. She was wigged out something terrible, according to reports.'

Shaun digested this, dragging on the cigarette.

'Shot with his own gun,' Dave said. 'She made a right mess of him too. Christ, you'd have to say there was something off about that tribe, wouldn't you?'

'Has been for a long, long time, Dave,' Shaun said. 'Now it's the end of the bloodline.'

'Yeah.'

'Christ. Charlie Manson now, is it? Well, maybe she wasn't too far wrong at that. So what's the latest word? Any chance of the case being reopened?'

Dave said, 'Depends on what Rick Stiles has to say, I guess. But of course, he'll probably clam up now that the threat's gone. At the end of the day it'll be up to the DPP, based on the recommendations of the cold-case unit, but I wouldn't be too hopeful. With the star witness out of play, where's it gonna go?'

'Nowhere,' Shaun said. So he would never clear his name now. Not conclusively.

'Afraid so,' Dave said.

'I'll bring the car up,' Jo said. 'Bye, Dave.' She seemed to sense that Dave wanted a private parting word with Shaun.

Dave raised an arm. 'Bye, Jo.'

When she'd gone, Dave said, 'Your story doesn't sit with me one hundred percent, Shaun.'

Here it comes. Shaun remained silent, waiting for the second shoe to drop.

Dave went on: 'For instance, a neighbour said she *thought* she saw a man get out of a maroon car and put something under the mat. Same neighbour also thought she saw another car pull up, and a man go into the house. But she's a woman in her eighties, and the report is uncorroborated . . . so far.'

Shaun said nothing: always the wisest policy in this situation.

'But, it's close enough. No-one's gonna bust your chops over it. I guess what really happened inside that house isn't important next to the fact that Terry Pritchett is now on a cold slab.'

'That's how I see it,' Shaun said, throwing down his butt and grinding it into the pavement.

They stood around for a minute before clasping hands. Dave's grip was fierce.

'She's a pistol, that Jo,' Dave said. 'You're on a dead-set winner there.'

'Bet on it.'

The maroon Prelude came into view along the service lane.

'Nice car too,' Dave said with a cunning flick of the eye. 'Well, that's all I wanted to get off my chest, man. Be cool. Catch you when.'

'Yeah, you too, Dave.'

Shaun watched his back as he went inside the building, hand raised in the air.

Good one, Dave. You'll go far in this caper.

Shaun was seated in a banquette with a pint of Bass when Wes came in the door, silhouetted from the bright sunshine outside. It was a recently reincarnated Irish pub called O'Toole's, in the heart of Brunswick. Shaun remembered it from at least three of its previous lives, but it seemed someone had made a fist of it this time. At 2 pm it was all go, suits having liquid lunches and a whole variety of the younger, more casual set, with some lilting Celt music unobtrusively adding to the pleasant ambience.

With everything that had been happening, he'd not had time for a proper debrief, or even to express his gratitude to Wes. But since the police investigation was largely over and done, now was that time.

Wes made straight for the bar. His right arm was in a sling, encased in plaster up to the elbow. Only his fingertips protruded.

'I'll have what he's got, love,' he said to the winsome Colleen behind the jump, throwing a nod at Shaun.

'What's the verdict?' Shaun said when he was seated opposite. Wes took a decent pull on his pint and wiped the froth from his lips with his good arm.

'Broken wrist,' Wes said. 'Snapped clean in half. Felt it pop as soon as I made contact.'

'That was the best punch I've ever seen unloaded,' Shaun said.

'Well, I only had one shot. Had to be a good one.'

'I thought you were never gonna do it,' Shaun said. 'I was stringing him along, trying to distract him . . .'

'Yeah,' Wes said, nodding. 'I was in the wings for ages, but when I spotted that fuckin' great shooter I thought, hold on a minute, Wes. Whoa up, son. Have to do this right first time, 'cause there'll be no second bite of the cherry.'

'I warned you he was armed up.'

'You did. But up close it seemed more dangerous than when you said it on the phone.'

They both laughed.

Wes swallowed some more Bass and said, 'You know, when I decked Bobby Sharples that time, it all came down to a *millisecond* when he was wide open. Bobby had terrific vision, he'd already had one bounce, and as I closed in from, uh, behind him, I saw he was aiming to go inboard. He selected a target, propped and was about to screw it across his body, and *that* was when I nailed him, when he propped. In his mind, he'd already delivered the ball. No vision, for *that* long.' He snapped his fingers. 'That was all I needed to bring him down. Same deal with this Pritchett bastard. If I'd made my move too early he would've seen me, even though I was behind him. He had vision as good as Bobby's. But then, your plan to distract him did the job. He lowered the shooter, momentarily took his eye off the ball, so to speak, and that was my cue. *Whammo*. Shit, it hurt, though.'

'Hurt him a lot more.'

'Yeah, but not *enough*. I couldn't fuckin' *believe* it when he came back from the dead. That guy's jaw was busted in at least three places, not to mention the concussion he would've suffered. It should've been lights out, good night. You have to give him credit for boxing on. He had more balls than Bobby Sharples, that's for sure.'

'He was running on automatic,' Shaun said.

'Maybe,' Wes said. 'Weird, huh? Anyway Jo fixed his liver good and proper.'

Shaun nodded.

'She all right?'

'Quiet,' Shaun said. 'Not overly flash. She'll have some problems, I guess. You're not really meant to go around stabbing people in the heart.' He could have added that she'd barely eaten or slept, despite dosing herself up with Prozac, and that she was given to silent, spontaneous crying jags.

Outside, they stood next to Wes's grubby, clapped-out Commodore.

'Still no sign of that big, fat bastard?' Wes said.

'Nope. He is AWOL.'

'Good. That pleases me no end.'

'Yeah. I'm sure he'd put in an appearance if he could.'

'If it hasn't happened by now, it isn't gonna happen,' Wes said.

'Yeah. Looks like. Uh, by the way, this . . . *car* of yours is about ready for the scrapyard too, Wes,' Shaun said.

'You got that right.'

They leaned on it, smiled at each other. A glacier of traffic moved steadily along the tramlines of Sydney Road.

'Open the trunk,' Shaun said, straightening.

'Why?'

'Just open it.'

Wes did as instructed. Shaun went to the back of the Prelude, which was parked behind Wes's car, and lifted its trunk. Wes watched him cast his eyes around cautiously. After a moment he returned, carrying a silver case. He put it in the Commodore's trunk and slammed it down.

'What's that?' Wes said.

'That's about . . . nine hundred and fifty thou. Close enough to a million.'

Wes's jaw fell open.

'Jesus, man, what the fuck—'

'Wes, listen. Hadn't been for you, Jo and I would both be in the ground by now, no question. You saved the day, man.'

'Yeah, but shit, a *million*—'

'Get used to it, Wes. It's all yours.' He lit a cigarette. 'Maybe I'm not doing you a real big favour, giving you tainted money.

A lot of people have died for it over the years, one way and another.'

Wes had no words. He was rubbing the bristles on his chin.

'Sounds a bit stupid,' Shaun said, 'but for me, it was never about the money anyway.'

'Well . . . what was it about then?' Wes said. His knowledge of the whole affair consisted of sensational but half-forgotten news items from long ago.

'That's the question, isn't it?' Shaun said, to the air, it seemed.

Wes nodded pensively without envisioning a possible answer. That was a place he definitely didn't want to visit.

'Get yourself a new car for starters,' Shaun said.

'Yeah,' Wes said. 'I will. That'll be top of the list.' He was thoroughly perplexed.

'Want some advice, from one who knows?' Shaun said after a bit.

'Sure. Go.'

'Engage a top brief. With the right representation you stand an even chance of getting a bond in this indecent exposure charge you've got coming up. Otherwise you'll hit the slammer for sure. Don't do it, Wes. Any prison jolt, even a few months, will screw up your life no end, especially for a sex rap. You don't wanna become a convict, do you?'

'Shit no,' Wes said.

'Go and get some proper counselling. That'll help when you're in court. You're not gonna go flashing your nasty any more, are you?'

'Certainly not.'

'I mean, you don't *have* to, do you?'

'I'm not a mental case, if that's what you mean.'

'That is what I mean. Give it away, man. Get your shit together. Get some *romance* in your life.'

'Ha. That's easy for you to say.'

'Jo's the first serious woman I've ever had, Wes.'

'Yeah? Bullshit.'

'Nope. And I just . . . stumbled into it. If I can manage that, after eleven years in the slot, you can do it with a leg in the air.'

'I am no good with women,' Wes pronounced with a sigh.

'Why? You're all right around Jo.'

'Yeah, but . . . see, there's no pressure on me. She's with *you*. So I can safely lust after her from a distance. I haven't had a girlfriend since I used to shag Brenda Michaels behind the local pavilion when I was *fifteen*. Mate, I learned all my social skills in the locker room. Put me anywhere with a bunch of swinging dicks, at a sportsmen's night or even in front of a TV camera, and I'm your boy. I'm a star. But if I have to go head-to-head with a person of the opposite gender, I'm out of business. I'm lost. I get . . . tongue-tied. I don't know the moves. Can't read the play. I have no confidence, no idea what to *do* with a woman. They have a different . . . configuration, up here.' He tapped his head.

'Time you learned it,' Shaun said. 'Christ, Wes, you're an intelligent, talented guy. Why toss it away?'

'I know, I know,' Wes said. 'What do you suggest? Got anyone lined up? Jo's twin sister, for example?'

'You wish. Listen, you dope, you're a rich man. Put an ad in the paper, then stand back to avoid the stampede. *Christ*.'

Wes thought long and hard about the whole deal, occasionally glancing over at Shaun as if to confirm he was serious and still on it. He was giving the impression he realised this was a significant moment for him.

'That's three things I have to do,' he said.

'It's no big deal. You've only got to turn your whole life around.'

Wes nodded. Soon enough, a resigned sort of smile formed on his face.

'All right—you got it,' he said.

'Is that a commitment?'

'Sure. Want me to write it in blood?'

Shaun grinned at him. 'Nah, I guess you've already done that.'

When he returned home Jo was in the lounge, sitting on the sofa with a magazine on her lap.

'How are you doin'?' he said, sitting alongside her and bringing one of her hands to his lips. The hand was as weightless as a baby's. She was visibly thinner, and her eyelids were on the verge of closing down.

She leaned into him. 'Tired. *So* tired. Just had another pill. I should go to bed soon.'

'You do that.'

'How'd it go with Wes?'

'Fine. He's promised to be a good lad from now on.'

She managed a pathetic laugh. 'That's nice. Think he can do it?'

'Don't see why not. Money can solve many problems.'

'Hmm,' she said a bit dubiously. 'Maybe. Let's hope. Oh, Dave Wrigley rang. Wants you to buzz him.'

'Uh-huh. Want me to carry you upstairs first?'

'Yes, please.'

She was out to it before she hit the sheets.

When he had him on the line, Dave said, with no preamble, 'Thought you'd be interested in some ballistic results. The shotgun pellets that killed Stan Petrakos came from double-aught, one-eighty grain shells fired from a sawn-off twelve gauge. Same as the pellets dug out of Rick Stiles' walls. No surprise there. But get this: they also ran comparative tests on the pellets used to shoot George and Stephanie. They are *exactly* the same. Even the spread's identical. Shotgun ballistics're not as reliable, or conclusive, as for regular bullets, but they're pretty accurate all the same. There's not much doubt that Stan's gun was the murder weapon back in '92.'

'Is that so?' Shaun said.

'So the tech guys say. It may be enough to reopen the case, or not. First there'll have to be a new coronial inquiry, after which it's up to the DPP. But Stan being dead makes it a tough call. I wouldn't be too optimistic. On top of that I imagine they're a bit busy at present with all that drug squad stuff hitting the fan.'

Shaun put down the phone and thought about it. In his heart he really didn't want the whole deal opened up again, but if the powers that be decided to, then he would have to accept that. From what Dave had told him it was a long shot anyway. He was now remembering Dave's advice to put it all behind him, and the more he thought about it the more he saw the wisdom of his words. If he was moving forward with Jo at his side, he did not want to be dragging all that baggage behind him, and nor did she. She was going to be fragile for a while yet. It was going to be a testing time for the relationship. In any case, there was nothing left to prove to himself, or to her, or to anyone; and that was the only real issue. The rest was all legalities. He made a conscious decision to cut it all loose, now and forever, and straightaway his spirits rose.

In a couple of hours he went upstairs to check on her. She was awake and staring at the ceiling. He sat on the edge of the bed, and she gave him her hand to squeeze.

'Want anything?' he said.

There was a glimmer of interest. 'Cup of tea?'

'Coming up. How about a couple of burgers and some fries to go with that?'

She filled her cheeks in an expression of mock-nausea.

'I keep playing it over and over in my mind,' she said after a silence. 'Can't get rid of it.'

'I know,' he said, squeezing the soft hand. 'Give it time, and some TLC. You'll be fine, baby. I guarantee it.'

She nodded as she squeezed his hand a little more firmly.

But even as she did so tears were silently filling her eyes and spilling down onto the pillow. Her expression did not change: she was releasing tears, nothing more. He passed her a box of tissues.

'Have you ever been to Proserpine?' he said while she cleaned herself up.

'Proserpine? In Queensland? No, why?'

'Well, I'm told it's pretty close to paradise. You rent a boat, one of those big motorised yachts, and cruise around. Drop anchor whenever you want, jump in for a swim when it gets too hot . . . go spear-fishing in this blue water that's so clear you can see right through it, all the way. I'm told the coral trout up there are the sweetest fish you'll ever eat.'

'Yeah?' she said, wiping her eyes, showing some interest.

'Yeah. At night, you barbecue the fish on deck, wash it down with a crisp, dry wine that's been chilled in the icebox. You can sleep, or whatever, under the stars, and it's a sky like no other, I'm told.'

'Is that so?'

'It is.'

'"Or whatever"?' She managed to arch an eyebrow.

'Definitely.'

She sniffed. 'Hmm. So, when is this happening?'

'Soon. I'll arrange it tomorrow. When does the university year end?'

'November.'

'November it is. Then maybe we can head for Italy, see if we can't chase down some long-lost relatives.'

She gave him a big smile—an enormous effort. 'Wouldn't that be something?'

At close proximity he lost himself once more inside those moist, mint-green pools that stared back at him like a mirror image. Amazing. Even when she was in the throes of post-trauma and depression, she filled him with a barely controllable excitement and longing.

'Everything all right in there?' he murmured, moving a strand of her hair from her damp face.

She responded with an almost imperceptible nod. It seemed a huge effort. But her eyes said it all. They told him that, for all its improbable origins in a rough bush cabin far from anywhere, for good or otherwise their future together was cemented with the blood of Terry Pritchett. They had somehow beaten the odds.

And now they were one and the same.